ALL THESE GIRLS

ALSO BY ELLEN SLEZAK

Last Year's Jesus

A Novel

ALL THESE GIRLS | *Ellen Slezak*

NEW YORK

Library of Congress Cataloging-in-Publication Data

Slezak, Ellen.
    All these girls : a novel / Ellen Slezak.—1st ed.
      p. cm.
    ISBN 0-7868-6742-6
    1. Women—Michigan—Fiction.   2. Upper Peninsula (Mich.)—Fiction.
  3. Loss (Psychology)—Fiction.   4. Women travelers—Fiction.
  5. Nieces—Fiction.   6. Aunts—Fiction.   I. Title.

    PS3619.L57A78   2004
    813'.6—dc22

                         2003057031

Hyperion books are available for special promotions and premiums. For details contact Michael Rentas, Manager, Inventory and Premium Sales, Hyperion, 77 West 66th Street, 11th floor, New York, New York 10023, or call 212-456-0133.

FIRST EDITION

10 9 8 7 6 5 4 3 2 1

To my nieces and in memory of my aunts
Mary Makowski Virgilio and Anna Slezak Opalewski

ACKNOWLEDGMENTS

ALTHOUGH THIS NOVEL is set in Michigan, I have taken liberties in creating a fictional town and its surroundings. As a result, my versions of real places cannot be mapped exactly.

I owe thanks to many people and organizations for their help during the years I wrote this novel.

The MacDowell Colony and the Centrum Arts Center were generous in giving me uninterrupted time to work. The Sewanee Writers' Conference gave me support in other important ways. My thanks to them all.

I am grateful to Laurie Liss, who not only sees to it that my work is published, but is also an astute reader along the way.

Many thanks to the many good folks at Hyperion, beginning with Ellen Archer. I am grateful also to Leigh Haber, my first editor there, and to Leslie Wells, who took over as my editor when Leigh moved on. Elisa Lee, Ben Loehnen, and Karin Maake—thank you.

I'm also grateful to Greg Grauman for sharing his basketball coaching expertise.

Many writers read many earlier drafts of this work with an eye to helping me improve it. My heartfelt thanks to Susan Messer, Carol Slezak, and Diana Wagman, who read the manuscript at various stages, and to Chris Hale and Adrianne Harun, who read at every stage along the way.

Above all, and as ever, thanks to my husband, Brian Hamill.

THE CROWS

The woman who has grown old
And knows desire must die,
Yet turns to love again,
Hears the crows' cry.

She is a stem long hardened,
A weed that no scythe mows.
The heart's laughter will be to her
The crying of the crows,

Who slide in the air with the same voice
Over what yields not, and what yields,
Alike in spring, and when there is only bitter
Winter-burning in the fields.

—LOUISE BOGAN

PART | I

*M*OST PEOPLE RINGED around an open grave don't see the grave diggers, but they're always there. Two, three, sometimes four of them. They may be off to the side, behind a tree, or in a pickup twenty yards away. They stay close enough to hear the drift of prayers and see the white shock and red-rimmed eyes on the faces gathered around the grave, but they don't intrude on private sorrow. While the loved one's friends and family are at the site, the grave diggers are stolid. They don't smoke or swear. Or even talk much. They keep the backhoe out of sight. They'll do their work when the mourners leave.

But if lamenters linger much too long, the grave diggers approach, shovels in plain view. They'd like to be more patient, but there may be half a dozen burials that day and two graves to prepare for the next. Moving in on mourners this way, grave diggers, it is fair to say, have stood next to grief in almost every form. They don't judge it or partake in it. They are paid to do a job: dig, then fill, the grave. That is the commitment they meet. They leave emotion to the living and the loving left behind.

Three women were left behind to mourn Melissa Golden's sudden death: Gloria Dreslinski, her aunt; Elizabeth Brannigan, her half sister; and Candy Golden, her teenaged daughter. That late November when Melissa died, the three met at Grimaldi's Funeral Home on the east side of Detroit, just a few miles from where Candy and Melissa had lived, which was hundreds of miles from Glo's Chicago bungalow, and thousands of miles from Elizabeth's Los Angeles apartment.

Glo, Elizabeth, and Candy might offer a collective shrug if anyone asked exactly when they'd been together last. A second cousin's wedding fifteen years ago, when Candy was still in diapers? A picnic to celebrate an uncle's ninetieth birthday five years after that? Glo's own husband, Stan, had died just a month before Melissa, but neither Elizabeth nor Candy had traveled to Chicago to console her. Stan had been seventy-six, thirteen years older than Glo, and he'd suffered a stroke. Elizabeth had just moved from Chicago to Los Angeles—the first phone call she received after driving cross-country was the news of her uncle's death; Candy had a basketball game the Saturday of Stan's funeral. Glo hadn't expected them to take what would have been great pains to be there. Melissa had driven the three hundred miles from Detroit to Chicago to support her aunt, but it was Glo, dry-eyed, who offered her niece a tissue at the grave site. Stan's death had been expected. His funeral had been a small and tidy affair.

But Melissa's passing was different. She was just thirty-eight. She was killed in a traffic accident—there was nothing expected about it. Parlor C at Grimaldi's, the largest room for visitation, was crowded with mourners—unexpected tragedy exerting its magnetic force. *So young,* the visitors murmured, looking at the closed casket, glad it was she who'd died and not them, secretly wondering what she might have done to deserve it, and *that poor girl,* looking at Candy, an orphan now. She had never known her father.

Besides Glo and Elizabeth, many of Melissa's AA friends came to Parlor C. One of them was drunk, the precarious balance of her new-found sobriety upset by the death of her sponsor and friend. She stumbled as she approached the casket and Candy, a few feet away, smelled the woman's boozy breath and thought back to the time when her mother's redolence had been forty-proof, too.

Candy's teachers from All Saints High School and her friends and teammates on the All Saints Ravens varsity basketball team also came to Grimaldi's. Her teammates shoved their hands under their armpits and looked down at their scuffed, flat, black shoes and plain skirts and blouses, which their mothers had made them dig out of closets and drawers, telling them it was the appropriate attire for a funeral home.

Once there, they discovered their mothers were wrong. All these girls, bound up in sober clothes that didn't fit, weren't themselves. The selves that could have been comfortable with their friend, even at a funeral home in front of her mother's coffin. Instead they became girls who were stifled. Girls who couldn't hug Candy and cry and tell her how very very very sad they were that she didn't have a mom or a dad. Girls who couldn't make fun of Mr. Morrisey, a guidance counselor at All Saints, who carried his briefcase into the funeral home as if he were a bank president or a congressman, instead of a man who administered standardized career tests and tried to convince girls to tell him their troubles. Girls who couldn't rescue Amy Prokoff, whom everybody liked, from the chair she sat on next to her mom, whom hardly anybody did. Girls so uncomfortable that they didn't even notice Coach D standing alone in a corner next to an arrangement of two dozen yellow tulips. His hands, heavy without a basketball giving them purpose, were rooted in his pockets. His neck, bare without the whistle that usually hung around it, drooped in consort with the pale green stems.

When Glo came out of the ladies' room on the lower level of Grimaldi's Funeral Home, she saw her grandniece, Candy, in the coffee room off to the side feeding coins into the silver slot of a Coke machine and then studying the soft drink choices on the illuminated buttons.

"Have you eaten anything today, Candy?" Glo came up behind her and put her hand under the girl's elbow, though she stood firm.

"I'm just thirsty." Candy pushed a button—COKE—but the machine gave up nothing from its refrigerated depths.

"You'll ruin your dinner with those sugary drinks. Your mother wouldn't want that."

Candy leaned into the SPRITE button, still no response, before correcting Glo. "My mother had M&Ms and Dr Pepper for dinner the night before she died."

Glo ignored the rebuke. "Your friend Amy Prokoff's mother, Anita—I believe that's her name—has invited people over to her house after the rosary tonight. She's prepared cold cuts and casseroles and such."

Candy kicked the Coke machine. "Whatever." She liked Amy enough to ignore her nosy mother, who issued opinions as if they were orders and then waited for thanks.

"And Elizabeth and you and I need to discuss where you'll stay."

That was worth turning around for, so Candy did. "What do you mean? I'm staying home. In the apartment. I mailed the rent for my mom last week. State starts next week. I need this all to be over. I'm missing practice. I need to get back to the team."

Glo wished she could take back her words. Stan had often told her during their fourteen years together that she was abrupt, bordering on insensitive. She shouldn't have brought up the subject here, this way, and Elizabeth should be part of the conversation also. Elizabeth, thirty-six, was closer in age to Candy. She was a guidance counselor and a basketball coach. She'd relate better to the girl. Not that Elizabeth had been much help so far. Even now, she sat upstairs alone in a corner, not tending to Candy, or praying at her sister's coffin, or greeting those who came to pay respects and trying to help them feel more comfortable in the face of such loss. Glo had deep faith that God's reasons for taking Melissa so young would be revealed in time. Meanwhile, she hoped God was up to figuring out exactly where this girl was going to live.

Damage done, Glo continued, "It's not realistic to think you can live in that apartment alone, Candy. While Elizabeth and I are here it's fine for the three of us, but we need to consider the future. I think you'd like Chicago and you're welcome to live with me, though Elizabeth, in L.A., could be a better choice, since you have things in common, like basketball, and she is, of course, closer in age."

"I'm not leaving Detroit. I'm not leaving my team. I'm not living with either one of you." Candy pressed the COKE button again. "What's Elizabeth doing here anyway? She didn't even like my mom. Plus, somebody should pump a gallon of Prozac into her. The way she's just looking down and barely moving and not talking? She gives me the creeps." Candy hadn't seen Elizabeth in five years. Her aunt used to be lots of fun. She used to look really great—she was tall like Candy. She used to laugh a lot, and when she had, she'd thrown her head back, aiming up at the sky as if she needed more space for how good she felt. Candy remembered being a little kid and trying to laugh that way, too. Now? The best Candy could say was that Elizabeth hadn't shrunk. All yesterday and today, Elizabeth had approached Candy every hour or so and then backed away without saying anything. Candy gave up on Coke and pressed the DASANI button. She'd drink water, a healthy choice. Maybe then Glo would shut up. *Where was she going to live?*

Candy hadn't been worrying about that. Forced to now, she thought that she would rather die than live with either of them. They were her only family, but they hadn't helped her mom the way they should have. Elizabeth hadn't helped her at all. Her mom hadn't seen it that way, but Candy wasn't afraid to say it was so. Moving in with Glo or Elizabeth would be a betrayal of her mom. She would not do it.

Glo nudged the machine, trying to help her grandniece. "Elizabeth has had a shock. Her husband, Leo, left her. I don't believe in all that true romance and heart business, but even I could see they cared for each other. Her divorce just became final. She'll perk up soon."

"You think she'd be used to husbands leaving her by now." Candy stared over Glo's shoulder at an arrangement of daisies that hadn't yet been brought upstairs. She hadn't even met Elizabeth's last husband, Leo—her third. Elizabeth wasn't talking to Candy's mom by the time she'd married the guy. More than almost anything her mom had wanted Elizabeth to see her sober. "I don't blame my sister for how she is toward me. I wore her out. I did awful things, and those are the things I remember. I can only imagine the things I've blacked out. I just wish she'd come around to see you like she used to."

"Forget it, Mom. She's useless. I don't need Elizabeth." They'd had that conversation just a few weeks ago. Candy changed her mind about the water and selected Diet Coke, pushing the button with her left hand. As she did so, she felt something digging into the palm of her right hand. Glo pressed a rosary there. All the prayers and tears and flowers and sorrow were like fresh marrow for Glo's bones. That gave Candy the creeps, too. She stuffed the rosary in her pocket and turned back to the machine, pushing hard. She heard steps, and she looked over her shoulder to see her friend Amy Prokoff; Amy's mom, Anita; and Elizabeth coming toward her, single file. She jabbed the Coke buttons randomly. Damn it. She wanted *something* to drink.

Why had her aunts even bothered to come? She and Elizabeth and Glo were freaks right now—tattooed by a run of tragedy that was hard to believe. Glo's husband dead? Elizabeth divorced again? Her mom killed? All within a month? Living with either of them now would only remind her that she was alone. It was their duty to offer. It was their job to say, come. But they couldn't make up for all those years missing by showing up now. She didn't want them. She didn't need them. She wouldn't live with either one of them.

Elizabeth, last in line, looked at Candy backed up against the Coke machine and facing Glo and Anita Prokoff as if they were a firing squad. She thought about trying to extract her niece from that position, but Anita Prokoff spread her arms, blocking access, and attempted to herd Candy and Glo upstairs like cattle, chiding them as she did. "We wondered where you two had gone off to. Father McLaughlin is waiting to start the rosary." While Amy ducked under the corral of her mother's arms and stood next to Candy, Elizabeth backed away as if those arms were barbed wire.

Glo didn't care too much for Anita Prokoff so far, but she recognized a fellow acolyte in the doctrine of efficient daily living, and she aimed to keep an open mind. "Candy and I were just discussing her living situation. It's something we need to decide sooner, not later."

Anita sniffed and turned her head, once, twice, three times, look-

ing at Glo, Elizabeth, and Candy. "I assumed you or your niece would
move to Detroit and take care of Candy."

"I doubt that's possible. Elizabeth?" Glo's voice was firm.

"I just arrived in L.A. I started my new job a week ago. I can't
move to Detroit now." Candy butted the Coke machine with her
shoulder, adding a thud to Elizabeth's refusal. "But Los Angeles is
possible. I mean, we can make arrangements for her to come there?
With me?" Elizabeth spoke in questions. "Or maybe Candy could
move to Chicago with you, Glo. Stan is gone. You have plenty of
room."

Candy listened. They weren't going to move to Detroit for her.
And she wasn't going to give up basketball at All Saints to live with ei-
ther one of them. "I'm not leaving Detroit. I'm not leaving my team.
State starts next week. I don't have time for this." Candy kicked the
Coke machine with her heel, her protest ending in a thump while Glo
murmured at the same time, "I've already told her she's welcome."

"Candy can't leave. All Saints is favored to win State. The tournament starts next week. You can't make her go anywhere else. She has
friends here." Amy Prokoff looked at Glo and Elizabeth, disbelieving,
and said slowly and loudly, "It's not fair to make her move because
her mom died." She cried after that.

Anita Prokoff reached out to her daughter. "It's okay, honey. Nobody is going to make Candy move. Ladies," she lectured, "your niece
is important to our community—to All Saints High School. She's had
her picture in the *Free Press* twice already this season. She has colleges
calling her. Candy, tell them about the recruiting." Candy shrugged.

"Mom?" Amy let go of Candy and grabbed her mother's arm instead. "She should live with us this year. She can share my room."

Candy watched Anita Prokoff take in Amy's suggestion. She
sensed her measuring, imagining another *Free Press* headline, "Bas-

ketball Star Saved by Selfless Woman," calculating the percentage of praise she'd receive for the good deed. Candy had missed three practices since her mom died. She needed to get back on court.

Anita Prokoff straightened Candy's collar. Candy flattened herself, wanting to disappear inside the Coke machine's refrigerated depths. She jerked sideways, feeling the voltage of Anita's fingertips on her neck, and shook her head, *No, I don't think so,* at Amy's suggestion. She turned and faced the behemoth machine and punched buttons randomly, harder and harder, finally kicking the glowing, humming, stubborn, cold machine that clearly wasn't going to deliver anything at all, much less what she wanted. Even though she'd paid.

Her head was too full of feeling. Crying wouldn't help, but she felt the pressure of tears coming again. Her face was already taut with salt trails, her eyelids heavy and tight—how much more could she cry before her skin disintegrated? In what world was her mom's dying this way possible? She whispered: *I'd rather be dead.*

If she could, she'd conjure buckets of blood that would splatter on Anita, Glo, and Elizabeth; she'd will wicked whispers to tunnel into their brains and torment them to death. She summoned all her strength. She concentrated: *Get away. Leave me alone.*

She looked over her shoulder. They were still there. She kicked the Coke machine. Hit it with her open palms and then pummeled it with tight fists. The State tournament started next week. She wasn't ready. She needed to get back on court with Coach D. She needed to shoot and run. Her mom was dead. Her aunts didn't want her. She turned and spoke to them all: *I won't live with you.*

CHAPTER 2

PEOPLE EVERYWHERE STRUGGLE to come to happiness of any sort. The happiness is not the important part of the tale. Nor is it a fixed state. It is, instead, a turning, toward or away from, things, people, ideas that invite hope or invite despair. The blows a person is dealt, the things that toss and turn her, are the more interesting story. How will they mark her? With sorrow carried, bitterness borne, anger insistent? These are all possible. Will she turn again toward hope? That is possible, too.

The five years when her mother was sober were good ones for Candy Golden. Her happiness fit. Her mother was there. Those same years for Elizabeth Brannigan were also full and good—too much so, she sometimes thought. The ease of living with Leo, of a marriage finally right, felt big and loose. She worried about the sheer plenty of it. It wasn't something she'd known before. Gloria Dreslinski's happiness fit another way. Barely. It pinched. Her life with Stan, she thought, fell just short.

But before the autumn when Melissa, Leo, and Stan left them, Candy, Elizabeth, and Glo each sailed on an even keel.

Look closely at Candy Golden, for instance. Folks in Detroit said they'd never seen a high school basketball player like her. And if they were to see her play, folks anywhere else would say the same. Candy Golden appeared thin as a shoelace, but, lithe and muscled, she was not easy at all to tie up in the post. She was five feet eleven inches, with arms so long she could open the front door of a Volkswagen from the backseat while barely stretching, and hands large enough to hold a puppy in her palm.

And she was beautiful. Almost everybody agreed about that, too. Some thought it a shame that she joined the others on her team and twisted her coffee-with-cream-colored hair into dreadlocks for the State tournament, but others thought that only added to her aggressive beauty. She had a straight, perfectly proportioned nose—nothing buttonlike about it. Her dark brown eyes were set in milk-pale skin that showed off a handful of tiny freckles. She had a generous mouth and wine-colored lips, and when she smiled she looked both regal and friendly. She smiled often, and often while stealing a pass and then racing downcourt, double-pumping to lose the defender crawling up her like a vine, and then reversing midshot to bank her layup soft and safe for two, or while nailing a three from the baseline, wrist flopping, long fingers extending in perfect follow-through, as she watched her shot nestle through net, a second left on the clock, and the All Saints Ravens no longer a point behind.

She stuck out her tongue like Michael when she drove to the basket. Then she reversed like Iverson, posting two on the fastbreak started off her steal. She missed free throws like Shaq when she stood at the line. (This was the only flaw in her game, and she was all the better for it. It gave the college coaches recruiting her something they thought they could fix.) She'd played point guard all her life—she wanted the ball in her hands—and she used her command of the court to quiet anybody who suggested she switch. Still, she was tall enough and tough enough and team player enough to plug the big hole left at center when Kim McVitty fouled out early and Marlene Washington was too chickenshit to bang around in the post. Competition in the league in which the Ravens played being such, Candy could be versatile at this point in her basketball career, at least for five minutes per game.

And with all that, plus a name like Candy Golden, the girl was a legend.

The All Saints Ravens won the State title a little less than a month after Melissa Golden's death. All the Ravens rose to the challenge, inspired by the relentless drive, the ruthless aggression, and the adamant team play of their motherless captain, Candy Golden. People marveled when Candy, so stricken, so recently, posted record numbers on offense and defense.

The Ravens had been run by Coach D since Candy had enrolled at All Saints as a freshman, and he knew he was damn lucky to have her. She could have gone to any high school in Detroit. Or in the suburbs. Private or public. It wouldn't have mattered what it cost. Recruiting starts early and money is not a problem when you're as good as Candy Golden. For players as good as she was, there are always ways around the rules.

Candy and Coach D broke the rules frequently after the season ended. The violation began in February, after he stopped her in the hallway between English and physics class.

"Golden? You doing anything tonight?"

"What do you mean?" Candy shifted her books from arm to hip and continued to unwrap the Mounds bar that Amy Prokoff, dieting again, hadn't wanted at lunch. She'd been eating junk food since the season ended in December. A candy bar or a bag of chips gave her momentary pleasure. Without that she'd have no pleasure at all.

"Meet me here in the gym at seven. I want to work with you on free throws. I've got a new theory. Of course, we all know it's psychological"—he tapped his forehead—"but this goes beyond that. Do your homework first. And don't tell anybody. I'm not supposed to work with players one-on-one, especially off-season."

Candy had been dreading the weeks and months ahead. She was living at the Prokoffs' house. January had been brutal and boring with the letdown from the season over, and the tract of time before her too easily filled with thoughts of the two things she missed: her mom and basketball. She was glad to have something to do that night.

When she arrived at the gym, Coach D was waiting for her, whistle around neck, basketball in hand. He walked to the free-throw line. "Your problem is you haven't thought enough about success. You don't visualize the ball going in time after time after time. You need to make the shot a part of the movie in your head. And every time it's in your power to make the movie end the exact same way—ball through hoop. Everything leading up to it is exactly the same, too. You dribble three or four or seven times, whatever you choose, I don't give a damn, but always the same. You bend your knees. You use your legs. You extend your arm. Always the same. Always. Shot after shot. One hundred and fifty times a day. Always going in. When you start to see it happen in your mind, you'll start to see it happen at the line." He sneezed four times and swiped at his nose with the sleeve of his shirt. "Sorry, allergies."

Candy shrugged, unimpressed. Nothing new here. Consistency. Practice. She stuck out a hand. "Give me the ball."

"No ball."

"What do you mean?"

"I mean you're going to shoot without the ball."

"That's stupid."

"A lot less stupid than shooting fifty-five percent from the free-throw line."

"So you expect me to just go through the motions? For how long?"

"As long as it takes."

It sounded dumb. A big waste. But summer ball didn't start until June, and there were a lot of evenings to fill between now and then. Candy pantomimed a dribble and then bent her knees and released the invisible ball quickly, feeling like an asshole, glad nobody was around to see.

"So you only dribbled once?" Coach D pointed at her hands.

"You said it didn't matter."

"I never thought you'd choose once. Try three times." Coach D smacked the leather ball against the gleaming varnished floor and then he sneezed twice. "That will give you time to settle yourself if you need settling. But not so much time that you'll start thinking too much, especially if it's a crucial point in the game."

Candy did as told, feeling three times as stupid. He made her do it that first night for fifteen minutes without the ball. After that, he told her to sit on the floor and cross her legs and close her eyes. "Oh geez, Coach."

"No talking, Golden. Phil Jackson does this—are you saying Phil Jackson doesn't know what he's doing?"

"It hasn't worked with Shaq."

"Shaq should lose fifty pounds—that would solve a lot of his problems." Coach D's hand drifted down to his own gut, which lapped over his faded sweats. "Be quiet now. I want you to think of safe calm places. I want you to imagine a place where you feel completely at peace and at ease. It could be a lake or a mountaintop or a field. Most people use nature."

Candy didn't. The place she felt safest and most comfortable was where she was that moment. On the gym floor. She thought about that. After a few minutes that seemed like many more, she squinted one eye open. Coach D stared at the ceiling, and then he reached his finger to his tongue and pulled something off it, maybe a stray hair, Candy couldn't tell, but clearly something bothered him. He sneezed—five times this round—and then he finally explained, "I took in a stray cat last week, and it turns out I'm allergic, but I like the little bugger so I'm trying to cure myself by swallowing a few cat hairs every hour." He sneezed again. "So far it's not working." If she didn't know what a great coach he was, Candy figured she'd probably think he was a retard.

Coach D didn't let her touch the basketball until they'd been there almost an hour, and then it was a defensive drill. He banged the ball off the glass. She read the setup and shot, planted her feet shoulder width apart and mustered her muscles to tighten and explode on cue, propelling her up to meet the ball as it crashed off the glass, seeking the timing that would reward her with the ball at the peak of her leap. He shot from the top of the key, purposely missing, so she could leap and snatch the rebound. Bang, leap, snatch, grasp, thud. After ten tries, her legs ached. She hadn't worked out since State. She panted, doubled over, and pulled on the hem of her shorts. Coach D cut into her break with his whistle.

"Golden, where the hell is your timing? My grandmother could jump higher than that and she broke a hip six months ago." He shrilled his whistle again. "Sprints. Suicides." He pointed to the baseline.

In practice, in season, she would have moaned. But that night she ran suicide sprints stoically—dashing from baseline, where Coach D planted himself, to free-throw line, dropping and doing five push-ups. Sprinting back to baseline, dropping for five more push-ups. Racing to half-court, dropping, five more. Back to baseline, more of a lope than a sprint now, exhausted, dropping, her push-ups wobbly, upper body, lower body, every muscle shivering. Counting herself down— five, four, three, two, one—to nothing. It was February 8. Her mom had died on November 28. Seventy-three days ago. She didn't want to know that number, but every day since the accident, upon waking, she added one to the indelible total from the day before. And one. It was too easy. If only the math were harder, maybe she could stop.

She moved more slowly now, but not dogging it, still hustling all the way downcourt to the opposite baseline, meeting the floor with her palms flat and muscles trembling, forcing her biceps to push her body up and lower it slowly, wishing instead that she could fuse herself to the floor, that she could extinguish all anguish by pressing herself into the gleaming varnished boards. But every time she made her mark, Coach D whistled, pulling her to her feet and back to the baseline where he waited to get in her face, not giving a damn that she was exhausted. Demanding that she go on. He was Bobby Knight without the sweater and the rage, a hard-ass who wouldn't let her stop. But that night in the gym, his callousness morphed into compassion by some alchemy of whistle shrill and sweat and closeness and command. Or by something much simpler: he was there. So Candy continued.

From the February after her mom died to mid-June, when she left for two weeks at the Red Star Elite Basketball Camp in Terre Haute,

Indiana, Candy and Coach D met at All Saints' gym on Tuesday and Thursday evenings. And though they never talked about it, and she never thanked him for it, Candy knew that with Coach D at her side and the basketball, imaginary or real, in her hand, she got settled enough inside the gym to continue outside the gym.

When she got back from Red Star in July, she heard that Coach D had left for northern Michigan at the end of June. He hadn't mentioned that he was going away for so long, but he had a brother who lived up there. He'd told her that once, so she didn't give it much thought. She played club ball in Troy the rest of the month, so she was busy—it was a long commute from the east side of Detroit to the northwest suburbs. When that was over, with Coach D still on vacation and Raven basketball tryouts and practices ready to begin in a couple of weeks, she shot around and scrimmaged and played pickup games with her friend Jimmy, who went to public school—Denby— and with a few other guys who could handle that she was better than they were. Sometimes she just shot for hours in the Prokoffs' backyard. She played Horse with the little kids next door. She hung out with Amy and Jimmy. Glo called every other week and reminded her to go to church and say her prayers. And Elizabeth called three times, never catching Candy in, and leaving messages that she'd try again soon, but she didn't. No complaints there. Candy messed with Anita Prokoff—breaking curfew and other house rules just for the pleasure of watching her itch. Up until the end of July things had been decent.

But then things quieted down enough for her to hear the whispers swirling around her, and to notice that people looked at her differently. And then she was called into a meeting at school with Ms. Hogan, the principal; Sister Anne, her favorite teacher; and Mr. Morrisey, that stupid dick, that lousy guidance counselor, that geeky dweeb. And in that meeting they told her that Morrisey was taking over as coach of the Ravens and that Coach D had resigned. She wouldn't have come willingly if she'd known any of that. She'd been blindsided.

"So, Candy," Ms. Hogan started, "how have you spent your time this summer?"

"Hanging out with Amy Prokoff and earlier I worked out with Coach D. And I went to Red Star in Terre Haute and played in Troy for a while. And I'm coaching a kids' team at Clark." Candy had totally bailed on Amy there, but she hoped to shake them off her back by mentioning volunteer work.

"Working out with a coach in the school gym off-season? Technically, that's not allowed, you know." Ms. Hogan ignored her charitable offering.

"Well, it wasn't official or anything. It's been a tough year, Ms. Hogan."

"It's not uncommon for a young girl to try to replace a missing parent with a parent figure. Have you gone to that grief support group at St. Matthew that I told you about, Candy?" Mr. Morrisey's Adam's apple bobbed above the collar of his navy blue Izod shirt, which he wore buttoned up tight. He folded his hands on his briefcase, in front of him on the table, as he spoke.

"My strength comes from within." Candy opened the Coke she'd brought with her, the hiss punctuating her point.

Sister Anne changed the subject. "Have you read any of the summer reading list I gave you at the end of class? I think you'll really like *Pride and Prejudice*." She'd reached out and patted Candy's hand.

Morrisey changed it back. "When you worked out with Coach D was it just you or did Amy Prokoff come along?"

"Amy doesn't like Coach D. He won't put her on varsity because she doesn't work hard. And now she's too old to play JV—it's embarrassing when you're a senior."

"So she didn't come with you?"

"Why would she?"

Mr. Morrisey ignored her question. "So what did you do. Drills? One-on-one? Shoot-arounds?"

"All that." Candy took a slug of Coke.

"Contact?"

"What?" Her face got hot and she choked a little.

"Was there physical contact?" Morrisey's Adam's apple stayed very still.

Where in the hell was Coach D? How come he wasn't there to back her up? A few days later, she still hadn't figured it out. Oh, there wasn't *any* question about her loyalty, and no way she'd *ever* play for Morrisey. It was like that night at the funeral home with her aunts, when, as confused as she'd been, she knew it wouldn't be right to live with either of them. No, she corrected herself, it was lots worse. It was basketball. It was important.

Like niece, like aunt—Elizabeth Brannigan was a remarkably pretty woman. She was slender and tall, though not outlandishly so. Her nose wasn't large and her eyes weren't small. Her hair wasn't too thin or too curly, but was instead a thick rich brown with an inch-wide natural golden hank that often fell in her eyes. True, her clothes were on the frayed and sloppy side and at first glance that was a distraction, but anybody who looked a second longer saw past that. Her first two husbands, Matthew, then Ben, had described her as having untamed beauty, as if she were a waterfall carving out a mountain crevice or a pasture schooning with grass. They'd bought her tight, low-cut shirts and lacy lingerie for which she was completely un-suited. She'd been young enough then to pretend she was grateful.

But her third husband, Leo, had taken a closer look. "Careless," he'd said after they'd known each other a month. "You have the most careless beauty I've ever seen." She remembered how she'd pushed her bangs, which needed a trim, out from behind her glasses, which were taped on the left side from a crash she'd absorbed during a pickup game the day before, and examined Leo right back, needing to know if he thought that mattered. "Careless?" She saw he wasn't insulting or complaining or suggesting she change. "I can live with that."

Elizabeth blew the whistle around her neck and motioned the freshman girls clustered under the basket to form a line at the top of the key. They played outside—the seniors had the inside gym, where it was cooler. The June sun at one o'clock in Los Angeles didn't so much shine as brand—its rays turning cells squamous and chopping breath short.

The principal of Our Lady of Sorrows Academy for Girls had come to Elizabeth's guidance counselor office just ten minutes earlier, begging her to sub for the phys ed teacher, who'd left to tend to her suddenly sick toddler daughter. "Elizabeth, please do this for me. Do some basketball drills with them. Maybe you'll discover some hidden talent for next year's team. Run them around for fifty minutes. Tire them out. I'll owe you."

"The school year is over in four days, Janice. You won't have time to pay me back." Elizabeth grabbed her whistle from her desk drawer even as she grumbled. The woman was her boss. The line between re-quest and order was inscribed on her monthly paycheck.

"You"—Elizabeth pointed at the first girl in line facing her—"dribble toward me. Everybody else watch. Notice how I plant myself before her and refuse to give ground. It's called taking the charge, girls. It's all about establishing position. It's called playing defense. She'll get the foul, while I stand firm." Elizabeth gave a short shrill of her whistle and motioned the girl to come at her.

The clumsy girl wound up and ran, dribbling wildly to shoulder height. It wasn't until she was a foot away that Elizabeth read the fierceness in her eyes, and realized she'd misjudged the speed with which the skinny thing moved. Seeing it, Elizabeth flinched and then gave ground, backpedaling, adding her own backward motion to the reckless forward velocity coming at her. She never would have dreamed that the girl, just a wisp, maybe even anorexic, would hit her with such force. Bone on bone, the student knocked her down, grinding Elizabeth's shoulder into concrete.

Six weeks later, at the end of July, while walking home from Ralph's grocery store carrying two heavy sacks through her Hollywood neighborhood near Sunset and LaBrea, a traffic-jammed spot marked by an abundance of fast food, hookers, guitar shops, and sticky, gum-spotted sidewalks, her aching shoulder called that day right back. If she'd given her injury some attention—heat, ice, rest—it would have healed in a few weeks. Instead she ignored it, not even altering her weight-lifting routine. She went to Gold's Hollywood Gym and hoisted 50 pounds of dumbbell over her head to work her shoulders, and then flattened herself onto the ripped synthetic-leather-covered bench and pressed 110 pounds up and down, and then again nine more times, two more sets, half the time fearful that it would all come crashing down and mark her permanently. The other half wishing it would, wishing her wounds visible so that she'd reap sympathy, if only from herself. She crept reluctantly out of bed each morning, her joints tight even in sleep, so that she ached on waking. Once vertical, she felt askew—her blood heavy, her head light. She'd lost 10 pounds since she'd moved to Los Angeles from Chicago right after her divorce, right before Melissa's death. The 135 pounds she now weighed were not enough for her five feet eight inches, but the weight loss only made her feel lesser, not lighter. She lumbered everywhere.

Literally. The transmission on her fifteen-year-old Toyota Cressida had blown soon after she'd driven it cross-country, so she had to walk or take the bus, a biped freak in speedy L.A. She remembered how heavy her foot had felt on the accelerator as she fled Chicago, putting distance between herself and her failed marriage. The marriage to Leo. The one that had been based on more than whimsy or sex. The one that should have lasted.

At thirty-six, she was too young to have already divorced three husbands. She knew that looked bad. "Troubled is the definition of marriage," she used to laugh and tell her friends in Detroit and Chicago after her first two marriages. "Oh, Elizabeth," they'd laugh back, "for you it sure seems that way." But when she and Leo split up after four years, nobody laughed, least of all her. Leo, the right man. Finally. Their marriage doomed by circumstance, no by *need,* beyond their control. He'd realized he wanted children. She'd always known she didn't. Whose fault was any of that? Might as well blame him for having brown eyes, her for green. Nobody who knew the whole story could help but feel that they'd both been dealt a blow. They hadn't lied to each other in the beginning. It wasn't her fault or his that he'd changed his mind and forced it to an end.

The phone rang as she entered her apartment with her groceries. She let the answering machine take it, then obeyed as Glo demanded, "Pick up that phone, Elizabeth. I need to talk to you *now.*" Glo would have made a good principal.

"I'm here. What's wrong? Are you okay?" A can of soup rolled out of the bag and off the table where she'd dumped the sacks and nailed Elizabeth's toe. "Damn it."

"Please. Watch your language. I'm fine. It's not me you need to worry about. It's Candy. When did you last talk to her?"

"I don't know. I left a message a while ago, maybe last week." Elizabeth thought it must have been June when she called and Anita Prokoff had said Candy was in Indiana at basketball camp. "She never calls me back."

"I thought as much. I call her the first and third Wednesday of every month. You need to get a schedule, Elizabeth. Your life will run more smoothly if you plan ahead."

"Right. Plan." Elizabeth looked at the foot-high stack of *Hollywood Recycler*s on the table next to the groceries. She'd been meaning to look through the classifieds and find herself a used car. Meaning to do so for the past three months. "So, what's the deal with Candy?"

"She quit the basketball team. She refuses to play this upcoming year. It's her senior year, Elizabeth. She has stacks of letters recruiting her for college. She'll receive full scholarships to all the best schools, and yet she refuses to go to practice when it starts next week."

"Why?"

"Her coach quit. Somebody else is taking his place."

"And why is that?" Elizabeth moved the phone away, protecting her eardrum from the slice of Glo's sudden intake of breath. "Glo, tell me what you heard and where you heard it."

"Anita Prokoff called. Candy's coach resigned. *In June.* I'm furious that they didn't tell us this beforehand. Candy didn't find out until yesterday. She's quitting to protest his resignation, which she believes was forced."

"Why did he resign? Why the secrecy? What is she protesting?"

"They're accusing him. And her. It's his fault. He's thirty years old, after all. She's seventeen, Elizabeth. It can't be." Glo's voice wavered. "Can it?"

"Glo, you're not making sense. Tell me exactly what Anita said." Elizabeth was afraid of the sense Glo was making, and she closed her eyes as her aunt continued.

"She said they think Candy and that man had relations." Glo whispered. Elizabeth heard her aunt's words come over the phone line in suspiration, a sigh, ashamed. Was there some sense of longing in them, too?

Elizabeth imagined Candy's coach preying on her naïve bravado, transforming the honest sweat of the gym to something perverse in his bed—the girl too young to know she should gird herself against his attention instead of tease it. The weight of the allegation, true or not, settled sadly. Such a thing would be hard for a seventeen-year-old to carry or shed. "What does Candy say?"

"She's not talking. But he's left town. She spent a lot of time alone with that man this year." Finding somewhere to pin blame, Glo's voice became firm, each word a hammer. "They *allowed* her to do that. I blame them. I blame every single one of them."

Elizabeth, hearing this thirdhand, knew there was reason to remain skeptical. She'd worked in high schools for ten years. She'd seen how rumors started. How somebody looking way too hard for trouble spots a flaw in the truth and encourages others to pick at it until they've created a rent large enough for everything but the truth to show through. Voyeurs all.

Then again, just this past June at Our Lady of Sorrows, Elizabeth had watched as three of the one hundred graduating seniors reached over their own protruding bellies as they shook the principal's hand and claimed diplomas. Clearly, high school girls had sex. And Elizabeth had seen more than one male colleague become intoxicated by the fresh skin and adulation of a sixteen-year-old girl gazing up at him over a Bunsen burner or Shakespeare sonnet. Most never acted on it, but clearly, too, thirty- and forty- and fifty-year-old teachers were sometimes aching to have sex with those sycophantic students.

"Elizabeth, listen to me. Anita Prokoff wants her out of the house if she's not playing basketball. Do you know what it was like to listen to that woman accuse me of neglect? I have *not* been negligent. I write and call regularly. Candy was living in the best place for her this year. But now, you and I, we've got to set everything straight."

Elizabeth wondered which sin was worse, to admit (to herself, at least) that she hadn't done right by her niece? Or to be in such denial about it, as Glo was. "What do you have in mind, Glo?"

"We'll pick her up and take her out of town for a week and get to the truth. I don't know where we'll go. I haven't planned it yet. The problem with that girl has everything to do with morals and faith. I need you to come along. Not for help with morals or faith, but I want a hand with the drive."

Elizabeth imagined being in the company of her reckless niece and sure-footed aunt. The timing wasn't right. She'd stumbled around for eight months now. She needed to gain traction on her own before she tried to help somebody else. She shouldn't subject herself to them or them to her. "Glo, you should go to her, but this isn't a good time for me. Like you almost said, I'm immoral. What help would I be?"

"Elizabeth, the girl is in trouble. Melissa named you guardian. You have responsibilities."

At the mention of her sister, Elizabeth flared. "She named me *co*-guardian with you. I'm officially relinquishing my half of the post. I give you free rein. Go ahead and guard. Send her to reform school. To a convent. I'll back you up. I'd send money if I had some."

"Candy wants to stay in Detroit with Amy for her senior year, but the Prokoffs will have nothing of that right now. I'm sure I can convince them to keep her, but only if she straightens up and plays ball. Elizabeth, if she doesn't live there, where will she go? If she doesn't play ball, what will become of her? I know I offered to let her move in with me when Melissa died, but clearly I'm not equipped to raise a teenaged girl. Elizabeth, I don't *want* to raise a teenaged girl."

"She's already raised, Glo. She's seventeen. I'm sure she's bluffing. She'll play ball this year. And if she doesn't want to, there's nothing we can do to force her."

"If we don't get this girl back on track, she's going to be living with one of us."

"Quit with the 'we' and the 'us,' Glo. I'm not up for any of this. I'll help convince her to stay in Detroit or to move in with you, but I'll be no good for her. I'm not even good for me." Elizabeth scraped frost off the cylinder of frozen juice melting and staining the unfinished wood table.

Glo ignored her. "Listen to me. *We* need to step up to our responsibilities in regard to this motherless girl. *We* are her only family."

"Melissa did not die thinking of me as family."

When their own mother, Glo's sister, had died of a heart attack while on her honeymoon in Florida with her fourth husband, Elizabeth had been twelve and Melissa fifteen. Elizabeth's father, Tony (their mother's third husband), was an intelligent and decent man. Melissa's father, Rick (their mother's second husband), didn't stick around long enough for anybody to form an opinion on the kind of man he was.

Though they had been old enough to stay home on their own, Tony had offered to move back into the house for two weeks and take care of Elizabeth and Melissa while their mom honeymooned with husband number four. It had been a year since the divorce, and though he saw Elizabeth regularly during that time, Tony said he missed daily life with her and Melissa. "You know, times like when we'd just sit around and watch TV or I'd pick them up and drop them off somewhere." Elizabeth had overheard him saying that to their mother. "Don't go getting all sentimental" was her mother's response.

When she died, Tony had simply stayed on. At least Elizabeth remembered that part as simple. The part about their mother's dying was much more complicated for her and Melissa, but their relief from the tempest of their mother's moods was simple, too. At the time, Glo had offered to move from Chicago to Detroit for a few months and help out with the girls, but Tony said it wasn't necessary, and Glo didn't press. Tony had been married to her sister for ten years before they divorced. He was a caring father and stepfather. He held a higher place than aunt. Glo went back to Chicago a week after the funeral.

When Melissa and Elizabeth were young, they'd played a game in which Melissa would claim Tony as her real dad if Elizabeth didn't successfully perform some Byzantine task at her command. "Run around the block five times in ten minutes and then make ten straight free throws and then recite the pledge of allegiance without taking a breath." Melissa would smack her hands together and shout "Go," and Elizabeth, six or seven at the time, would sprint to defend her claim to Tony. By the time Elizabeth was old enough to understand what Melissa was doing, she also understood that she, who never once met the rigors of these tests, was the lucky one in the equation of their family life.

Tony was not self-indulgent and short-tempered and dismissive and mildly drunk as their mother had often been. His neglect was benign. He worked at Oakwood Hospital, where he managed the second shift maintenance staff from 3:00 to 11:00 P.M., so that Elizabeth and Melissa came home after school every day to an empty house. Every few months, Elizabeth heard her dad on the phone with Melissa's father. Tony sometimes yelled at him to stay away if that's the attitude he had, and other times pleaded with him to pay some attention to Melissa, who had pushed and tested the limits before their mom died, and crashed through them once she was a teenager with a stepfather calling the shots.

"Come on, Elizabeth," Melissa would urge her little sister, wanting her to shotgun a beer to perform for her high school friends who had taken to hanging around their house, which had no parental supervision. They all laughed at Elizabeth who, still wearing her sweaty basketball clothes from practice after school, spun wildly, already drunk on the one Stroh's she'd sipped.

In the beginning, Melissa would kick her friends out of the house and clean up all the beer cans and cigarette butts before Tony got home from work at midnight, but after a few months she didn't bother with that charade, meaning that sometimes Tony came home to a party that he broke up with threats to call the cops and the stricter parents, as in the dads who worked days and moms who hadn't married four different men. Other times he walked in after the party to find Elizabeth tending to her drunken sister. (It had taken only two wicked bouts of hangover-induced nausea for Elizabeth to steer clear of Melissa and her friends and their beer.)

After three years of this, it was Elizabeth who, with Tony's backing, urged Melissa out the door to college. "You've got to get out of here, Mel. Go to Western—it's a party school. You'll like it."

"I don't know, Elizabeth. I don't like the idea of leaving you alone here." Elizabeth, fifteen, studied Melissa carefully. Did her sister honestly think she was a good influence? Melissa continued, "With Tony working so much, and me in Kalamazoo, you'll be alone here all the time. You'll be stuck here in Detroit."

"I'm fine alone. Maybe alone is how I'm meant to be. I'm at basketball practice a lot of the time anyway. And I'll be leaving soon. Just two more years and then I'm going to college, too. I'll get out of Detroit. If I can get in and Dad will pay, I'm going to UCLA. California, Mel. The ocean. Imagine visiting me there. I need more than this"— Elizabeth scraped frozen pizza cheese off her paper plate—"and you do, too."

"This house is pretty grim, isn't it? Tony doesn't really have a clue." Melissa took a pull from the Coke she drank with dinner. She'd wrecked a car while driving drunk the month before and the crash had scared her off beer for a while.

Elizabeth stood up for her father. "I didn't say that. Tony tries hard. He takes care of things. He comes home every night. He pays the bills. There's food and a phone and he's willing to pay for your college. We're okay, Mel. *I'm okay.* You've got to go."

"I guess so. I guess you're right."

"I *am* right. I'm fifteen, Mel. The worst is over. We did it. We raised ourselves." Elizabeth raised her water glass and clinked it on Melissa's Coke.

But twenty-one years later, while talking to Glo about the trouble Candy was in, Elizabeth could not forget Melissa's sober response: "You're right. But Elizabeth? I think we may have done a really bad job."

"Elizabeth. Are you still there?" Glo shouted into the phone again. "Elizabeth, you need to quit taking out your trouble with your sister—"

"Half sister," Elizabeth corrected.

Glo raised her voice, emphatic, "On your niece. You and Candy used to be close. What's wrong with you?"

"Candy doesn't like me. You saw that at Melissa's funeral. I won't have any influence on her. I'll make things worse."

Glo wouldn't hear it. "You have to come with me. I'll pay for your plane ticket out. And though I hoped you would agree to do the right thing before I mentioned this, I'll also give you Stan's car. It just sits there in the garage. I have my own car. I don't need his. Spend just a week with me and Candy. We'll go in August. The third week looks good. If you do this, you can drive back to California in a Cadillac— a Coupe de Ville. It's only five years old. It has only fifty thousand miles on it. It's in pristine condition. Stan kept it in the garage and barely drove it in winter. It's black. He told me once he thought you'd like it."

"So big dumb Stan wanted me to have his Cadillac?" From the moment they'd met, Elizabeth and Stan had had lavish fun insulting one another.

"Don't call him that."

"I say it with affection. He called me Lazy Lizzy and made fun of me because I was tall."

Ten minutes later Elizabeth hung up the phone. They'd gone back and forth, but they'd shared firm common ground: Glo *shouldn't* drive around alone with Candy; Candy *should* play basketball her senior year; Candy *shouldn't* have sex with her coach; and if Candy already had done that, she *should* get some help. Elizabeth missed plenty of nuance these days, and Glo was quicker to condemn than to care, but the same big picture came in clear to them both.

Glo hadn't had to sweeten the pot with the offer of Stan's car, and a Cadillac was not at all Elizabeth's style, but she'd take it. She could always trade it in. She was broke, and she was tired of trudging around L.A.

Gloria Dreslinski could still lay claim to beauty, too. Five feet nine inches tall, with a spine as straight as a schooner's mast, she would have appeared regal even if she were six inches shorter. Her thinness was not ascetic, but, still, the cords of her neck, the declivity of her collarbone, the jut of her hips, created edges. She wore her reddish-brown hair short (it was late to gray), and she wore her clothes ironed. The crease of her pants, the placket of her blouse, the cuffs of her sleeve, each of these had a cutting edge, part of the picture of angled elongation that she presented to the world. Her faith had edges also. She did not shy from stating her opinions. She was a devout Catholic—she called herself that, others would, too—but Gloria had made her deals. She felt her guilt. Her husband, Stan, was dead and she was not completely unhappy about that. Worse, she was thinking about sex.

A week after coercing Elizabeth to join her in saving Candy, Glo sat in a lawn chair in her Portage Park backyard on the northwest side of Chicago and watered the flowers that Stan had planted years ago. The cusp of late afternoon fell off to dusk while she sat, and the garden drooped with the weight of a day's heat not yet relieved by evening.

The neighbor's cat, a fat black longhair named Darcy, glided toward her, stopped, and then backed into her shins, unwilling to face her with his need. She reached down and stroked the animal, running her fingers along its ridge of soft spine, sure its indifference was affectation, something she understood. She'd spent much of the day working in the garden, listening to the buzz of bees on blooms, and now the added touch of Darcy made her think of Stan. Of sex with Stan. He was the only person with whom she'd ever had sex, after all.

She missed it. Sex, that is, not Stan. She liked living alone. She liked having her house back to herself. But lately the desire for physical contact warmed her in odd places—at the Jewel in aisle four choosing paper towels, or watching the delivery man unload his crates of Coke in aisle two, or at the bank waiting in line for the young teller to hit a switch that chimed and beckoned her, the next in line, to approach the window, finally open. Young, old, stranger, the neighbors' cat—it didn't seem to matter—she craved touch.

She and Stan had had sex 416 times. She wasn't proud to know that number. She hadn't planned to count. But she also hadn't planned to be forty-nine with no sexual experience when she married. Such a background was not normal. She knew that. Desire and sex were essential—the drive to them biological. She'd never denied that during her chaste years. And she certainly wouldn't do so now. How could she? But it irked Glo to think of their reactions if people suspected she'd been a virgin until age forty-nine. It's not as if there weren't other biological imperatives that people did not gratify. Violence, in certain situations, was a primal urge. Meat-eating, too. Yet those who didn't engage in these activities at age forty-nine were not judged harshly, were not laughed at behind their backs.

If the right man (Catholic) had presented himself to her and suggested sex at the right time (after their wedding ceremony), she would have been just like everybody else and had sex at age eighteen or twenty-two or some other less giggle-inducing age. But it hadn't happened for her that way.

When she and Stan had sex for the first time it had been, with her history (or make that lack of history), more than a typical momentous wedding night. The second, third, and fourth time they had sex invited comparison. By the time they'd been married for five months they'd had sex twenty-six times. The more Glo tried to forget the number, the larger and brighter it flashed in her mind each and every time she lay next to Stan, their coupling complete, their breathing falling steady again after first rising to keep up with sheer glee.

Glo suspected nobody looking at her—she was sixty-three after all and her mien was more puritanical than passionate—would believe that she'd had such pleasure in bed. She was glad about that. She had nothing *against* sex. She'd cast her vote *for* it. But intimate matters were to be shared only with one's spouse in ways that were not reliant upon speech. Whether they described it profanely or with reverence, people spoke entirely too much about sex. She hadn't shared her pleasure in it with anybody but the man she'd slept with for fourteen years. Now, ten months after Stan's death, the number 416 flickered off to the side, reminding her of pleasure past. Glo would not marry again. Of that she felt sure. With the brush of Darcy against her bare leg, she forgot, for a moment, all else she was sure of.

She shook her head, rattling another thought into place. The girls. The trip. Those details had fallen into place once Glo set her mind to them. In just two weeks, Elizabeth would fly to Chicago from L.A. They'd drive Stan's Cadillac and pick up Candy in Detroit, heading up north from there. North to Indian River, Michigan. North to the Cross in the Woods. She'd made her choice. They would make a pilgrimage to a shrine.

For years, Glo had dreamed of visiting it, but Stan had preferred other kinds of vacations. Glo hadn't pushed him toward the Cross. She'd been saving it. The time should be right, she'd thought. Her traveling companion devout. The occasion somehow sacred. Within one year of marrying him, she hadn't seen Stan as worthy of a shrine.

He had been a decent man—sturdy, loving, and easy—but she'd

found out too late that he wasn't devout. He'd worked as an accountant for the archdiocese of Chicago for more than forty-five years, but he might as well have kept the books for the Pussycat Gentlemen's Club over on Pulaski. He simply didn't believe, and this was a breach for which she had been unable to forgive him. She should have married a husband whose faith rivaled hers, whose beliefs burned. Stan's tepid faith wouldn't warm a gnat at noon in August.

As it was, it was almost worse that he'd been so good to her in other ways. It made her look rigid to others, even to herself. If he had been lazy or stupid, stubborn or angry, *everything* in her marriage would have felt hollow and wrong, and maybe she wouldn't have felt this one, deep, carved-out place in her chest. It would surely have spared her the hypocrisy she felt. For though it pained her when he decided not to go to Sunday morning Mass, when she returned home, she sat at the breakfast table with him—the table he'd set with matching place mats and napkins. She ate the breakfast he'd made. She thanked him for doing the dishes. And later that week or even that day, she had sex with him willingly, enthusiastically. It seemed to her irreconcilable to believe, as she most certainly did, in the virgin birth and a Savior who was celibate, and yet desire a man who should have been celebrating the Eucharist, not making pancakes for her at home. Her desire for Stan became an affront to herself.

She stayed with Stan for fourteen years, thinking all along that if he left her the very next minute, in many ways she'd consider it a gift, a release from the ambivalence that irritated her on good days, and caused her deep pain on others. She didn't see how her faith and her feeling could both be judged as good. For that, she'd have to meet a different man. A devout man. A man available for marriage, as well as for sex. At her age it seemed unlikely.

She had no illusions about the worthiness of her troubled niece and grandniece as companions on her shrine tour—next to them Stan seemed saintly. But their mission together was a worthy one. Plus, she wanted to get to the Cross in the Woods before she died, and at her age that could happen any time. She had heart trouble herself (probably genetic—her sister had died of a heart attack at the age of forty-six), and look at Stan: cleaning the gutters one day; a stroke the next; a funeral six months later. She'd sacrifice sacred for help with the drive.

The Indian River brochure showed the fifty-five-foot-tall cross with a bronze, seven-ton Jesus nailed to it, his head bent in pain and sorrow, looking down, not up at God his own father who had forsaken him. Glo looked at Jesus in the brochure, his arms forcibly outstretched, pleading for relief. She set down the hose and stood quickly, startling the cat, Darcy, who darted away. It was too hot, even at five o'clock. She'd come back and finish up when the sun set.

At the kitchen table, an hour later, Glo looked through a large pile of direct mail pleas from charitable organizations. In addition to her weekly twenty-dollar contribution to her parish church, St. Viator, she gave twenty dollars every month to one charitable cause or another. This month she opened her checkbook to SANE—Stop Abortion No Exceptions—and its full-color mailing.

She looked at the balance in her checkbook register, subtracted a sum to bring it up to date, and then circled the new balance—$274,635.89—in a thick green marker, a reminder to herself to call the young woman she liked at Fidelity Investments and talk to her about what to do with it. The check for $270,000—Stan's life insurance policy—had arrived just a few days ago. She stared at the large number circled in green, a sign of abundance. She didn't need the money. She'd invested in the stock market for years, carefully, with due diligence. Stan had, too. And after they'd married they'd invested some together—mostly technology stocks that they'd sold high enough and well before the bubble burst. There was money in her name, his name, their names. She had her pension after working for the archdiocese for almost forty years, and her Social Security would start soon enough. And now she had this life insurance money. It was really too much. She didn't need it. If she lost it tomorrow, her life would be no different from today.

Maybe she'd give it to a good cause, Danny Thomas's children's hospital in the South or to some school that helped children who didn't have all their arms and legs. Or she could give it to SANE—it wasn't logical to help sick or crippled children who weren't allowed to be born in the first place. SANE told the truth, and abortion was a grisly business in its eyes. In Glo's eyes, too, though she closed hers to the bloody proof that SANE splattered in its mailings. Instead, that day, as she did every so often, she stuffed the material into a larger envelope that she'd been putting together for Elizabeth. It contained a hodgepodge of printed matter that might help her niece: two small prayer booklets, a one-page fact sheet about a baby's pain upon being aborted, a brochure titled *A Handbook for Returning Catholics,* an essay from St. Viator's church bulletin on the importance of discipline in Catholic education, and a holy card with a picture of Mary—blond hair, blue robe, and white veil flowing—on the front, and a nine-day novena to her Immaculate Heart on the back.

Glo would post the envelope tomorrow. It would give Elizabeth reading material during her plane ride from Los Angeles to Chicago. The girl was resoundingly anti-life—she and Glo had sparred about the topic for years, though by this time neither rose high to the other's bait—and she had sinned gravely by marrying three times, not once in the church. Elizabeth's job at a Catholic high school was a charade, something she and Stan had in common. But the work of the Lord wasn't meant to be easy, and Glo took solace in the words of the Capuchin monk Father Solanus Casey as printed on a holy card in her wallet: "Do not pray for tasks equal to your powers. Pray for powers equal to your tasks."

Glo thought of Candy and Elizabeth, of those girls snarled in sins committed by them and to them. Her breathing, which ran ragged and angry when she thought of that coach, almost stopped as she pictured Candy. Glo felt as if she had a ten-pound sack of flour on her chest. She reminded herself to stay calm. This kind of anger wasn't good for her. But what desecration had the girl been part of? No matter how much her coach had pressed, Candy should have resisted. Glo felt righteous—*she* would have resisted. And Elizabeth? Three marriages? True, her mother, Glo's sister, had been a terrible role model in that respect. But Elizabeth shouldn't use that as an excuse. If she did, that is. Glo wasn't sure what explanations Elizabeth offered for her ill-considered choices. If the girl couldn't commit to any of those husbands, she should have committed to the institution of marriage—entered it and stuck to it whether she liked it or not. It wasn't complicated. Anyway, if her niece couldn't make it with as good a man as her last husband, Leo, there was something fundamentally wrong with her.

These girls were her tasks, no doubt, and though Glo didn't assume she was *guaranteed* success in assessing their problems and setting them straight, she prayed for the power. She truly prayed.

She wrote a note for Elizabeth's care package:

Dear Elizabeth—

Enclosed please find an inspirational booklet from our guides to the Holy Father and eternal salvation, the Salesian Fathers, Brothers, and Sisters. Also, some political information on the good work being done by some of our partners in saving unborn children's lives. These pictures may upset and disturb you, but if you pray for the strength to examine them fully and to admit your sins, I think you'll find that God will not abandon you. And isn't that a beautiful picture of the Blessed Mother? There's a prayer on the other side! I look forward to seeing you for our shrine tour. I will pray for your safe arrival. We'll have a good time as we take care of Candy while we visit the Cross in the Woods.

With love,

Glo

The phone rang as she sealed the envelope. She pushed back her chair and straightened her stiff right knee slowly, feeling the joint crack and creak open. When she finally got to the phone, after eight rings, she didn't recognize the voice that answered her hello.

"Mrs. Dreslinski?"

"Who's asking?"

"This is Anita Prokoff calling from Detroit. It's about Candy."

"What about her?" Glo wished she'd let the phone ring. This woman rarely had anything good to report.

"She's missing again, and I just got a phone call from her new basketball coach and it seems she didn't show up at his first team meeting this morning."

"What do you mean missing? What do you mean again?" Anita Prokoff was an alarmist.

"It's seven o'clock. She was supposed to be back by two. She and my daughter Amy are helping coach kids' summer basketball at Clark Elementary. But Amy came home without Candy."

"Amy shouldn't have done *that*." Glo heard her tone and softened her approach. Anita had fed and housed her grandniece for the past eight months, and the whole point of the shrine trip was to make sure she'd continue to do so. "Where does Amy think Candy might be?"

Anita Prokoff ignored the question. "I've asked Candy to obey the rules of our home."

Glo heard an edge in Anita Prokoff's voice. "Let's focus on the problem at hand, Anita. Are you suggesting we need to call the police?"

"Mrs. Dreslinski—"

"Please, I've asked you to call me Glo." Anita Prokoff's use of her surname was no sign of respect. The woman merely thought her old.

"Glo," Anita pronounced it from the back of her throat, the "g" congested as if she had an infection, "Candy is a big problem. There's no other way to say it. There's the situation with her coach, and there are boys, too. I don't know what she's done with them. She stays out past curfew. I don't know where she is all day. Amy says she's changed." Anita's voice became crisp down the stretch.

"Maybe Amy is in a rut," Glo spoke her mind again, and then backpedaled to politeness. "Seventeen is a difficult age. Remember, Candy lost her mother less than nine months ago. Have patience, Anita."

"My husband and I were happy to help out with Candy during

the school year last year, but if she's not playing basketball this year . . . before today we didn't believe she meant it. You have to realize that besides my Amy, I have a thirteen-year-old daughter. I'm concerned about Candy's influence on her. What I'm trying to say is . . ."

Glo interrupted, knowing exactly what Anita Prokoff was trying to say and knowing she'd take too long to say it. "You're saying that Candy can't live with you this year because she quit the basketball team."

"I'm glad you understand."

"Now Anita, I promise we'll straighten this out. Elizabeth and I will pick up Candy two weeks from today—Saturday, August seventeenth. I've made all the plans. We'll knock on your door by one in the afternoon. Tell Candy to be ready. She'll be a new girl when we bring her back. She'll play basketball and continue to live with you next year—make no mistake about that."

"Mrs. Dreslinski, what about the other issues?"

"Patience, Anita. Who among us is perfect before God? All we can do is pray for strength and forgiveness and understanding."

"Hold on, Mrs. Dreslinski, I think I hear Candy. Yes, she's at the back door. I'll put her on."

"No, no, Anita. Thank goodness she's home so you don't have to worry anymore. Candy and I will talk during our trip. Right now, I'm just glad I was able to help." Glo hung up in the middle of the woman's protest.

Relieved to be finished with that call, and sensing a slight turn to cool in the air filtering through the kitchen window, Glo went back outside and sat in her lawn chair, watching the arc of water from the garden hose lift up up up and pelt back down on the roses Stan had planted fourteen years ago. Their blooms were past full in late summer, not needing the attention she showered on them now.

CHAPTER 3

*I*N TIMES THAT had turned almost everyone into a nervous flyer, Elizabeth paled and perspired more than most as she boarded her plane, United Flight 130, the red-eye to Chicago. It was scheduled for departure at 11:15 P.M. to arrive at O'Hare the next morning at 5:06. Rushing toward dawn.

It hadn't been one full year since 9/11, but even before that day gave her better reason, she'd always expected each flight would be her last. More specifically, she thought she and everyone else had a finite number of safe trips assigned to them at birth—a grim, flight attendant–like fairy godmother pinning numbers to souls like distant death knells. If only she could discover her allotment, she could ground herself after flight eighty-three or ninety-six and avoid the fiery crash of number eighty-four or ninety-seven. Or maybe she would fly safely and land in one piece until her four hundred and seventy-seventh flight—way more flying than she planned to do. She wished she knew. This flight to Chicago and Glo would be her sixty-ninth. Caught in the grip of her own theory, she counted doggedly, superstitiously, even as she hoped the numbers would amount to nothing.

She gave herself a silent reminder to keep calm as she arrived at row fourteen and stuffed the bag she'd packed just a few hours earlier into the overhead bin. When she and Leo had gone to London after they married (her fifty-fifth flight), she'd spent two days packing—picking and choosing just the right combinations of colors, of shoes, of skirts and sweaters, just the right amount of underwear, socks, books, and T-shirts. She had packed thoughtfully, as if it mattered.

But not that evening. Not for United Flight 130. Instead, that evening she'd watched a drama outside her bedroom window and barely paid attention to her packing. When she and Glo and Candy arrived up north, she might open her bag and find twelve T-shirts and a slipper.

The drama was one she'd seen before, but it continued to engage her. Another of her nameless old neighbors in the six-story multiunit across the street had died. It was a regular apartment building turned ipso facto nursing home for the aging population it housed. Elizabeth often watched the old people who lived there as they came and went, making their daily rounds of shopping, walking in the park across the street, and sitting on the steps kibitzing. They were only a little older than Glo, she guessed, though she couldn't imagine Glo *ever* looking or acting like any of them. Glo moved with purpose from point A to B. She wasn't one to linger on porches or park benches, and she looked more fit at sixty-three than Elizabeth felt at thirty-six. In contrast, the old folks across the street seemed sodden with age. The men had torsos uninterrupted by waists, their belts wrapped arbitrarily near their middles. The women wore dresses bright with print, their legs sausaged into nylon stockings despite relentless heat, their surplus pounds jouncing in arms, stomachs, hips, even jowls.

Every few weeks, Elizabeth saw the EMS or fire truck parked in front of the building, saw the paramedics amble, not rush, toward the door, as if department protocol forbade hurrying to a victim so old. Or perhaps it was the old folks who set the rules, who knew how to die suddenly and unequivocally so that no medical intervention would rush in to eradicate the simple past pleasures of their lives or counter the certainty of their deaths.

Earlier that evening, as she packed, Elizabeth watched the paramedics roll a stretcher out of the building. On it was a body bagged in white, stiff and still like a statue ready for transport. There were no family members alongside tugging and crying and pleading, or pale and quiet and stricken. She wondered if maybe alone was the way to die—neat and efficient, with no breast-beating or tears from those around you to complicate the process.

It was definitely better than dying with a plane full of strangers. She buckled her seat belt and pulled it tightly across her lap before the flight attendant told her to do so. As the plane rumbled across the tarmac, she closed her eyes and began her ritual for a safe flight. First, she reached under her blouse and touched the neck of her T-shirt—a relic from the state high school basketball championship team she'd played on twenty years ago. She'd worn it the first time she'd flown and landed safely, eighteen years ago, and that was enough to wear it sixty-eight times since. Then as the engines keened to speed, she gave God a silent pep talk. *Come on now. Just one more today. Concentrate and you can do it. Not just for me. Do it for all the good people on this plane.*

Ten minutes later, she touched the neck of her T-shirt again and relaxed as Flight 130 leveled to cruising altitude. She was free now until it was time to land. The man to her right in the two-seat row already snored, his head turned toward her, his hot breath inches from her ear, as if they were sharing a bed, a pillow. The cabin lights had dimmed and the plane was unearthly quiet. Why wouldn't it be? They were in an unearthly place, flying thirty-eight thousand feet high, terra firma hidden beneath a cover of clouds that were themselves indiscernible at night.

She shifted in her seat, trying to escape her discomfort. Her shoulder still ached from her June run-in with the anorexic girl, denying her rest, and sending a stream of pain down her back that pooled and dripped to her hip. As she finally settled in a comfortable position, she was startled out of it by a teenager across the aisle who jerked her hands out and thrust her neck forward. Elizabeth instinctively looked around for somebody to lurch across the aisle and help the girl, who was obviously having a seizure, but then she noticed the CD player on the girl's tray and the tiny earphones puttied into her ears. She wasn't seizing at all, she was listening to some savagely named band whose lyrics probably encouraged her (as if she needed encouragement) to hate her parents. She looked to be about Candy's age. Watching her, Elizabeth tried to muster some authentic emotion about the mistake her niece had made by quitting basketball. (For now, she was compartmentalizing, as in ignoring, the suspicion about her niece and the coach.) Mostly she felt empathy, or maybe it was jealousy. She wished she could quit, too. But quit what? *Quit whining. Quit drooping. Wake up.* She answered her own question.

She turned to the envelope in her lap, another hodgepodge missive from Glo. It had arrived last week, but she'd been too busy to look at the contents. Elizabeth always reviewed Glo's packages carefully, wondering if she would ever surprise her by altering the script—her aunt's religious compulsion interested her, at least from a distance. Elizabeth had tucked a few other things she wanted to look over during the plane ride into the envelope also—the current issue of *Sports Illustrated*, a memo from Sorrows' principal about the beginning of the school year, and a card that had arrived from Leo just that morning. She took it out now.

It was a "birth" announcement. He'd adopted a little girl, Molly, it said. Four years old. The card was a photo of the two of them, the girl sitting on a tree branch, Leo beneath her, the photo cropped to show just his head and arms raised up, steadying the little girl's bottom, both of them laughing, the tree an oak with generous branches and deep green leaves. The oak that grew in front of the house he and Elizabeth had lived in together for the four years of their marriage. The little girl's face was fat. Her cheeks flushed red. Her mouth was open to a shaggy strand of black hair misplaced by the breeze. She clapped her hands, clearly not worried about falling, trusting Leo to hold on.

This was why Leo had left her. This girl was the reason they'd divorced—but it could have been any girl or boy. Leo had known when they'd married that she didn't want children. It hadn't been a problem then—he didn't want any either. But by year two of their marriage, Leo wasn't so sure anymore, and by year four, he was certain he'd changed his mind. He wanted a child. Or children. Biological, adopted, foster—he wasn't picky. He needed to be a parent. And she still needed not to be. And in their certainty (and on such an issue, certainly they both were entitled to that), they could not find a way to compromise. Despite the fact that these needs were unassailable, and the resulting divorce unavoidable, something nagged at her. If they'd continued to share the same feelings about children, they'd still be married, right? She wondered, remembering her conversation with

Melissa so long ago, "I think alone is how I'm meant to be." What kind of thing had that been for a fifteen-year-old to say?

If Flight 130 were to fall out of the sky that second, Leo, laughing and holding on to a stranger he'd chosen over her, would be the image she would pray over, bargain over, panic over, and hold tight to her chest as she died. That wouldn't do at all. She stuffed the photo back into Glo's envelope and pulled out Mary, the Virgin Mother, blond and blue-eyed on a holy card. A Barbie heaven blessed. Elizabeth clutched it instead.

Two hours later she woke, unsure if any time had passed. She took her glasses out of the seat pocket in front of her and struggled to see the face of her watch in the dimness. Whatever time it was, it was the middle of the night in L.A. But here, wherever here was, dawn infiltrated the dark beyond the window with thin rootlike streaks. Thirty minutes later Flight 130 touched down, the brakes straining, the wing flaps shuddering. Elizabeth touched the neck of her T-shirt twice, once on each side. Her sixty-ninth flight had been a success. Thanks be to God. As they traveled slowly, civilly, securely across the tarmac at O'Hare, she already dreaded number seventy.

The Blue Line el sped alongside the traffic-jammed expressway from O'Hare. The el was the quickest way out of the airport, and Elizabeth was glad that Glo, not wanting to deal with increased security, had suggested she take it. It was her last chance to be low energy and depressed. Once she got into the car with Glo and Candy, she would have to suck it up. Candy was an orphan. Glo a widow. Their troubles trumped hers—she wasn't too depressed to at least acknowledge that.

Elizabeth's old el stop at Irving and Pulaski straddled a freeway overpass about two miles from Glo's house. Nothing much on the platform had changed. Walter "Skippy" Jacobson's image, huge on a poster advertising his role as anchor on Fox News, still had holes poked through the eyeballs and a mustache Magic Markered above the smirky smile. Elizabeth grinned seeing it, and then took the stairs down from the platform, grin turning to grimace as the strap of her bag cut deep into her left shoulder, creating a symmetry of pain that was not pleasing at all.

Once at street level, she stopped and looked around. Even this early in the morning, the overpass trapped August's hot air to produce a kilnlike effect. Twenty yards away, where the sky broke free of the cement-and-reinforced-steel canopy, Elizabeth saw people walking languidly toward a bus. Clearly it was hot over there, too. She crossed Irving, dodging traffic. A westbound bus that would drop her almost directly at Glo's house shuddered to a stop in front of her, full even on an early Saturday morning.

She couldn't make herself get on. As the bus pulled away without her, muscle memory, brooding nostalgia, and the slightest bit of something else she hadn't felt in a while (was it merely consciousness?) pulled her east, toward Leo. Toward their bright blue house with white trim and crabgrass in the front yard. It was only six blocks from the el stop. She hadn't planned to do this, and she might regret it, and Glo would surely be irritated when she arrived late, but in that early-morning moment she wanted flesh-and-blood proof of Leo's happiness with his little girl. After that, she'd let him have it.

She looked down at the pigeon-shit-spattered sidewalks, hurrying to escape the underpass, eager for blue sky to appear. Just before it did, she looked up to see two pigeons homing directly in on each other, flying low, one heading back to its dingy dwelling, the other aiming for sky. She cringed, expecting them to crash, and was relieved when they didn't. One of them, feathered in grime, brushed against her arm. That couldn't be a good sign.

. . .

Elizabeth was sweating clear through her lucky T-shirt by the time she got to Leo's. She stood on the sidewalk, across the street, alone in the early morning, deciding whether to knock. Leo hadn't planted flowers, which he'd done every summer when they were together. Coarse crabgrass grew in place of flowers, but even it was ground down to dirt in a wide ring, like an urban crop circle.

Elizabeth really didn't have to knock. She still had keys to the house, the garage, and the back gate off the alley. She put her bag on the ground and fished her keychain out of her backpack, twisting off the old house keys, metal-warm in the heat of her hand, until the one key to her L.A. apartment was left with nothing to jangle against. Maybe Leo would look out the window and see her, would help her decide that it wasn't too early in the morning, too early in the divorce, to ring the bell.

She crossed the street and stood under the shade of the big oak that covered the eaves of the house. The leafy tree had been a blessing in the summer heat, and in winter, its branches, husked in snow, became radiant. She remembered the living room as she'd left it. Comfortable. Worn. Functional. Like a pair of sturdy, broken-in boots. An overstuffed chair that had belonged to Leo's grandma was in one corner, an Arts and Crafts rocker Elizabeth had found at a junk store in another. Lots of books, some shelved, many not. The floor was covered with a dark green straw mat they'd found together at a Lincoln Park garage sale for five dollars. They'd piled up pillows to hide the tear in the arm of the purple velvet couch, and always had fresh flowers that they'd sheared from a green-thumbed neighbor's overgrowth, which crept through the fence into their backyard. Thinking about it now, she wondered if she should have left it all for him. Those things that she'd collected, that they'd collected together, that, for her, had been the physical manifestation of their good life. Things that fit together surprisingly well given that they didn't match at all.

Leo had warned her that she was being hasty when she'd insisted he keep everything. Until right now she hadn't realized that he'd been right. Leo was in there with all their comfortable, useful, broken-in things. In their house. With his daughter. And what did she have? An empty apartment in a city she found barely tolerable, and a five-day trip with a religious-zealot aunt and a teenaged-phenom-athlete-slut niece to look forward to. Goddamn Leo. How come everything had worked out for him? She climbed the porch steps and rang the doorbell of her old home. She hoped she *would* wake Leo.

A woman wearing cutoffs and a tight black T-shirt answered the door on the first ring. In her arms was a baby, resting on her right hip. "Yes?" The baby screwed up its face to cry as the woman spoke.

"Oh." Elizabeth wobbled under what she hoped was only the weight of her suitcase. She felt a creep of sweat on her temple. "Is Leo home?"

"I'll get him. Come in. Do you need a glass of water?"

"Is that Leo's?" Elizabeth, confused, pointed to the baby in the woman's arm.

"No, this is Gracie, my girl. Say hello, Gracie." The woman raised the baby's floppy arm and waved it at Elizabeth. Gracie frowned and bleated. A child screamed in the back of the house, in the kitchen, and the woman cocked her head that way. "*That* would be Leo's girl. Molly. And that would be the first of her dozen daily tantrums."

Who was this woman? Why was she letting Elizabeth, a stranger to her, into the house? And offering up such personal information. "You know, on second thought, this is obviously not a good time. I'll just call Leo later." As Elizabeth backed out of the hallway she'd just stepped into, her bag caught on a table that had never been there before and knocked over a china saucer full of keys. The saucer shattered on the tile floor—a floor previously cushioned by an acute blue chenille rug. The baby wailed at the clamor. "Oh hell, I'm sorry." Elizabeth leaned down to pick up the mess, apologizing to the woman, but it was Leo who answered when she finally stood straight, various keys and large shards of china protruding from her palm like thorns and her shoulder blade throbbing from the sudden movement.

"Elizabeth? What are you doing here?"

A child, Molly of the oak-tree picture, though not laughing, ran out from the kitchen with jelly smeared on her face and hands, screaming for notice while simultaneously hitting Leo's bare legs with her sticky arms. Not waiting for Elizabeth's answer, Leo knelt to talk to the little girl. Elizabeth sniffed and caught a whiff of diapers and wet dog, not smells that had been part of the house when she lived there. As if on olfactory cue, a dog barked in the back. She looked at the girl's rear end, which was encaged in alligator-print pajama bottoms, and what looked to be proof of a diaper. Surely four was too old for that.

Leo had always been a morning person, his early-going easy. The minute he got out of bed, he'd showered and dressed and been wide awake. But that morning, red veins crawled through the whites of his eyes and he wore the oversized Jerry Jeff Walker T-shirt that he often slept in, the one from the 1977 tour. The hole in the back had grown bigger since she'd seen it last. His thick black hair stood up on one side, was flat on the other, and was greasy all over. He hadn't put in his contacts yet—his big silver-framed glasses were crooked and ten years out of style.

She examined the living room while he dealt with the girl—it looked worn and dingy, not warm and comforting as she'd remem-

bered outside. The formerly bright white walls were smeared with fin-
gerprints and streaked with crayon marks here and there. The aquar-
ium, empty of fish and water, was home now to black-tinged green
scum on glass walls. The hardwood floor, which they'd stripped and
sanded and polyurethaned until it gleamed, was dull and scratched in
deep grooves around the legs of the couch. When she'd lived here with
Leo, while it hadn't been house beautiful, its shabbiness had been gentle, self-deprecating. It had been shabby with books and the purloined
fresh-cut flowers and the creaking rocking chair with a thick pillow
on its seat. Shabby as in, Please sit down and read or listen to music,
and, Here, have a glass of wine. Not shabby as it was now. As in,
Damn, the dog wrecked the floor. As in, Sorry it stinks. As in, Oops,
don't sit there, it's sticky.

Leo knelt still on the cold tile floor, his arms embracing the girl,
who, unable to hit, cried louder. The woman with the baby, Gracie,
sat in the living room, nursing and watching cartoons on a tiny black-
and-white TV. Taking in the surroundings—the crying, nursing, hitting, wailing; the dog smell; the dingy walls—Elizabeth wondered,
How had it happened? How could this—all this noise and grime and
smell—be what Leo wanted more than he wanted her?

This scene with this troubled little girl was vintage Leo. He leapt
to "yes," trusting he'd always find a way, trusting he'd never deplete
his emotional stores, trusting thin ice. She loved that about him, but it
wasn't her way. She had become a cautious person—a lesson learned,
finally, from her first two marriages, and from her childhood, too.
Watching Leo that morning, though, she wondered if it weren't so
much cautiousness as mistrust that dictated her motions and moods.
She remembered Melissa's observation: *We raised ourselves. . . . We
may have done a really bad job.*

Elizabeth repeated to herself the question she'd asked on Flight

130: If not for this screaming little girl, she and Leo would still be married, right? This time she answered: she was no longer sure.

She stepped back again and placed the spilled keys, the broken plate, on the table. "I'm sorry, Leo. It's so early. What was I thinking? I should have called. You're busy, in the middle of . . ."

"No. Really. It's fine. Mornings are tough for Molly, but we're working on it." Leo looked into his daughter's eyes. "Molly, Dad needs you to take some deep breaths." He looked back up at Elizabeth. "We're working on rules and limits."

"Everybody needs those." Elizabeth changed the subject, pointing to the nursing mother. "So, that woman? You and she? The baby?" Her voice weakened, anticipating the answers to her half-asked questions.

"No, God no. Sally," Leo shook his head emphatically, "watches Molly while I work. Just for this summer—I have to find somebody else for fall. Remember John Durham? Young guy who teaches algebra at Lane Tech? Anyway, Sally is his wife. They needed extra money, but they just had the baby so she didn't want to get a full-time job right now. I needed somebody to take care of Molly. It worked out for everybody. I'm teaching driver's training at Lane this summer—the morning session. This is my last week before school starts full-time in September. That's John and Sally's baby, Gracie."

"Looks like one, big, happy family here." Elizabeth, relieved at the explanation, watched as Gracie cried and Sally switched the baby to her other breast.

"I'm sorry the house is such a mess. We're all still adjusting." Leo let go of Molly, who whimpered now instead of cried, and then stood and faced Elizabeth. "But listen, I haven't even introduced you properly." Molly, free of Leo's arms, turned her back and kicked the hallway wall. "Molly, turn around now. Stop kicking the wall and say hello to my friend Elizabeth."

Elizabeth knew she should crouch down and give the little girl something to look at, something to turn around for, but at least she was quiet now. She said hello from above and then talked to Leo. "So, you look good."

"Liar."

"I must look even worse. I've been up all night flying. I'm going on a trip with Glo."

"Oh, right. The shrine trip. She told me. Your niece, Candy, is in trouble."

"She told you?"

"Was it a secret?"

"You talk to Glo?"

"Every now and then. She watched Molly once when I was in a real pinch."

"She never mentioned it."

"She said you don't like to talk on the phone."

"I'd like to talk about that." They spoke in beats to the rhythm Molly set as she kicked the wall.

"Come in, Elizabeth, please. I'll get you some coffee. I don't have to leave for an hour."

A black sheep-sized dog ran into the hallway from the kitchen and jumped on Elizabeth before she could accept the invitation. The dog barked, then salivated, then blew its furnace breath in her face. She stood very still, not wanting to encourage it, trusting Leo, who knew just how afraid she was of dogs, to tell it to stop. Preoccupied with Molly, he didn't.

She inched away from the dog. "You know, Leo, this was not a good idea. I haven't slept. Glo is expecting me. I better go now. I'll call you sometime soon." She leaned down to pick up her bag and then remembered the house keys still in her pocket. "Oh, and here."

As Elizabeth reached out her hand to him, he stretched his own toward her. And for a second this is what she heard: the clink of three keys from one hand to another, the click of the dog's nails on the tile floor as he walked away, the muffled thud of the little girl's rhythmic kick against the wall, the baby Gracie's snorty suck in the living room. She imagined Leo taking it in, relishing this moment of ordered chaos, of something as close to silence as he would get for a while.

"Elizabeth?"

"Yes?"

"Molly is a really nice little girl." He closed his hands around the keys.

Elizabeth hoisted her bag to her shoulder, winced, and backed away.

CHAPTER 4

GLO WOKE THAT morning at four. By six, which was when she expected Elizabeth, she'd said her prayers; drunk her morning coffee (against doctor's orders); taken her cholesterol and blood pressure medication, her aspirin and diuretic, her calcium supplement (other than coffee, she was completely compliant); filled a small cooler with fruit and yogurt and carrots and a large thermos with coffee and carried them both to the car. She then read the newspaper from front to back, and triple-checked that the iron, hair dryer, and coffeemaker were all unplugged.

She was looking out the front window when Elizabeth finally arrived, struggling out of a cab with her bag. She opened the front door before Elizabeth even knocked. "You're more than an hour late."

"The plane was delayed."

"Nonsense. I called the airline. They said it arrived ten minutes early."

"Train. I said train. I took the subway here."

"Then why the cab?"

"Glo, please. No third degree. I'm sorry I'm late. But I've traveled almost two thousand miles and it's not even eight A.M. yet. How about a cup of coffee? Or even just a 'Hello, Elizabeth, how are you?' " Elizabeth was still too confused by her visit to Leo to tell Glo the truth.

Glo hadn't seen Elizabeth since Melissa's funeral in December, but she didn't need to ask how she was. She'd lost weight, and the skin under her eyes looked brittle and frail, as if it were about to molt. Standing on the porch, shoulders drooping, Elizabeth clearly needed help—Glo wasn't blind. But at the moment there wasn't time for concern. That could come later. "You've been better. I can see that. I've already had my morning coffee, but there's a thermos in the car for you, and we'll have plenty of time for hellos later. Right now, we need to get going to avoid the worst of rush hour. Everything is packed up. I'll have you know I got up at four A.M."

"It's Saturday. There's no rush hour. And I didn't sleep at all last night."

"Nonsense. People always say that and it turns out they were curled up like babies. You'll be fine. I'll drive first so you can take a nap." Glo moved her hands as she spoke, picking invisible pieces of lint off her blouse, running her finger along the part in her hair, pinching the sharp crease in her slacks, and then plucking car keys from her purse.

Roused by her aunt's feverish motion, Elizabeth grabbed the keys from her. "I'll caffeine up and drive first. That way I'll crash harder later. You can take over halfway, around Kalamazoo."

"Fine, fine. Whatever you want. This trip is my gift to you young people."

"Not just the trip, the car, too, right, Glo? You haven't changed your mind on that?"

The back end of Stan's Coupe de Ville stuck six inches out of the garage. Glo and Elizabeth entered the garage through the alley, sidling into the car because of the tight fit all around. As Elizabeth opened the door to the driver's side, she noticed that its black paint gleamed with a pinkish orange glow, a reflection of the early-morning sun.

The Cadillac was fully loaded with automatic options and religious paraphernalia: a CD player, a St. Christopher medal glued to one sun visor, an I LISTEN TO CHICAGO CATHOLIC RADIO sticker on the other, power locks and windows, cruise control, a dashboard Jesus figurine whose arms spread wide to the vehicle's occupants. Religion and luxury glided smoothly together down the road in Stan's Cadillac.

Elizabeth pointed to the dashboard Jesus and the sticker on the sun visor. "I didn't know big dumb Stan was into this kind of religious crap. I thought that was just you."

"I'm not going to ask you again, young lady. Please don't call him that. And don't use that kind of language. Especially when talking about religion. These are my things, not Stan's."

"Why do you care what I call him? Stan and I had an understanding. I actually liked the guy. It's you who didn't—at least in some ways. I didn't imagine that, did I?"

"Liking him has nothing to do with it. I was married to the man for fourteen years."

"Why?" Elizabeth sped up to beat a semi barreling at them as she merged the Cadillac onto the Kennedy.

"Why what? Some of us think one husband in a lifetime is plenty."

Or one too many, but Glo didn't say that. Elizabeth wasn't the one to whom she needed to confess. Besides, confession was meaning-less unless a person meant it, and Glo had mixed feelings about her guilt. Stan had always made fun of her prayers and devotion, calling her "Oh Holy One" when he was particularly angry or especially pleased with her. She flushed now, thinking of his caress, of the way he ran his fingers lightly down the length of her long leg as they lay to-gether, massaging her hip, humming to himself.

Glo positioned the air-conditioning vent so it blew directly on her face and waved her hand wildly in front of her own eyes. Sex was not enough to make a marriage. They'd met because Stan was at St. Mary's so often, helping to sort out the school's accounting ledger. "You gals at St. Mary's need a sugar daddy to help you replace that boiler," Stan had commented more than once as he'd worked out of a freezing, empty classroom one March preparing their books for inspection by the arch-diocese. Sister Assumpta, the principal, had laughed and sent Glo to bring Stan something hot to drink. Stan kept on his winter jacket and fingerless gloves as he worked on days when the boiler was on the fritz; on other days he was forced to loosen his tie, strip to his shirtsleeves, and Glo watched as his fingers moved nimbly on the ten-key calculator. Glo knew he'd been recently widowed, but he never mentioned his wife.

At first Glo thought that if only Sister Assumpta hadn't laughed at Stan's jokes and asked his opinion on everything from finances to fir-ing Miss Jenkins, who clearly was unable to control a roomful of teenaged girls, she would never have looked twice at Stan. He was nearly fifteen years older than she was, after all, and she had been a spinster long enough not to expect to end up anything but. But her boss, a nun no less, had flirted with Stan (Glo was sorry to say it, but it was true), and Glo found herself watching them curiously. When Stan asked Glo to go see a movie with him one afternoon after she'd brought him a cup of tea, she'd been surprised enough at the thought of being chosen over Sister Assumpta that she'd said yes. The next day, realizing that she was competing for a man with a nun, she wanted to back out, but she was not one to break a commitment. She blamed the beginning on Sister Assumpta. But she didn't blame the marriage on her. That had been Glo's doing—partly a reaction to her own parents' deaths the year before, to a sudden fear of turning fifty, and to curiosity about sex.

A few years into her marriage Glo had begun to imagine herself in the role of grieving widow, pale and sheathed in black, accepting condolences, offering them to others, showing her faith, preaching it when people marveled at her calmness and dignity in the midst of such loss, taking pains to hide her relief at her escape.

During her fifth year of marriage she'd made a list of what life would be like with and without Stan. *If he lived . . .* she had labeled one column. *If he didn't . . .* she had labeled another. *Must pray for patience. Must ask forgiveness. Must be kind.* She wrote these in column one. *Less cooking needed. More prayerful atmosphere. Sadness, but not overwhelming.* She added these to column two. When she was finished she ripped the list into tiny pieces and pushed them to the bottom of the kitchen wastebasket as if hiding a motive for a murder. She hadn't committed her yearning for his body to paper.

By the time Stan finally did die, they had been married long enough that some of the entries on her list had switched columns and others were long forgotten. With Stan gone, her hip ached and he wasn't there to help take her mind off the pain, and the lawn needed mowing but Glo didn't know how much Stan had paid the boy down the street to do it. She didn't even stop cooking, though she had less of an appetite.

Now Glo looked out the car window as Elizabeth sped east on I-90 until she merged onto I-94 past the steel factories in Gary, most of them abandoned now and filigreed by rust. They drove past Wolf Lake, which was divided by the freeway running through its middle and ringed by more industry, these plants smaller and still active, smoke billowing from them and drifting over the lake, which on that early morning held small boats from which people fished, apparently oblivious to the traffic and industry surrounding them, or maybe just resigned to it. Could they possibly think it pretty? A quarter mile up ahead, Glo saw a state police officer pull a silver station wagon off the road. She was staring at the officer and the station wagon when Elizabeth swerved violently.

"My goodness. What was that for?"

"Something sharp in the middle of the road."

"Well, slow down. You're lucky that's not you with the police. You're going eighty." Glo tightened her seat belt as she spoke.

"I'm trying to get us there on time."

"Just get us there alive."

"Do you worry about dying, Glo?"

"When I'm in the car with you, I do."

"Come on, be serious."

"I have a will. You and Candy will get everything."

"A will? You're only sixty." Glo and Stan had worked in Catholic schools all their lives. Elizabeth knew there wouldn't be much to leave behind.

"Sixty-three."

"That's still too young. Talk to me about your will when you're ninety and I'm visiting you in the nursing home."

"Are you going to put me in a nursing home?" Glo laughed.

"I said I'd visit." Elizabeth laughed, too. "But really, Glo, do you think about dying?"

"I'm comfortable with the state of my soul. I trust in God. I know what I want."

"What's that?" A car passed Elizabeth on the left and its driver honked and pointed at the Cadillac, laughing.

Glo looked at her niece, unsure if the question was about her statement or the passing driver, but Elizabeth, in profile, was solemn, so Glo told her. "I want to die at home in a prayerful manner. I want a priest at my side. I want you girls around me, too. You and Candy. You're my only relatives now. I want you to see me off. I want to bear any pain I may have with dignity. I want to feel every minute of my death. I want to see that white light. I want to know God." Glo reached over and pulled a stray hair off Elizabeth's shoulder. She held it up, the long brown strand dark against the sunlight. "I certainly don't want to die in an accident on I-94."

Glo flicked the hair to the floor and reached into her purse for her favorite rosary—wooden beads and a silver crucifix that gleamed— the one that had been blessed by the pope during his visit to Chicago more than twenty years ago. She began her creed, fingering the crucifix. Keeping her place bead by bead, she looked out the window, murmuring prayers in answer to Elizabeth's question. As they continued east, steel plants gave way to Lake Michigan vacation homes, then to farmland, and everything was flat and limp green, even the chlorophyll tuckered out by the August heat.

The car slowed and veered right, jostling Glo awake. She opened her eyes slowly against the glare of sun unimpeded by the passenger-side sun visor Elizabeth must have lowered while she slept. Her niece had *some* good instincts. Glo was glad to see those surface even in the girl's current sunken state. She reached into her purse for a tissue and wiped the sides of her mouth, then fingered her hair, which was flat on the side where she'd slumped against the window.

Elizabeth turned left onto the two-lane highway at the end of the exit ramp. "I'm starving. We're near a town called Mayville. Maybe they have a Dairy Queen. I want a chocolate malt."

"It's ten-thirty in the morning."

"Your point?"

"You've lost some weight—it's strange that you don't look better for it—still you need to be careful or you'll put it back on. It gets harder when you get older. I'm lucky not to have that problem. I've always been very trim. But your own mother was heavy and these things are often genetic."

"I got my mother's tendency to get married too often—that's my genetic jackpot. It's Melissa who leaned toward fat if she wasn't really careful." Glo's hair still wasn't gray, Elizabeth noticed, taking her eyes off the empty road and examining her aunt's roots but finding no sign of faux color. She hoped she'd look as good as Glo when she turned sixty-three. Since she barely looked better than her older aunt now, that wasn't likely. "Hey, Glo, I might just get onion rings, too."

"Don't be a smart aleck, and keep your eyes on the road. Go ahead and eat what you want, but your face is rather full for your being on the tall and thin side."

Elizabeth ignored her. "Do you remember Ben? My second husband? His parents owned a mom-and-pop Dairy Queen–type place in downstate Illinois. They named it after him when he was a baby—Frosty Ben's. Turns out he was lactose intolerant. We always used to laugh about that, but think what it must have been like for him as a kid."

"I don't believe that lactose business. People get a stomachache and they swear off a perfectly healthy food. It's wasteful." Glo looked in the mirror on the sun visor, applied lipstick, pinched her cheeks to bring out some color, and then touched up her hair with her fingertips.

"Oh no, it's real, Glo. Apparently, it's a genetic mutation that allows people to tolerate milk after they leave babyhood. So he never mutated. . . . Hmmm . . . I wish I'd thought that one through. He'd get severe cramps at even a pat of butter or sip of milk. We couldn't have a cake at our wedding. Maybe that was a sign of trouble to come."

"I don't think you should blame your failures on genetics and cake."

Elizabeth thought again of her mother's marriage record. "I could probably make a case for it, but I won't. I know I married the second time because I was ashamed that it didn't work out the first time. Melissa called that one from the start. And then she did a good job of helping it end. Melissa was very insightful when she wasn't very drunk."

"I don't know what drove you and your sister apart. Besides the drink, I mean. You girls never told me anything."

"Besides the drink? There wasn't room for anything besides that. But there are some things you'd probably rather not hear. Look," Elizabeth thumped the steering wheel and whooped, "I knew we'd find one." She pulled into the empty gravel parking lot of the Frosty Cream on the side of the two-lane highway and turned sharply right, butting the Coupe de Ville against a green-painted picnic table in a spatter of gritty dust.

Glo opened her door and stretched a leg out slowly, stiff from the drive. She hadn't slept well the night before and she felt it in her bones that morning, mostly up and down her right side. She felt limber enough on her left. She imagined her body divided, the one thousand extra milligrams of calcium and vitamin D she forced herself to swal-

low every morning shunted left, while on the right her skeletal structure rusted like those abandoned steel plants, her very bones slowly
crumbling to calcified dust. Her run-of-the-mill heart disease was
nothing compared to the chronic ache of her entire right side. She
used her hands to lever herself up and out of the car and then took
deep breaths of the humid August atmosphere, acclimating her body
to its release from air-conditioning. She looked ahead, expecting Elizabeth to be at the window ordering already, but was surprised to see
her niece on the other side of the car, inching herself out even more
slowly than Glo had, gradually reestablishing trust with her limbs. She
remembered how clumsily Elizabeth had gotten out of the cab.

"What's the matter with you?"

"Basketball injury. A kid knocked me down and I tore something
in my shoulder blade. The pain moves down my back and to my hip.
It mostly hurts when I sit for a long time. Or if I carry something. Or
turn. Or stand."

"You should see a doctor for that."

"Maybe we can get a two-for-one. You're not too speedy yourself.
Come on, Glo. I'm buying."

Elizabeth stepped free of the car and stopped stock-still after
she'd turned to close the door. "Glo? What is this on the side of the
car?" She remembered the honking and laughing on the expressway
and the glow she'd chalked up to sunlight in the garage a few hours
ago. It hadn't been sunlight at all. The side of the Coupe de Ville was
a roving billboard for something, though she couldn't tell what at such
a close angle. Elizabeth stepped back, looked, then asked again.
"Glo?"

"Yes?"

"Tell me we aren't driving around Michigan in a black Cadillac
with a hot dog painted on the side."

"I can't really do that now, can I?"

"Skipper's Red Hots?" Elizabeth read the name aloud.

"The owner, Tony, was a friend of Stan's. He paid Stan two hundred dollars a month to drive around this way. It would have been a good deal for Stan, but Skipper's went out of business a month after Stan had paid to get this done."

The colors were off—the hot dog was pale pink in a garish gold bun with a ribbon of ketchup more rusty than red on top. Elizabeth walked around to Glo's side. The hot dog there had a worm of AstroTurf-green relish on top.

"So this is the car you're giving me? A hot dog car?" Elizabeth imagined parking the car in the Sorrows parking lot—the students gathering around it, pointing, laughing, and making phallic jokes at her expense.

"I told Stan not to do it. You can have it painted over."

"And what's that going to cost?"

"Oh, much more than Stan was willing to pay. He didn't even earn back enough money to make up for what he paid to have it done. He wasn't about to pay more to get it off."

"Glo, do you understand now why I call him big dumb Stan?"

They were at the Frosty Cream window by then. Looking in, they saw a young girl, obviously pregnant, reading *CosmoGIRL* and drinking from a carton-sized paper Coke cup. She set the cup and magazine aside as Glo and Elizabeth said hello. Glo wasn't hungry. Not for ice cream. She'd like a tuna sandwich in about an hour. Maybe at Denny's or Big Boy's. Someplace where she could sit down and be waited on and use the ladies' room afterward.

The girl—how old was she? Glo had given up trying to guess women's and girls' ages. The ones Elizabeth's age no longer had clothes or haircuts that signaled their position as mothers or career women. They all looked as if they were free for a movie on Friday night, for drinking and dancing and dating on Saturday. These women, like Elizabeth, refused to get matronly. Were they twenty-eight? Thirty-two? Forty-four? Who could tell? They all wore the same shoes.

But the Frosty Cream employee was not thirty-two or even twenty-two. And she was too young to have a baby. That much was clear to Glo.

"Welcome to Frosty Cream. May I take your order, please?" The girl's red polyester uniform shrink-wrapped her bulging belly as she moved closer to the window and addressed Glo. Her name tag—SUZY—was pinned to the pocket of her smock-top, which was stretched tightly over her breasts.

"I'll have a small coffee with cream."

"Would you like French fries with that, ma'am?"

"With what?"

"Your coffee."

"I think not."

"My boss, Pete, says I have to ask." Suzy shrugged.

"Then you've done your job." Both Glo and Suzy turned to Elizabeth, who looked up at the menu, rapt.

"I'll have a large chocolate malt and a large order of onion rings."

"Would you like French fries with that, ma'am?"

"With my onion rings?"

"They're only seventy-nine cents. I just had some. They're really good. You and your grandmother could share." Suzy took a big gulp of her Coke.

"Well, sure. Why not?" Elizabeth turned to Glo, laughing. "What do you say, Grandma? Will you eat some of my French fries?"

Suzy took another pull on her soda before preparing their order. Glo and Elizabeth watched as she measured the malt powder three times before being satisfied she'd gotten it right, and then held the tin canister under the malt mixing stick, staring up at the wall and shifting her weight from foot to foot.

After a minute, Glo cleared her throat. "Hello, young lady, are you awake? That malt is mixed enough. And you need to start the fried food. We don't have all day. And I'm not her grandmother, by the way."

Suzy handed Elizabeth her malt. "You can go sit down. When your onion rings and fries are ready, I'll call you back." She set two cups of coffee on the countertop, one golden with cream, the other ebony. "Here's your coffee, ma'am. I know you're not her grandmother. I was just trying to make her feel younger. But I forgot that would make you even older."

Glo pushed the black coffee back at her. "We only ordered one."

"I know that, too. But I couldn't remember if you wanted it black or with cream, so I made it both ways." Suzy looked pleased at her ingenuity.

Elizabeth carried the drinks to the picnic table out front. "I don't think Suzy's kid is going to get into the gifted program at Mayville Elementary School." Glo laughed and sipped her coffee as they waited for Elizabeth's food. Every once in a while a car whizzed past and once in an even longer while a truck rumbled down the county road, but otherwise it was quiet—the Mayville Frosty Cream was just a little too far inland to get the summer tourists, and not near enough to Kalamazoo to get that bigger city's spillover.

"Speaking of Melissa, we might as well use this opportunity to talk about Candy."

Elizabeth, who had been concentrating on her malt, looked at Glo, puzzled, and then got up to fetch her onion rings and fries as Suzy leaned her head out the order window and bellowed like a barn animal. "Melissa?" Elizabeth questioned her aunt as she returned with a tray of hot greasy food.

"In the car. You mentioned her name. The point is, we have to make sure we're both working toward the same goal with Candy. We need to use this trip to its best advantage. The girl needs us to show her the way. Or she needs me to do that. Given your history, it will be best if you stick to driving and let me do most of the talking and example-setting."

"I don't think this visit to a shrine is going to save anybody, Glo. You need to be realistic about that."

"What we *both* need to be realistic about is that she is throwing away her future by quitting basketball. And that she needs somewhere to live if the Prokoffs won't let her stay with them. I don't think she'll agree to live with either of us."

"That's Candy's choice. And Anita Prokoff's, too. But ultimately, if Candy has to leave Detroit because she won't play basketball, she's just going to have to move to Chicago with you. She's seventeen. She's too young to live alone. You might like living with her, Glo. I bet you're lonely." Elizabeth had seen other star players at high schools she'd taught at get burned out by the time they reached senior year. High school sports had changed from when she played. The pressure was intense. This situation with her coach might even be Candy's excuse to cover a change of heart about the game. Since their phone call weeks earlier, she and Glo hadn't talked about the incident with the coach. Elizabeth, usually forthright enough about sex, didn't feel up to opening that conversation with Glo. Her aunt would have to take the lead. She wondered if Glo and Stan had had sex very often or at all.

"Nonsense. I haven't been lonely a day in my life. The girl would be unhappy with me. If it comes to that, she'd go with you. But the point is, it's not going to come to that."

"With me? You don't trust me to talk to her, but you'd send her to live with me?"

"You're closer in age. She could go to school where you teach. Or you could move back to Detroit and get a job there. I would, of course, help out financially. Her mother named us coguardians. I'm not going to abscond on my responsibility."

"No, no, no, Glo. I swear I'm not being a jerk about this—it's just a really bad time. Last November at the funeral home when I offered I meant it. I would have taken her in then even though I was operating more or less in shock. But now? Now, I'd welcome shock. I'd embrace it. I'd run to it. Things are just not so good for me, Glo. I can barely handle administering standardized career tests to these girls I deal with from eight until three every day. If Candy quits basketball, she'll have to go to school somewhere in Chicago. With you, but not with me. I would make things worse for her." Elizabeth sucked fiercely on her malt.

Two or three years ago, Elizabeth could have handled Candy. Maybe even helped her. She dealt with high school girls every day. She had been the counselor kids wanted to talk to—as much as any high school kid wanted to talk to anybody older. At Lane Tech in Chicago, when she'd been assigned juniors whose last names began with the letters "A" through "H," she'd had Serbiaks and Johnsons and Vicaris stopping her in the hallway between classes and asking for her help with a teacher or her opinion of a college or seeking her sympathy about boyfriends or girlfriends who'd broken their hearts. She'd been effective because while she acknowledged the students' feelings about their situations, she was also pragmatic.

For instance, when Ana Gomez had come to her office and insisted that Mrs. Barski was flunking her in trigonometry because she didn't like Latinas, Elizabeth arranged for her to be tutored by senior Virginia Povliak, whom Mrs. Barski had recently nominated for Math honors and a citizenship award. Ana had grumbled at first. She had imagined a showdown culminating in Mrs. Barski's firing for being a bigot, but Elizabeth knew Mrs. Barski as an authoritarian who was hard on everybody. A month later when her F had climbed to a B-, Ana had been content merely to complain about how much she hated trig. When Donny Freehan's father, a single parent who was understandably concerned about his extremely intelligent and mildly delinquent son, insisted that the boy enlist in the army instead of wasting his time at college, she'd convinced him to support Donny in applying to the University of Illinois via its ROTC program. Neither Donny nor his father saluted her for it, but Elizabeth had seen the deep split between the two coming, and she knew she'd done good work there.

Leo had worked at Lane Tech also. It was a large school. With 3,500 students enrolled, and afternoon and morning sessions overlapping and competing for space, they rarely saw each other, but he'd told her that he'd heard the kids talking about how they appreciated her, or at least, didn't see her as a total loser the way they did many of the counselors. Leo, more genetically optimistic than she was, became a realist, too, when, before they'd married, she'd told him the story of the breach between herself and Melissa. "What went on between you and your sister is one thing, but you need to get right with your niece, Elizabeth. Detroit and Chicago are not that far away. You need to go there."

She'd meant to, but then the first cracks in the solid face of their marriage began tentacling to its heart. She'd felt the fissures before he had. She'd noticed him looking at fathers with their sons or daughters in the park down the block, saw how happy he was goofing around with the neighborhood kids at the summer block party. It scared her, and making sure things stayed good with Leo was the commitment she'd chosen to attend to—she didn't trust herself to put things right in two places. Melissa had been sober then, and Candy didn't need an aunt who was perched on the precipice of another failing marriage.

And now, in L.A., at Our Lady of Sorrows? If Glo only knew how little aptitude Elizabeth had with young girls, she'd let Candy live in a cardboard box on the street before sending her to L.A. Elizabeth felt she was no longer fit to counsel anyone. This year at Sorrows was proof of that. Elizabeth felt a thicket of shame forming in her chest. The very last week of school, which in the Hollywood version of life would have been when the Sorrows girls finally came to understand what a wonderful person and rich resource they had in their guidance counselor, had been particularly upsetting.

She'd made no meaningful inroads with her students. True, she'd copied transcripts for them, and told them which courses were required, but that was about it—they hadn't asked for help of any other kind. Not that Janice, the school principal, necessarily wanted her to offer any. She'd been nervous enough about hiring Elizabeth, who, on her application, had admitted to being divorced without adding "three times." But Elizabeth had been recommended by a mutual Wayne State University friend who had moved to L.A. after college, and Janice had been desperate to find somebody to fill the spot suddenly vacated when the former counselor, five months pregnant with twins, was forced to go on complete bed rest. Joining the faculty in the middle of the first semester, Elizabeth found the other teachers didn't have room for her in their web of friendships already spun.

At least, Elizabeth had thought, early in June, the day after she'd subbed for the phys ed teacher and hurt her shoulder, the year was almost over. But she'd let down her defenses too soon, because when she came to work that day, she'd found a pile of dog shit outside her office door. That was bad. Worse, some prankster had placed her office desk nameplate in front of it.

There was an explanation. At night, when Sorrows was finally empty of all extracurricular activity, the janitor let loose two German shepherd guard dogs that patrolled the halls freely. Dogs being dogs, there was sometimes an accident. The janitor knew this and checked the hallways carefully each morning before opening the school to anybody else. On that particular morning, the janitor had been home sick and his replacement hadn't known to clean up after the dogs. Elizabeth could see how some smart-ass student hadn't been able to ignore the temptation. So there it was, her name—Ms. Elizabeth Brannigan—right in front of the dog's heap.

Elizabeth hadn't known about it until third period. She'd been late that morning and gone straight to first period assembly, and right after that she'd gone into a meeting in the vice principal's office. It was ten o'clock by the time she went to her office. It was obvious that word had spread: a steady stream of students just happened to be wandering past her out-of-the-way workspace. Preoccupied as she'd been with the full day of work ahead and her late start, Elizabeth had almost stepped in the pile. She'd stopped just in time, only because she'd heard a whispered gasp. She never found out who had done her that favor.

The next day she'd come to school early and walked in stealthily so that nobody would see her or the large bouquet of flowers she carried. She'd bought her favorite, tulips—bright yellow ones in a brilliant blue vase—that she placed on the same spot on the floor outside her office. She placed her nameplate in front of it. She wanted them all to think an alternate faction supported her. There was, of course, no such faction. She barely knew the kids she was supposed to counsel. She'd given them no reason to like her. The truth is, Elizabeth had walked into Sorrows every day feeling she could not have entered a place with a name more suited to her mood.

"Elizabeth?" Glo watched her niece sucking her malt, her face all concentration, as if there were some secret in the bottom of the paper cup. "Get this through your head. Candy *must* play basketball her senior year. Anita Prokoff tells me she has recruitment letters from a hundred colleges. We can't let her lose this opportunity. You know how good she is, don't you? They have a professional league for women now, I hear. It's called the NWA or something like that. Don't you know about this? What kind of coach are you?"

"The kind that doesn't force a pipe dream about the WNBA down a kid's throat." Elizabeth drained her malt, her straw vacuuming up every drop. "A malt finished. Isn't that just the saddest sound?"

"Candy is seventeen. She's too young to make such a decision. Her mother is dead. Who knows what went on with that coach of hers. If she doesn't play basketball and go to college, the next thing you know she'll be doing those drugs, that Ecstasy. She'll end up d-e-a-d on a dance floor. She needs some faith and some role models. She can look at us and see what to do. She can look at your troubles with all your marriages and judge for herself. She can look at me with my faith and one husband—"

"Whom you complained about constantly. 'Stan doesn't go to Mass. Stan doesn't pray.' And what do you know about ecstasy?" Elizabeth pointed her straw at Glo.

"That's even more to the point. I stayed true to my marriage vows even though it was difficult for me. Candy needs to stay true to basketball even if it's hard for her to do so. And we can show her that. I know boys slip drugs into girls' sodas at those parties. I read the paper. I watch *20/20* and *Primetime Live.* Has anybody told her to make sure she opens her own soda?" Glo reached for her purse and searched for something inside it, finally pulling out a booklet that she waved in Elizabeth's face. "And another thing. In light of these rumors we've heard about her, you also need to talk to her about . . ." Glo cleared her throat. She looked down at her coffee and over at the Cadillac and up at the sky, "About . . . you know."

"No, I don't know. About what?"

Glo pushed the booklet, *Pure Love,* across the picnic bench and watched her niece flip through the pages. Glo read the subheads upside down—"Isn't Everybody Else Doing It?" and "Does How I Dress Really Make a Difference to Men?" and "Rewrapping the Gift of Your Virginity If You've Already Fallen."

Glo wished somebody had given her such advice, or any advice, before she'd married Stan. As embarrassed as she would have been, she could have used some reassurance. But nobody talked about sex to a forty-nine-year-old virgin.

Instead, the night before she married Stan, Glo had been alone in her house feeling nervous and uncertain and scared to death that Stan would find her foolish and unattractive on their wedding night, and, worse than that, that she'd have to face him the next morning if he did. He was a widower—he was experienced. Before she so much as unbuttoned one button on her blouse in front of a man, Glo had felt ashamed. That she had gone from this to feeling confident and eager to have sex with Stan was something that she counted as a blessing, as a gift from God. That Stan had loved her 416 times was something she took as his duty and her due. God had provided finally, if imperfectly.

She looked across the table at Elizabeth, who read the booklet while chewing on the straw from her malt. Glo didn't kid herself that a woman who had been married three times hadn't also had sex out of wedlock. She felt a pang of jealousy. If only she were thirty years younger, she might be as able as Elizabeth to indulge herself, to make her choices based on what pleased her instead of what was right. Elizabeth wasn't the best person to talk to Candy about a woman's gift and her responsibilities—to remind her that sex outside marriage was wrong, and maybe even sinful, but that sex that resulted in babies when a woman was married was sacred—the babies perfect gifts from God the father. Glo knew Elizabeth would not put it that way. But she also knew she could not say the words herself.

"So you don't want me to talk to Candy in general, but you do want me to talk to Candy specifically about this?" Elizabeth held up *Pure Love*.

"Yes, about you know . . ."

"It's not called 'you know,' Glo. Say it. Say 'sex.' Say it, and I'll do it. Talk to her, I mean."

"I'll not only say it, I'll tell you something else—sex is for creating children, which is probably why all your marriages failed."

"Yours, too?"

"Don't get smart with me. I was past childbearing age. And my marriage did not fail. I was married for fourteen years, and you don't know as much about my marriage as you think you do. But you? Look at Leo. You couldn't find a better man. I thought you'd finally got it right when you married him. Now he's adopted that poor little girl all on his own, and he'll be happier for it, even though she needs a good spanking as far as I'm concerned. But you, what do you have? Look at you."

Glo followed her own rhetorical command. Sadness enveloped her niece. When she smiled or laughed, there was a noncommittal looseness, a detachment—only her surface seemed to respond, while her deeper muscles remained lax. Her dark brown hair was longer than it had been at Melissa's funeral, and shaggier. Hair escaped the barrette that she used to gather it crookedly in the back, and her bangs edged over her glasses like an untrimmed lawn. Her nose was long and strong, a nose fit for her height, and her posture had always been excellent, characteristics she'd inherited from her mother and from Glo, who was a proud five feet nine inches tall. But her wide mouth was her father's, complete with full lips that turned often into an expansive smile, or used to, and her eyes were his, too, sea green, bright, hopeful, though not that day at the Frosty Cream. Glo remembered her brother-in-law as a decent, intelligent, happy man, everybody's favorite, and her niece Elizabeth was a very pretty woman—it was no wonder three men had married her. And before now, for all her mistakes, there had been very little that was tentative about her. This nimbus of uncertainty currently surrounding Elizabeth was all the more disturbing for how alien to her it was.

Glo reached across the picnic table and pushed the hank of hair out of her niece's eyes—she still had that gold streak in front. "Elizabeth, I'm sorry. But you can help Candy and yourself on this trip. You clearly don't want her in Los Angeles with you, and you're not about to move back to Detroit to care for her. If you do the right thing by trying to help me convince her to do the right thing, then you may find your own way easier."

"Do you think it counts, Glo?"

"Do I think what counts?"

"Counts as helping if we manipulate Candy in one way so we can avoid helping her another way that would be much harder on us? And do you really think she had sex with that bastard coach?"

"Language, please. I try not to even think about that man—about that possibility. But I know our intentions are pure."

"I think they're anything but."

Glo pulled her hand back, frustrated by Elizabeth's accusation. "You have no right to judge me. If you're not going along with this, then go back to Los Angeles right now. I can't have you working against me. Are you going to help me convince Candy to play basketball and live with the Prokoffs again this year?"

Elizabeth thought about subjecting a seventeen-year-old girl whose mother had died a little over eight months ago to the lonely hollow of her life in Los Angeles. She and Melissa hadn't fared well, even when Tony had stepped in and done his best. She was a long way from being strong enough to pull herself *and* Candy out of the mucky rut they'd independently sunk into. It was like when the flight attendant, before a plane took off, warned adults to fasten their own oxygen masks before attending to their children. It would be better for Candy to stay with the family in Detroit this upcoming school year. To have a curfew and a home-cooked meal. Better for her to have more than she or Melissa had at her age. She nodded at Glo, "I'll do what I can."

With that, Glo and Elizabeth shook hands at the Frosty Cream in Mayville, Michigan. They had seven days, five hundred some miles, and a visit to one giant shrine to make Candy renounce her loyalty and anything else she might feel toward her coach and agree to play basketball during her senior year at All Saints.

Business settled, malt finished, deal struck, they got up from the picnic table, threw their trash in the basket, and walked to the car, stopping when they heard a sobbing screech from Suzy, at the order window, pleading with them to come back.

CHAPTER 5

GLO RAN, REACHING the order window before Elizabeth did, and then watched as her niece got to the girl first through the Employees Only door.

Suzy lay on her back on the gray linoleum floor, her knees bent to her belly, her shiny red smock streaked with chocolate sauce that dripped from an upended container on the counter above. Eyes closed, Suzy cried and swatted the air until she found a handful of Elizabeth's hair and pulled. "It hurts. I think my water broke. Or I'm bleeding. I'm scared. What should I do?"

Suzy's skin was custard-colored, her forehead perspiring. She looked bad, jaundiced. Elizabeth thought of the vampirelike qualities of a baby—how it would drain a woman's body of every ounce of nutrition and hemoglobin it needed to survive with no concern for its host's well-being. Every child was willing to be motherless from the start, she thought.

"It's okay." Elizabeth stroked Suzy's clammy forehead once, and then pulled back her hand. "We'll get help. You'll be okay. The baby will be, too."

The girl cried, "It's my fault. I never wanted the baby. It must have heard me say it. But now I do. I want the baby. I want the baby." She pulled Elizabeth's hair harder, gripping with both hands, clamping her in place, gasping more than breathing.

"Glo, get in here and call 911."

The girl opened her eyes, shook her head. "The phone is broken. The repair guy is coming later. My mom is coming by to check on me in an hour. It hurts really bad." She pulled her knees up tighter and let go of Elizabeth's hair, closing her eyes again and slipping her hand into the slot between her groin and protruding belly while she cried.

"Glo, check if she's bleeding." Elizabeth rubbed her own sore head and looked up at her aunt, who watched through the window.

"I will not. What does that matter? Either way, we need to get her to the hospital. You know where the hospital is, don't you?" Glo called down to Suzy, who opened her eyes and nodded. "Elizabeth, I'll stay here and wait for the mother. You'll drive her to the hospital. We'll put her in the backseat. She should stay prone. Suzy, when is your baby due?" Glo took charge.

"In three months. On Thanksgiving. I want to name it Pilgrim."

"Well, Suzy, don't you worry. We'll get you and Pilgrim to the hospital right now."

Except for her belly, Suzy was slight. Glo and Elizabeth half slid, half lifted her out of the cramped Frosty Cream kitchen after Glo pulled the car up to within a few feet of the door. Together they cradled her into the backseat, Glo first placing a Frosty Cream dish towel under where Suzy's rear would go on the backseat.

"Glo, please, there's no time for that."

"Nonsense. Stan would not want his Coupe de Ville bled upon by an unwed mother. Move that cooler away from her head. Put it in the trunk."

"Glo, she can hear you."

"Well, she knows she's not married. Straighten that dish towel out for me."

"Oh, for God's sake, he's dead. He can't complain about a little bit of blood in his Cadillac," Elizabeth grumbled as she patted down the dish towel and then lifted the cooler from the car.

Suzy winced as Elizabeth spoke, and Glo patted her shoulder. "Never you mind her. You're going to be fine. Don't worry. Your little Pilgrim will be fine, too. We'll see to that. You haven't hurt your baby." Suzy had advanced to mute terror, but she nodded, her forehead now pale as paper, her breathing labored.

When Elizabeth sat in the driver's seat, Suzy found her voice again. "No, I want her to take me and Pilgrim." She clutched Glo's hand and sobbed, refusing to let go until Elizabeth got out of the car. So it was Glo who backed out of the lot in a skitter of gravel and a cloud of dust, and Elizabeth who watched from the side of the highway until the grit settled at her feet.

She stood for a while on the shoulder of the road, looking left and right for traffic, hoping Suzy's mother would arrive early. Hot and tired, she headed back to the Frosty Cream to get out of the sun. It was almost noon. If she were in L.A., she'd be out walking on some errand or other, the heat laserlike, piercing her lungs, burning a distinct hole in her comfort. Here in Mayville, she felt a different discomfort as a drape of humid Midwest haze settled on her, another sodden weight to carry.

Once inside the Frosty Cream, she examined the small space—the brown-spotted bananas hanging on a wooden rack, a day of life left in them yet, the aluminum-colored soft-serve ice cream machine humming with cool, the bins full of nuts and M&Ms, the other bins thick with sauces—chocolate, cherry, pineapple—and tiny metal ladles hanging off their sides, the sugar wafer cones stacked in a leaning tower on the counter, and the Crock-Pot of hot fudge simmering next to it. Chocolate sauce still dripped from the container Suzy had knocked over, but mostly the Frosty Cream was organized and neat. She understood how Suzy could enter this orderly sweetness every day and pretend she didn't have a problem, hoping the baby would magically disappear before it announced its presence to everybody else.

Pregnant teens often lived in that fog of hopeful denial. Elizabeth knew this from her years as a guidance counselor and from working as a volunteer at Planned Parenthood when she'd lived in Chicago. She'd answered the information hotline at the main office, and had also worked at the clinic, where abortions were performed, holding the hands of girls, some of them seeming young enough to need help tying ribbons on their braids. Denial was a major factor in many of those cases, certainly with the girls who showed up expecting to terminate a pregnancy when they were twenty or thirty weeks along, as if only then, when they could no longer hide it from their parents and teachers and friends, only then, when it was too late, would they consider the option that might have been best for them from the start. Before then, they would have faced a pregnant Virgin Mary herself and denied they were going to have a baby, too.

Suzy's eleventh hour change of heart, her concern for her baby as she lay bleeding on the Frosty Cream floor, had probably just been a desperate bargain for her own life, an affirmation of love that she hoped would save her in the midst of crisis. Come November, she might sneak away and have her baby alone in a corner somewhere, and then abandon it, or smother it, or leave it at a fire station. Or come November, Suzy might take her Pilgrim home, nurture and love and raise the baby on her own, send her or him to Harvard on a scholarship, and thirty years later become the proud mom of a Supreme Court justice. There was no way to know with these things.

But whichever way it went in the future, what was most likely *today* was that once the doctor attended to her, once the panic and emergency and blurriness were blotted out by a few deep breaths and a steady heartbeat, Suzy would go back to her general unease about her little Pilgrim and avoid dealing with the fact that, ready or not, it would be born. It was emergencies that made people become other, whether better or worse, than they normally were. Crisis averted, people soon enough scurried back to the confines of their common selves.

Elizabeth had seen it in herself—with her first husband, Matthew, for instance. She'd been twenty-four when they married. He'd pursued her, wooed her, pushed for marriage until she'd said yes, intoxicated by the proof of being wanted so much. But within a year, she knew the marriage was a mistake, that his courtship had been a solo dance that she'd enjoyed as it swirled around her. He had worked so hard to win her, while she was left to breathe effortlessly, to sit back and enjoy being wanted so much. She'd soon realized that they had little in common, and even less that they cared enough to disagree about.

And then he'd felt a lump under his arm. He'd made her feel it, too—in retrospect, it was the most intimate gesture she'd made toward his body. And amid doctors talking of lymph nodes and cancers and tumors and ultrasounds, for ten full days she'd been wrecked and certain she'd founder without him. Certain she'd gotten it all wrong, that their marriage was a gift she should have cherished and *would* cherish from now on. During those ten days, she took long walks alone, imagining herself as a young widow, berating God for taking Matthew from her before she'd understood her true feelings. With test results pending, she loved him doggedly, truly, deeply. But when they'd gotten the good news that it wasn't cancer, she had been taken aback at how quickly she wanted out of the room again.

Within a few months of that, she asked him for a divorce, and she was surprised at how readily he agreed. Surprised until he got married again, six months later, to a nurse he'd met during the cancer scare. That episode of fickleness notwithstanding, Elizabeth took full responsibility for the failure of her first marriage—she'd been too young, had treated it all too lightly.

Elizabeth rinsed out a dishcloth in the sink, cleaning while she waited for Suzy's mother. She wiped up the counter in streaky swipes, too tired for straight lines. She hadn't slept in almost thirty hours. She found a mop and bucket and swabbed the chocolate syrup from the floor. She notched down the fan, which whirled and rattled and shook on top of the soft-serve machine, until it pointed at the damp floor. She lifted her hair off her neck. Then she slid down and sat on the floor against the cupboards. Ten minutes later, she slept sprawled out flat on the Frosty Cream floor with the fan spitting hot air on her sweaty face, and the ache in her shoulder lending her rest an air of endurance instead of ease.

Elizabeth woke to a voice. She didn't know where she was or how long she'd been wherever that happened to be. She sat up too quickly and gasped at the pain that sliced through her shoulder. She looked around, saw the ice cream cones, the chocolate sauce, and, remembering now, stood to greet Suzy's mother in her most reassuring voice.

Then she tuned in to the clash and clatter of voices and laughter and feet slapping and scuffing and running and adult admonishment and she realized this wouldn't be Suzy's mother after all. This would be Frosty Cream business. She checked her watch. She'd slept for twenty minutes. Her wake-up call was a Little League team, ten or fifteen girls and boys. She looked again. They were awfully young—make that T-ball.

She came out to stop the woman who led the kids to the Frosty Cream order window. "No, no. Sorry. We're closed for business here. Get back on your bus." The kids ignored her and the woman looked puzzled and placed her order there in the middle of the parking lot.

"We'll just take twenty small cones for the kids and be on our way back to Benton Harbor."

"That's eighty miles from here."

"T-ball championships. We lost. And look, little kids. God bless 'em, they don't care." The kids ran around the parking lot, one-size-fits-all T-shirts swooping like evening gowns to the ankles of the slight ones, stretched too tight on the biggest. One chubby pigtailed girl crawled around Elizabeth's feet, jumping up on her knees, tongue hanging out, begging for notice. The coach explained, "She thinks she's a dog."

"Well, get me a newspaper, and I'll swat her on the nose."

The woman busted out a laugh. "That's a good one. You must have a houseful of little ones yourself."

"My house is a studio apartment and I've got no children, little or big." Elizabeth looked down at the panting girl who still pulled her pant leg. "Go away, Fido—go play with the other doggies." The girl yelped and clawed at her jeans while Elizabeth explained to the woman, "Listen, I don't know how to work the machines here or what things cost."

"How do you keep your job?"

"Oh, I don't work here. The regular employee had to leave. She had an emergency. I'm just waiting for her mother. It's a long story."

"My name is Diane." The woman held out her hand. "Tell me about it while we get the kids some ice cream."

A half hour later, Elizabeth and Diane sat on the picnic bench licking their own cones while the kids, having finished theirs, ran around the parking lot and played catch in the field behind the Frosty Cream. "Aren't you afraid they'll run onto the highway?" Elizabeth sat on the edge of her seat, ready to leap off and save a child from disaster, while Diane ignored them.

"Nah. They're six years old. They all live in places like this. They know better. Kids aren't dumb. A kid has a strong impulse to stay alive, something parents who worry too much forget. You take that Suzy girl you told me about. She'll be fine and the baby will be, too. It is very hard to kill somebody off, even a three-month-premature baby. Very hard. Even a tiny baby has a big will to live."

Elizabeth dripped chocolate ice cream on her shirt and, not seeing a napkin, leaned down and licked it off before she remembered she wasn't alone. She smiled sheepishly at Diane. "You think?"

"I do. The thing about death is, it doesn't come when you expect it. Maybe when you're eighty or ninety it does, but not other deaths. The accidents. The tragedies. They'll never happen while you're watching, so there's no point in keeping your eyes wide open."

"Actually, with that logic, you should always be on the lookout. That would ward it off."

A car turned into the Frosty Cream lot and Diane swiveled quickly, making sure the kids stayed back. The driver didn't get out, just turned his car around and took off the other way, apparently lost. Turning back to Elizabeth, Diane objected. "But that would be a form of death itself, don't you think?"

"I think there are a million different ways to live, and that could be one of them."

"Seems a waste to me." Diane stood up and blew the whistle around her neck. "We've got to go. But it was nice talking to you." The kids clustered around the picnic bench and at Diane's direction lobbed a wobbly "Thank you for the ice cream" at Elizabeth, who reached out and patted the head of the doggy girl, sticky-faced with soft serve, who whimpered at her leg again.

By the time Glo got Suzy to Sacred Heart Hospital (not much time at all; she drove fast, and the moaning girl gave good directions), Suzy had color back in her face, her cries had beveled off the sharp edge of pain, and her breathing was steady. Still, the emergency room nurse took her in immediately and hooked her up to a fetal monitor and paged the ob-gyn on call. When the nurse found out Glo wasn't a relative, she told her she'd have to wait outside.

"I'll call your mother and have her come here instead of the Frosty Cream. I'll wait until she gets here, just in case. But you're going to be fine now." Suzy gave Glo her boss's phone number, too, and then asked the nurse if they had the latest issue of *CosmoGIRL*.

Once she reached Suzy's mother, who sounded more annoyed than worried, Pete, the Frosty Cream owner, who groaned and said he never would have hired that girl if he'd known she was pregnant, and Anita Prokoff, who wasn't home but even in her recorded phone message made the mother and the Frosty Cream owner sound mellow in comparison, Glo sat and waited on a bench outside the Sacred Heart emergency room doors.

She was glad it was a Catholic hospital. She liked the idea that at a Catholic hospital the baby had some standing, and that the little one, even if it did die, wouldn't be set aside, its skin and bones and blood used to patch up somebody else's trouble, someone who could be an alcoholic or a drug addict or a glutton or an adulterer or any other kind of sinner. She opened her purse and took out her rosary and began the five Joyful Mysteries, especially appropriate in the case of Suzy and Pilgrim—the Annunciation that Mary was with child, the Nativity, the Presentation of the baby Jesus—asking God to watch over and protect them both.

When Stan had had his stroke, she'd sat outside Mother Cabrini Hospital and prayed—the Sorrowful Mysteries then—for she'd seen Stan's death coming in the stillness of his body and in his labored breath. She'd left Stan alone in intensive care after a few hours and gone outside, where she sat on a bench with only her sweater to warm her, though it was forty degrees, and the wind beelined to her bones. The sun had shone defiantly despite the cold, all glare, no comfort.

Glo's leg had ached badly as she prayed to the wind that day, and she offered up her pain to help Stan, wondering if it were too little, too late. She pledged that if Stan didn't die that day, if Stan became an invalid, she'd care for him, see Christ in him, tend to him with love and patience. She adjusted her prayers accordingly outside Cabrini, switching to the Glorious Mysteries, which were miracle based—the Holy Ghost descending, Jesus rising, Mary assumed body and soul into heaven—a more aggressive defense against the beeping machines hooked up to Stan.

She imagined that others would be put off if they knew the truth of her—that with Stan alive, she'd often hoped for a life without him. And she knew then that if Stan died, she'd have to live with the guilt of hope fulfilled. Sitting on that cold concrete bench, on a day so sunny she winced, she prayed for assurance that she wasn't responsible, and for forgiveness.

When she checked in again on Suzy, the girl's mother had arrived. Glo introduced herself. Amid mumbled thanks and questions about the state of Suzy's health and the baby's, Glo found out there had been no blood or broken water, Suzy had simply drunk too much Coke and lost control of her bladder and then panicked and hyperventilated, thinking something was wrong. The nurse announced that everything looked just fine but they'd keep her for observation all afternoon, and as Suzy was asking if the TV got cable, Glo backed out of the curtained cubicle.

When she got to the Coupe de Ville, she took a pencil from her purse and lifted the corner of the towel on the backseat, holding the offending cloth out in front of her—let's see if Elizabeth objected to the precaution now. She threw the towel in the trash and drove back to the Frosty Cream. When she arrived, Elizabeth was asleep on top of a picnic table under an oak tree while a balding man with drooping shoulders yelled into a cell phone about somebody working a double shift. Glo shook Elizabeth's shoulder firmly.

"Ow. Damn, Glo. That hurt." Elizabeth rubbed her shoulder with one hand, her eyes with the other.

"Language, please. We're almost four hours late. Let's get going. The girl, Suzy, she's fine. And the baby is, too. Not that you care."

"I care. What do you mean by that? I care."

"I mean if you've got a maternal bone in your body, it was broken long ago."

Back on the road, Glo drove, looking over at Elizabeth every now and then as her niece tried to get comfortable in the reclining seat. Glo was eager to get to Candy and Detroit. Eager to put everything in place for the school year, so they could all get back to their respective homes where, Lord knows, they each had troubles to tend. Glo had high hopes for the trip, but looking at Elizabeth—seeing the chocolate stain on her shirt, the purple tinge under her eyes, the crease in her brow—for now, she merely prayed her crumpled niece would get some blessed sleep.

CHAPTER 6

*A*S GLO OBEYED the speed limit and drove out of Mayville four hours late to pick up Candy, Candy lay on the twin bed in her friend Amy Prokoff's room about two hundred miles east, bouncing a softball-sized, fiber-filled, red-and-blue Pistons basketball off the ceiling in between spinning it on her right index finger, eating potato chips, and waiting for her freshly polished toenails to dry and her friend Jimmy to call.

"Come in, Anita," she called out when she heard a knock on her door, knowing it was Amy's mother coming to give her shit about one thing or another. She ticked off the Prokoff house rules she was breaking just lying there that Saturday afternoon: no eating in the bedroom; no basketballs tossed against the wall; no spilling nail polish on the white shag carpet—well, Anita didn't actually have that rule yet. Candy reached down and tossed a dirty sock over the metallic blue spill she'd made ten minutes ago. She thought about hiding the potato chips, too. Fuck it. Anita would sniff them out anyway.

Anita Prokoff edged her head around the door frame and in her hands-on-hips voice reminded Candy she was not allowed to bounce a basketball in the house. "Think fast, Anita." Candy faked a pass and laughed as Amy's mom ducked behind the door.

Mrs. Prokoff didn't like it that Candy called her Anita, which was why Candy did it. She'd irritated Anita (the feeling was mutual) without even trying from the minute she moved in with the Prokoffs last December, but she'd begun tormenting her in earnest just a couple of weeks ago, right after she'd been called to the meeting with Morrisey and Ms. Hogan and Sister Anne. Before that meeting, on the surface, things had been normal. But then she'd found out that Anita Prokoff was a big part of the reason Coach D had been fired. They said Coach D had resigned, but she didn't believe that. When he left town in June, it hadn't been for some planned vacation as they'd implied. He'd been *forced* to resign. He'd slunk away while she was gone. And they'd compelled him to do it. She was pissed at them all.

She wished she could forget that meeting. Forget that day three weeks ago when Ms. Hogan, Mr. Morrisey, and Sister Anne had each called her at nine in the morning and told her they needed to meet with her that afternoon. All three right in a row, like they were the stooges and couldn't remember the plan. *We need to discuss your basketball plans and come up with a support system for you this year, Candy.* Ms. Hogan was a basketball fan, so Candy wasn't surprised to hear her mention hoops. *We want to check in with you, Candy, and get a pulse point on how you're doing this summer without your mom.* Mr. Morrisey carried his briefcase and wore a suit to work and said stuff like "pulse point" as if he worked for IBM instead of a Catholic girls' high school. By the time Sister Anne, whom Candy really liked, called, she cut her off in midphrase. "Everybody is worried about me and yes, I'll come to a meeting today at two so you can all see that I'm okay."

That afternoon, once Morrisey asked those questions about "physical contact," Candy finally understood what was going on. But she couldn't believe it at first. She'd never done anything with Coach D but play basketball. He'd never given her any advice that was useful beyond the perimeter of the basketball court. He didn't even ask her about her homework or her grades. Besides the morning he'd shown up at her door to tell her that her mom was dead, and in the bus on the way to or from games, she'd never seen him outside of the gym or school hallways.

After Morrisey, with his questions about contact, had made the point of the meeting clear without actually saying it, Candy had looked at Sister Anne, who'd nodded her head and said, "Tell the truth, Candy. You're just a child. Whatever you've done, you've done nothing wrong. Mrs. Prokoff suggested that—"

"Mrs. Prokoff? Is Mrs. Prokoff the reason all this started? Anita Prokoff doesn't know shit." Sister Anne had raised an eyebrow, but they all let that slide, and Candy continued, "She doesn't know her own daughter made herself puke after dinner last night. You can't listen to Mrs. Prokoff. She watches TV all day. Her brain is, like, infected with Jenny Jones and Montel. She sees stuff that isn't there. She's just mad at me because I break her stupid curfew and eat junk food in the bedroom. This is all my fault. Coach D is my *coach*."

Morrisey wouldn't drop it. "Did he drive you home after your workouts?"

Morrisey's wife was a doctor and he never knew whether to hide or trumpet that fact. Candy imagined him naked, having sex with his doctor wife—his briefcase at his side—his Adam's apple bigger than his dick. Or maybe the doctor wife thought he was a loser just like every girl at All Saints did. Maybe she refused to have sex with him.

"No, he drives me home after we stop at the Chandler Park Motel." She got up from the table. "You're all sick. You know that? Especially you," Candy pointed at Mr. Morrisey. "And you," Candy pointed at Sister Anne. "Forget *Pride and Prejudice*. I'll read *Lolita* instead. That's what you're all thinking, right?" They looked at the table, not at Candy. "I'm not talking to you about Coach D. When he gets back from vacation next week, you can talk to us both." What was the point of telling them the truth? That nothing had happened. They didn't deserve it. They'd think she was protecting Coach D. People went that way too fast. Even nuns.

"Candy." Ms. Hogan had taken over. "This is not just about Mrs. Prokoff. Other people this summer have also been concerned. There's something else you should know, Candy: Coach D isn't coming back. He resigned. Mr. Morrisey will take over as interim coach while we search for a permanent replacement." At that, Candy slammed her Coke can on the table, and Morrisey swept his briefcase away from the spray. Ms. Hogan continued, insisting, "He's qualified. He coached college women at Sienna Heights when his wife was in medical school at Michigan."

"He coached an intramural team of players who sucked too much to make their shitty little college team. He thinks that's impressive? I am not impressed. We're good enough to win State again, but not with him coaching. I won't play for him."

"That's how you feel now. You just need some time." Sister Anne reached out for Candy's hand.

"I'll die before I feel differently." Candy shoved her fists in her pockets. She meant it. Just as she'd been sure she wouldn't leave Detroit to live with Glo or Elizabeth last fall, she was sure she would never play ball for Morrisey.

Morrisey, briefcase on his lap now, searched for something in it and then held out a sheaf of stapled papers to Candy. "I've put together a playbook. I'm calling a general meeting and light workout for Saturday, August third. You'll want to be there."

"No. I won't." Candy grabbed the playbook, but only so she could throw it on the floor and kick the stupid Xeroxed papers out of her way as she left the room.

Three weeks later, she hadn't changed her mind. She would not play ball for Morrisey. It was nonnegotiable. If they thought she would, they'd find out differently on tip-off. Oh, she heard them whispering about her. About how she loved basketball and would never stay away. About how she missed her mother and wasn't thinking straight. About how she was eating too much junk. About how she'd been "acting out" all summer. About how quitting was another sign of that. The whispers about her and Coach D were worse than any of those, but so far nobody'd had the balls to say it flat out. Let them think whatever they wanted. She *did* love basketball and she *did* miss her mother. Other than that, they were full of shit. She felt her jeans digging into her waist, keeping her honest—they got the junk food part right, too.

Everything was confused. But this much was clear to Candy: people wanted to believe the worst. And sex with your thirty-year-old basketball coach—well, that was pretty bad. Almost as bad as your mother dying just like that. As if her mother hadn't deserved more than five full years when she was sober so she could actually look at her daughter without wobbling or passing out or closing her eyes to the wreckage she'd made for Candy, her own kid, to climb through.

They were way off base about her, if they thought she didn't know enough about men to stay away from them. When her mother had been drinking, there'd often been men around, some of them drunk enough themselves that it hardly mattered—they'd ignored Candy and hung on her mother. Candy would shut herself in her room as soon as she'd hear a car veer into the driveway and then she'd peek out her bedroom window to see if the guy weaved and stumbled as he walked. If he did, she didn't worry. The less drunk ones were the bigger problem. They thought they could save her mother, save her daughter. They'd look with pity at Candy as if they were Jesus H. Christ arriving to deliver salvation.

Candy could handle dismissal, anger, puzzlement, maybe even disgust—but when people turned on her all concerned-looking, it made her want to smack them. These men didn't even know her. How dare they think she'd take their help.

She hoped none of those concerned-looking sober guys was her father. When she was twelve, her mother, drink in hand, assured her once again that no, her father had been a nice enough man, but long gone, somebody she hadn't wanted to marry, somebody who was married already when she'd known him. He'd been in the military, her mother said, and had died in Desert Storm. "I heard that from a very reliable source. That was 1991, honey. The Gulf War. You were only three then. You wouldn't remember."

That conversation had been in 1997, when Candy was in sixth grade. She hadn't been sure she'd believed the story. "I was six in 1991, Mom. Plus, we studied that war in school. Like, five guys died in Desert Storm. I mean five American guys," she corrected herself and thought a minute. "Hold on. Are you saying my dad was an Iraqi?" She looked up from the book about New Guinea she was reading for a geography report that was due the next day.

"God, no. Not that there's anything wrong with the Iraqi people, and Bush had no business bombing them. Don't you ever let me catch you voting for a Bush—he's got sons who are going to be even worse than he is. Apples don't fall far from trees."

Candy reached for another book in the stack of homework before her and knocked over her mother's drink. "Yes they do."

Her mother pretended not to hear that. "No, your father was American through and through. Maybe some Irish in him, which accounts for your coloring, those freckles." Her mother had reached out, tilted up Candy's chin. "You're beautiful, honey, you know that? I'd kill for skin like yours. Your father and I used to drink at the Shamrock Inn. And he must have been athletic, because you surely didn't get those genes from me. Clean up that mess for me, will you, honey?" Melissa pointed at the spilled drink leaking through the table crack.

"Elizabeth is a good athlete." Her aunt had been by three times already that week, working with Candy on her left-handed layup.

"Oh yes, Elizabeth."

"Well, if my dad was an American who died in Desert Storm, then that is just really bad luck because what are the odds of that?" Candy set a sponge in the middle of the pool of vodka on the kitchen table and watched the puddle shrink.

"You're looking at it all wrong, honey. It wasn't bad luck. It was the long shot coming through."

Her mom had poured herself another drink then, so Candy had figured it was a mixed-up lie. But later, sober and clearheaded, her mother stuck to the story and Candy decided it could be true. In any case, it was all she had.

Anita Prokoff stuck her head around the open bedroom door again, slowly this time, "Your aunt Gloria, Mrs. Dreslinski, called while I was out." Candy thanked the good luck that had made the phone ring while she was in the shower. "She left a message. She and your aunt Elizabeth got held up near Kalamazoo. She didn't say why. They won't get here until four at the earliest. And you got another half dozen letters from colleges—all Division I teams, I noticed." She pointed at the potato chips, "I've asked you not to eat in here, Candy."

Candy ate a potato chip, slowly, staring at Anita, before she answered, "Anita, I've got to tell you, I really don't care." Candy threw the Pistons basketball right at her, no faking, and laughed as Anita yelped, the Nerflike ball caroming off her head, her hands swatting air. Candy shook her head in disgust—fucking spastic—no wonder Amy sucked at sports.

She went out to shoot around in the backyard a while later. The Prokoffs' basketball setup was sweet—regulation height, and they'd even let Amy and Candy paint a free-throw line, center line, baseline, three point arc, and key. True, the driveway had one big crack down the middle that made the ball skew wildly if you didn't snatch the rebound directly off the boards, but even that was good for Candy's game. Expect the unexpected. Take nothing for granted. Grab the ball.

She and her aunt Elizabeth had played for hours on a much more cracked-up driveway back when Elizabeth lived in Detroit. That was after Elizabeth's first divorce and during the two years of her second marriage. Candy had been seven when Elizabeth had introduced her to basketball, playing with her and coaching her, and twelve when her aunt had stopped. Back then, Elizabeth would show up on Saturday afternoons, Thursday evenings, on Sunday mornings, unannounced— she was family after all. They'd play one-on-one and do drills and shoot for hours and then Elizabeth would take her to Big Boy for a malt or to a thrift store or to a movie.

Even when they weren't on the court, she had talked basketball and strategy to Candy. Lectured her on the importance of defense. Told her one rebound was worth two shots. Get the ball, she'd said. Close the passing lanes, disrupt the dribble, get your hand in your opponent's face before the shot goes up. Once it does, read the angle of the shot, stake your position, box out, crash the boards, grab the rebound, and protect the ball. Defense creates offense. Be single-minded on defense. You cannot be successful if you *only* want to score. Scoring alone is empty glory. A frill. Today's fashion. But when you learn to stop your opponent from scoring, you become absolutely essential to the game. Michael, Magic, Bird, Kareem, Bill Russell—every legend played defense. Do you want to be *essential*? Do you want to be *effective*? Candy, who had been eating a hot fudge brownie, swiped the whipped cream off her chin and paid attention to her aunt. She remembered Elizabeth's emphasis. What kind of player do you want to be, Candy? You *choose*, Candy. You always have a *choice*.

Candy, short for her age at the time, and still not sure which was front court or back, perched on the edge of the red leather booth, kicking her legs metronomically, staring at her aunt, hoping her ice cream wouldn't melt before Elizabeth finished, and nodding her head as if she got it, laughing when Elizabeth did, even when she didn't see what was so funny. She had liked the attention, the unslurred words from her aunt, who didn't stink of beer or rambling apology.

Years later at All Saints High School, a perennial basketball powerhouse in Detroit, on her way to becoming the first freshman in twenty years to make the starting varsity lineup, Candy listened as Coach D began practice by introducing himself. "In case you're wondering, the 'D' is for defense. On my team, you will learn to play it because there is *nothing* more important than it. Defense wins championships. You will learn to defend. Or you will not be on my team." Candy, understanding, had looked down at the highly varnished gym floor and smiled.

When Elizabeth married her second husband, Candy, almost ten years old, a junior bridesmaid garnished in violet satin flounces, her silver braces gleaming, had cried during the whole wedding reception, knowing how her aunt would have less time for her, and also because her mom, drunk, kept stumbling and apologizing and landing in the open arms of Elizabeth's new husband, Ben, on the dance floor.

Waiting for Glo and Elizabeth to arrive that Saturday afternoon, Candy saw the Prokoffs' neighbor girl, twelve-year-old Lily Parks, in the yard next door and waved her over to play. Lily was no good at basketball, but she'd feed Candy for hours some days, expecting nothing in return, which was pretty much all Candy offered her.

"Hey, Lil, climb over the fence and help me out."

"Can my brother come, too?" Candy hadn't seen nine-year-old Gordon, who shot out from behind the garage, a smirk on his bony ratlike face.

"Sure, bring the brat over." Gordon gave Candy the finger. She faked a pass at his head, but unlike Anita Prokoff, he stood his ground. She gave him a grudging point for that.

They'd been shooting for twenty minutes when Candy heard a car in the driveway. Knowing her aunts were due, she stopped the game and told the kids to go home, ignoring Gordon, who said it was no fair and that she was only quitting because he was going to win, which made Candy and Lily roll their eyes, since he'd barely hit the rim yet, much less scored a point. She helped Lily over the fence. Gordon refused a boost and climbed over on his own, falling into the gladiolas on the other side.

Candy went out front, dribbling left to right, between her legs, behind her back, stutter stepping and putting on a show for Elizabeth and Glo, and then she let out a whoop when she saw it was Jimmy. Much better. She and Jimmy had hung out a lot that summer. He was a year younger than Candy and he'd sat the bench on Denby's basketball team last year. This year, a junior, he might not even get to do that. He wasn't good enough for Candy to take pride in beating him routinely when they went one-on-one. Mostly they didn't play basketball together. Mostly they drove around listening to music, stopping at Ram's Horn for burgers or gyros, and then catching a late movie at the Galaxy.

The other guys she hung around with weren't friends like Jimmy. They liked her in other ways, and last winter and then spring, Candy liked two of them right back. She'd gone out with Jerry Maiz in February and March, but they broke up because he said he "needed someone who needed him more." When he told her that, Candy looked sad, batted her eyes, and hung on to his arm desperately before pushing him away and saying so long. She and Rick Overman were together in April and May, but then she saw him eating pizza at Shields with Janey Morse on a night when he'd canceled a date with Candy, using the excuse that he had to stay home and baby-sit his little brother. She hadn't even cared that much, she was off to Indiana for Red Star the next week anyway, but it pissed her off that he'd lied. He should have told her the truth.

She hadn't had sex. Not with Jerry or with Rick or with anybody. They'd both wanted her to, but the way she saw it, it wasn't as if she were going to turn forty next week and had to hook up with a ton of guys before she was too old to enjoy it. Besides, Jerry and Rick had both wanted to do it in the car, and that wasn't for her. It was not private, and sex should be private. She'd known way more than she'd wanted to know about her mom's sex life before she got sober. She was going to keep her own sex life, once she had one, to herself. Maybe this year, without basketball, she'd have time for a boyfriend. Maybe she'd have sex. In a bed. With clean sheets. Not in a car.

And not with Jimmy. He was a friend, and that was better than a boyfriend. Waiting for Glo and Elizabeth and getting Jimmy instead was a good sign. She passed him the ball and he caught it with one hand, pocketing his keys with the other, and scudding the ball back to her all in one clean motion. Not bad. Maybe he'd make Denby's team after all.

"Where have you been the past couple of weeks? I've been looking for you." Candy dribbled them back up the drive to the hoop.

"Just around. I don't know. Busy, I guess."

"Shoot with me while I wait for my aunts to come and pick me up. I'm going on vacation with them."

"I heard you had to leave town."

"Who'd you hear that from? I don't *have* to leave town." Candy stopped dribbling, hearing an accusation in his voice where there was usually only laughs or thanks or invitation. She passed him the ball, a bullet from four feet away.

"My mom ran into Mrs. Prokoff at Farmer Jack a few days ago. She's glad to be getting rid of you." Jimmy held on to the ball, faked left, dribbled once right, and pulled up for a ten-foot jumper that clanked off the rim, a brick for all his work.

"Well, it's not like this trip with my aunts Glo and Elizabeth will be any fun, but as far as Anita Prokoff goes, the feeling is completely mutual." Candy hoped Anita was listening at the open kitchen window.

"I heard you quit the team."

"Actually, I didn't. There's no team to quit. They fired Coach D. Morrisey is a loser. Only an idiot who's also a big loser would play for him." Candy swished from twenty feet out, Jimmy's hand in her face no distraction.

"Coach D resigned. They had to find somebody else on short notice."

"They forced him out. I'm not playing for anybody else. Unlike others, I believe in loyalty."

"What is he, like, your father?" While Candy stiffened, in defensive position, Jimmy flew past her with the ball and leapt, reversing midair, switching right to left hand, and shoving his hip hard into her, a flagrant foul that leveled her, as the ball angled sharply off the backboard and dropped cleanly through the nylon net. When he came down to earth, he finished his question, "Or your fucking boyfriend?"

Knocked down to concrete by his blow, Candy lay still, confused by the jut of Jimmy's body and words. Her elbow was a hinge sending pain up and down her arm. Jimmy pounced, straddling her and pinning her down, cuffing her arms to her sides. He whispered in her ear. "So you like to fuck your coach? Was it as good as all the other guys you've fucked? Everybody knows you did it with him. They know that's why he ran away."

Candy went limp. There it was. In the plain words she'd been holding her breath against. Before Jimmy said it flat out, she'd told herself nobody who knew her could *really* think such a thing was true. She imagined Coach D lying next to her, his paunch inflating his black-and-gold All Saints sweatshirt (she would *not* imagine him naked), a whistle around his neck, his hair stuck up all weird because he pulled it when he was thinking. How could anybody think she'd have sex with him?

The only time he'd ever touched her in a way that didn't have to do with basketball was when he'd come to tell her that her mom was dead. He'd knocked on the apartment door at eight in the morning. It was November 28. It was cold. He'd looked bad, ugly. His chin all stubbly. His eyes rimmed with red. His fingers, white without gloves, rubbing his temples. Before he'd said a word, she'd known. Known because she'd been awake all night waiting for her mother to come home. Known because the house had been so still. Known because she'd done her reading and learned that most alcoholics relapse. Known because it had always lurked clear to her that her mother would get drunk again and die. That morning when Coach D had knocked, knowing all those things had helped Candy for the moment. They'd helped her worry more for her coach than for herself. They'd helped her open her arms and hold him while he cried.

When he'd finally stopped crying so hard, which was when he noticed she wasn't crying, she'd asked her question. "Did she hurt anybody else?"

"Nobody was hurt except her. She wouldn't hurt anybody."

"Yeah, right. Driving drunk. That doesn't hurt a soul."

"Golden?" He'd noticed that she was angry. "Your mom wasn't drunk. She got hit by a guy who was speeding and ran a red light."

By then she'd traveled too far down the flinty path she'd chosen to admit her mistake. She felt foolish. How could she feel something as trivial as foolish when her mother was dead? What kind of a person was she? She was more mixed-up than she'd ever been. She watched Coach D watching her. And then it all fell apart. She fell apart. And she knew that it wouldn't have mattered if her mother had been drinking. Knew it wouldn't have mattered if her mother had killed a busload of little disabled kids while she was at it. At that moment of understanding what Coach D was saying, Candy knew that what mattered was that she was alone, and that her mother, whom she didn't want to live without, was, too.

She doubled over, almost falling off the couch, but he caught her. She wailed and tried to wrench herself away from him, but his arms were locked tight and he wouldn't loosen them even a little until she yielded to his comfort. His voice in her ear was low and sibilant, a wisp of comfort. "Sshhh, it will be okay," over and over again, both of them knowing it really wouldn't be.

How long had that gone on? Three seconds? Thirty minutes? She didn't know, but at some point he let her go and told her exactly what had happened. "The police showed up at All Saints this morning looking for you. They thought you'd be at school already. They were going to come here to tell you, but Ms. Hogan thought it would be better coming from somebody you knew. Morrisey was coming to tell you. Hogan thinks I'm odd, but cops or a guy you hate telling you this— she knew that wouldn't be right." He rubbed his eyes and inhaled deeply. "Sister Anne is on a retreat with a bunch of sophomores or else it would have been her who came to tell you. I know you like her. It should have been her who came to tell you. You like her." He repeated himself helplessly.

"How did it happen, Coach?" Candy's question came out cracked up in jagged bits that she wished she could ask another way: *did it happen?* That would be her choice—that there was some chance he was wrong. That somebody else's mother was dead; that some other girl cried; some other coach rubbed his eyes. But she knew he'd only rearrange the words: *it did happen.* He was probably doing it now. He was speaking. Her arms felt too heavy to swat the words away.

"Your mom got off her shift late. The manager said there was a party of twenty that didn't settle up until after one A.M. She was waiting for her tip. She stopped at the 7-Eleven just a couple of miles up Mack on the way home. She bought a Dr Pepper. This guy, he ran a red. He fell asleep at the wheel. He hit her full force coming through the intersection at Outer Drive. The cops said it was instantaneous. She didn't suffer. Just so you know. The cops said that twice."

"She drank too much soda. We both do. I told her to drink more water." Candy's voice caught in her chest as if there were a giant claw holding it there. She doubled over once more, and Coach D caught her again. And then the doorbell rang and after that she couldn't remember much more about that first day—about when she'd cried and when she'd breathed and when she hadn't. But she did know she'd never forget that instead of shock and sorrow and devastation, her first emotions upon learning of her mother's death had been anger and resignation—what she'd always expected to happen finally had. At least the waiting was over.

In April, she had slipped and told the truth to Amy about working out with Coach D on Tuesday and Thursday nights. He'd asked her not to mention it, but once she'd made the mistake, she told Amy how her game, so good, was even better now. She described how Coach D worked with her on her free throws and fadeaways. How he timed her in sprints. How he drilled her. Now she regretted putting it that way.

"It really is weird that you spend so much time with him, Candy." A few days later, she and Amy were still talking about it as they walked to Clark Elementary, where they were volunteer coaches for a seven-and-eight-year-old boys' basketball team.

"Why? He's my coach." Candy held out a large bag of Nacho Cheese Doritos to Amy, who took one and nibbled it for half a block.

"You're already the best player ever. You don't need to work that much extra. Plus, you shouldn't be working out with him—my mom says you're both asking for trouble because it's not allowed by the high school athletic association rules."

"I'm an orphan. They'll take pity." Then, realizing what she'd just heard, Candy grabbed Amy's backpack strap and stopped her. "You told your mom? I can't believe you did that. Jesus, Amy, you're going to get me in trouble."

Amy pulled her strap back. "It came out accidentally. I didn't mean to tell her. I'm sorry. Do you really think you're an orphan? Do you believe that story from your mom about your father's dying in Desert Storm?"

"Actually, I do. But it was just a figure of speech, Amy. Don't be so fucking literal all the time. And don't listen to that shit from your mother. Coach D and I play basketball. That's it. It's my future. Why is it so weird to everybody that I take the game seriously?"

"I think it's mostly him, not you, that everybody thinks is weird. My mom drove by his house the other day, and she said he still has that chicken coop in his front yard and it smells even from the street. My mom worries that you don't know what you're doing because you're so sad that your mom died. But she doesn't trust Coach D. Do you think he raises chickens?"

That's one reason Candy liked Amy so much—her friend said what she was thinking—there was no filter to her truth. "Well, your mom doesn't have to trust him. I trust him. I think he raises parrots, or some other kind of bird, but not chickens. And your mom thinks everything smells."

"What's it like, Candy? I mean not having your mother or anybody, really?"

"It's fine." While Candy admired Amy's candor, she wasn't about to engage in it herself. "I don't dwell on it. I have basketball."

Or at least she used to. She wanted to. Since that meeting at the end of July, when she'd learned Morrisey was taking over, Candy had been thinking that there must be some way to get Coach D to return to the Ravens, but now, flat on her back on the Prokoffs' driveway with

Jimmy holding her down and whispering in her ear, spelling it out for her in four letters—*so you like to fuck your coach*—Candy quit thinking. With her now-certain knowledge of how wrong they all were, and as pissed off as she'd ever been, she drew herself together and turned into the Jethro of a girl she was. The one she usually saved for tip-off. The one who could push up her pelvis and shoulders and break free of Jimmy's arms, flip him off her and onto his back before he realized she'd come alive to fight, aching elbow and all. She straddled him and jabbed her knee into his puny little crotch and said "Fuck you, Jimmy" over and over again, even as he cried for her to stop.

She hated him as much as she hated Anita Prokoff and Mr. Morrisey. As much as she hated Coach D, who'd run away and made them all so certain they were right, while she was left alone, too embarrassed by the charge to defend herself outright. As much as she hated the aunts who had left her alone with her own mother drunk and then dead and who, even today, if they hadn't been four hours late, could have spared her this moment.

Elizabeth and Glo should have moved to Detroit. Or they should have insisted she move and live with one of them. She wouldn't have betrayed her mom by saying yes, but they should have made some large gesture to try to prove they really wanted her. Even Morrisey and Anita Prokoff—two people who didn't like her at all—had made large gestures. Her aunts were so small.

She looked up and saw Lily and Gordon watching her. Gordon smirking, eyebrows raised. Lily horrified, mouth open in a circle of fear. In a loud raspy whisper that she wanted Gordon and Lily to hear so they'd know plenty young just how free and fluid hate could be, Candy stared at them and said once, then twice, then one more time to be sure they got it, "Fuck you stupid little kids, too."

CHAPTER | 7

*T*HE PROKOFF KITCHEN was insistently red and white. A border of stenciled hearts, flower-laden, ringed the large red-walled room, where a round white-laminate-topped table was set with red plastic plates, red-and-white-checked place mats, white-plastic-handled flatware, and a pot of blood-red blooming tulips bookended by ceramic crowing rooster candlesticks, red candles stuck in the cocks' open throats. Waist-high white-painted wainscoting was edged with more stenciled hearts, the pattern carried out on the tiebacks that held open red cotton curtains, dish towels that hung from sink cupboards on red plastic hooks, and potholders stacked like pancakes next to a wood block full of knives. The room looked not so much cheery as hemorrhaging.

Elizabeth stared at the ceramic birds silenced midcrow. She and

Glo and Candy had filed into the kitchen for dinner because Anita Prokoff, on her way out the door to her bridge game, had come upstairs and suggested they do so. Elizabeth wasn't hungry and Glo was in the middle of her evening prayers, but Anita's suggestions seemed as negotiable as an IRS deadline, so they'd dutifully filed down for dinner. How had Candy found the strength to defy this woman? The girl had a boldness that Elizabeth hadn't seen in her five years ago. Then again, after living with an alcoholic mother for so long, maneuvering around a control freak like Anita Prokoff might be as easy for Candy as shooting free throws. Or maybe Candy got the yips when she shot free throws. Elizabeth didn't know much about her anymore off court or on.

If Suzy hadn't wet her pants, they'd be on the road right now, instead of sitting awkwardly in the Prokoffs' blood-colored kitchen. But the delay had put them hours behind and Glo hadn't wanted to drive at night. Candy had barely acknowledged them when they'd first arrived. Glo had hugged the girl with a persistence that surprised Elizabeth—it was as if her aunt depended upon the embrace. Candy offered nothing in return, holding herself stiffly before disengaging from Glo and excusing herself to go upstairs to pack.

"You haven't packed?" Hug accomplished, Glo chastised her grandniece, who shrugged. Glo stepped back and took a better look at the girl. "My goodness, what have you done with your hair?" She reached for a dreadlock, but thinking better of it, picked a stray hair off her own blouse instead. "It looks like something I should use to scrape the mud off my shoes. And one, two, three . . . how many holes do you have in your ear?" Glo reached out to touch a silver stud, but again drew her hand back before her flesh met any part of Candy's bad-girl accoutrements. "When did you do that? And why? Who allowed you?" Glo glowered at Anita Prokoff, who glowered right back. "Why aren't you packed? What if we'd gotten here at one o'clock as planned and wanted to leave right away?"

"You didn't, did you?"

As Candy challenged her grandaunt, Elizabeth spoke up. "Glo, leave her alone. Those are dreadlocks—she looks good." Candy looked anything but, and it wasn't the dreadlocks' fault. Her face was broken out, and she looked chubbier all the way around, although that could be because she wore very short shorts that were also very tight. Sequined stars twinkled up and down the sides of them. Her niece looked like someone Elizabeth might find on her street corner in L.A.—a wannabe Rastafarian hooker. "Candy, we're sorry we're late. We had to help a pregnant young girl at an ice-cream stand in a little town we stopped in. Glo and I will get a hotel room for tonight. We'll get an early start tomorrow morning."

"Tomorrow is Sunday," Glo corrected her. "We'll need to go to Mass first."

"We'll stop on the road. We'll pass through Flint. It's a big enough city. We'll find a Mass there." Elizabeth answered Glo's protest.

"This is not going the way I planned." Glo sank into an easy chair.

Anita Prokoff piped up, "I find Candy often upsets the plan."

"Hey, I didn't get that ice-cream girl pregnant," Candy said, defending herself.

Elizabeth stepped in to referee, turning to Anita Prokoff. "Can you recommend a hotel?"

"Why don't you stay here? Amy and my younger daughter, Julia, are both staying overnight at friends' houses. I've got a bridge game tonight and my husband is out of town on business. You won't be in anybody's way. You and Mrs. Dreslinski can sleep in Julia's room—

she has twin beds. Candy will take you upstairs and you can relax and freshen up."

"We couldn't put you out that way." Elizabeth yearned for an anonymous hotel room.

"Of course we could. Just thank the woman, Elizabeth," Glo spoke up.

"Then it's settled. I don't have to leave until six and I'll have dinner on the table for you before I go." Anita Prokoff straightened a cushion on the couch.

"Please, we'll get our own dinner." Elizabeth didn't believe Anita Prokoff's hospitality would come without some price.

"No, no. I'll take care of it. I don't like others in my kitchen. I'll start something now. Go. Relax." Anita Prokoff clapped her hands and pointed as she left the room.

It was the first time Glo, Elizabeth, and Candy had seen one another since Melissa's funeral.

Glo, flustered by all the upsets to her schedule, mumbled about her suitcase in the trunk of the car, the cooler there, too, the yogurt in it gone bad by now, and the Cross in the Woods. She was tired. Her leg ached and Candy looked like a stranger. A cheap and common stranger with tangled-up hair who easily could have done the shameful things implied. Good Lord, you leave somebody alone for nine months and look what happens. She should have visited the Cross in the Woods with Stan.

Elizabeth, certain no good could come from a trip with such a mixed-up beginning, stared at her niece, too, trying to remember if she'd always looked so much like her mother. Melissa had had those same full, deep red lips, the same dark eyes. She kneaded her shoulder as she looked at Candy, who, Zeppo-like, massaged her elbow.

Candy, wondering if she could get through a week without talking to either of these women, rubbed her sore elbow unconsciously. She felt pushed and pulled. She was glad to be escaping Anita Prokoff and the rumor that coiled around her, but she was also determined not to let Glo or Elizabeth off the hook. They hadn't done shit for her. They barely deserved politeness, much less forgiveness. She wished she were out back, being called a slut by Jimmy. Who would have guessed that would be better than this?

It was five o'clock. Each felt the challenge of being together. It had been easier with Anita Prokoff there—at least then they had her duty-laden, discomfiting generosity to guard against.

Elizabeth broke the silence. "Glo, are you sure we wouldn't be better off in a hotel tonight?" Her aunt's eyelids were half closed.

"Don't be silly. The woman offered. Let's just sit still a minute and talk." Glo didn't move out of the armchair she'd sunk into. She didn't look up. She sighed after she spoke. She really wanted anything *but* conversation right then. She wanted her rosary and her prayer-book, which were in her purse at her feet. She felt as if her blood were trying, and failing, to flow uphill.

Candy thought Glo looked about as tired as her mom had when she'd returned from Stan's funeral last October. Her mom had driven to Chicago and back in the same day, so that she'd miss only one day of work, leaving Detroit at four in the morning and getting home after eleven that night. Candy, waiting for her, jumped right in with a play-by-play of her game that day. She'd made twelve assists, a record. Her mom listened closely and asked questions, laughing at Candy's imitation of a player on the other team who sucked, and then reminded her not to be arrogant or a show-off. After a while, Candy realized her mom had just spent five hours on the road alone at night after being at a funeral all day. She had a crease in her forehead that Candy hadn't noticed before. Candy took her coat and told her to sit on the couch.

She went to the kitchen to make her a cup of tea. When she came back to the living room, her mom was asleep.

Candy pushed a footstool toward Glo, and then seeing her grandaunt grasping air near her feet, she reached down and handed Glo her purse. "I'll go upstairs and pack. When Elizabeth brings in your stuff, I'll show her your room." Candy left. Glo was old. And tired. No point being a total bitch to her.

An hour later, Anita Prokoff called them to dinner. Pint-sized white cardboard cartons of chow mein, beef and broccoli, and shrimp fried rice stood next to a quart-sized red-and-white cylinder of hot and sour soup. Anita had apologized when she'd come upstairs to tell Glo and Elizabeth that dinner was served. "I couldn't cook after all. I got a phone call from my sister. She and her husband are having financial trouble. They don't budget—I've been telling her for years they need to. She comes to me for advice, but she never listens. So, anyway, I ordered Chinese for you. I hope you don't mind." Anita was dressed for her night out, pink lipstick outlining her thin lips, her hair coiffed carefully, faux casual. She wore dangling handcrafted silver earrings and linen pants.

Elizabeth, sitting on a twin bed with Rugrat and My Little Pony stickers decorating the white headboard, looked at her, confused. Mind? That she was putting them up and ordering Chinese for them? Should she offer money for dinner? Glo's voice yanked her back to earth, "I've never eaten Chinese in my life." It came out half boast, half complaint, with no room left for thanks.

"So, Glo, what's the deal with the big Jesus we're going to see? It sounds sort of cool in a lame way." Candy balanced a broccoli floret on chopstick tips and pointed it at her aunt.

Glo pointed a fork full of chow mein back at her. "It's not 'cool,'

Candy. Show some respect for your faith. Mrs. Prokoff told me you refuse to go to Sunday Mass with them. When you're with me, you'll be going to Sunday Mass." She put her fork down and looked at Elizabeth. "You didn't take that cooler out of the trunk, did you? I'd like yogurt tomorrow morning."

"I think people should just forget Mass and spend more time thinking." Candy sometimes went and sat in an empty church. The silent space there was big enough for her.

"You young people with all your talk of 'thinking' are wrong." Glo slurped her soup, wincing at the sour heat. "God wants you to be *praying* and *doing*. There's no need to think. He'll place what you need squarely in front of you until you either pick it up and prove yourself worthy or ignore it and prove yourself not. Take you, Candy. Your mother died. You think that's sad and you feel sorry for yourself. I understand that. But God is watching what you do with it. My advice to you is to stop thinking and start praying for forgiveness for your sins, which, by the way, could be why God took your mother in the first place." Glo reached for the broccoli. "God doesn't go around taking people's mothers willy-nilly. Do you understand what I'm saying?"

The room went quiet. A breeze shushed through the open window and blew the napkin off Glo's lap. She bent to pick it up, blood rushing to her head. She'd gone too far. She'd said something cruel that she didn't even believe. These girls, for all their smart talk, were in trouble, were bereft. Surely God wouldn't hold it against them that they didn't worship by the book. But no matter how forgiving God might be, Glo thought they should do better. Stan should have, too. He'd made it impossible for her to fully love him anywhere but in bed. In the spectrum of sins committed, where did they all stand? Doctrine was important. She believed that. But these girls before her, and Stan gone, and her desire thwarted—those were also important.

She usually felt sure and certain, but being with Elizabeth and Candy for an hour had already churned up feelings she couldn't reconcile. And now she'd gone and blamed Candy for her mother's death. She had to rise to a much better self and apologize for that. She smoothed her napkin on her lap, her spine straight. Did she have a better self? She was so tired. She began her apology, "I'm sorry, I just—" but Elizabeth cut her off.

"Jesus, Glo. Stop it, Glo. Why would you say something like that? God isn't punishing Candy."

"You're right. I was too blunt. I just wanted the girl to understand that she has a choice. And she has to exercise it to save her mortal soul. Do you hear me, Candy? What do you have to say for yourself?" Glo looked over the stifled roosters at her grandniece. The girl's head was bowed, absorbing her counsel.

Candy looked up and pointed her chopsticks. "Could you pass that chow mein, please?"

At ten o'clock Elizabeth heard Candy leave her bedroom and tramp downstairs. Her niece made no pretense of walking softly. Glo, asleep in the twin bed next to Elizabeth—frilly blue bedspread pulled up to her chin even in the heat—breathed a soft rattle. The day had taken its toll on Glo—by nine her gaze had been unfocused, her opinions delivered without her usual insistence. She seemed grateful when Elizabeth suggested she go to sleep.

Elizabeth, her shoulder pain prominent in the distraction-free zone of night, lay squarely on a wide ledge of insomnia, no danger of falling off it into sleep. She might as well see what Candy was up to. She got out of bed, pulled on her shorts, stuck her feet in her tennis shoes, and went downstairs. Once there, Elizabeth watched out the back door in the dark kitchen as Candy got her bike from the garage and rode away. Elizabeth ran two steps at a time back to the bedroom, grabbed the Coupe de Ville keys from Glo's purse, and left out the front door to follow her niece.

The reflectors on Candy's pedals rotated steady as a Ferris wheel as she rode the dark neighborhood streets, but when she turned onto Mack Avenue, the light was diluted by neon-signed bars and restaurants, by traffic, by streetlights bright. Mack was big and busy—Candy was a fool to ride it at night, with no helmet even. Elizabeth followed in stops and starts, allowing Candy to pedal ahead for a few blocks and then coming up behind her slowly, keeping her distance so Candy wouldn't notice the car. Driving that way, it would be a miracle if she wasn't arrested. A slowly moving Cadillac with a hot dog painted on it tailing a teenaged girl was not exactly discreet. Four blocks later, Candy turned into the parking lot of a twenty-four-hour Kroger and chained her bike to a spike of the black wrought-iron fence that enclosed the parking lot.

Elizabeth remembered Glo's plea for yogurt. Could Candy be thoughtful enough to do something about it? Doubtful. Her niece was probably just hungry, though she'd eaten twice as much as anybody else at dinner and sat on the back porch afterward with a bag of potato chips and a Coke. At her mother's funeral, Candy had moved like a cat on the veldt—all big muscle and gliding power. Her body had changed since then—she looked uncomfortable in it, slightly inflated, muscle no longer the first thing an onlooker noticed. Elizabeth watched the automatic doors of Kroger close behind her niece. She parked at the far end of the lot and walked in after her.

The grocery store at night was less frantic than during the day, less frivolous, too. At night, it met essential needs, most shoppers instinctively cutting flabby daytime purchases. On that Saturday after ten, the one cashier on duty studied her fingernails in between swiping small orders.

Candy didn't plan to purchase anything. For the past few weeks, she'd been coming to Kroger to steal things out of people's shopping carts. Not steal as in take them out of the store. But steal as in ruin some dinners, frustrate some parent packing a lunch later that week, screw up a birthday cake that somebody's grandma planned to make from scratch. She wanted to fuck up some stuff for people. She'd probably eat something, too, since she was there anyway.

The compulsive eating had started after her mom died. After State was over. Compulsive is what others would call it—it wasn't the right word at all. Purposeful eating. That's what she'd call it. She called the shots. She changed the shape of her body. Literally. Nobody could stop her. Nobody could keep the pads of flesh from growing on her thighs and stomach. They tried. Anita Prokoff urged second helpings of green beans and salad, while keeping the bread and pasta at the end of the table farthest from Candy, but Candy just reached past her. She didn't even have to get out of her chair.

Once the season was over and she didn't have anything but her twice-a-week, secret practice sessions with Coach D, there were many hours of the day when Candy was alone. Anita had a full-time job and Amy was involved in a bunch of extracurriculars. So during those after-school hours, she chose as company a bag of Oreos and a half gallon of milk or Chunky Monkey with hot fudge topping or a few Hot Pockets. She occupied herself this way. She filled up. She didn't have to think about everything that was wrong while she ate. Instead, she felt the pleasure of food. Sweet, salty, hot, cold, smooth, crunchy—her sense of taste was not complicated by her mom's death, her aunts' neglect, her coach's betrayal. She didn't want to think any-more, and thoughts intruded when she didn't have food to ward them off. She knew the eating, purposeful or not, said something about her to others. It said she was a stupid cliché: a fucked-up teen with a dead mom and low self-esteem stuffing junk down her cake-hole. She thought herself more interesting than that. And she would be again. But not now.

That night at Kroger, she walked down aisle eight, "Baking Needs," swinging a basket on her arm. She watched a woman, about Elizabeth's age, put a bag of Nestlé's chocolate chips in her shopping cart. Candy, pretending to examine varieties of Crisco, also saw walnuts, flour, granulated sugar, and vanilla in the woman's cart. The woman walked away from her cart and toward the brown sugar boxes lined up on the shelf like dominoes. Watching the woman closely, moving as she did, Candy approached the shopping cart and in a fluid motion reached in and removed the small bottle of vanilla extract. She continued down the aisle, turned up aisle seven, and walked over to the meat section.

A man shopped there. A little boy, maybe two years old, was strapped into the seat of his cart. This one would be a challenge—the man paid more attention to his cart, holding, as it did, the irreplaceable cargo of his kid, along with two pounds of ground turkey. What was that kid doing up so late, anyway? From a few feet away, while the man looked down for two seconds at the scrap of a shopping list in his hand, she reached into the cart and in one facile motion took the turkey and put it in her own hand basket. The toddler laughed as she did so, and the man looked up from his list and made a googly face and kissed the boy's forehead.

Candy spent more time in the beer, wine, and soda aisle than in any other. She had to be careful there, because the clinking bottles called attention to her presence. But still she reached in for a six-pack of beer here, a bottle of Chablis there, taking care of her business in the gaps between people's focus and distraction—that millisecond in which they stared up from the list in hand to the aisle sign that hung from the fluorescent-lit ceiling, eyes wide and blinking, as if they couldn't believe they were exactly where they needed to be.

When she was ten, she used to steal her mother's booze and pour it down the sink. That was before her mother'd stopped drinking five years ago. Actually, five years, eight months, and thirteen days ago, if you counted the time since she'd been dead, which Candy often did. Stealing her mother's alcohol had been easy, but pointless. It only made her leave the house, drunk and driving, to find more. Her mother had been sober two full years before Candy allowed herself to believe it might stick. Now, she wished she hadn't wasted those years looking for a bottle hidden, sniffing surreptitiously to catch a whiff of alcohol on her mother's breath, or staring in the window of the bar where her mother used to drink for hours, even though she had told Candy she was meeting her sponsor for coffee at the Clock.

Candy pretended to examine the price of a case of Budweiser as a woman slowly pushed a wobbly-wheeled cart down the aisle. When the woman left the cart and went to look at the Pepsi display, Candy walked past it and saw that it already held a six-pack of Diet Coke, a two-pound bag of plain M&Ms, a half dozen cinnamon-raisin bagels, a box of granola bars, and two bags of baby carrots, peeled, cleaned, and ready to crunch. She looked again at the woman, who stood staring at the shelf full of soda as if it held some secret that would save her if she concentrated hard enough. Candy remembered the first few months after her mother quit drinking. How she had kept herself occupied with food, often sending Candy to the grocery store alone, not wanting the temptation of this aisle. How, in the beginning, she'd seemed so much weaker physically as a sober person than she had as a drunk. Candy walked past the woman's cart without reaching in, and went two aisles over to the Bath and Beauty section. She picked out a lavender-scented bar and walked back to the soda aisle where the rickety-looking woman still stood and stared. Then, as the woman reached up for a liter jug, needing both hands to lift it off the shelf, Candy slipped the violet-colored cake of soap under the carrots in her basket.

She smiled at the thought of the woman arriving home, smelling the soap even before she unpacked her bag of groceries. She chortled at pictures of all the other shoppers finding key items missing from their bags, incensed at the bagger's mistake, and then checking their receipts and cursing themselves instead for forgetting. Tired people with yet another petty problem to deal with. Good, let them join the crowd; though she felt her problems were far from petty.

Yogurt, Elizabeth reminded herself as she tailed her niece. That could be her excuse if she ran into Candy. She watched, curious, as her niece pulled things out of people's shopping carts and then placed a bar of soap in a brittle-looking woman's basket.

After that, Candy roamed around the store and ate. Elizabeth watched as her niece walked pigeon-toed down the cereal aisle, fitting each foot into the confines of the gray-and-white-square-tiled floor, and then grabbing a box of granola bars off the shelf, eating one, and throwing the wrapper on the floor. Candy put the open box in the Dairy section next to a carton of cottage cheese. She went to Produce then and selected a Granny Smith from a gleaming green pyramid of apples, took a bite, and placed the remainder amid a mound of navel oranges. Then she peeled a banana, gobbled half, and jammed the rest into a dusty heap of baking potatoes. She left the Produce section and wandered back toward Dairy, and that's when Elizabeth saw that the store manager, his white shirt gone gray with wear, skinny black tie tucked into the placket, was following Candy, too.

Hoping to head off the trouble sure to come, Elizabeth backtracked and picked up the half-eaten apple and banana, and the open box of granola bars. She heard the hiss of a soda being opened and hurried to that aisle in time to see her niece chugging from a two-liter bottle of A&W Root Beer. The manager approached Candy from behind, but Elizabeth faced her first. "Oh good, you found the root beer."

Candy stopped drinking and let out a loud belch in Elizabeth's face. "Huh?"

"Soda was the only thing left on our list."

"Excuse me, young lady," the manager reached up to tap Candy's shoulder—short guys always got the night shift. "I've been watching you on the video screens at the desk. We prosecute shoplifters here." He took a step back as Candy turned and faced him full on. Elizabeth recognized the raising of the eyebrows, widening of the eyes, and involuntary smile of a man facing a beautiful woman. Candy hadn't said or done a thing, and she looked far from her best, but the man's reaction was textbook.

Elizabeth stepped in front of him as Candy opened a bag of sour cream and onion potato chips. "What are you talking about? Shoplifting? There's no shoplifting going on here. My niece and I haven't left the store, have we? So she had a bite of fruit? It's a blood sugar thing—she's diabetic. We'll be leaving after we pay for these things." Elizabeth pointed at the fruit, already brown around its teeth-marked edges, in her basket. "Come on, Candy. Time to go." Candy swiped her mouth with the back of her hand, burped again, this time toward the manager, and followed Elizabeth.

Out of the manager's earshot, Elizabeth demanded answers: "Is the burping necessary? How about leaving us a little dignity?" They walked through the Bakery section on their way to checkout, and when Candy stopped to stare at a shelf of doughnuts, Elizabeth moved to block her reach. "Cut it out with the eating and the taking things from carts or putting things in. What the hell is this all about?"

"I'm keeping people on their toes. Upsetting their equilibrium. It's a service, really. The eating part has no point—I'm just really really hungry. And I didn't ask you to defend me."

"I notice you didn't stop me."

"My mouth was full."

"Jesus, Candy, I came here all the way from L.A., and I'm going on this trip with you, and now I just saved you from being arrested. You could cut the smart-ass routine for a second."

"Oh, sorry. I forgot. You're here for me. You're a fucking saint. St. Bitch. That's who you are. Glo, too."

"You swear too much. You *were* shoplifting and you *could* be arrested for it."

"Like you said, I didn't leave the store. Would you rather I was out in the parking lot having sex and doing drugs?"

"*Have* you been out in the parking lot having sex?"

Candy snorted. "Hah! That's what you and everybody else want to know."

"Listen, I know you're angry at me because I walked away from your mother—"

Candy cut her off. "Don't be an egomaniac, Elizabeth. This has nothing to do with you. Or with my mother."

"Fine."

"You were such an asshole to her."

"You don't know what happened, Candy."

"Yes, I do know. She told me."

"What did she tell you?"

"Everything. She told me everything she ever remembered she did when she was drunk. Including have sex with your stupid husband. What was he? Your fourth? Your sixth? Who can keep track with you?"

Elizabeth stiffened and jerked her hand away from her niece so that she wouldn't strike her. It was after 11:00 P.M. Had she flown from L.A. that day? Or the day before? When had she seen Leo? What was his little girl's name again? Tired as she was, she thought she actually could muster the energy to hit this girl in front of her. The impulse, examined, diminished, and Elizabeth turned from Candy to the doughnuts displayed behind a plastic cupboard door. The wax paper lining the tin trays was crooked and spotted with sugar residue, only a few long johns and jelly doughnuts left from the long day of shopping, barely enough sugar and fried lard to keep a night shift awake. She reached in for a jelly doughnut, tore it, red jam oozing like a wound, and handed half to Candy. "He was my second husband. Your mother told you about her and Benjamin?"

"She was defending you. I said you were an asshole for never coming around anymore. I said that for years, by the way. So she finally explained. It was a lame reason. That guy was a jerk. My mom was a drunk. You were almost divorced from him anyway. It's just sex. She was your sister."

"Half sister." Elizabeth breathed in righteous anger.

"She was the good half. You should have listened to her when she got sober. She tried really hard with you. I told her you turned into an asshole. But she wouldn't blame you. I didn't—I don't—give a shit about you, Elizabeth."

Elizabeth banged the Plexiglas door open and shut—Candy didn't know what she was talking about. When Elizabeth had realized Ben was cheating again, she'd been glad. It had given her an unassailable reason to leave him. But then she'd found out the other woman was Melissa. And that was an out she'd never asked for. Now, almost six years later, Elizabeth saw that she'd become the bad guy in this story with Melissa, even though Melissa had been the one to sleep with her husband—no jury would acquit her of that. Even though Melissa had worn her down, year-after-year full of booze—all sides would stipulate to that, too. But then, there had been Candy. Twelve years old, sober, and still working on her jump shot when Elizabeth last spent time with her. She remembered Leo's reaction—incredulous—when she'd told him about Melissa and Candy. *Come on, Elizabeth, it's not like you have to travel to Sydney, Australia. She's in Detroit. And you're in Chicago. Even Amtrak goes there. You need to go there.* No jury would acquit Elizabeth either. "So, your mom told you everything?"

"Everything she remembered."

"You should have met my third husband, Leo."

"Whatever." Candy licked a splot of jelly off her finger.

"He adopted a little girl. I think she has emotional problems. He's a good guy."

"Then I'm not surprised he dumped you."

"There are no perfect people, Candy."

"There are lots of people who aren't as fucked up as you. I know why you and Glo are here now. I'm *not* stupid and I'm *not* playing basketball this year. Don't worry because I'm also *not* about to move in with either one of you." Candy spoke forcefully. She knew exactly what she wanted at that moment: *Not to be like any of them.* Glo, Elizabeth, Mr. Morrisey, Anita Prokoff, even Coach D.

She wanted to be better than them. Better even than her mom had been. She didn't know yet what quitting basketball had to do with any of that. She'd quit because she was so pissed at Morrisey. So pissed at Coach D. And so embarrassed about something she hadn't even done. And now *they* all wanted her to play again, and that was a good enough reason not to. But what had she done to herself by quitting? She wondered if this was how a crazy person felt—one second certain, the next second stupid, the next one so mad she wanted to punch her aunt or herself in the face.

"When Anita Prokoff kicks me out, I'll live under an overpass before I move to Chicago or L.A." Candy spoke loudly, competing with the droning whirr of the large buffing machine gliding over the floor near a display of cakes nearby. A young man didn't so much guide the machine as barely restrain it. The chemical smell of floor wax added a sharper edge to the aroma of burned sugar and lard that coated the cakes and pies and doughnuts.

"You say that now, but this is all very complicated."

"It's not complicated at all. I'm taking a stand." Candy spoke with her mouth full.

"It looks more like you're running away."

"I'm sticking with my coach. *I'm* not the kind of person who abandons somebody because of a mistake."

"So you're saying your coach made a mistake?"

"I think it's obvious." Had Candy just confirmed the rumor? Elizabeth kept quiet, hoping for more, but what followed was cryptic. "Coach D never should have left me alone to face this shit. You two would get along just fine."

They were interrupted by a crash. The buffer had escaped, gliding over the tile floor like a puck on ice, slamming the cake stand to their left into the bread rack behind it so that birthday wishes in devil's food, angel food, buttercream, and German chocolate tumbled at their feet. Candy, nonplussed, reached down, picked up a cracked plastic carton, and ate a messy handful of cake, while Elizabeth leaned down to help the young man, who mumbled, *"Lo siento, Lo siento,"* and rubbed his shin where the buffer had bounced back and cracked it, all while looking over his shoulder at the short, dim-shirted manager who hastened their way. When Elizabeth straightened up, Candy was gone.

Elizabeth went to checkout. Let Candy do whatever it is Candy did. Have sex, eat crap, steal fruit—Elizabeth didn't care. St. Bitch? Was her niece right about that? She'd had three husbands. No children. Was there something wrong with her—a chromosome missing, some DNA disturbed, a hormonal imbalance, not enough estrogen, too much testosterone? Or was it something immeasurable? Heartlessness or selfishness. St. Bitch? Forget Melissa and Benjamin and their soap-opera sex. What kind of woman let a husband who was an idiot keep her from a niece who wasn't? What kind of woman didn't want a kid so much that she let a man she loved and lived with easily leave her? Her break from Leo had her questioning everything about herself, until she was left with few unpolluted feelings. Everything was tainted with guilt or shortcoming. Good or bad, she wanted to feel something pure and plain again and then *follow through* on it. In some warp of twisted logic, it almost felt like progress to have wanted to hit Candy at the cake stand a minute ago. As Elizabeth swiped her credit card, Candy came up behind her and placed four cartons of yogurt on the belt.

Anita Prokoff pulled her car into the driveway as Elizabeth parked the Coupe de Ville on the street in front of the house. Candy had climbed into the car without a complaint or question. They'd put her bike in the trunk. "Oh how nice. You ladies went out for a drive in the hot dog car?" Anita Prokoff, obviously not in the habit of waiting for answers, enthused, "Isn't it a glorious evening?"

Candy looked up at the sky, wide open over the treetops and chimneys of the old brick neighborhood with its patches of porches where people leaned and perched and watched one another's business every day. With all that open sky, it was amazing that this is where she gazed up at it. In Detroit. With no mom. With no basketball coach or team anymore. With two aunts who really wanted her to be well taken care of. By somebody else.

Elizabeth saw Candy's mouth quiver and then hold firm. She looked up, too. The sky was hazy with city light. She saw no glory in it, just an endless expanse of dimness that didn't offer even the conviction of true dark. She went inside without saying goodnight. At least Glo would be sleeping—a mere presence she could pretend wasn't there. She was tired of company. Tired of staying awake. She wanted to be alone.

But Glo was wide awake, kneeling by the window where a breeze fluttered the sheer curtain. A bluish-white shaft of street light illuminated her, diffusing her image. Her lips moved, the soft murmur of her prayer wrapping around the rosary beads in her hand. It should have been a pretty picture, the flutter of breeze, the sheer of curtain, the shaft of light, the strength of devotion, but Glo's shoulders sagged in her blue bathrobe, which was faded and worn to the color of dust, and her face was somber and shadowed, as if she carried sorrowful mysteries close to her heart.

And she might, Elizabeth thought, watching Glo from the bedroom doorway. Just because she could not see them, did not mean they were not there.

CHAPTER 8

"CANDY. THINK FAST." Anita Prokoff threw a basketball to her as Candy heaved a bag into the tremendous trunk of the Coupe de Ville. It was seven in the morning. Candy, needing more sleep and less everybody urging her to move or think, didn't try to catch the ball, merely stepped out of its path. When it hit Elizabeth in the shoulder, Candy laughed. "Good shot, Anita," she said, adding under her breath, "for a fucking spastic."

Elizabeth yelped and then chased the ball that bounced into the street. She tossed an easy shot into the open trunk. "Good idea to bring a ball. We'll shoot around on the road. I haven't seen your game in a long time."

"I do believe seats were available." Candy leaned down and tightened the worn Velcro strap of her Teva, which came undone about ninety times a day. How could Elizabeth act as if this were all normal?

Just showing up after five straight years of staying away. Coming in for the funeral didn't count.

With the last bag loaded in the trunk and Glo's yogurt in the cooler, Candy, resigned, opened the car door and ducked into the backseat. She felt a jolt of hope when she heard her name being called from down the block. The voice was too faint to identify, but clearly somebody was charging toward her. Somebody who might liberate her from this trip, from her aunts, from the giant Cross in the Woods. She looked up, willing to accept salvation. But it was only Amy, on her bike, pedaling fast and shouting again, her voice recognizable now.

"Candy, wait."

"What?"

"I wanted to say good-bye."

"Okay. Bye." Candy ducked back into the car, hoping Amy wouldn't try to hug her.

"Come over here." Amy motioned to the street, out of earshot of Glo and Elizabeth and her mother, and Candy, curious, followed. "My mom called over to Kim's house last night and told me you were leaving this morning. And then Kim and I were talking about it and I just want you to know before you leave that I believe you that nothing happened with Coach D."

"I don't care who believes me."

"I'm the only one who does."

Candy raised her voice, exasperated. "He's thirty. He eats cat hair. He's really weird everywhere but on the court. How can people think I'd do it with him?"

"Ssshhh"—Amy pointed at her mother, Glo, and Elizabeth— "they'll hear you. Listen, just make sure you come back, okay? Stay with us again this year. Don't agree to anything else. And don't quit basketball."

Candy edged away. "Who told you to say all this? My aunts? Your mom?"

"No, it's just me. My mom wants you out of the house." Amy took Candy's arm, cradling her elbow as if she were fifty and needed help walking, guiding her to the car. Once there, Amy stopped and faced her, and Candy saw how like her mother Amy was, butting in, and how unlike her she was, too. Amy didn't do nice stuff because she wanted credit or wanted something in return. She did nice stuff be-cause she was nice. She let Amy hug her when they got back to the car and as she did, she saw Elizabeth looking at them closely, puzzled, as if it were a surprise that anybody could like Candy enough to make a special trip to say good-bye and then hug her, too. Candy hugged Amy back hard and whispered in her ear, "When you see Jimmy, tell him I said he's a dick."

The backseat of the Coupe de Ville was big as a couch and Candy had it all to herself while Elizabeth drove. From there, Candy could see the dashboard glowing green and red. There were buttons and vents and computer-generated LED displays for just about everything: if your seat is too cold, press this; if your feet are too warm, try that; volume up for me, down for you, no problem. Fix your makeup in this lighted mirror. Check your direction on this computerized com-pass. Just ask and the Cadillac will answer. And presiding over it all was Glo's dashboard Jesus, feet firmly glued to leather, sacred heart glowing inside his pure white robe, opening his arms to the road just traveled, to them all.

Candy eased herself into the corner, pillowing her sore elbow into the soft leather. She was wearing her SEE NO EVIL, HEAR NO EVIL, SPEAK NO EVIL T-shirt. She'd pinned a button reading ASK ME ABOUT MY VOW OF SILENCE to the third monkey's head. She had on the same shorts as yesterday, stretched out for a second day of wear. She'd hoped they'd feel more comfortable that way, but they still dug into her waist. No wonder. In addition to the Oreos and Hot Pockets, she hadn't strapped on an ankle weight, run a mile, or done a push-up in more than three weeks. Clearly she'd turn fat if she never played basketball again. But tight shorts or not, she was ready for a heaping plate of eggs and bacon and pancakes. Maybe a couple of Pop-Tarts, too.

Elizabeth wore jeans and a T-shirt, but one that hung loose and conveyed no message. When she and Candy had come downstairs with their bags that morning, Glo had disapproved. "You're going to Mass like that?" Glo wore light green knit pants and a matching sweater, beige sandals, and lipstick, but her complaint about their clothes was proffered without conviction—it was easy to ignore. Candy studied her grandaunt's face in the sideview mirror from the backseat. She looked a little raggedy this morning, even for an old lady. Her red lipstick had already saturated the filigreed wrinkles of her lips and her beige powder had crept into the bigger, deeper wrinkles rutted on the sides of her mouth, outlining her jaw, making it look as if it were attached to her cheeks by a hinge. As Candy watched her in the mirror, Glo took five pills one by one, a swig of bottled water with each, her lipstick splotchy by the time she was done. She looked stunned by the day started too soon. Too bad. It was her idea to leave so early.

Candy looked away quickly as Glo caught her glance in the mirror. Too late. Glo turned around. "Mrs. Prokoff says you had college coaches scouting you last season. You'll get even more coming to see you this season, I'm sure."

"Then they'll be coming to see me sit on the couch and watch TV."

"Oh, stop that nonsense. You'll play. Why wouldn't you play?"

"Why would I?"

"That coach who left your team high and dry is not a good reason to quit. He does not deserve your loyalty. Your loyalty should go to your teachers, your school, your teammates, and yourself. Anita Prokoff said a Notre Dame scout came to watch you last year. Notre Dame, Candy. It does not get better than that."

"Glo, get this straight. First: I am not playing basketball this year. Second: as if I'd *ever* go to Notre Dame. Domers suck."

"God gave you great talent, young lady."

"God can have it back."

"God doesn't like a smart aleck, especially on Sunday."

"Glo, give it a rest." Elizabeth thought her aunt's approach—obtuse denial accompanied by lecture—to Candy's resistance was futile. She wasn't going to listen to anything they said straight out. Elizabeth hit a button she thought was the radio and a blast of hot air hit her face. She tried another button and, success, baroque music oozed like caulk, sealing the car from all other sound.

Candy tuned out the grind of organ and thought seriously about not playing basketball this year. She'd played the end of last season in a complete zone, adamantly rejecting any outside interference in the form of sympathy or concern. The concentration she'd attained had been impenetrable—the now, the ball, the game—that was all that had mattered to her. Her stats during the State tournament had gone up in every category. She had been unstoppable.

This was a heightened, not a new, focus. It was during her sophomore year that she'd begun to understand that she saw the floor in a way that others didn't. She saw the open court as vast. Saw geometry in the half court. Get the ball and produce. Give and go to create an angle too acute to defend. Sprint past defenders. Knife toward the basket. Always keen. Always patient. She'd griped about Coach D's visualization and meditation exercises but, truth is, she'd read the great coaches. *Chop wood, carry water*. In *Sacred Hoops*, that's what Phil Jackson said the Buddhists said. *Be quick, but don't hurry*. That's what John Wooden advised. When she thought too hard about these things, they seemed like riddles, but when she played, they were the answers that catapulted her game to another level. She anticipated her opponents' intentions and stepped into the passing lane for an easy steal, or doubled down in the post and stoppered an attack on the way. She heard crowd noise when she played, but it existed only as a hum behind the cone around her where every important voice came through easy and amplified: her own, commanding a teammate; Coach D's, directing from the bench; Kim McVitty's, pleading for the ball in the post; or an opponent's, cursing or panting or celebrating. In the flow of play, Candy, even minus her mother, could react. Fans might call it instinct. Teammates, dedication. Candy didn't name it any more than she named the functions of her kidneys, liver, heart, or bones. It was who she was. No. It was who she used to be.

In the backseat of the Cadillac, thinking about the power she held on court, Candy began to better understand the command she held by staying off it. What was it they had learned in physics? For every action, there is an equal and opposite reaction. Quitting had upset the people around her. If she put some thought into it, she could manipulate them even as they thought they were yanking her chains and winching her back on court. She wasn't powerless without basketball. She just needed to step back and study how to use the new power. Glo couldn't force her to play. Neither could Anita Prokoff, Mr. Morrisey, Ms. Hogan, or Sister Anne. And Elizabeth? At least she seemed to get that it was useless. That *she* was useless.

For a long while, except for the muted music, the car was quiet—

Elizabeth didn't talk and Glo stared out the window. It was foggy as they drove north on I-75 toward Flint. Elizabeth fiddled with the switches and buttons for defroster and lights. "How do I know?" Glo said when Elizabeth asked her how to turn things on. "I was not about to drive a hot dog car around a neighborhood where people knew me. All the gizmos on this car confused Stan, too. He had some of the features disconnected because the dashboard was always buzzing or dinging or lighting up and he didn't know why. He drove my car more often than he drove this one. That really irritated me."

"You shouldn't use lights in fog. It's not good for the drivers coming toward you." Candy remembered driver's training class and the *Laws of the Road* booklet that she'd memorized for her written test at the DMV.

"That's just for high beams. Regulars are okay." Elizabeth corrected her as she found the button that helped light their way.

Candy stretched out, feet up on the seat, and watched out the window as the weighty industry of auto factories and tool-and-die shops gave way to shopping malls and office buildings with smoked glass windows and then to the rolling hills of Oakland County, where the All Saints Ravens went to play the rich girls at Mercy and Marian and Lahser.

The final game of the regular season last year had been against archrival Mercy, and the team had traveled up this same stretch of I-75 in their bus during a snowstorm—everybody nervous from the weather and the need to beat Mercy. Candy, her mom just dead, sat alone. Her teammates knew enough not to buddy up to trouble before a big game. Candy didn't think about the game or her mom during the bus ride. She just watched the snow drive toward the bus window, and noticed that in the instant before it should splat on glass, it got caught in a vortex that swirled it up and away. The old yellow bus rattled along in the slow lane of I-75, clanking and straining, no grace or deftness to its motion, merely making its way.

Coach D had come and sat with her before they exited the freeway, which made Candy sit up straighter, her shoulders a frame. All that past week, one teacher or another had made a point of getting her alone and giving her advice, wanting her to confide, inviting her to soak a shoulder with tears. Their faces while they talked resembled the plaster cast of the saints standing guard in the church, eyes wide and beseeching. Morrisey had put his arm around her shoulder when he'd seen her outside the cafeteria. Even Sister Anne had tried to break in on her distress, stopping her in the hallway, giving her a Bible, inscribed with love, a Post-it note stuck on Job, another on the Psalms, inviting her to pray, assuring her she was not alone, and then checking her watch and hurrying away when she saw she was late for class. Candy girded herself against Coach D on the bus that day, hoping that at least he'd be klutzy enough that his attempt at sympathy would make her laugh.

"You know, Golden, I'm a birder." He tapped a rolled-up newspaper on his knee as he spoke.

"A what?"

"I watch birds."

"Oh yeah. They say you have a chicken coop in your front yard and that it stinks."

"Who says that?"

"Amy Prokoff. Her mom told her."

"Her mother is—forgive me—an ass."

"Amy is my friend."

"She's too passive." The bus lurched and Coach D dropped his newspaper. Candy leaned down to get it for him. *The Copperwood*

Crier—News from Up North read the masthead. He saw her reading it. "You ever been up north, Golden?"

"Name one person in Michigan who hasn't. Even the poor kids get shipped up there to charity camps."

"I see your point. I usually go up there in the summer. My brother has a place he lets me use near Copperwood. I subscribe to this local paper during the rest of the year because it has a bird sightings column."

"So, birds, Coach?"

"I had homing pigeons when I was a kid. My dad helped me. We built hutches for them. It was a good thing—something we did together. But I moved on from pigeons. I'm interested in rare birds now. I've gone birding all over Michigan. I'm secretary of the Detroit chapter of the Audubon Society. People think that because I'm a guy in a sweatshirt I go home and watch ESPN, but, Golden, I don't even have cable. I watch birds."

"I thought it was only old people who do that kind of thing."

"That's my point about the game tonight, exactly. So you see what I'm getting at?"

Candy wondered if he were having some sort of brain seizure that made him talk nonsense. "Honestly, Coach, I have no idea."

"Mercy thinks you're our main scoring threat."

"That's because I am."

"Not tonight, Golden. I don't want you to even think about shooting. The ball comes into your hands, you get rid of it. They'll collapse on you, but little do they know you don't want the ball, you don't have the ball, you won't get the ball, you won't shoot the ball. They think they know you inside out, Golden, but they don't. Because tonight we're introducing a new Candy Golden. The one who doesn't score."

"That might just confuse them enough that they win."

"No. They won't know what to make of it. They'll think one thing. They'll see another. They won't adjust in time. Another thing, on that man-to-man when their shooting guard has the ball, you've got to swing off on the weak side and be ready to double team with Lasser. You missed that rotation more than once in practice the other day. We can make some stops if you do your job. We'll get this game if we hold Dietz under twenty."

"I hate Dietz." Candy stamped her feet, which were going numb in the drafty bus.

"Don't blame you for that. What'd she do, score twenty-four on you last time around?"

"Twenty-two." Candy corrected him quickly. "Plus, remember how she took out Marlene last game? Marlene was like six feet in the air and Dietz goes for her and not the ball. That is nasty shit."

"I agree. If she were my player, I'd suspend her the first time she did that and kick her off the team the next. But forget about that. And forget about shooting, too. Pressure defense. No backing off. No slacking off. We'll have to grind this one out with Washington's ankle weak, McVitty's shot gone to hell, and you being silent, but we're going to be a wall on defense. If you pull down ten rebounds—four offensive—we'll win this game."

Candy pulled down fifteen rebounds, seven offensive. She scored only eight points, fifteen below her season average. But freed from the burden of creating her shot, she roamed easily during a game in which she'd been afraid she would trudge under the weight of her mother's absence in the stands. Coach D was right—they won. The All Saints Ravens would go into the State Championship playoffs undefeated. On the dark bus ride back to Detroit after they'd beaten Dietz and

Mercy, Coach D had merely nodded as he walked past the empty seat next to Candy. She'd thanked him for that, too.

Driving up north with her aunts that Sunday morning, she thought about how he was the best coach in Detroit. The best coach in Michigan. He was also the only adult who hadn't asked that she favor him with her grief. And it wasn't because he'd seen her collapse with it on the morning he'd delivered the news about her mom. When she was with her friends she laughed about what a freak he was. But that was a pose. She did not laugh at him when she was alone. So what if he ate cat hair and raised chickens and watched birds? All those months in the gym after State, after her mom died, she'd played ball with him, and played attentively. Everywhere else that semester, she'd avoided thought or pushed it out of her mind by stuffing her mouth. But on those evenings he'd demanded that she sit and think before she stood and moved. He'd saved her ass that semester. Her mind, too. She knew it in her heart.

She didn't understand how he could have run off, leaving her to deal with people like Morrisey. She would never run away. He was probably up north himself right now. He'd told her he went to his brother's place. She imagined running into him. She thought about what she'd say if she did, but came up with nothing. Nothing—that's all she expected anymore.

Elizabeth drove the Coupe de Ville past the exits for Mercy and Marian and Lahser, and before too long they approached the dingy, smoke-tinged outskirts of another auto town—Flint, Michigan. It wouldn't be anybody's choice for a postcard. Candy closed her eyes to the scenery—she'd lived in Detroit all her life. Nothing in Flint could surprise her.

CHAPTER 9

PEOPLE FILLED THE pews of St. Anne just north of the Flint River at 8:30, even though Mass didn't start until 9:00. Glo felt a thrill as Elizabeth idled in a long line of cars waiting to pull into the parking lot. It was like a shopping mall at Christmas. At St. Viator back in Chicago, she worshiped at nine o'clock Mass on Sunday with, perhaps, one hundred other parishioners. Most of them were even more senior a citizen than she, hobbling in on a walker or a cane, or, if lucky, the arm of a visiting granddaughter or -son.

But here at St. Anne, many of the parishioners didn't walk in at all. Instead they skipped and ran and giggled and pulled on their mothers' jackets, their fathers' pant legs. Yes, there were children, lots of them. Glo couldn't remember the last time she'd seen so many youngsters going to Mass. Teenagers, too, walked in the main doors, dipped fingers in holy water, and blessed themselves. Not that she was the only older woman. She noticed her peers, grandchildren underfoot or tugging at hands. "Look at that, girls. Children and young people, like you."

"Look, Glo, they're not all white either. Kind of nice to see that for a change." Elizabeth stopped at a space marked COMPACT ONLY.

"Nonsense. The church is very receptive to our African-American friends." She wagged a finger at Elizabeth. "You can't park here. It's much too small. Keep going."

"There's lots of black girls at All Saints." Candy stuck her head into the front seat, bookended by her aunts, and looked out at the crowd as Elizabeth ignored Glo and inched the Coupe de Ville into the tight spot.

Glo swatted one of Candy's ragged dreadlocks when it swung too near her shoulder. "Honestly, your hair looks like something you should use to tie up an old boat. I suppose one of those black girls did this to it."

"Marlene Washington's aunt did it for me. It was a team thing. We all did it for State finals. I'm the only white girl who kept it though. In some people's hair it didn't really take. I was lucky."

"Luck is often a matter of opinion." Glo patted her own hair and lowered the visor to check it in the mirror. Good, her part was neat, her scalp showing through straight as a lane divider.

Elizabeth tapped the DO IT YOURSELF: GOD CAN'T BE EVERYWHERE bumper sticker on a yellow Neon in front of them. "Look at that. I made it." She turned the key, cut the engine, and they began the painstaking challenge of squeezing out of the car.

Glo had been in plenty of Catholic churches, but St. Anne was unlike them all. There was no gold and gilt. Little statuary. No filigree. She didn't see the Blessed Sacrament anywhere. The church had plain white walls, wood beams supporting the apse, and a hardwood floor.

Four simple stained-glass windows shot beams of color onto the un-adorned dark-wood pews. Small, wood-carved stations of the cross hung at eye level, the yards of open space above them left bare.

Glo marched to the first pew facing the altar on the left side of the main aisle. It was fronted by a row of choir pews perpendicular to it—that is, facing the main aisle, not the altar. The choir members, white and black, stood in those pews just in front of Glo and the girls. They talked and mingled with one another and with members of the con-gregation. A young boy sat at a drum kit, not ten feet from Glo, fixing an orange-and-green-and-white stole around his neck, the colors clashing with his royal blue choir robe. An older woman adjusted her robe with one hand and tapped a mike hanging from the ceiling on a ligament of wire with her other. A young woman next to the drummer carried a newborn baby in a sling across her chest. The baby bleated as its mother pinned up her auburn curls, her cheeks bright red in the skim pallor of her smiling face.

It wasn't just the choir members who chattered. The whole church was a buzz of greeting, the noise a presence. People skipped from pew to pew, extending hands or hugs, mingling as if they were holding cocktails instead of hymnals. Glo thought of the haunting quiet of St. Viator, where she could sink into her prayers with no distraction. She'd applauded the friendliness in the parking lot, but inside it just wasn't proper.

She would lead by example. Glo lowered the kneeler and nudged Elizabeth to her right, Candy to her left, into place on it. She drew her rosary from her purse as if it were magician's silk and wrapped it around her clasped hands, welcoming the familiar finish of the ellipti-cal beads in her fingers, these almost-weightless stepping-stones to prayer. Stan had given the rosary to her for their fifth anniversary. It had been blessed by Pope John Paul II when he visited Chicago more than twenty years ago. Stan had planned to display the rosary with his other Chicago souvenirs—a foul ball he'd caught at a Cubs' game in 1964, a campaign sign from Mayor Daley (the despot father, not the tongue-twisted son), a newspaper column autographed by Mike Royko—but then he'd watched her pray one day, and then the next day and the day after that also. He had studied her, he said, and she didn't seem to be there when she prayed. Where do you go, Glo?

He asked her more than once. And once while they lay in bed, having just made love—complementing each other in a way they couldn't once standing. His body, in its sixties when they'd met and growing ever older, was not a disappointment to her. She hadn't known a younger man, after all. And the way Stan took her in, the way his touch—so welcome on her knee, her back, her breast—conveyed a fragile yearning for her, made her sense the act sacred. If only his touch, which signified his devotion, could have lingered and transformed itself into faith. *If only*. She thought it often. If only this one thing: Stan with true faith; she never would have wished him gone. It would have been the thing that protected her from the simple things he did that frayed the edges of their marriage. She had needed Stan to be something other than he was. She did not know exactly what he'd needed from her.

And when he asked again, "Where do you go, Glo? What is your prayer?" she didn't tell him. She wasn't being cagey. She simply didn't comprehend. She didn't "go" anywhere. She wasn't transported. She was earthbound, steady, rooted—she was merely doing her duty. He'd done the right thing in giving her his blessed rosary, and she'd thanked him truly for it.

At St. Anne that morning, she closed her eyes, her fingers kneading the beads, counting on them to calm her. She barely finished her first Glory Be when a choir member in front of her turned and said, "Hi, I'm Josie. Is this your first time at Father Jim's Mass?"

"At *what*?" Glo questioned the interruption.

"Father Jim's Mass—I drive in from Saginaw for it. You ladies will love it. He's wonderful. So joyous. And the music." The woman clasped her hands, be-ringed on four fingers, and looked heavenward.

Glo was not comfortable. Praising a priest in the house of God was vain at best. Father Jim, however good a priest he might be, should not be the focus of the celebration of the Blessed Sacrament. Surely Christ did not die for their sins so that this woman Josie could drive fifty miles and swoon. Glo nudged Elizabeth and whispered, "We need to find a different church."

"No way. A bird in the hand, Glo."

"It's not respectful."

"Relax. God likes joy."

"This much joy is sinful."

Candy, looking pained after the man next to her hugged her, weighed in. "I'm with Glo. Let's get out of here."

But it was too late. The drummer began his beat and the choir crooned and then belted out "Holy Holy Holy, Lord God Almighty," all while swaying and clapping. The congregation turned toward the aisle like sunflowers to noon and watched as a sandal-footed priest danced toward the altar, waving and clasping hands, politician-like, as he progressed. Glo looked at Candy, then Elizabeth, for support. The people on either side of them had grabbed the girls' hands, holding them up as if they were contenders in a heavyweight fight. A man sitting behind Glo tapped her on the shoulder and urged her to take her nieces' hands, and before she could politely invite him to mind his own business, he began to sway. Everybody did. The whole church became an undulating mass. The whole church, *except* her nieces.

Candy and Elizabeth, seawalls against the crash of camaraderie on either side, stood firm. When Elizabeth hissed, "I am *not* swaying," Glo gave her an I-told-you-so look.

Glo wrapped her rosary tightly around her hand. She bowed her head. She tried to find her prayerful mind amid the noise and showy rapture. Father Jim boomed, interrupting her, "Let's get out of these bloody pews and say 'hello' to each other on this glorious morning."

Glo felt faint. These "bloody" pews? She knelt and held her head. She felt the kneeler sag on either side and looked right, then left. She saw Elizabeth and Candy next to her, looking down, not touching her. The three of them, together, a citadel holding strong while bombarded by joy. In the midst of her discomfort and displeasure, Glo felt proud of her flinty nieces.

Father Jim was a sham. Elizabeth knew the type, though this one pushed it to an outer limit. Part televangelist, part Vegas showman, he was an arrogant dandy intent on upstaging God, or anybody else who dared intrude on his limelight. He was handsome in a game-show-host kind of way—forty or so, with tanned skin, and eyes so blue they must be colored by contacts. She wished he would stay still, would stop walking around and high-fiving his flock. She gave thanks that at least his glad hands were too slick to rest a moment on her and Glo and Candy.

When Father Jim finally stopped walking, he started talking. That was worse. He called all the children to him. More rustle and talk as parents urged their reluctant six- and eight- and ten-year-olds to the altar, as if they'd never heard of pedophiliac priests. With the children gathered around him, Father Jim continued his stage act, asking this question: "Who is more important? The pope? Or Father Jim?"

Elizabeth watched Father Jim clamp his hands on a young girl's shoulders and heard him ask the question again. What an egomaniac.

The girl, maybe eight years old, looked confused, "I guess, like, it's a tie?"

Father Jim did a phony spit take and let loose a phonier laugh and put his arm around the guileless girl's shoulder. "The most important person is the one who serves God by tending to his neighbor. By loving his neighbor. By accepting and working to understand his neighbor, whether that neighbor is the homeless man under the freeway viaduct or the checker at the grocery store or his mom or dad. Serve *others* and *you* become important. We don't need to listen to this stuff from Rome about this or that church law. People," Father Jim commanded the congregation, with counterfeit smile and bleached teeth, "quit worrying about whether you've done your Easter duty and start worrying about whether you stuck out a hand to lift up a fallen stranger. That's how you become important."

The baby in the choir woman's sling cried as Father Jim landed on his up note. Elizabeth felt Glo stiffen next to her as the mother opened her choir robe and nursed her infant. Elizabeth doubted lactation had ever occurred at Glo's old, cold parish. Father Jim looked at the choir member nursing and smiled. "Look at that. That leads directly to what I'm here to tell you today. Kids, you go sit down." He shooed the children off the altar. "Folks, we need to talk about something important that's coming up, something divisive, something political that shouldn't be political at all. Something that should be in God's hands only. We're marching on Lansing next week. We're marching to protect the life of that nursing baby. That newborn baby who just a few months ago could have been murdered by its own mother." The nursing choir member's pale skin flushed red and she leaned over her baby, her body a cave, warding off his bludgeoning words.

"Let me ask you something, fellow servants of God." Father Jim was on the move again, roaming off the altar, walking toward the choir, past the choir, toward the congregation, toward her, Elizabeth realized, horrified. She willed herself invisible, but Father Jim fixed his simulated-blue gaze on her. When he put his arm on her sore shoulder, she flinched. "Look at this woman. Here, let me help you out of that pew. Come with me. Let the people see you." Elizabeth didn't budge, and he pulled her harder. "Please. Show yourself this morning. Help me bring the word to our neighbors. Don't be afraid. Come. Please. You, too." He reached out for Candy.

This was what came of sitting in the front row. Elizabeth dug her elbow into Glo's side, searching for a point of blame, as she gave in to the insistent priest and climbed out of the pew to face the congregation, grabbing Candy's belt loop and yanking her along.

Father Jim tugged them up the altar steps, turned them around, and posed them like spokesmodels, one on each side, as he continued his speech. "Who among you can look at this woman," he nodded at Elizabeth, "and say she is not equipped to raise a child? Or this one," he put a hand on Candy's dreaded head, "and say she is? Who is to choose? You? Me? The pope? Justice Scalia? No. None of these. It's a choice for these women only."

Elizabeth raised an eyebrow. In her experience, Catholics who spoke of mothers murdering their babies in one breath did not say something reasonable with the next. Besides, what did Father Jim, clad in sandals, ego, and celibacy, know about babies and the women who had them?

Father Jim bellowed again, "You're surprised to hear me say that? Don't be. But listen hard, my friends. Let's say, hypothetically, of course, that the choice has already been made for these two young women. Let's say," Father Jim wrapped his arm around Elizabeth's waist, and put a hand on Candy's shoulder, "that these two women are pregnant. It happens. We all know it can happen. And this one will have her baby," he squeezed Elizabeth, "and this one won't." He looked sideways at Candy. "I'm here to tell you that's okay." As the congregation let forth a puzzled "Hmmm?" Father Jim continued, "But not the way you think. It's okay as long as God takes her baby in a natural way. As long as God safely delivers hers into the world."

He looked and pointed right and left and right again but quickly so that it was no longer clear to Elizabeth whether she or Candy represented the hypothetical mother or sad victim of a miscarriage. Elizabeth saw the kente-clothed drummer looking at Candy's ass, his drumsticks resting on his thigh. She saw Candy slip a foot out of her broken-strapped Teva and provocatively scratch the back of her calf with an electric-blue toenail. She heard Father Jim harangue, "Here at St. Anne, we're not like all those other Catholics. Blindly following the Holy See. We recognize that these women have a choice to make. But only *before* they hold that life in their wombs. After that they might as well be cold-blooded murderers. Let's tell the truth here, people. They are cold-blooded murderers."

Elizabeth tried to keep it straight: miscarriage, sad; abortion, bad; birth control, a good idea? Was that his point? The congregation murmured, a little puzzled, but clearly chilled by his stark accusations. A feeble "Amen" drifted up from a pew in the back. Father Jim held Candy by the arm now, his hand a cup for her elbow, just as Amy had supported it earlier that morning. What had Amy and Candy whispered about? They'd been so somber. Why did that gesture, Amy's hand supporting Candy's arm, and now Father Jim's supporting it, strike Elizabeth so? The gesture impressed upon her. She remembered Amy's face, full of kindness. Remembered Candy's face break a little, guard lowered, as she listened to her friend whisper in her ear. As she accepted.

Hand cupping elbow. The muscle memory became a kinesthetic

compass that directed Elizabeth back almost eighteen years. Back to the feeling of her own hand supporting Melissa's elbow. That solicitous gesture. Let me help you. Let me hold you. She'd been only eighteen years old herself. Melissa was barely twenty-one—she'd start her junior year at Western in two weeks. Elizabeth was flying to L.A. to start her freshman year at UCLA sooner than that.

They'd gone to the Michigan State Fair at 7 Mile and Woodward—walked off the Detroit streets and onto fairgrounds that promised to display life unlike the city mode in which they lived. Strolled from canvas tents full of three-foot-long zucchinis and blue-ribbon cherry pies to coliseum-like edifices with dirt floors and cowboys roping steer. They'd been eating and laughing—all the food fried, all the laughter forced.

Melissa was pregnant—just two months. They'd stayed up late for nights, crying about it, talking about it, debating what to do about it. Melissa, deeply ambivalent, had decided to have an abortion. "That's fine," Elizabeth supported her. "I can go with you. You're going to be okay." She'd argued with Melissa against that choice for three days. It wasn't that she disapproved of it. She didn't. She also didn't think it was what her sister wanted.

She'd gotten to know her sister well that summer. She and Melissa had moved in together after Tony had died in June three months after he'd refused all treatment for an intestinal malignancy that the doctors admitted was inoperable. He'd said yes to morphine at the end, and Elizabeth remembered how, in a narcotic-tinged state, he'd held her hand and assured her that she'd be all right when he died but that Melissa might not be. "You'll want to walk away from her," he'd told Elizabeth, "and that's going to be easier than you think—the hard part is walking back." He'd said it so serenely—his face free of concern—just stating the facts.

But that August day, worn out, Elizabeth wasn't going anywhere. She and Melissa both felt relieved that Melissa had made any choice at all. The state fair, Melissa had said, now that I know what to do, let's just forget about it and go to the fair. Elizabeth agreed enthusiastically. A great idea. It would be fun. Cotton candy. The midway. Pigs and horses and tomatoes and pies. Cold beer.

Or maybe not. Melissa had stopped drinking when she'd realized she was pregnant. Elizabeth had read that as one clue that her sister might want the baby. Her sister's drinking had moved from high school and college partying to a deeper place, as if the alcohol no longer wore off in fumes of embarrassing behavior or slurred speech, but sank deeper, so that Melissa's very blood was thick with it and demanded more the next morning, afternoon, evening—the need becoming physiological. It was a hot day. A beer would taste good. Melissa could drink safely—no worry about hurting the stem cells that could become a baby. Melissa had called Planned Parenthood that morning. In just three days, there would be no more potential baby, all cells would be gone.

They'd stepped into the swine barn to look at prize-winning hogs and sows. They'd walked aimlessly—the fair wasn't much fun after all. In the barn, the heat mingled the smells of shit and hay and sweat into a sodden fetid assault. They stopped in front of a huge grunting animal—hog, sow, pig—what was the difference anyway? Elizabeth didn't know. This one had dark pudgy bristles of hair, and its snout trumpeted bad intent. The sign said it was SPUNKY from Midland, Michigan. Dow Chemical was headquartered there. It might be a genetic mutant. Maybe it was supposed to be tiny and lovable and soft and clean and pink, instead of brutish and threatening.

Melissa, standing next to her, stared at Spunky, and then she shuddered once like a pane rattled by gusts, and began to cry. It was at that moment that Elizabeth placed her hand under her sister's elbow and guided her out of the barn, toward an umbrella-covered table spattered with sticky residue and greasy remains of midway food. She talked to Melissa quietly, keeping a hand on her arm, as if her touch were the key to keeping things whole.

"Tell me, Mel. Tell me what you *really* want to do." Melissa wanted to have the baby. And raise it. Elizabeth took her hand off Melissa's arm and extracted a napkin from the dispenser on the table. She spit on it and tried to clean up the spills, thick and sticky. She said the right thing while she did. "That's good, Mel. If you need to have the baby, you should have the baby. And I can help you raise the baby, too. I don't have to go away to school. I'll go to Wayne. I'll get a deferment." Elizabeth looked directly at her sister and offered her help, though she wasn't sure she *could* do any of that. She wasn't sure of anything except how hard this would be for them all. For her. For her sister. For the baby. The loudspeaker above them squawked, a child lost, could the mother please come fetch him from the First Aid tent next to the Poultry and Goat Barn. They heard a soft sizzle of sound as the speaker shut down.

The drummer's silky whisk, a shushing beat, brought Elizabeth back to St. Anne. Candy moved to it, hula-hipped, flirting with the boy as Father Jim implored the crowd. Elizabeth hunched her shoulders, embarrassed by Candy's display. But there was something else, too. Something else about Candy. The weight gain, the loyalty to her coach, the rumors about him, the sneaking out with other boys that Anita Prokoff had mentioned to Glo, the quitting basketball, the whispered conference with her friend, the hand on her elbow. Candy and Amy. Melissa and Elizabeth. The friends. The sisters. The mother. The daughter.

Her niece was pregnant. That must be what this was all about.

Father Jim didn't let up. "We'll be marching on Lansing next week to deliver a message to the pope and to these women. Let us help you beforehand with birth control, even abstinence. Hey, did you ever think about that?" He smiled and looked at Elizabeth as the crowd chuckled appreciatively. "We will not allow these women to become killers. We will save them from themselves. So join us in Lansing next week. March with us to save the babies.

"I ask each of you today to think of these women"—Father Jim pulled Elizabeth and Candy close to his green satin vestments, and the drummer leaned forward in his seat, still brushing a soft patter, still looking at Candy's ass—"and pray that she has the courage to admit that come a certain point, she has no choice."

Father Jim, done with them, his props, patted them on the back and sent them to their pew. Candy smirked and wiggled on the way. Elizabeth, setting aside her epiphany (she couldn't think about it in the obliterating bluster of Father Jim), looked at her watch. They'd been there thirty minutes and he hadn't yet recited the Kyrie. What the hell would this man do with his sermon if he spent this much time on his opening salvo? Even someone as devout as Glo would need divine intervention to get through a Mass this long. Especially someone as devout as Glo. As she edged back into her pew, Elizabeth prayed for a miracle.

It took an hour and thirty minutes to get it. After communion, the deacon made an announcement: "The owner of a black Cadillac with a hot dog painted on its side"—people laughed—"your lights are on."

Elizabeth jumped up, free at last, and edged out of the pew. She whispered to Glo that she'd wait for her in the parking lot, but her aunt came right behind her and Candy followed. The three women, their senses battered, walked down the main aisle, grateful to escape Father Jim and his showy assault of love and eager to be on their way up north.

PART | II

LOVELY, MICHIGAN, SITUATED in the upper portion of the lower peninsula, was not. Lovely, that is. Some of its 2,172 residents might have argued that point, but they were either chronic civic boosters or people who had an overpriced house for sale. Most small towns up north had a degree of either charm or utility—a main street where a visitor could buy a jar of jelly with a ribbon tied around the lid and a slab of chocolate walnut fudge, or where a resident could find a ballpoint pen and a ball-peen hammer. But not Lovely. Its Main Street had diminished storefront by storefront in the 1990s, when the big retailers that had already taken over the most economically viable communities in America began to bigfoot less promising places, and finally even stamped on spots like Lovely.

From a natural beauty point of view, there was no more glorious place on earth than the area *surrounding* Lovely, but the town itself was flat and duneless and rocky. Its originally skimpy forests had been stripped clean by a sawmill that flourished in the 1950s and '60s and then closed shop, leaving behind clear-cut unemployment. Enveloped as it was by a batch of towns that boasted cherry and apple orchards that were neat and straight as the pins on a silicon chip, freshwater lakes full of even fresher fish, mountainous sand dunes that dipped to create perfect bowls of sound while the grasses holding them together rustled faintly and promised a Great Lake nearby, forests of pines so tall they dwarfed the birches bleached white and rising in no small glory of their own, and only seventy-five miles southwest of one of Michigan's grandest tourist attractions, the Cross in the Woods in Indian River, Lovely was the gooseneck on the pipeline filled with vacationers streaming toward or returning from the glory of the wonderland above. It was only the intermittent clog of these people who were forced to stop and spend a few dollars in Lovely that kept the town's IGA market, Granny's Restaurant, and Mar-Jo Motel in business.

Now add to all this the cruel trick of its name—a hurdle too high, a red flag in the face of the bullishly beautiful towns to Lovely's north and south and east and west, and even in the old days, before the sawmill closed down, before the Goods-4-Less warehouse store came to Copperwood, twenty miles east, and tempted the locals to spend their money there instead of at Lovely's Main Street establishments such as Sallee's Hardware and Lawson's Ladies Dresses, where neither nostalgia nor 50 percent off had rustled up enough customers to keep them wobbling on their last legs for more than a few weeks—and it's clear that Lovely, Michigan, was plain screwed.

So it was that the people of Lovely took matters into their own hands by placing their trust in Roger Sallee, a hardworking man, former proprietor of Sallee's Hardware who now punched a time clock at

Goods-4-Less as a retail clerk, a job he was bitter about because it required he wear a blue smock and answer such questions as "Do you carry Hoovers and Crock-Pots?" all while making minimum wage. He was more comfortable in his role as Mar-Jo Motel manager. The two jobs tired him out, but he had a goal and no other way to reach it—he was trying desperately to amass enough money to flee Lovely and the unfair obligation forced upon him by the state, which wouldn't acknowledge that his ex-wife was living in sin and refusing to marry her live-in boyfriend simply to hold him up for alimony.

Roger's belief that he could meet his personal challenges through hard work and ingenuity helped him view the town's troubles as solvable, too. At Roger's urging, and after years of watching tourists blaze through on the way to pledge their prayers (and, more important, their tourist dollars) to the Cross in the Woods, Lovely made a choice. It would build a shrine of its own, a tribute to Our Lady of Guadalupe. It had worked for Indian River, so whether Catholic or Lutheran or First AME or Baptist or even the two Jewish families who lived a mile up Route 51, the residents of Lovely hoped it could work for them. The group of concerned citizens who spearheaded the cause quickly realized they couldn't afford anything along the scale of a seven-ton bronze Jesus on a fifty-five-foot redwood tree cross, so they formed teams and searched Lovely and the surrounding area for a natural religious phenomenon—something that could be interpreted as holy to those blinded by devotion—a rock in the shape of the Virgin Mary, a tree that loomed like Lucifer stricken, a field full of cabbages that grew in the shape of John the Baptist's head, even one lousy stalk of corn that could be mistaken for a crucified Jesus would do. But, no go in Lovely.

Giving up on a natural wonder, the committee ordered a statue from Roger's cousin in Milwaukee, who would make it for them cheap. Roger showed them pictures of the statues of the Seven Dwarfs that his cousin had sculpted and everybody agreed they'd never seen a dumber-looking Dopey or a Sleepy who seemed more likely to nod off while standing. The committee had great plans for the outdoor structure and the satellite shrines that would be part of Our Lady of Guadalupe. The committee held bake sales and raffles, and so far it had collected $246.78 for its efforts.

Roger placed that money in a separate account, held in name by the Committee to Build the Guadalupe Shrine (CBGS), on which he was the sole signatory. The people of Lovely trusted him not to put his mitts on their shrine money—his faith was true and strong, and if his other desires were, too, they were willing to accept that—but behind his back they made plans to change the structure of the CBGS account as soon as it reached five hundred dollars. With Roger, the thinking went, you got what you saw. He wore his flaws outright, an admirable trait.

The good news that summer was that Roger had talked the old Lawson couple into donating a parcel of land for the Guadalupe shrine, next to the Sunnyview Senior Center, right on Main Street, Route 51. It was the length of four storefronts that had been razed ten years ago, the lots left vacant, a blotch in any other town though not much more unattractive than anything else in Lovely. The lots had been surrounded by a fence that teenagers scaled easily and sat behind on Saturday nights, smoking dope and cigarettes and drinking beer, prisoners of their hometown, no matter on which side of the chain link they were. The kids had to find another place to drink and smoke that summer because the Lawsons had paid to tear down the fence, fill in the hole, pour a concrete slab, and erect a red-and-white-striped canvas canopy to shelter a few folding tables and chairs and a ragtag collection of religious memorabilia that most people donated to the Guadalupe shrine instead of money.

However, until the shrine was finished, there were still only a few reasons people stopped in Lovely: they needed gas; they were falling asleep at the wheel; every other motel within a hundred miles was booked.

Glo, Elizabeth, and Candy didn't know any of that when they ended up there. From Flint and St. Anne that morning, they'd driven straight to Indian River and the Cross in the Woods—that is, *almost* to the Cross in the Woods. Glo asked Elizabeth not to exit I-75 too near the shrine because she wanted her first view of it to be when she was in her most prayerful mind, not when she was worried about checking into their hotel and getting settled.

As it turned out, that was a valid worry. Glo had made a mistake, one that she wouldn't have forgiven in somebody else. She'd made a reservation at the Best Western outside Cheboygan, just ten miles from Indian River. (Her friend Sarah Lewis from St. Viator had stayed there when she visited the Cross the summer before.) But when they got there, it turned out that Glo didn't have a confirmation number or the name of the clerk who'd helped her or the date she'd called to make the reservation or even the price of the two rooms she'd reserved. Actually, she did have all this, but it was written on a leftover memo pad from Stan's office—*Stanley Dreslinski, CPA, Archdiocese of Chicago*— and left stuck to her refrigerator in Chicago with a magnet in the shape of a cow.

"But I called almost three weeks ago. Please, check under my name again. Maybe the clerk misspelled it. He wasn't efficient at all, but he assured me there was space. He said I probably didn't even

need a reservation. But I *did* make one. I'm very thorough." Glo trans-
ferred her annoyance with herself to the clerk, who clicked and
clacked commandingly on the Best Western keyboard.

"*If* you called, he never should have said that. We're booked and
everybody else is, too. Everybody goes up north in summer."

"Come on, Glo. We'll go somewhere else. It's okay." Elizabeth
tapped her aunt on the shoulder. Candy spun the basketball on her
finger.

Glo ignored her niece and looked at the woman next to her who'd
checked in with the other clerk on duty. The woman smiled at Glo after reading a confirmation number from a computer printout she
plucked from a briefcase full of manila folders with glossy red, green,
yellow, and blue tabs that were a dash of sentience in the anesthesia-
colored Best Western lobby. Glo, knowing she was just as organized as
that woman and angry at herself, tried one more time. "I booked two
rooms, but we can squeeze into one. I'll settle for that. Really"—Glo
adjusted her reading glasses so she could see the clerk's name tag—
"Ramona, it is your duty to honor my reservation."

"Without a confirmation number or your name in here"—Ramona
tapped her monitor with a pencil—"I just don't believe you have one."

"Are you calling me a liar, young lady?"

"No ma'am. I'd get fired if I did that."

"Fine." Glo gave up. "Just book us into a hotel nearby."

"I can't do that. Petoskey, Otsego, Traverse City, even Copperwood—I just checked for another customer—honest, everybody is full."

"Copperwood?" Candy slapped the spinning ball to a stop.
"We're near Copperwood?"

"It's just fifty miles away." Ramona turned a map toward Candy
and pointed to the town with the tip of her pen.

Candy pointed to a decent-sized speck on the map that was just a half-inch west of Copperwood. "What about this place?" She turned the map back to Ramona. "Are there any hotels there?"

"Lovely? Myself, personally, I've never been there, but I've heard it's kind of gross."

Proprietors Marvin and Josie Klopski had opened the Mar-Jo Motel in Lovely some thirty years ago, and though it didn't do particularly well when times were good, it did well enough to keep it open when times were not. Their steady, if low, expectations were not that difficult to meet. They should have put a large portion of their small profit into capital improvements, or even run-of-the-mill maintenance, but instead, they bought themselves a time-share condo in Tampa Bay, where they went every May through September, never mind the heat and humidity in Florida then or the brutal Michigan winters they endured upon return.

When they first drove past the Mar-Jo, Glo noticed the salmon-colored paint on the cinder-block walls peeling in a psoriasis-like pattern and the built-in pool, a once perfect circle of blue, marred by its rim of cracked cement and surrounded by a half dozen rusty lawn chairs with torn webbing just waiting for a hot breeze to make them flap and scratch the legs of a pale girl, the lone sunbather.

"Oh my goodness, we can't stay there." Glo looked out the window as Elizabeth drove slowly past the Mar-Jo. Glo looked up and read a banner spanning the street. It announced the "CBGS Pageant and Taco Dinner Fundraiser" next Saturday. Elizabeth turned the car around a few blocks later, down at the other end of Main Street near a large red-and-white-striped tent. Across from the tent was an empty parking lot bordered on one side by a vacant building with graffitied plywood on its one window and on the other side by a cracked concrete basketball court, the fading white crescent at the top of the key on both ends ghostly.

Elizabeth, ignoring Glo, pulled into the Mar-Jo parking lot, serpentining around the potholes and parking the Coupe de Ville next to the office, where a sign read VAC C , as if it were an abbreviated reminder to get immunized before dipping a toe in the putrescent pool.

"We've tried five other places, Glo. The Best Western clerk was right. This is it. If they have rooms, we're taking them. You can stay in the car. I'll check." Elizabeth cut the engine and then glanced back at Candy. She wondered how her niece felt—if she suffered from morning sickness or exhaustion or regret. She waited for her to weigh in with some complaint about the Mar-Jo, but after lobbying at the Cheboygan Best Western to come to this town, Candy picked fiercely and silently at a chip of blue nail polish on her big toe and offered no additional opinion about where they'd sleep that night.

"No. I made the mistake. I have to take care of it." Glo eased out of the car and walked to the office. She examined the smudged glass door, trying to find a clean spot to push it open, and then nudged it with her shoulder. She entered gingerly, holding her breath for an instant and then exhaling and taking a look around. The brown wood-look paneling made the small lobby seem even smaller than it was. An inch of coffee in the glass pot that seemed embedded on the burner of the Mr. Coffee gave the over-air-conditioned air a barbed edge. The coffeemaker sat atop a card table that was covered with a red plastic cloth spotted with cigarette burns. A single peach-colored plastic rose, its petals coated with dust, bloomed in a thick white glass vase next to Mr. Coffee. The check-in counter was protected by a frosted Plexiglas shield with a sliding window. The shield was bordered by stained-glass-look contact paper, translucent, though there was little light to spare in the windowless lobby. A SNOOPY FOR PRESIDENT bumper sticker hung crookedly on the wood paneling beneath the shield.

As she looked around, Glo heard a loud voice behind the frosted window, which was closed to customers. "*Si, me gusta jamón.*" The voice, a man's, repeated this four times, once each after a smooth, professionally accented voice said it first. The repeating voice was halting, but gained confidence by the third time. Still the man pronounced each syllable of each word separately, as if he didn't believe they belonged together. Glo cleared her throat, but the voice now repeated "*Tengo hambre*" and didn't respond. Finally, she knocked on the window. At that, it rattled open right away, releasing a cone of smoke. She coughed and the face behind the smoke said, "Does this bother you? The cigarette? I really have to quit. I am sorry." The man in the window reached through and stubbed out his cigarette in a brimming ashtray whose sides were crusted with tar.

"Now, where were we? *¡Hola!* Welcome to the Mar-Jo Motel. *Me llamo es* Roger Sallee. And how may I help a beautiful woman—*¡mucho linda!*—such as yourself?" Glo stepped back from his greeting and almost fell into a scuffed orange laminate chair laden with women's magazines and cracked in a jagged shard along its back. Roger Sallee reached farther through the window as she stumbled. Half in, half out, like a sandbag on a rail, he grabbed her left hand and looked into her eyes. "I am sorry again. Here I am paying you compliments, and you do not even know me. Of course, I have been waiting for you."

"Pardon me?" Glo was confused. His speech pattern was somehow formal, as if English were his second language.

"I have been expecting you."

"But . . ." She never would have called this place for a reservation.

"I made a novena." Roger made the sign of the cross as he spoke.

"I asked for the arrival of somebody in particular today. And here you are. God has provided."

"You've spent nine days praying for me to come here?" Glo waved her right hand through the smoky motes that further dimmed the lobby.

"Not exactly you, but you are not alone, right? And you are a Catholic, yes?"

"Right. Yes." Glo twisted the gold cross around her neck, and Roger smiled, triumphant, as if he'd just converted her.

"Your daughter? You are here with your daughter?"

"My niece."

"And how old is she?"

Her hand still in his, Glo, before thinking how odd it was that he asked, answered, "Thirty-six"—she hesitated—"I think."

"Hmmm . . . I wanted someone younger, but I guess we should be glad for her that she is not sixteen. With the younger girls, I want to weep."

"My seventeen-year-old grandniece is with us also."

"Ahhh . . . so I weep after all. It *is* a younger girl." Roger put his other hand to his brow and lowered his head.

"What *are* you talking about?"

"Your grandniece? She is with child? Pregnant? *Embarazo,* no?"

"*No.*" Glo pulled her hand from his and stepped back again, surefooted. "Mr. . . . what was your name?"

"Sallee, but call me Roger, please. *¿Cómo se llama?* I have upset you. No, of course you do not speak Spanish. Please, sit." He pointed to the cracked chair full of magazines.

Glo stayed standing. "You have not upset me. But nobody in that car," Glo pointed to the painted hot dog, impressionistic through the smudged glass door, and whispered, "is having a baby."

Roger looked puzzled. "Are you sure? I need a pregnant girl and I usually get what I want. So," he looked at her left hand, "Miss . . . ?"

"Dreslinski. And it's 'Mrs.' My husband is dead. What do you mean you *need* a pregnant girl?"

"It must have been a long time ago. His death, I mean. I can see you have reached the final stage of acceptance." Roger looked up from her finger. "The girl is for my fund-raising pageant next Saturday."

"It was almost nine months ago." Glo threaded her ringless fingers together in front of her chest as she remembered the banner that spanned Main Street.

Roger Sallee reached into his shirt pocket, took out a pack of Merit Menthol, and lit one. "My condolences, Mrs. Dreslinski."

"I don't believe in excess, Mr. Sallee. And I'm not partial to jewelry." Glo unzipped her purse and looked for a tissue—the smoke in the airless lobby caused her eyes to water.

"Please, Mrs. Dreslinski, call me Roger." He walked away from the cutout counter window and opened the plywood door that separated the office from the lobby. The door's brown veneer finish peeled up from the bottom in spiky strips. Its EMPLOYEES ONLY sign seemed superfluous to Glo. The Mar-Jo's public space was so grimy and off-putting, she couldn't imagine anybody unauthorized willingly opening a door on things the Mar-Jo hid from view. As Roger entered the lobby, Glo stepped back one more time and bumped into the orange chair again, this time dropping her purse. The contents spilled onto the worn carpet, her checkbook falling open, her lipstick rolling underneath the chair, and her wallet, fat with the cash and coin she carried for the trip, ending up near Roger's shoe. As she bent down to pick up her things, Roger squatted next to her and helped. She saw him look closely at the large, bright green balance, $274,635.89, in her checkbook as he straightened some twenties in her billfold that had gone askew.

Glo took a better look at Roger as he stood and handed back her things. His face, wider than it was long, looked like a reflection in a fun-house mirror. His hair was more pepper than salt, and he parted it far over on the left. It was thick and puffy, and had the appearance of perching on top of, instead of growing out of, his scalp. Wide head notwithstanding, Roger Sallee had entirely more hair than he needed. His light blue Banlon shirt, on the other hand, was not quite enough for his strapping chest, which strained mightily against the slightly clingy fabric, as if demanding, "Notice my pectorals. Regard my biceps. Behold my broad shoulders." Head, hair, upper body, he seemed a large man, a man physically heightened. He had presence. But there was a problem: Roger Sallee was six-plus feet of muscle, confidence, vanity, and nicotine stuffed into a five-foot-five-inch frame.

Examining Roger, Glo felt many things: confused, embarrassed, and oddly attracted. But mostly, at that moment, Glo felt guilty for being tall. She tried to make amends. He'd offered his name—she'd give him hers. "Well then, Roger, you may call me Glo. It's short for Gloria."

"Gloria." He issued it forth like an anthem, clearing the air in the smoky little room, even as he exhaled and added toxins to it. "That is a wondrous name. Every week at Mass, to hear your name honored by Our Lord."

"Everybody calls me Glo."

"Then only *I* will call you Gloria." He reached for her hand again, though she stood steady. "Tell me, Gloria, why did you come to Lovely?"

"My nieces and I need a room. Two rooms, actually."

"No, that is not the reason, Gloria."

Glo noticed that he proclaimed things—many men did, especially the shorter ones—as if to remind others that they'd met no challenge, deserved no kudos, for possessing height. But there was something else about the way he spoke that added to the impression. What was it? Roger squeezed her hand. "Do not be afraid, Gloria. I will not betray you."

That was it. Glo heard it clearly. *Do not, will not.* He didn't say *don't.* He wouldn't say *won't.* His speech was stilted and formal. Perhaps he thought he sounded commanding that way—why say one word when he could issue two? Or maybe it was old-world manners upon meeting a new acquaintance. As their conversation continued, perhaps he'd allow himself the shortcut of *I'm* or *it's,* but for now, he demanded Glo bear with him on his longer route.

"Please, Roger, we've been to five hotels in the past two hours."

"Oh, I will give you a room. But, Gloria, that is clearly *not* why you are here." He poured three inches of burned coffee into a Styrofoam cup, which he handed to Glo along with a packet of Cremora, bowing obsequiously as if it were the finest tea in the most fragile china. "I think that you have been sent here to help the cause."

"And what cause is that?" Glo, trained to be polite to those she didn't know well, sprinkled white powder in the slick of pitchy coffee and watched it congeal in waxy circles.

"I have a few." He opened his battered brown briefcase, its cardboard edges showing through the leatherlike finish, which was on the counter next to the ashtray, and handed her a sheet of lime green paper, pointing at the black block letters that headlined it. "I am the president of the committee that is building a shrine here in town. I am in charge of our pageant next Saturday—maybe you saw our banner across Route 51? I also have a personal financial obligation that I am taking care of," he said this as if it were an item on a grocery list, and then snapped his fingers. "Oh, and, as you heard, I am teaching myself Spanish."

"You sound very busy."

"There is more. My novena." He gave her another piece of paper, this one orange, with a prayer printed on it. "I have been praying for nine days—nine days, Gloria. Six times a day. I need a pregnant girl so I can dedicate my shrine realistically. I want complete authenticity, a purity of offering. I completed my last prayer thirty minutes before you walked through the door. I was certain you were somehow the answer."

"I'm sorry to disappoint you. I'm here with my nieces to visit the Cross in the Woods."

"Our shrine will honor Our Lady of Guadalupe. It is down the block, near the senior center. Did you see the red-and-white canvas tent?" Glo nodded, and Roger continued, "Herb and Ginny Lawson donated the land. He laid the cement slab. We raised the tent. We have a statue on order—it arrives tomorrow. It is ten feet tall." Roger reached up. Arms extended, he seemed almost average height.

"The brochure says the Cross in the Woods is fifty-five feet tall." Glo spoke without thinking, and then realizing she'd belittled his statue and stature, attempted to purchase forgiveness. "Perhaps I could make a small contribution."

"Money is always very welcome, Gloria, but we need *you*, not only your money." Roger took her left hand again. Glo tightened her grip on her purse with her right. He stared up at her, insisting she look down at him.

No man had paid this much attention to Glo since Stan had looked up from his adding machine at St. Mary's High School so long ago. Roger put his other hand on top of hers, sandwiching her palm. Neon numbers flashed in her mind, the ten-key Stan had used to find the balance, the 14 years of marriage, the 416 times they'd had sex, the 5 hotels she'd been in and out of in the past 2 hours. The cinder of warmth in her face turned to an ember. *Don't be silly,* she scolded herself, feeling the flush. She took a sip of coffee. Having simmered all day, it was reduced to scalding bitterness and caffeine. She felt even warmer.

"It will be a beautiful shrine, Gloria. Lovely. Open air. Big timbers supporting a roof that rises high to God. A simple but striking statue of Our Lady of Guadalupe—modest, humble—nothing hulking about it. You know the story of Our Lady?" Roger kissed her hand, released it gently, and then launched into his story without waiting for her answer. "Juan Diego was a simple peasant in Mexico. He wore a peasant's cloak. He was not a young man, Gloria. He was fifty-seven." Roger bowed his head and made the sign of the cross. "That is my age, Gloria. More proof that my mission is just. When Our Lady appeared to him, he heard music. Imagine. You are walking. In the woods. In the mountains. You hear something. Strings? Trumpets? And then a vision. Our Blessed Mother, the Virgin of Guadalupe—it is her first appearance in the Americas—she is swollen with child. *Embarazo.* And you, poor and frightened in your cloak, bow down before her as roses bloom in the rocky soil around you. And when she leaves, her portrait, brilliant and lovely, appears—it is miraculous—on your threadbare cloak. And almost five centuries later the image is still vivid and brilliant and on display in Mexico City.

"And Gloria, something else, and this is really what made me choose the Virgin of Guadalupe over St. Sebastian, whom I also considered for our shrine. Do you know the fastest-growing segment of the Catholic Church? The people who have larger families than anybody else? In Chicago, Gloria, in Michigan, in California, wherever you go in this great good land, it is the Hispanic people. And where can those wonderful, beautiful, devout, Spanish-speaking people find a Midwest shrine that is for them?" He lit another cigarette, jabbing the embered end in the air as punctuation and warning not to try to interrupt his lecture. "I will tell you. Right here. In Lovely. And *hablo español*. I will speak to them in Spanish, welcome them, encourage them to spend their *dinero* in Lovely and not anywhere else. And you know what this all proves?" Again, he rushed to answer. "Sound morals can lead to sound business, Gloria."

"I've never been to Mexico City." Glo ducked his lively cigarette and tried to find a way into the conversation.

"You are here instead. You did not bring me the pregnant virgin I prayed for, but your arrival here today is still in answer to my prayers. It is not mere coincidence. Read this." Roger reached into his briefcase again and pulled out a laminated card. Glo looked at the title printed on it, "A Prayer to Motherhood." She read a few lines, *"In your humanity and person you sanctified motherhood from the first instant of conception through all stages, for our salvation . . . avert your just anger from the enemies of life . . ."*

Glo looked up after reading and saw Roger stubbing out another cigarette. Even in the bitterest cold, she'd sent Stan to smoke his daily cigar in the garage—she had a heart condition, however under control her doctor assured her it was. She took a deep breath, allowing the hazy air, a combination of dust motes and Roger's smoky exhale, to fill her lungs. She thought of Suzy in Mayville at the Frosty Cream. She thought of Elizabeth, of all her marriages, of all the men she'd been with and no children even to show for it. She thought of Candy and the trouble she was in—her coach vanished, her reputation, too. She tried not to think of herself with Stan, herself touched. Her left hand was warm still from when Roger had held it. She relaxed her grip on her purse. She let her breath out slowly. Maybe Roger was right. Maybe God *had* brought them to Lovely for a reason.

The lobby door opened and the bells attached jangled. It was

Candy. Before her grandniece said a word, Glo saw Roger look the girl up and down, saw him turn to her and raise his brow, skeptical. She looked at Candy more closely. And in the smoky lobby of the Mar-Jo, it was as if she could finally see clearly what she'd missed before. The shorts grown too tight. The slightly swelling middle. The ferocious appetite. Why had Candy really quit basketball? Why had her coach fled? She thought of how the charlatan priest at St. Anne had used Candy to make his pregnant point. She looked again at the laminated prayer in her hand . . . *you sanctified motherhood from the first instant of conception . . .*

Candy jerked her head toward Roger, her dreadlocks swinging. One ropey strand settled in the middle of her face and swung gently back and forth like a pendulum as she spoke. "What's the deal, Glo? I feel nauseous. And I'm really tired of waiting in the car. Can we please just get a room? Can this guy help us?"

Why, they *were* the answer to Roger's novena. Her grandniece was pregnant. That's why Candy had quit her team. It explained so many things. Glo reached out and tucked a woven rope of hair behind Candy's ear. "Yes, I really think he can."

CHAPTER 11

ELIZABETH NOTICED THE surprise on the face of the muscle-bound motel clerk who came out of the Mar-Jo office and approached the car with Glo, but she thought little of it. The hot-dog-garnished Cadillac had that effect on people. She waited for the joke sure to come, reminding herself to be gracious when it did—the poor guy was so short, she'd give him a break. But, apparently, it wasn't the hot dog that made an impression on the little man. He whistled, "You are three tall girls. I am going to call you the *Niña,* the *Pinta,* and the *Santa Maria.*" He took a drag on his cigarette and laughed as he exhaled into Elizabeth's chest.

Elizabeth's sympathy evaporated. "And I'm going to call you the dinghy."

"Are you calling me short?" The man looked as if he wanted to stub out his cigarette on her forehead.

Elizabeth raised her chin a little higher. Let him jump like a terrier and try. "Are you calling me a Spanish sailing vessel?"

"Stop it, Elizabeth." Glo stepped between the two while Candy smirked in the background. "This is Roger Sallee, girls, and he has a room for us."

The Mar-Jo had a half dozen vacant rooms, but, as it turned out, only one of those, number 107, didn't have some major flaw—a jammed lock, a cracked shower stall, a clogged pipe, a broken TV— that kept Roger from renting it. Elizabeth protested as Roger reached for their bags—they didn't need his help—but Glo pointed at her blue Samsonite in the deep trunk, asked that he be careful with it, and added that she hoped it wasn't too heavy. At that, he laughed, picked up Candy's stuffed canvas duffel, and nudged Elizabeth, instructing her to hang her bag on him, too. She slung the sagging weight over her good shoulder and shuffled away.

Candy called out instructions to Roger as he strode off to their room: "When you're done with those, go back to the car and get the cooler. And my backpack in the backseat? You can get that, too, okay?"

Roger stopped and his gaze lingered on her T-shirt—the three monkeys, hands across eyes, ears, and mouth—stretched tight across her chest. He sighed. "You are just a child."

"I'll be eighteen in March."

"All you girls are so selfish."

"Hey, you offered."

"Have some shame, at least." Roger walked away, shaking his head, bags crisscrossed over his shoulders and lodged under his arms, moving easily, a human dolly.

Candy lingered near the car. Why was he so cranky? Probably be-cause he worked at the Mar-Jo Motel, which was clearly a dump. A third-world refugee would see that. She'd stayed in decent hotels when she'd traveled for basketball. She'd been named *Parade* and *USA Today* All-American the past two years. People treated you pretty good when that happened. She'd flown to Paris the summer before her sophomore year for the Red Star Elite International Tournament and to Washington, D.C., for the All-American Nationals the summer after that. Those hotels had thick carpets that were vacuumed every day so that when you walked barefoot your feet got cleaner, and chartered buses whose gears shifted smoothly while the air-conditioning kept everybody comfortable. The arenas the buses dropped them off at were packed with fans, little kids with faces painted red, white, and blue, begging for autographs or a pat on the head. Candy usually stopped and talked to the kids, signing whatever they stuck in front of her—a hat, a scrap of paper, a stuffed animal worn from years of clutching, sometimes even an arm or a leg. She told the girls not to budge when the boys tried to kick them off the court and to take the charge when somebody drove the basket on them.

She'd been invited to play in Italy and Spain just last summer. Her mom said no to that. She'd limited Candy's travel and the amount of college recruiting they'd listen to. "I don't want you getting turned upside down by all this. And I don't want you away from home for a whole summer. We'll pay attention to the recruiters next year. You'll travel plenty in college." After so many years of wondering if her mom would come home at all or what sorry-ass shape she'd be in when she did, Candy had been glad to sit still in Detroit with her mom making sense. When Candy came home on any given day last summer, after she'd been hanging out with Amy or Jimmy, or if she'd had a date, or been at a basketball camp, her mom would be sitting on the porch waiting for her, drinking something—soda or coffee or iced tea. She had given up alcohol, but she couldn't let go of the glass.

Her mom, who never missed a home game, had traveled with her to the Nationals in D.C., scraping the money together and taking two days off her job waiting tables. Once her mom quit drinking, Candy had liked looking up in the stands and seeing her. She usually sat alone. She'd bring a book or magazine and read until the game started and then she'd look up and catch Candy's eye right before tip-off. She'd nod once. That's all. One nod. The other parents hollered and demanded restitution when the ref fucked up and cheered wildly when their daughters scored. But not her mom. At first Candy thought that odd—her mother drunk had been big and loud, harassing the fans around her when she thought they weren't enthusiastic enough. She embarrassed Candy all through grade school whenever she came to games. She'd stumble as she climbed the bleachers to the top row, and she'd call out, her voice slopping over the crowd—"I love you, honey"—when Candy lined up to take a free throw. In the first few months after her mom stopped drinking, during a close game, the court trimmed with cheerleaders, Candy had figured her mom would be the leader of the desperately cheering mob. But instead she sat quietly, her gaze steady. So she stood out again, but this time not because of the flotsam in her wake as she crashed left and right, and Candy appreciated the even keel.

Candy kicked a loose stone in the Mar-Jo Motel parking lot that afternoon in Lovely. It skittered, then arced airborne toward the pool, landing near the bare feet of the girl who sat reading a thick book. The girl looked up at the clack on concrete. "Hey, watch it." She pushed up the heavy black frames of her yellow-lensed glasses as she warned Candy.

"Sorry. Accident. Cool glasses."

"I got them in Chicago last month when I visited my grandma. My mom hates them."

"Does everything look yellow?"

"It's more like just coated and sort of dull."

"What are you reading?" When the girl held up *The New American Bible*, Candy turned away.

"Why are you leaving?" The girl called to her back.

"I'm not into it. And I'm traveling with my religious freak grandaunt, so I don't need to be around even more Bible stuff."

"I'm not into it either. I'm just trying to make sure that I'm doing the right thing." The girl fidgeted with a gold angel pin stuck to the strap of her bright pink tank top. She wore light blue and gray and black camouflage pants cut off at the knee. She crossed and uncrossed her thick white legs, her skin so pale against the militarily spotted fabric that it looked bleached. "I'm just not sure. My mom thinks it's right, though."

"Mothers."

"I'm Alex, by the way."

"Candy." The girls waved wanly at each other.

"I mean, I know I'm only sixteen, but so? I could raise my baby." Alex dropped one hand to her lap and raised the other to her forehead, shoving a strand of wispy orange-colored hair out of her eyes. A breeze bloomed, hot and humid, and pushed a bank of bulky gray clouds over the sun, giving no relief from the thick air, but changing the color of the surroundings so that Alex's hair didn't glint and glare anymore.

"Oh, I get it. You're pregnant."

"Just eight weeks. I want to have it. My mom thinks that's a bad idea. We live in the UP, but we're driving around the lower peninsula for a few days without my father and brothers around so we can really talk about it. How about you?"

"I'm not pregnant."

"Lucky."

"I'm pro-choice though, don't worry. I think it's cool if you do decide to do that." Candy saw Alex wince behind her yellow lenses. "Not cool. I'm sorry. Wrong word. I just mean I don't think it's a sin or anything no matter what it says in there." Candy pointed to the Bible. "Why are you reading that anyway?"

"That short guy, Roger, who runs this place gave it to me yesterday. He's been bugging me to play the Virgin Mary in some pageant he's running later this week. It's freaky. Like he assumes I'm pregnant. He doesn't know that I am. I mean don't think I tell everybody I meet just because I already told you. My mom really yelled at him this morning—told him to leave us alone. He'll probably find somebody else to bother. He's into religion, too. Maybe he'll hook up with your aunt."

Candy laughed. "She's sixty or seventy. I kind of doubt it." She changed the subject. "So you and your mom purposely came here?" Candy opened her arms to encompass the full decrepitude of the Mar-Jo.

"No, we're stuck here because my mom messed up and didn't make reservations anywhere else. She went to Copperwood this afternoon to see a movie."

"So that town Copperwood really is close?" Coach D's brother lived there or near there. If she ran into Coach D up here, Candy thought she could force him to admit how wrong he was to run away and then beg him to return. She looked at the Bible in Alex's lap. It would be a miracle if she ran into him. And an even bigger miracle if she stooped to begging.

"Copperwood is right up that road, like twenty minutes away. Me and my mom go there almost every day. Today I told her I wanted to be alone. I don't, that's why I'm talking so much to you, but I could tell she's losing it, and I thought it might help her to get away from me. So, listen to this." Alex read from the Bible, " 'Your hands have formed me and fashioned me; will you then turn and destroy me?' That's Job."

"This nun back home in Detroit told me to read Job."

"What do you think it means?"

"It means different things to different people. It doesn't mean you have to feel like shit because you're sixteen and you don't want a baby."

"But like I told you, I think I do want a baby." Alex lifted the Bible to her brow, a visor, as the cloud moved on, and her hair glared again.

"Well, you shouldn't feel like shit about that either. But in that passage, the 'you' isn't really you." Candy pointed at Alex.

"Still, you've got to admit. I don't really like the idea of taking care of a baby forever or even for a full day. But it's a baby. What did it ever do to deserve this? Who knows who it could turn into?"

"Well, it could turn into a Hitler or a Bobby Knight or a Playboy bunny, so you might as well not think like that."

"Why are you saying my baby would turn out bad?"

"I'm saying you don't ever know. This girl I know back home at school, she had an abortion this year. She had to sneak and do it. I mean her mom knew, but not her dad because he wouldn't have allowed it. But her dad found out and he was really pissed at her and at her mom and he ends up divorcing her mom because of it. Or maybe that was just his excuse, because three months later he's living with this girl who's like twenty and then *she* gets pregnant and has an abortion, but my friend's dad doesn't leave *her*. He's such a loser. So you should just do what you want because other people, they say one thing

today and swear by another thing tomorrow. That's what I think."
Alex looked skeptical, but Candy pressed on. "If I were pregnant and
didn't want an abortion, there's no way I'd get one and not because
some pushy short guy gave me a Bible and told me I'd go to hell. Or
even because of my mom. But because I decided not to. It's your baby.
You decide. Don't listen to them."

"That's easy for you to say."

Candy shrugged. "I guess."

Alex stared at her bare feet, her breathing a series of little sighs
that lifted her white shoulders. Candy understood those sighs. She
knew that sometimes, even on big stuff where you knew they'd screw
it up, you went along with what the adults came up with because you
were too confused not to. It had been like that when they'd tried to
figure out where she should live her senior year. Five days after her
mom died, she'd gone back to practice. Coach D ran them hard that
day. Lots of sprints because six players didn't make at least seven of
ten free throws. More sprints during practice whenever anybody
fucked up and didn't listen to what he said, didn't make the switch on
the man-to-man they played, or took a shot before they'd set up on offense and made two passes.

Candy ran up and down the court, glad for a script, following orders, listening for the whistle. Glo was meeting with Ms. Hogan and
Mr. Morrisey and Sister Anne even as Candy ran her sprints. Amy
Prokoff's mom was at the meeting, too. They'd hatch some plan that
they'd spring on her after practice. She imagined them sitting around
a table, hands folded in front of them, discussing her life as if she were
an assignment. Nobody invited her to the meeting, which was fine by
her—it would make it that much easier to bitch about the decision
they landed on. She didn't feel up to being indignant about every op-

tion presented. Did she want Glo or Elizabeth to move to Detroit and into her mom's apartment so she could just keep her life going as is? Or would she rather *never* live in that apartment again? Did she want to live with an aunt who was an asshole or a grandaunt who was old and into religion? At the funeral home she'd sworn to them all that she wouldn't leave Detroit or live with either Glo or Elizabeth. And she'd been right to do so, she reminded herself. That was being loyal to her mom. But could she really live at Amy's house, with Amy's mom? She wasn't sure. She felt split in two—each half of her hostile to the other half.

In biology class freshman year, Sister Miriam had taught them about the Rh factor and how a woman's own blood could be incompatible with her baby's. Candy had listened, curious. When it came to pregnancy, everybody made a big deal about how women should talk to their babies in utero, play music or read books to them even before they were born. They made a big deal about how women *wanted* to do this, did it as naturally as they slept and woke and ate each day. Nobody ever mentioned fierce physiological fights with slow poisoning from blood cell to blood cell. If the wrong antigen coated the wrong cell, somebody, baby or mother, was in big trouble. A baby was a foreign body—how come nobody ever talked about that?

At the Mar-Jo that afternoon, Candy looked at Alex's outside garish colors. Her hair, glasses, skin, and camouflage pants clashed. Maybe she'd been invaded by tissue and cells and blood that didn't match her own. Maybe everything about her was a fight. She must be tired. Maybe Alex should listen to her mother.

Or maybe not. Coach D's forced resignation proved how stupid Candy had been to sign over her future to Anita Prokoff, two absentee aunts, and a few teachers. Alex should fuck up her life on her own—she shouldn't let others do it for her, do it to her. Why should Alex's mother or a Bible-toting midget loser like Roger be the ones who spoke for her? And forget *speaking* anyway. She would *do* something for Alex. This girl sitting in front of her was an opportunity to seize. This girl was a way to prove she was like her mom. Strong.

Her mom who had stopped drinking. Her mom who had driven six hundred miles round trip to go to Glo's husband's funeral. Her mom who had reached out to Elizabeth 1,000 times and would have reached out time number 1,001 if she hadn't been stopped by a guy who was asleep at the wheel. Her mom, minus the eighteen years of drinking, was somebody to admire. Her mom would have done something for Alex. She would, too. She would not leave this girl alone in trouble. Right there at the Mar-Jo pool, she swore she would think of something to help Alex, whether Alex wanted her to or not.

"Candy." Both girls looked up as they heard a shout from the other end of the parking lot. Elizabeth walked toward them, dribbling a basketball, the twang of it echoing in the humid afternoon.

"Is that your religious-freak aunt?" Alex closed the Bible and sat up straighter.

"No, that's my been-divorced-three-times-depressed aunt, Elizabeth. The religious freak is my grandaunt, Glo."

"Where's your mom?"

"She's dead."

"Oh. Sorry. It's good you have aunts to live with."

"I don't live with them."

"Why not?"

When Candy didn't answer right away, Alex looked at her over the top of her glasses, which had slipped down her nose. "This girl where I go to school has to live with her grandmother because her parents died. Her grandmother is old, but if you've got an aunt like that who is younger, it wouldn't be so bad. So why is it that you don't live with her?"

Elizabeth came closer then, and Candy used the distraction of her approach to ignore Alex's repeated question. Her aunt smelled good and her hair was damp and her clothes were clean. Elizabeth put on a show, her feet shuffling, weaving around imaginary opponents and dribbling behind her back and between her legs. Candy turned back to Alex. "This is very unlike her. Like I said, she's usually extremely depressed."

"So is that why you don't live with her? Is she, like, in a mental institution?"

"She should be."

"Who's your friend?" Elizabeth stopped dribbling when she came close. "Somebody you know from home?"

"From home? Here?"

"People always run into people they know when they go up north. It's a Michigan phenomenon. Statistically speaking, either you, me, or Glo is bound to see somebody we know while here. If there's anybody in particular you want to see, concentrate on that, put some psychic energy into it. This one time, when your mom and I were kids . . ."

"Psychic energy? You've been in California too long." Candy pictured Coach D whistling for sprints and she kicked the stone that lay near Alex's feet. It skipped up and hit Elizabeth in the shin. "Alex, Elizabeth. She lives in the UP." Candy bobbled her head between the two.

Elizabeth shook Alex's hand as she rubbed her shin. She glanced at the book in the girl's lap. "Beach reading?"

"Roger gave it to me."

"What's his deal?" Elizabeth didn't wait for an answer. "He's in the room with Glo right now. I left when they started to pray. He said this place has a weight room in the back, outside. I'm sure it's a lame setup, but maybe we can work out together later. I think I'm getting energy from disliking him—maybe I should thank him for being such an arrogant windbag." Elizabeth pointed at Candy. "We're sharing a bed. You better take a shower before the day is over. And I hope you don't snore."

"This trip just gets better and better."

"Let's go to that court down the road and shoot around. Alex, you come, too."

"I don't play." Alex pushed her glasses up the slope of her nose.

"That's okay. Candy doesn't either anymore."

"I'll come over in a little while. I want to wait for my mom."

Candy, unbalanced by Alex's questions, followed her aunt without complaint.

Elizabeth was determined to make Candy confess her pregnancy sooner, not later. It wasn't something that could wait. She was seventeen. Three months seemed liked an eternity to most seventeen-year-olds. Candy might not hear the clock ticking toward too late until the alarm went off and it already was.

Once Melissa had passed her three-month point and decided to continue her pregnancy, Elizabeth had played a new role, no longer her sister's confidante and sounding board, more a silent partner who helped with logistics. She'd deferred her UCLA admission and went to Wayne State University. UCLA would still be there when she was a sophomore. First things first: she had to help her sister get the baby born. Melissa didn't ask her to do that, but she didn't try to dissuade her either. Melissa dropped out of Western and they lived together in an apartment on the Cass Corridor near WSU and Harper Hospital and Melissa's waitressing job—they didn't have a car, they could walk everywhere they needed to go, and they pretended to each other that they didn't want to go anywhere else. That fall and winter, waiting for Candy to arrive, their lives were predictable and quiet and sober. They did for the baby on the way the things they hadn't done for themselves.

Elizabeth went with Melissa to her monthly ob-gyn appointments, watching as the doctor coated her sister's tightening belly with goo and ran a microphone over it, the baby's heartbeat pulsing through the small, tiled examination room in a staticky beat that spelled something different to each of the women who listened—the ob-gyn unmoved by yet another future that she might or might not deliver depending on something as arbitrary as her on-call schedule, Melissa expectant, literally and figuratively, and Elizabeth resigned and confused, hopeful yet skeptical that they could outmaneuver some doom she sensed with the coming of the baby. She worked hard to hide that from Melissa—to be only supportive.

"That's normal," the doctor said when Elizabeth questioned the speedy heartbeat. What had her name been—that doctor who had been absolutely unwilling to feign enthusiasm? She couldn't remember, but she remembered clearly the woman's handwriting on the chart that Elizabeth plucked from the metal basket on the examination room door and read to Melissa at the beginning of each visit. "That doctor will be pissed," Melissa would warn even as she leaned forward to learn more about herself. Elizabeth scoffed, reminding her sister that there was nothing in that chart they weren't entitled to know. The doctor's handwriting—fat, childish, and slanting left—had inspired little confidence, but Elizabeth had been glad for how legible it was.

"Melissa, look at this note, 'first pregnancy, unproven vagina.' That's what it says you have." Melissa rolled her eyes and made a joke about how she'd proven her vagina plenty of times, thank you very much. They laughed nervously.

Elizabeth looked at Candy walking alongside her down the deserted street in Lovely—this girl had no idea what she was in for. Candy held the basketball in front of her, cradling it low to her stomach. A shield. Candy's confessing her pregnancy voluntarily would be best, but if Elizabeth needed to confront her head on, she would. They walked on the gravel shoulder of the two-lane highway leading in and out of town. Candy resisted when Elizabeth pulled her closer as a semi sped by and spit a handful of grit at them.

"So, Candy, talk to me. You seem depressed. I wonder why."

"As you may remember, I'm an orphan."

"Come on. I'm serious. You know I'm sorry about your mom."

"How would I know that? How many times have you talked to me since she died, Elizabeth? I'm thinking maybe it's zero. And before that, how many times did you accept my mom's apology and be her friend, her fucking sister, like she wanted? Again, I think zero is the number. So I guess that's just about how sorry you are."

"I was going through a difficult divorce."

"You're *always* going through a difficult divorce."

Elizabeth ignored that. "And before that with your mom, well, if I'd known. If your mom had known the accident was coming. I mean of course, I would have . . . but you never know, do you? I mean that semi that just sped by could have killed us both."

"This is you trying to make me feel better? And you're a guidance counselor?"

"I'm not a very good one lately."

"No shit." Candy spun the ball on her index finger.

"But still, it seems to me that with you right now there's more than just depression about your mom."

"Just?"

"You know what I mean. I think there's something else on your mind."

"Quit thinking. There's not."

"You're getting a little chubby, you know."

"Jesus, Elizabeth, you must *really* suck at your job."

"Weight gain or loss can be a sign of depression or maybe something else."

"So what if I do get fat? I should love my body however it is, right? Isn't that what *Guidance Counseling for Dummies* would tell you to say? That I shouldn't buy into exploitive and unattainable images of beauty based on anorexic models? It's my body, right? I should love it and all the flesh I come wrapped in? You know, I think I will get fat. Really fat."

"Okay, okay, I'll shut up. But you're right about one thing. It *is* your body. Don't forget that, Candy. No matter what other people tell you." Elizabeth jammed her hands in her pockets. This wasn't going well.

A few minutes later, a carved wood sign, weathered and askew at the foot of the driveway, announced their arrival at Lovely Recreation Center. After an hour in Lovely, the sad-sack basketball court, its wood backboards splintered with white paint and rot, its baskets with bent rims and rusty chain-link nets, was no surprise. The recreation center building at the west end of the court was made of gray concrete block and treated wood painted brown. A spotted tin roof canopied it. A hand-printed sign on the door, shimmering silver because of its duct-taped borders, read LOVELY COMMUNITY REC CENTER. HOURS: M-W-F 1:00–5:00. The "M" and the "F" had been crossed out with a thick black marker—the Rec Center's initially paltry assistance to the community dwindling to almost nothing. A Coke machine stood to the left of the door, its heft and glow and hum the first bright light they'd seen in Lovely. Two picnic tables and an empty sandbox were planted in a treeless patch of dried-out grass on the east end of the basketball court. A swing set stuck next to the picnic tables had no seats at the end of its heavy metal chains.

Beyond the court on the north side, a shallow ditch lined with dried grass separated the Rec Center from a cemetery. Not that anybody would confuse the two. From center court, Elizabeth took in the cemetery's Seuss-like trees, jutting gravestones crooked with age, and the formerly imposing marble mausoleums, now softened to a chalky matte, their previously tight right angles curved by years of Michigan weather. Grass grew tall around many of the gravestones and mausoleums, the paths between them too narrow for the mowers to get close. It was the prettiest place she'd seen in Lovely so far.

Just beyond the closest cluster of gravestones and mausoleums, Elizabeth saw a man walking with a stick. As she watched, he crouched and appeared to crawl along the ground for a few feet. Upright again, he walked on. Was he collecting trash? His movements seemed too fluid, too purposeful for the stick to be a cane. Maybe he was searching for an ancestor's gravesite. She turned to Candy. "Do you ever visit your mom's grave?"

Candy flung the ball at the backboard, a line drive that rattled the rotting wood and ricocheted right back at her. "What did I tell you, Elizabeth? You don't get to talk to me about that."

"Let's talk about something else then." Elizabeth stuck a hand in Candy's face as her niece squared off for a long shot. The ball banked hard, clanged on metal, and then, fluke or forgiving rim, rattled through the hoop on the strength of its own velocity. Elizabeth ran down the ball, checked it, and, dribbling hard left to right, crossing over to keep Candy off balance, added, "Tell me more about your coach."

"What about him?"

"What does he look like?"

"Why would you ask that?" Candy hacked Elizabeth's forearm hard and she shot an air ball.

Calling foul, Elizabeth checked the ball again. "I thought girls your age liked cute guys."

"He's not a guy. He's my coach. He *was* my coach. And he's sure not cute."

"So where did he go when he quit?" With Candy hand-checking her all the way, Elizabeth backed into the basket and let go a soft hook over her right shoulder for two. "Call me Kareem."

"Call you old—who shoots that shot anymore? I don't know where Coach D went. But he didn't quit. He got fired."

"That's not what I heard."

"Do you believe everything you hear?"

"I don't believe in being naïve. Come on, tell me. What does he look like?"

Coach D's appearance seemed a safer subject than most that Elizabeth brought up, so Candy gave in. "He's got that guy beer belly thing actually, which doesn't make sense because he gets a lot of exercise. He's weird, too. He eats cat hair and—"

"Cat hair?" Elizabeth swiped at the ball.

"Long story, and he raises birds." Candy crisscrossed, protecting it.

"Well, idiosyncratic people can be very attractive. And coaching doesn't give you much exercise. You mostly stand around and yell and blow a whistle. I'm coaching JV at Sorrows. The team sucks."

"JVs always suck. Everybody good makes Varsity. Coach D isn't 'attractive.' If our team sucked, he'd just be an overweight guy who raised birds and coached a bunch of girls."

Elizabeth reached in again and this time got the ball. She drove past Candy, pulled up at the top of the key, and let loose a soft jump shot. The net jingled, tallying two. She leaned over, sucking air and pulling on her shorts, her back to Candy, tired and trying to hide it. After a few seconds, she turned around and lobbed the ball to her niece, who waited at half-court. "Men who work at all-girls schools have to be extra careful."

"Of what?" Candy, playing dumb, faked left, drove right, and scored an easy layup as Elizabeth took the bait.

"Of rumor, innuendo, impropriety, impulse. Plenty of them would be happy to sleep with a girl your age."

"Well, that works out fine because plenty of girls my age would be happy to sleep with them, too."

"See, Candy, it's that kind of talk that gets your coach fired and starts people spreading rumors about you."

"Rumors can't change truth. I know what they say about Coach D and me."

"And what's that?"

"That we had sex."

"And did you?"

"See, Elizabeth, I really shouldn't have to answer that. Especially to somebody like you who is nothing to me. Should I?"

"No."

"And you shouldn't ask it, should you?"

"In a perfect world, no."

"Well, let's pretend it is a perfect world. And not perfectly fucked up. Let's just play some ball here. Or better yet, you keep shooting.

I'm going back to the motel. I have to pee, and I want to make sure that girl Alex is still coming. I feel bad for her."

"She seemed nice."

"She *is* nice. She's pregnant."

"Oh really?" Elizabeth hoped for more.

"The two aren't mutually exclusive, you know."

"Give me a break, Candy. I never said they were. Go ahead. Go get your friend. Check on Glo, too, while you're there. I think she and Roger need a chaperone. And take some money out of my wallet. I'll buy us Cokes." Elizabeth leaned down to tie her loosened shoelace as Candy walked away. It had been an odd day—what were the chances of running into two such irritating men as Father Jim and Roger Sallee? And after seeing Leo yesterday? It's as if the gods were reminding her what a good guy Leo had been. She didn't need that reminder. The gods should quit rubbing it in.

A second later, crouching close to concrete, she heard a shout, then a whoosh, and then she felt the whomp of a golf ball hit straight and sure—a line drive directly into the meat of her calf, just inches from her head, which was bent to her shoe. She fell back, hands trussed around legs, spine curved like the spindle of a rocker.

It was the pure velocity of the ball that knocked her down right then. The pain itself was not instantaneous. In the first few seconds, as she rocked there, numb, Elizabeth imagined the other possibilities and felt lucky. Golf ball thumping temple, setting up internal brain bleeding, future life as vegetable. Golf ball shattering teeth and mouth, future life of wired jaw and puréed food. Golf ball smashing eye socket, force permanently implanting it there, future life of kids in the neighborhood pointing at her, a grotesque, the golf ball–eyed lady. When the first spike of hot-edged pain did finally travel up and down her nerve endings to arrive at her conscious mind, the shock of it was buffered by the alternatives she'd just envisioned, even as the strength of it kept her clutching her leg and rocking like an upended beetle.

Before she could sit up, before Candy said a word or made a move to help her, she heard a shout again, very close, and then heard footsteps running toward them. A man approached—the man she'd seen from a distance in the cemetery, the stick that she hadn't been able to name, obviously, from the Titleist imprinted on her calf, a golf club. The man waved the club wildly as he ran. Elizabeth instinctively wrapped her arms around her skull and ducked. Huffing to a stop at her prostrate body, the man crouched over her.

"My God, I'm lucky. That's a doozy—I could have killed you."

"Can we not talk about your good luck right now?" Elizabeth's voice sounded strange, as if even her vocal cords winced.

She directed her attention at the man instead of the pain commuting up and down her leg. He was large, not just tall, though he was that, too. The very heft of him camouflaged his age. He might be thirty. He could be fifty. He wore a red-and-white-striped golf shirt, wrinkled khakis, and red wristbands. A pair of binoculars hung around his neck, the strap hidden in a sunburned slot of flesh. He looked up at the sky after he knelt over Elizabeth, shielding his eyes, and his neck stretched taut revealed thin white lines that were untouched by the sun, making his flesh there seem a mere extension of his striped shirt. He repositioned himself so the sun wasn't in his eyes. They both looked at the flank of Elizabeth's right calf, where a fist-sized bruise rose tentatively from the canvas of her skin. The bruise, a hotspot, literally, was pink and mottled with purple and deep red specks with hazy edges that were suspended beneath the surface warmth. Its center, the point of impact, was a circle of white, as if the brute force of the golf ball had squeezed all corpuscular activity to the perimeter. Objectively speaking, it was pretty.

The man's voice pulled her back to the present, to the pain.

"I was practicing over in the empty part of the cemetery. I shanked it worse than I ever have before. It went completely perpendicular to the direction I hit it. I only started golfing last week. There's a whole big part of that cemetery without any graves yet. I didn't think I'd do any harm. I'm really sorry about this. My name is John, by the way." He stuck out his hand and Elizabeth, holding her leg and rocking, freed a few fingers to shake it as he continued. "Now you need to get home and RICE that bruise. That's Rest, Ice, Compression, Elevation. RICE, get it? Don't get that confused with BRAT, which is banana, rice, applesauce, and toast—that's for when you have stomach trouble." He laughed at his joke. "Anyway, that's going to swell. Give it a couple of hours and it will look like you had a softball implanted in your calf. Your daughter here," he nodded up at Candy without looking at her, "should pull your car up as close as she can and take you straight home. You shouldn't drive on this. It will hurt to apply pressure to the brakes." He stood and looked up at Candy for the first time. "Go get . . ." He stopped midsentence, the brunt of recognition snapping his head back as if he'd been punched. "Golden?" he said. "Golden? What the hell are you doing here?" He looked down at his shoes.

Candy, frozen white, went blank, forgetting all her plans for what she was going to say and do when she saw Coach D. She thawed enough to whisper, "She's not my mother, Coach," and then she ran, faster than she had in weeks, back toward the Mar-Jo.

Elizabeth watched as her niece turned and ran off the court. And sure, very sure, there could be only one reason for Candy's shock and retreat, and many reasons, all incriminating and actionable, for the coach's downward gaze—he'd had sex with her niece, he had followed them to Lovely, he was stalking the girl, he wanted to have sex with her again, he was sick, he was a pervert—Elizabeth was ready for the beefy man, the criminal pig, when he crouched to help her.

Arm cocked behind her ear, her fist wound tight and hard around her anger at his exploitation—no, call it what it was, his *crime*—and Candy's stupidity, she let loose and punched him in the face. She struck him again and then, as he covered his face with his hands, she hoisted herself to a stand and kicked out her right leg, which even bruised had more strength than her left, anger trumping pain. She kicked him hard, in the shin first, but then she got him in the crotch. Making contact once, she kicked him again, and once more, until he folded to the ground, moaning, but not loud enough to satisfy her. She aimed for his ribs next but stopped midkick when she saw the golf club, its shaft gleaming silver at center court.

The coincidence of his presence here must mean something. She would punish this coach, firmly, quickly, more painfully than she already had. The selfish bastard had left Candy in the lurch. Left her without basketball. Left her with a baby. She'd leave him with something, too. She'd whack his knee with that club. She leaned down and reached over Coach D's prone body, using it as a lever to extend her reach. But as she touched the club, he woke to her intention and jutted his hip, upending her, his body a bulwark, so that Elizabeth was back on the ground where she'd started, though this time she lay next to Coach D, who, curled fetal still, reached for the golf club himself and held it far away from her.

The pain in her calf merged with the ache in her fist. Her knuckles stung. She wished Candy were present to see the lengths she'd gone to for her. She'd almost crippled a man on her behalf. She wanted credit for that. She breathed heavily from the exertion, and began flexing various body parts, wondering if she'd done further damage to herself.

"Are you insane? What the hell are you doing? It was an accident. I didn't purposely hit you with that golf ball." Coach D raised himself up on an elbow as he folded accusation and apology into interrogation.

"This has nothing to do with a golf ball."

"Who *are* you?"

"Her aunt." Elizabeth sat up and cocked her head in the direction Candy had run.

"Oh—"

"Oh?" She cut him off. "Is that what you have to say for yourself? 'Oh.' She's seventeen. That's statutory rape, you bastard, and don't think we won't press charges. And then you have the nerve to follow her here. Are you stalking my niece?" As she spoke, Coach D scrambled to his feet, leaned down, grabbed her wrists hard, and yanked her to her feet. "Get your hands off me. You're hurting me. Again. You're hurting me *again*." Elizabeth squirmed, but she couldn't break free.

He loosened his grip and tightened his voice. "I did not have sex or do *anything* wrong with your niece. I will take any test you want to prove it. Lie detector. DNA. Litmus. Rorschach. There is *nothing* to that story. Golden and I were player and coach. Always. And *only*."

"So what kind of coach deserts his star player and team?"

"I was told to leave."

"Why did you listen if you're innocent?"

"Because they were only insinuating. Because I couldn't stand to hear it if they ever got past that stage. Because what if some girl lied? Because some parent besides Anita Prokoff, and believe me she was bad enough, was bound to get involved. Because if anything ever went on record, I'd never coach again. Because going away would eventually leave them with nothing much to talk about and then something else would happen instead and they could all talk about that. There were fifty good reasons to go. Do you want all the others?"

"Something else did happen. She's pregnant. And by running off, you've really made things worse for her."

His shoulders slumped with that news, but his voice tightened. "Are you sure?"

"She hasn't told me flat out. But, yes, I'm sure. I don't know who the father is." Elizabeth glared at him. "I mean, once I've truly dismissed the possibility of its being you." She did believe him though. A person didn't get divorced three times without knowing the way around a lie or evasion. This man hadn't had sex with Candy. Elizabeth had hurt him for nothing.

"What's your name?" Coach D let go of her wrists.

"Elizabeth Brannigan."

"What do you go by?"

"Go by?"

"Liz? Betty? Lizzy? Eliza? Beth?"

"It's Elizabeth."

"So, Elizabeth, what are you and Golden doing in Lovely? How'd you find me? Nobody knew I was here."

"We didn't find you. We weren't looking for you. We got stuck here. Why are you here?" A bird chittered in a tree to their right and Coach D looked up. Elizabeth noticed the binoculars that banged against his chest when he moved, and a small guide, *Birds of Michigan*, peeking out of his shirt pocket. "Oh, right, Candy said you're into birds. I guess there are a lot of those up here."

"I'm secretary of the Detroit chapter of the Audubon Society." He patted the guide in his pocket. "My brother lives in Copperwood and he has a hunting cabin just a couple miles outside of Lovely, and I'm living in it for the summer. It's a strange time for me, with everything going on, but I'm glad to be here. I need to be here." He looked over at the cemetery. His voice trembled the littlest bit. He changed the subject. "Golden never mentioned she had an aunt."

"We're not close."

"Shame. It was a tough season for her with her mom gone. Her mom was your sister?"

"Half sister."

"Guess it was tough for you, too. Sorry."

"I managed."

"So what was the deal? Didn't Golden want to live with you? She didn't seem too happy at the Prokoffs' house."

"I live in L.A. It was complicated. I thought it was better to stay away. But I was probably wrong."

"So I guess you made things worse for her also, right?"

Elizabeth sat on the court. She examined her calf. Her bruise was swollen and hard, hot to her touch. The edges of the deeper red and purple clots had become more precise as they moved closer to the surface. She studied her trauma closely as it came into focus, as if the answer to his question glimmered there.

CHAPTER 12

"*E*XHALE SLOWLY, TWO, three . . . feel it here, four, five." Glo felt Roger's fingertips in the ditch of her back between the jut of her shoulder blades as she slowly, to his count, pulled the metal bar behind her head, her hands gripping the tattered black foam rubber padding that had been duct taped to its ends. Behind Roger, a woman, a man, a young boy, and a pale young girl wearing a clash of colors waited for a turn at the Flex Performance Systems station where Glo pulled and breathed and felt.

Roger had made introductions before they'd started. The young girl was Alex and she was a guest at the Mar-Jo. The others, Claudia, Dexter, and Henry, were residents of Lovely. Claudia had a short shock of white hair that was surely premature—she wasn't much older than Elizabeth—and every visible inch of her, even lips, eyelids, and earlobes, was freckled. Glo thought she should come with instructions, like an official payroll check, about which color, brown or white, was the background. Roger introduced her as a waitress at Granny's Restaurant. "Ask for me when you eat there," Claudia said as she shook Glo's hand, "and I'll bring you an extra big slice of cherry pie. Ours is the best in Michigan." Dexter, the teenaged boy, smirked as Claudia said that, and she reached out and smacked the back of his head, not too hard, but enough to send the Tigers baseball cap he wore backward flying onto the dumbbell rack. Henry, who looked as if he should start for the Lakers, ran after it and handed it back to Dexter. "Don't be a smart-ass to Claudia," he warned the boy, adjusting the purple bandanna he wore wrapped tightly around his head. Dexter looked at his feet and mumbled something and when Henry turned his back, he gave him the finger, and Claudia smacked that, too.

The Flex machine with its stations for five different exercises was the focal point of the Mar-Jo's outdoor gym, which also included a rack of dumbbells, some miniature, others worthy of Henry's biceps, and two benches with upright stanchions welded to them to hold what Roger told them were forty-five-pound Universal bars for free-weight bench pressing. "I can bench two-fifty-five," Roger boasted. He took a deep breath and held a pose, his chest straining to be paroled from his shirt. The pack of Merit Menthol in his breast pocket looked implanted. "But you," he reached for Glo's hand, "when I am done with you, you will be able to lift what is here today, in front of you"—he pointed to the forty-five-pound bar—"and you are going to have to remember what a great accomplishment that will be. You must not compare yourself to me. I am a case unto myself."

Back lat pulldowns, Roger called them as he'd demonstrated the first exercise and how to breathe in and out deeply, to do three sets of ten repetitions slowly, focusing on the muscle. He explained things clearly and he was patient with Alex even when she yanked the bar down too hard and fast and then lost her grip, which sent plates crashing. For Glo, Roger placed the pin at twenty pounds. Learning from Alex's mishap, Glo lifted and lowered the two ten-pound plates slowly, trying to feel the moving mass of muscle beneath her skin, but there was too little effort involved—she could have lifted twice the amount. Instead of her own muscles straining, she felt Roger's touch. She leaned back into it—maybe she should lift even *less,* so she'd feel that *more.* After two more reps, Roger patted her shoulder and moved away to work with Claudia.

He'd told her about his Introduction to Strength Training class after he'd carried in their luggage and talked to Glo about his Guadalupe shrine. They were alone. Candy dawdled outside and Elizabeth immediately excused herself to take a shower. Roger gave Glo a tour of the room, pointing to the air conditioner, the radio, the television, his hand on her arm the whole time. After that, he sat on the edge of one of the double beds, and while Glo sat on the other, facing him, he talked about his work in Lovely. He'd founded the Committee to Build the Guadalupe Shrine just a few months earlier. He wanted to call it the Guadalupe Action System. "It is a catchier name," he told Glo, "but everybody said it would be known as GAS and made fun of. The CBGS has dignity. We are in need of money, but I sense things about to change there. The dollars will come. God, through good people," he looked at Glo's purse, "will provide. Our shrine dedication next Saturday is a big event for us. It is a fund-raiser. We are selling tickets and the response has been very good. The statue we commissioned from my cousin will arrive tomorrow or Tuesday morning. With it in plaster cast and your grandniece in motion, it will be a beautiful ceremony. If you will only grant me permission to ask the young girl to be part of our tableau, or if you prefer to ask her yourself, I would be indebted to you always."

Glo's knees had aligned with Roger's in the narrow corridor of space between the two beds. She wondered where Candy had been when she became pregnant? A car? A party? Someplace like the Mar-Jo—a room with thin worn carpets, faded bedspreads thinner still, and dusty drapes? A room where the air had been exhaled one time too many? She pictured hands on Candy's leg, pictured them moving up toward what they wanted. She stopped, willing away the image. Glo had never been in a hotel room with any man but Stan. She remembered Stan's hands on her leg, and she willed away that image, too. She wouldn't yearn for something she no longer had.

Roger's gold cross was visible in the open neck of his shirt. She wondered how different her life would have been if she'd married a man of active faith. A man committed to the Church and God and not just to his wife. *Committed to his wife*—most women would give a lot to have a man like that. But here was a devout man before her. Stan should have been so, too. She opened her purse, taking out her rosary and the Ziploc sandwich bag she'd stuffed with her prayer cards, devotional booklets, and daily missal. She placed them at her side, sentries.

Roger had interrupted her thoughts. "So, Gloria, perhaps you will come to my strength training class later today? It is in my gym, behind the motel. Outside. It is yet another thing I do. All kinds of people, younger and older, men and women, attend. They come from town, too—it is not only the motel guests. It is two dollars per class." He squeezed her arm. "You seem very strong. Really, you are a remarkable woman."

Glo hadn't disagreed. But strength training? She shifted her weight on the bed slightly to the left to compensate for the ache in her right hip, another in a series of continual adjustments she made. Getting older often seemed merely a matter of millimeter by millimeter going off plumb. Roger took her hand and held it between his own hands, his touch light and dry, his palms warm. Glo looked at him directly; she had nothing to hide. "I'll come to your class. And as to Candy's being the Guadalupe Virgin, I'm honored that you want her for the role. I'll make sure that she is, too."

When Elizabeth had walked out of the bathroom, a rush of steam preceding her, her shampoo scent overpowering the stale air, her shirt damp in splotches where her wet hair hung, Glo quickly took back her hand from Roger and picked up her daily missal. She opened it to the day's reading, August 18, the "Mass of a Martyr Not a Bishop," and read aloud from the Epistle, James, chapter one: "For he who hesitates is like a wave of the sea, driven and carried about by the wind. Therefore, let not such a one think that he will receive anything from the Lord being a double-minded man, unstable in all his ways. . . ."

When Glo finished reading, Roger looked up at Elizabeth. "Do you see the relevance here? Do you listen to your aunt? Do you realize the value of her teaching, of her faith? Without faith, you are unstable. You are of two minds. With faith, you are able. You are one."

Two hours later, doing her third set of lat pulldowns, while Roger urged Alex to slow down as she raised and lowered a dumbbell over her head, Glo thought about James's epistle. She would not hesitate. She would ask Candy about the baby. It was fruitless to expect the girl to confide or confess. There was no time for that. Candy had a great decision before her: to raise the child or to put it up for adoption with Catholic Social Services. Of course, adoption was the acceptable answer. Life wasn't *that* complicated. She paused and exhaled slowly, two, three, four, the light weight easily perched across her capable back. She felt her hands covered by another's hands. Roger had returned.

Glo allowed him to offer help she didn't need. She leaned back into him as he encouraged her, the weight moving easily as they both pulled down. She hadn't been touched by a man since Stan's death last October. And for months before that, it was she who touched him. His stroke-afflicted body, circuits shorted, muscles flaccid, speech all but gone, could not reciprocate. If she leaned into Roger's touch at that moment, who could blame her? She wouldn't condemn herself for that. Nobody else should either.

Coach D drove Elizabeth back to the Mar-Jo, saying it was the least he could do. Putting emphasis on least, she didn't disagree. Her bruise had swollen to a hard pack of blood vessels fighting to escape the boundary of her skin. It felt as if her heart beat there. Her shirt was torn at the neckline where Coach D had grabbed it to hold her off, her knuckles ached, and her right elbow was shredded in delicate red lines from where she'd fallen to the ground—all this aggression's price and wasted at that.

"Here it is," she pointed at the Mar-Jo driveway and he turned in.

"Wow, you're really going first class."

"I told you we got stuck here. At least we didn't *choose* to live in this rundown town."

"Actually, I'm stuck here, too. I'm waiting for something important to happen, otherwise I'd have come back to Detroit a while ago. I'm not as big an asshole as you think." Before Elizabeth could ask what he was waiting for or exactly how big an asshole he thought she thought he was, he was out of the car and striding toward the back of the Mar-Jo. He asked if she needed help, but he didn't slow down. "I've heard the guy who runs this place has a gym out back. I want to check it out. I need something else to do while I'm stuck in Lovely." He stopped and pointed to her calf. "Golf isn't my game."

Elizabeth went to room 107, girding herself for the possibility that she'd find Glo *and* Roger there. She had reconciled herself to a week with her niece and her aunt, but she hadn't counted on somebody like Roger being around. He amplified Glo's religious claptrap. She imagined the next few days—one of them preaching, the other imploring her to listen. They'd begun their tag-team evangelism already. When she'd come out of the shower, right before she went to the Rec Center with Candy, he was still in the room. Glo had immediately read to her from the Bible, and when she had finished, Roger lectured her on how deep Glo's faith ran. What nerve. He'd known her aunt for twenty minutes. She'd received Glo's religious missives for twenty years—she'd been dunked in that depth.

After Glo had read the Epistle for the day and Roger seconded it, Elizabeth, unwilling to let him go unchallenged, had picked up a section of the newspaper that she'd tossed on the bed. No way was she going to accept some parabolic teaching that gave them leave to think they were better than anybody else, and she certainly wasn't going to take pointers about appreciating *her* aunt from him. He was presumptuous. Why had Glo allied herself with him? Elizabeth found what she was looking for in the paper and read her horoscope aloud to Roger and Glo: "Pisces: You'll journey and arrive at your destination. Accept others as they are." It was perfectly apt for the day. She tossed the newspaper on the bed with a flourish, and announced, triumphant, "Don't you two lecture me about relevance. You'll find relevance wherever you look for it. The Bible doesn't corner the market on it."

Except, in this case, it did. Elizabeth's horoscope had actually said that she would "meet someone she'd heard about" and that she was prone to injury that day and she should accept help offered. It didn't fit at all. She felt mildly bad about lying to Glo, but she would eagerly tell a bigger lie than that to beat Roger. She picked up the basketball from the closet, bounced it five times on the carpet just an inch from Roger's feet, which were smaller than her own, until he stepped back, and then she moved to the door. "I'm going to find Candy and shoot around with her at that court down the street."

Her aunt wasn't in the room when Elizabeth returned to the Mar-Jo with Coach D. The newspaper was on the bed where she'd left it, open to her horoscope, which was creepily accurate after all. Elizabeth limped around back to check out the weight room. "Glo?" Elizabeth raised her voice upon arrival, incredulous at the sight of Glo prone on the free-weight bench. Roger spotting, leaned over her. Their faces were inverted, lips to eyes to eyes to lips, but they were startlingly close, as Glo raised and lowered the bar.

A severely freckled woman came up to Elizabeth and offered her hand. "I'm Claudia. She's your aunt, right? I hope I'm like that when I'm sixty-something, trying new things, working out, healthy. You look like her a little bit. I heard that you three tall gals had come to town."

Elizabeth, distracted, ignored the friendly woman and limped past her toward Glo. Reps completed, Glo sat up and breathed heavily, and then turned to smile at Roger.

"What are you doing, Glo?" Elizabeth tapped her aunt on the shoulder.

"I'm training my strength. This is Roger's class. I'm taking it. It's not expensive." Glo looked over at Coach D. "Who's he? Where's Candy?"

"You're paying him for this?" Elizabeth heard a groan and turned to see a large black man struggling to control a set of eighty-pound dumbbells. The veins in his arms bulged, as if they'd been inflated. His biceps rose to the occasion and then failed with a flourish, the dumb-bells thudding down to the rubber mat that coated the cement.

"It's only two dollars a class," Glo said.

"I've lifted for years. I would have taught you for free."

"Well, how was I to know that? You never offered. He did. Why are you ignoring my question about that man? And where's Candy?"

"So, Elizabeth, you came to take my class? I am honored." Roger inserted himself into their conversation, sparing Elizabeth the need to answer Glo, and she was glad enough for that. She'd break Coach D's presence to Glo gently. Even without suspecting that Candy was pregnant, Glo would certainly feel the same pure shot of anger that Elizabeth had upon learning who he was, and she would rather spare Glo that. The woman was sixty-three. She took five daily medications for her heart—Elizabeth had seen her do so the past two mornings—Glo didn't need to unexpectedly face the man who, rumor had it, had had sex with Candy. As to where Candy was, Elizabeth wished she knew.

"Don't flatter yourself, Roger." Elizabeth looked around for Coach D. He talked to a young boy whose acne was the only color in his pale face and to Alex, whose equally pale complexion was blemish free. "I don't need your class. I've lifted for years."

"Really? I was a runner-up for the alternate Olympic weight squad back in the seventies. I can bench two fifty-five. How much do you lift?" He stood with his shoulders completely squared, as if he were hung on a rod in a closet.

"Plenty. Adjusting for my weight and upper-body gender difference, I'm sure I'm stronger than you are."

"Will you put your money where your mouth is?" Roger rubbed his thumb and index finger together.

What a money-grubbing cretin he was, hovering to make a buck. Things were complicated enough with Candy pregnant, the last thing

Elizabeth needed was the challenge of protecting Glo from a two-bit scam artist. The first thing she needed was to get her aunt and her niece back to basics: the Cross in the Woods; Candy playing ball; Candy living at the Prokoffs' house next year. There were too many distractions in Lovely. Elizabeth ignored Roger and spoke to her aunt. "Glo, let's leave this place. Now. We'll drive somewhere—anywhere—else. We'll camp. We'll go to Canada. Let's just get out of this town."

"Leave now?" Glo, drawn to Roger, but not blind to him, considered the idea.

"Leave now?" Roger glared at Elizabeth, and then reminded Glo, "Gloria, my friend, you promised. Your niece. My pageant. Gloria, I prayed for your arrival." He took her hand as he mentioned his novena, massaging a vulnerable spot.

"I did promise him that I'd ask Candy to be part of his shrine dedication . . ." Glo liked the feel of his hand on her hand, his hand on her back. She remembered the feel of his knee brushing her knee in the room earlier. His novena had been answered, his request granted, his beliefs dovetailed hers, hand in glove, tongue in groove, they fit in a way she'd often dreamed of and never known. Her spirit *and* flesh were weak for him. Elizabeth was right even if she didn't know the reason why. Glo sighed. She should remove herself from the temptation of Roger.

"Glo, we don't have as much time as you think." Elizabeth stepped between Roger and Glo. "What about our mission? What about what we vowed to do for Candy? We should leave here and concentrate on that." Glo needed to know she was well on her way to becoming a *great*-grandaunt.

Glo, thinking of her pregnant grandniece, shook her head. "Maybe the mission has changed. There are things you don't know . . ." She stopped. She should talk to Candy about her pregnancy before she told Elizabeth it was so. She owed her grandniece that much. "Maybe we should move on. I want to do what's best."

"What's best is to get the hell out of here." Elizabeth was encouraged. She hadn't expected Glo to even consider the idea.

"Gloria, you promised me." Roger pouted, coming between them again, taking Glo's hand again, too. "Your aunt has to stay."

"She has a point, Roger." Glo felt a swell of pleasure from her stomach to her knees as he put his other hand on top of hers. She was glad to be sitting. "But then, I did promise you."

Elizabeth turned away, embarrassed by their contact. Claudia, the friendly freckled woman, came over, and Elizabeth pumped her for information about Roger. "I've been in this place for two hours. Am I the only one who sees what a fraud that guy is?" She jerked her thumb over her shoulder at Roger, and then stuck out her hand to the woman. "I'm Elizabeth Brannigan, by the way—sorry I brushed you off when I got here. I was just surprised to see my aunt with that guy. That guy . . ." When Elizabeth muttered that last part through clenched teeth, Claudia laughed.

"I didn't take offense. And Roger? He's okay. He actually does a lot of good around here. You'll get used to his style. And he has his troubles like everybody else. Anyway, we have history with him here in Lovely. One way or the other, he's ours."

"He's not mine. Or hers." Elizabeth pointed at Glo.

"I don't know about that. I think she likes him." Claudia and Elizabeth stood side by side watching Glo and Roger with their heads together again.

At the bench, Roger pressed Glo. "I know your word is important to you, Gloria. So let me help you keep it. You and I," he spoke loudly and pointed at Elizabeth, "we will have a competition. You say you are stronger than I am? Fine, let us bench press for the honor of staying in Lovely. Your aunt promised me, but I will release her from that commitment if you can outlift me. Three clean reps of your maximum onetime lift. I told you mine is two fifty-five. I did it just Friday. You will see it recorded right over there"—he pointed at a clipboard hanging on a nail driven into a wood post—"and I will have to trust you to be honest about your ability. We will each have a spotter, but if his fingers even brush the bar, the other one wins. If you win, you can take your aunt and niece and leave Lovely and I will not try to stop you. I will not even charge you for the room. When I win, you have to stay through next Saturday, and you and Gloria must promise to work with me to convince the girl to be my Virgin of Guadalupe. If we are both successful, I will give you the tie."

"Tell me, exactly how short are you, Roger?" Elizabeth flexed her biceps and felt her chest expand. She wouldn't back down from this bulldog masquerading as a man.

Candy ran blindly from the Rec Center basketball court. Seeing Coach D made her feel like a fool, a stupid girl, a slut. She'd thought she wanted to see him, convince him to come back and coach the Ravens, but the surprise of him in Lovely and not in Copperwood, where she'd planned to find him, threw her. The Copperwood idea had been a dream, an impossibility—how would she have found him there? Gone door to door asking people if they'd seen a big guy who liked birds? Had she been sending out psychic energy like Elizabeth said? Is that why she'd run into him in Lovely? The coincidence gave her the creeps.

More than that, it confused her. What was she supposed to do? None of her imagined meetings with him had included an actual conversation. What good was a coincidence that came with no instructions? Seeing him made her feel as humiliated as if she *had* fucked him. Seeing him made her feel sick. It had been hard to stand up to the teachers and Elizabeth and Jimmy when they were insinuating and then even when they said stuff outright. But it was even harder than that to look at Coach D and think that he'd heard those things, too, to think that he might think that she might think it would have been a good idea to have sex. She ran faster. She didn't think that at all.

So why had she run away? That's what he had done. That's what all the rest of them did. She was better than that. She was better than all of them. She pounded her thighs with her fists and ran faster still. Ten minutes later, her chest stabbed with the pain of going too far, too fast, she slowed and then stopped. She bent over, pulling the hem of her shorts, which rode up her ass. Damn it. They were tight. And she was hungry. So they would only get tighter. That's how that would go. She walked back toward town.

The storefronts on Main Street were mostly empty and dusty or boarded up, the plywood graffitied with harmless messages—AS + HK and NAH NAH NAH NAH . . . GOODBYE—the vandals in Lovely so dumb they didn't even know how to spray paint a threat. She walked past the Standard Federal Bank—it looked like somebody's house. She wouldn't trust some place with ruffled curtains on the window with her money. The Sunnyview Senior Center, on the other hand, was squat and square and plain, and it had small windows that were high off the ground, as if the old folks were flight risks. Stupid town couldn't get anything right. The IGA was down the block. She had ten bucks in her pocket. She'd get something to eat.

A handwritten sign on the grocery store door read OPEN 7:00 A.M. TO 9:00 P.M. EVERY DAY IN SUMMER. NO SHIRT, NO SHOES? WE'LL SELL YOU BOTH! Before going in, Candy peeked through the large white sale signs pasted to the plate-glass windows. Though the lights were less bright than Kroger, the aisles narrower, and the floor wood slat not tile, the IGA, too, promised organized abundance. Each layer of goods on each shelf was a circus of color, shape, and size. The wrappers and containers flashed brightly—aisles of cookies, dish soap, bread, and mustard—a picture of plenty that left no room for want.

The cashier looked more bored than the one at Kroger had the night before. Candy put a bag of Doritos in her basket. She was buying for real. The IGA was empty of customers—she couldn't fuck stuff up for some other shopper right now even if she wanted to. She added a box of chocolate doughnuts to her basket and then remembered she needed a toothbrush. She needed toothpaste and shampoo and deodorant, too, but she'd just take all that from Elizabeth or Glo. She wished she'd taken a shower that morning. She was starting to gross herself out. She didn't blame Elizabeth for not wanting to share a bed with her. She walked over to the toiletries aisle.

Next to the toothbrushes, she saw a stack of e.p.t. pregnancy tests. There were twelve of them. There were four toothbrushes. Stupid town. The e.p.t. box had a bright yellow headline: 99% ACCURATE*. She looked all over the box trying to find the meaning of the asterisk. Did Alex know there was an asterisk? How sure was Alex that she really was pregnant? Maybe they didn't even have e.p.t. kits in the little UP town where Alex came from. Candy felt bad for her. Her mom shouldn't be pushing her to get rid of the baby. If Alex wanted to have a baby, she should have it. Candy thought that would be a really stupid thing to do—yeah, sure, go to high school with diapers in your backpack—but so what? It should be up to Alex. She'd buy Alex this e.p.t. thing so she could double-check. Maybe Alex was the asterisk. Then she saw the price, $12.99. Candy looked around— the bored cashier blew a bubble and turned the page of a magazine. Candy crushed the e.p.t. box so it was almost flat and stuck it in the back waistband of her shorts. It dug into her back—there was no extra room in her shorts, but at least that kept it securely in place. She sucked in her stomach, walked up to the cashier, paid for her junk food, and then backed out the door.

The Mar-Jo gym rats divided themselves in favor of Elizabeth and Roger. Henry, the biggest and strongest, spotted for Roger, and Coach D volunteered to do the same for Elizabeth. Claudia enthusiastically urged on Elizabeth. Alex did, too, though wanly—the girl seemed determinedly lethargic, as if she'd saw off her own feet to save herself the trouble of walking. The teenaged boy, Dexter, aligned himself with Roger, and Glo hovered in the six-foot-wide aisle between the two benches, straddling a gap. Her DNA and common sense versus her faith and desire. She was attracted to Roger, and that alone was good reason to cheer her niece on. *Good reason,* she reminded herself, even as she admired the cut of Roger's biceps as he reached toward the weight.

Elizabeth was honest about her normal lift. She did three sets of twelve reps of 110 pounds three times a week at Gold's Hollywood Gym back home. That was just about 80 percent of her onetime maximum lift of 140. That was good for a woman. It wasn't bad for anybody else either. But she doubted she could lift 140 once today, much less three times. Her shoulder was injured. This would probably mess it up more. Still, she'd try. If she met Roger's challenge, Glo would feel she had permission to leave, that she was even obligated to do so. There would be public pressure, all these people were witness to the deal struck. She didn't feel bad at all about trying to get her aunt away from him. Roger was interested in Glo, all right, but it wasn't for her mind (he didn't seem like the kind of man who gave much credit to anybody else's intelligence) or her body (please, she was sixty-three). And that left one thing—money. Glo didn't have any, but he didn't know that. He'd seen them drive up in a hot dog–painted Cadillac and must have imagined it meant more. Roger was transparent in his need and greed. Getting her aunt and niece out of Lovely would give Elizabeth a chance to set both Glo and Candy straight. She shook her head, rueful—things were really out of whack if she was the stable one in their trio.

Elizabeth dropped down flat on the bench. She took a deep breath. She lifted her 140 pounds.

Roger lifted at the same time, thrusting his 255 pounds into the airspace above his head. They both inhaled loudly, delivering oxygen to muscles quickly taxed. He took shorter, sharper breaths, as if he were in labor. On the way up, for her first rep, Elizabeth felt her chest become rigid with the effort of hoisting so much. Once she'd made it to the top, her elbows straight but not locked, she controlled the descent of the bar. Downward motion controlled could be transformed into strength that went back the other way. Downward motion indulged would lock her into a position out of which it would be impossible to climb.

It was 6:00 P.M. Dusk fell slowly, a counterbalance to all the weight rising more slowly still. Only the connotation of cool came up from concrete—a hand there proved the heat it held would linger much longer. It was quiet now. The atmosphere changed. Both Elizabeth and Roger strained. Coach D and Henry hovered over them, behind the benches, hands cupped under the respective bars, but careful not to touch unless the lifter called for help. Glo felt her back tensing for both her niece and Roger. They looked inhuman in their struggle. Elizabeth had a bruise on her calf that Glo hadn't noticed before. Swollen and gleaming, it looked alien, ugly. She looked at Elizabeth's face. Contorted in concentration, it looked alien, too. She didn't look at Roger. Glo's destination was in her niece's hands, and also in her wrists, her arms, her chest. Glo wouldn't tease herself by looking at Roger. The lifters each made it back up and down again. Dexter shouted, "That's two."

Elizabeth, bar lifted halfway up, in her third and final rep, arched her back more acutely, and felt her abdominal muscles tighten. Her body was allied—every ligament and tendon, every muscle and bone was directed at the task of lifting the weight upon her. She thought her wrists might splinter before they reached the zenith toward which she aimed. She heard Roger breathing next to her. Too quickly. He must be in trouble. Maybe he'd hyperventilate. *Quit it.* She couldn't waste thought on him. She was almost there. She was going to make it. *Concentrate.* Three more inches of effort and she could drive them out of Lovely intact.

Candy crept around the Mar-Jo. Where was everybody? She heard somebody in the back shout "That's two," and she went that way. She peeked around the corner and saw Elizabeth on her back. Her skinny aunt lifted more weight than Candy thought physically possible. Candy didn't bench close to that and she was taller and fifteen pounds heavier. She sucked in her stomach. Maybe twenty. She crept closer. Coach D spotted for Elizabeth, but he looked up at the sky, instead of down at the bench. Elizabeth's eyes bulged and her back, raised high off the bench, looked as if it could snap any second. Nothing about this picture of strain and effort was pretty. And then Candy saw Elizabeth's calf. Her bruise seemed to beat as if her heart had been transplanted there. It looked alive.

Candy dropped her bag of groceries. "Oh my God, your leg looks repulsive."

Hearing her, Elizabeth faltered. Her calf throbbed. The bar, which she'd been just inches shy of lifting all the way, slipped down a little. Her elbows jutted awkwardly to the side. The bar slipped down farther, faster, and she panicked. *Where the hell was her spotter?* She looked up at Coach D, imploring him to get a grip, though she couldn't catch a breath to say so as the bar headed for her windpipe. He stared up in the distance. She heard a crow caw. She saw two birds flying overhead. Saw his gaze on them. Birds. He was watching birds while she was pinned beneath dead weight. She squeaked out a yelp, and Claudia rushed over, which woke Coach D to his duty, and he finally helped her lift the heavy weight.

Elizabeth lay still for a few seconds, her muscles thawing, not trusting the sudden relief. When she sat up, she was greeted by Roger, who clasped his arms above his head in victory and taunted her with a juvenile "Yesssssss," before adding that they should all meet him tomorrow for a pageant organizing meeting at the Guadalupe shrine tent on Main Street at two. Glo smiled at him, and then she turned to Elizabeth and raised her eyebrows and shoulders in a no-jury-can-convict-me-I-was-ready-to-leave-if-you'd-only-literally-carried-your-weight apology. They both looked at Candy, who had no idea that she'd just bound them all to Lovely and herself to the role of the pregnant Virgin of Guadalupe.

Candy didn't like how quiet it was and how they looked at her as if she'd just flashed them or done something else she'd get in trouble for. She turned to leave, first bending to pick up her Doritos and doughnuts. As she did, the e.p.t. kit worked its way up out of the waistband of her shorts and fell to the ground.

She wouldn't have thought it possible, but the quiet got quieter. Coach D, Alex, Roger, her aunts, and other people she didn't even know circled around the little cardboard box as if it were a campfire and they had frostbite. Some skinny, ugly guy with zits blushed fiercely as he looked down. Candy felt her own face becoming hot—

how was she supposed to explain this, without busting Alex? She already felt bad about telling Elizabeth that Alex was pregnant.

Elizabeth spoke first. "This is awkward."

"It's not what—" Candy began to set them straight, but Alex cut her off.

"You swore you couldn't be pregnant like me. You lied to me. But everything *I* told *you* was true." Alex stepped up to Candy until she was just inches from her face and she clamped her teeth together as if she wanted to keep from biting her, but then she wilted and her face got all baggy and she began to cry, and then she ran away.

Glo interrupted. "Awkward? You call it awkward? I'd say that's an understatement. That other young girl is pregnant? What exactly is going on here?"

"This is going to be hard for you to hear, Glo." Elizabeth stepped up to her aunt; Candy's secret was laid out on the cement, it was a little late for discretion. "But it's something you need to know. She's pregnant. Candy is pregnant."

"Well, I know *that*. By the way"—Glo turned to Candy—"you'll be playing the Virgin of Guadalupe in Roger's shrine dedication."

Elizabeth also jerked around to face Candy. "You told *her* and not *me*?"

Glo corrected her before Candy had a chance to. "Nobody told anybody anything. But I'm not an idiot. Look at her." Glo waved her hand over Candy's body as if she were a magician introducing her assistant. In so doing, she felt a swell of sympathy for Candy. The girl looked chastened, unsure, and her ratty mat of hair was dull, though twilight glowed. Even at seventeen and as physically fit as her grandniece was, it couldn't be easy on the body to be pregnant. "And she quit basketball. And that man, her coach, ran away. I can put two and two together as well as anybody else." She stopped, suspicious, and pointed at Coach D. "Who is he? Why is he listening to this conversation? Why are the rest of you? Don't you have anything better to do?" Dexter and Claudia shook their heads no.

Coach D ignored her question. His forehead was wrinkled—he looked as if he were searching for the answer to a crossword puzzle clue. Dexter had gone past his embarrassment and now acted like the prurient fifteen-year-old boy he was, leering at Candy's chest. Roger turned his head from Glo to Elizabeth to Candy, clearly not wanting to miss a thing. A blind woman could see that he was trying to figure out how this turn of events might benefit him. Only Henry had been polite enough to walk away from a conversation that was clearly none of his business. He adjusted his bandanna and then he re-racked weights, the clink of metal plate on plate interrupting and underscoring the conversation. Claudia stepped over and patted Candy's arm. "Oh honey, I had a baby at sixteen. I know exactly how you feel."

Candy put her hands to her head and pressed. How she felt was as if she'd been abducted by aliens. Nothing made sense. Was that what this freckled freak meant?

Coach D, his forehead smoothed out now, stepped forward and answered Glo's question. "My name is John, ma'am. I know your grandniece from Detroit. I was her coach."

It took Glo a few seconds to understand. Her coach? What gall. Had he followed them there? Had he and Candy planned some tryst? He wasn't her grandniece's coach. He was the father of her grandniece's child. The father of Glo's great-grandniece or nephew. How dare he introduce himself as Candy's "coach." Glo thought she would have spit at him if her mouth weren't so dry. She raised her hand to strike him instead, and as she did Henry dropped a forty-five-pound plate, which rolled off the rubber mat toward them all until it landed with a gritty clang near Candy's feet.

Elizabeth caught Glo's hand, as Coach D backed away from it. "No, Glo, it's not what you think. They didn't . . . he didn't. He's not the father. You can say he's cowardly for running away and letting her face those rumors alone, but he's not a statutory rapist."

"Why should I believe you? Or him? Who is the father? I want to know." Glo glared at Elizabeth and then at every man in the group. One by one, each looked sheepishly down at his fly, as if it were unzippered.

Candy, mortified, mumbled at her grandaunt, "We didn't do anything."

Coach D came forward again, but this time he spoke to Candy. "Golden, we need to talk. Meet me tomorrow morning on the court. At ten. We'll shoot around and straighten things out."

"She's not meeting *you* anywhere, young man." Glo wagged a finger at the coach. Elizabeth stepped between them again, and then everybody talked at once and grabbed Candy's arms or patted her head or pointed at her. *She's too young. Tell her again that she has to be in my pageant. How do we know he's telling the truth? This freshman last year had a baby in the bathroom. My oldest weighed nine pounds and my third was a preemie. We have a pageant rehearsal meeting tomorrow at two. At least that explains why she quit.*

Candy put her hands over her ears. She was sick of it. Sick of them. She kicked in frustration and caught the edge of the e.p.t. box. It flew high enough to clear Roger's head, which wasn't very high at all, but as everybody watched the arc of the crushed cardboard box, Candy ran away. Again. She would find Alex. She would tell Alex the truth because Alex was another girl who'd gotten screwed. But the rest of them didn't deserve it. Let them think she was pregnant. If it made them unhappy, that was fine by her.

CHAPTER 13

*W*HEN THERE WAS no answer to her knock on Alex's door, Candy walked down Main Street. She'd rather stay on her feet alone for hours than sit on her ass in that depressing hotel room with Glo and Elizabeth. She walked along the side of the road toward the Rec Center. Night settled in. It was difficult to see, but at least that meant she didn't have to look away from anything. Traffic on the road was sparse, but every so often a car or truck illuminated the shoulder of the road, and she moved ahead easily in the lingering glow.

When she got to the Rec Center, the basketball court was dark, too—there were no bulbs in the battered housings of the lampposts in the corners of the court. She should have brought the ball. She could have challenged herself with the dark. She wouldn't admit it to Elizabeth, but it had felt good to shoot around that afternoon.

The argument over her nonexistent baby or fetus or fingernail of tissue or whatever you wanted to call it had no effect on her. She didn't care one way or another about it. She didn't think she would even if she were pregnant. Whatever somebody needed to do was fine with her. She didn't like how Glo and those anti-abortion people spoke for God. How did they know what God wanted? It's not as if God never allowed a baby, born or not, to die. But Elizabeth and all those pro people? For all their talk about choice, Candy didn't think they truly believed a teenager should ever have a baby. It was as if they had some secret formula—income divided by age, or number of SUVs owned times years married plus money in the bank—that qualified you to give birth. Whatever their equation, it was one no high school girl could solve or equal.

She should have lied and ratted out Coach D back there in the weight room. He'd done it to her, leaving her to that asshole Morrisey. Not just her, but the whole team. For all she knew, Coach D might want to have sex with her. Still, she'd meet him tomorrow, and she'd shoot with him. She would ignore his explanations and his lecture on how she had to play for Morrisey this year. She'd just let him run down the ball and feed her. Catch and shoot. She'd get her rhythm going. She wouldn't think. Catch and shoot. She wouldn't listen. A second left on the clock. The game on the line. That ball where it should be—in her hands. She paced the baseline, picturing it all, and then turned on the spot, squaring up to the basket, shooting an imaginary ball, ending with a perfect follow-through, her right arm extended, her wrist bent, her fingers curled around the dark. Never missing.

The follow-through was the first thing that had set her apart from other kids. It was so simple. It was the most important thing. In every sport. You cocked your arm behind your ear to throw a strike. Extended your racquet behind your hips, knee high, to hit cross-court. Raised your stick behind your head to propel the puck down ice. Held your arm in the air like an "L," basketball nestled there, hands spread wide, to shoot a jumper. Then you thrust your arm forward, past your ear, didn't stop, and slashed it across your body until it rested on your opposite hip. Swung your racquet low to high, and wrapped it around your opposite shoulder. Drove your blade through, the puck no obstacle. Extended your arm with wrist cocked still, fingers arced in a gentle grasp of the sphere-shaped air where the basketball used to be.

For all its simplicity, the follow-through was not a natural motion. When she coached at Clark with Amy, Candy watched five-year-olds stop their motion midthrow—most girls and boys halting their hands at their ears as if an electric fence jolted them to a stop. They almost all "threw like a girl." She hated that phrase. It wasn't even accurate. Boy or girl, a kid had to be taught, told again and again, to keep the arm going up or forward or out. It was a rare kid who followed through on instinct. Candy's follow-through had always been as natural as sleep.

She moved from her baseline pantomime to center court and sat cross-legged like a campfire girl, facing the cemetery from which Coach D had hit his golf ball earlier that day. Her pupils had adjusted to the dark. The crumbling white marble mausoleum where Coach D had been hanging around glowed dully. The smaller monuments were murky shadows.

Anita Prokoff had forced her to visit her mom's grave on New Year's day, just a month after her mom had died. She'd said it was important that Candy acknowledge her loss, as if waking up every day in the Prokoffs' house weren't acknowledgment enough. Candy went to the cemetery for the same reason she did everything except play basketball—to get it over with. Amy had come along. It was Amy who told her mother they should wait in the car once they got there. So Candy had trudged alone through a crust of old snow, her feet cracking the gray-speckled surface and sinking to the layer below with each step, as if the grave called for her.

Getting closer to her mom's grave, which, thanks to Anita's visit a few days before, had been cleared of snow and sprouted a bouquet of pink plastic tulips gathered with blue ribbon, Candy thought it would have been better to have Amy or even Anita at her side. It would have been a distraction. Instead she zeroed in on the slab that marked the location of her mother's body. It was so small. Her mom lived her hard life and got this place mat–sized piece of marble for all her trouble? Anita cut the car's engine, and in the abruptly resulting silence, Candy felt as if she'd been jerked off her feet in a net. She tried to become smaller and stiller to avoid becoming more tightly entangled.

The silence at the cemetery that day had felt the opposite of the silence she heard and felt on court. On court, it was like wind that invited her to roam in all the space it cleared. It heightened her other senses, too. She felt the seams of the ball, the slight dip between leather segments cleaved together. She saw the pattern of the play before her—the open passing lane she could rocket the ball through, the baseline unprotected, inviting a drive, the defense collapsed, the wing open. She felt the momentum of a teammate cutting, felt the gap she moved toward, and she connected those dots with a bounce through traffic, a forty-five-degree angled whip, or a lofty beginning of an alley-oop heading toward a hand held high. On court, opportunities and feelings were amplified in the absence of sound. But the cemetery silence stifled and blanketed—it gave no rise to chance. Every so often it was pierced by the screech of a bird as it flew by, and to Candy it sounded as if bones long buried protested their fate. Unnerved that morning, Candy had stared past her mother's marble slab for a minute, fulfilling her duty, and then she'd tramped back to Anita Prokoff's car, eager to hear some pious chatter.

The silence at center court that night in Lovely didn't amplify or oppress. Instead, it sedated. She wished her mom was with her in Lovely to hear it. She had missed too much by drinking. By dying. And though Candy was grateful that her mom had sobered up in time to show and tell her plenty, it killed her that she had died too soon to hear everything Candy wanted to say in return.

A breeze stirred the leaves of a big maple near the mausoleum and the tree crickets chirped predictably in the rustle left behind. She could count the beats between the rub of their wings. Every so often a car sped past on the road behind her, adding to the quilt of night noise. But then another sound, the faint hum of an engine, joined the spell. She looked behind her, puzzled, though it clearly didn't come from the road. She leaned forward and squinted into the dark. It came from the cemetery. As near as she could tell, it seeped through the cracks in the walls of the largest old mausoleum. The one Coach D had crept around that afternoon. Yes, she was sure of it. A car sped by and nicked the engine-humming sound for a second or two and then one semi and another roared past, their cargo-laden trailers a barrage that annihilated everything except the dust they stirred. When the particles settled, the mausoleum hum had been sopped up by the dark. Candy wondered if she'd heard it at all.

She lay back, long limbs lengthening as she stretched. *Focus, Candy. Focus. She could do this. Concentration leads to anticipation, recognition, execution, completion. It was so on court. Maybe off court, too.* She'd step up to the thing that needed to be done. Alex needed time to figure out whether she wanted that baby. She'd help Alex. There must be some way to use Glo's and Elizabeth's mistake and buy some time for Alex. This was a moment to seize. She couldn't count on Elizabeth's getting everything so wrong again. Elizabeth wasn't that stupid, and, after busting her at Kroger last night, she

might watch more closely. She'd have to distract a lot of people—
Alex's mom, Glo, Elizabeth, Roger—if she was going to help Alex.
And she was going to help Alex. She was her mother's daughter. She
was Elizabeth's *half* niece; she was Glo's *grand*niece. Those links were
weak.

This assumption they'd made about her being pregnant was a
good start. She hadn't had sex yet. She could have let it get to that
with either Jerry Maiz or Rick Overman, but it was hard to arrange
for sex when you were seventeen. Alex probably thought it romantic,
and that's what got her into trouble. All these girls deciding they loved
their boyfriends just because their bodies felt so good together. All
these girls convincing themselves that sex was beautiful and special,
just like those stupid books said it should be, even as they were sneaking around and lying so they could hook up.

Those stupid books—*Pure Love*—one of them had been titled.
Sister Miriam gave it to them during biology class. What did love have
to do with biology? "Purity knows no regrets," the book said. The
Blessed Mother Mary was the ideal role model for a young girl, it said.
So my goal here is to have a virgin birth? Sister Miriam hadn't liked it
when Candy asked that question. The whole discussion irritated
Candy—talk about setting up a girl for failure. She wished adults
would just leave kids her age alone—when they got involved they
fucked things up worse. Take Alex's mom pushing her to have an
abortion. That was crazy. Candy needed to turn that woman's attention away from her daughter. Distract her for a while.

Now she was thinking. Back on track. She knew a couple of ways
to divert attention. By stealth, where the distraction involved minimal
movement and no fanfare, the act taking place in some hidden pocket
of time or place. Or by activity—everything out in the open, strength
and speed the operative forces—enough motion created that people

made a choice and looked the wrong way. Her grocery-store switching, for instance, was the first type. On court, it was more often the second.

She ran through the list of inbound plays that Coach D had diagrammed for the Ravens last year. Blue Series, plays 11–30; Green Series, plays 11–30; Box Series, plays 11–30; and the Sideline Series, 1, 2, 3, and 5. (Why no four? they'd asked. He had bad luck with that lousy number, he'd answered.) For all the codes and talk of "series," there were only four inbound plays—Coach D thought the different numbers would help confuse the other team, make them think the All Saints Ravens had more than they did. All of the plays, baseline or sideline, counted on the players breaking and switching. The one and two guards cutting to the wing, the four and five players angling to position in the post. At the beginning of the play, they lined up waiting for the command of the three, who stepped out of bounds and slapped the ball against the flat of her palm, demanding their attention. She'd make the call then, "Green 19," and they'd begin the flurry of diagrammed movement, hoping to get a step on the opponent and, crisp, fast, and with authority, put the ball in play. Candy loved that beginning slap of the ball, that smack of leather on skin that twanged off the palm and signaled something about to happen.

She also loved how during a game, everybody—fans and players alike—was in the moment, for the moment. People reacting more than thinking. It was almost the complete opposite at the grocery store, where shoppers stared at overloaded shelves, fixated on what they might want later that day, that week, that month.

The crickets' unsynthesized chirp took center court again. Such a steady strum, but then they had no choice but to rub their wings together. Their instinct was so strong. Instincts were. That's what her own mom had said when she talked to Candy about sex, augmenting the abstinence that All Saints preached with lessons about condoms, pills, diaphragms, and blow jobs. "Mom, please, stop," Candy had begged that evening during her freshman year of high school, as her mother placed a condom over her hand and pulled it up her arm to her elbow like a glove, proof positive that it would always be big enough. That Candy should call his bluff if some boy she wanted to have sex with fed her some line about how a condom felt too tight.

At least her mom hadn't talked too much about love and feelings and stuff like that. She'd stuck to practical issues. "Candy, when you do have sex, you'll have a strong *urge* to do it. You'll feel like you *must*. Like you'll die if you don't. Your brain will turn off. That's why you have to think and talk about this now. *Before* you have sex. You haven't had sex yet, have you?" Her mom had looked at her searchingly and when Candy shook her head no, she continued. "When you do, I hope you really care for the person. And I hope you have fun. I want it to be wonderful. Sex *is* wonderful. But use a condom and foam. I want you to be safer."

"Than what?"

"Than I was, for one thing."

"Do you wish you hadn't gotten pregnant?"

"No. That turned out very good. But for you, for now and even ten years from now, by all means avoid it. Pregnancy, I mean," her mom had continued that day, the condom on her arm glistening. "Don't have a baby unless you're sure you want one. And you should be lots older—in your thirties—before you decide that."

"You were twenty-one, Mom."

"I was well on my way to being a drunk, honey. All bets were off with me. I'm just lucky I thought straight for nine months and that Elizabeth was around to help. But I also don't want you for a minute to believe all that talk about how abortion screws up your life. It doesn't have to. I know plenty of secure and happy women who've had abortions. And plenty of truly sad ones who haven't. If abortion were the worst tragedy a woman ever faced, she'd be lucky. Most women are destined for sorrow much greater than an abortion."

"Did you ever think of having one with me?"

"No. Never." Her mom hadn't hesitated. "The thought never entered my mind. I was gifted with you and I knew it even then. Not for one second did I think of anything but having you."

Candy felt a flood of warmth at her mother's words. With all her mom had been through. With all the men she'd been with, it must mean something that her mom had been so sure from the start.

On the floor, during a game, when All Saints was down and the clock chipped away at their chance to win, Candy never felt unsure. She'd sacrifice anything for the good of her team. When trouble brewed on court, Candy begged for a cup of it to run over on her. She felt powerful.

She felt the same way in Lovely that night. Too bad she wasn't pregnant. She could display her invincibility if she were. A baby? An abortion? Whichever she'd choose, she'd do it with such confidence that people would marvel. How could somebody so young be so sure of herself? That's what they'd say. Candy looked up at the Lovely sky, challenging it to throw a bolt. Wait a minute—maybe it already had. They all *thought* she was pregnant. That bolt was good enough. *No, that was even better.*

Alex said her mom cried when she told her she was pregnant. Sobbed as if she'd just found out Alex had a brain tumor. Alex stood there watching her mom cry and felt like throwing up and felt guilty and felt what else could she do but what her mom wanted? Her mom had five kids before she was thirty. Alex said she'd do anything to make her mom feel less bad. But, at the very least, Alex should get more time to figure out what *she* wanted.

Candy got up and walked back to the Mar-Jo. She needed to find Alex, and tell her that she hadn't lied to her. That it was all a mistake they could use to Alex's advantage. She'd have to keep Glo and Elizabeth in the dark for a few more days, but tough shit for them. It was just like them both to get all bothered and involved in a problem that didn't exist, her baby, after ignoring one that did, her, for the past nine months. She'd agree to be the Virgin Mary for Roger's sorry-ass shrine because that would give her more time in Lovely with Alex. With every step she took along the road back toward the motel, Candy felt more and more sure that she could help Alex, that she was even meant to help her.

When she reached the Mar-Jo, Candy went to Alex's room again. Candy towered over the woman who answered the door. "Oh. Hi. Is Alex around? Are you her mom?"

"I'm Hillary Johnston. Yes, I'm her mother."

"I'm her friend, Candy."

"She mentioned you." All of Hillary Johnston's features—nose, chin, ears, brow—were sharp, as if she'd been whittled. And she was tiny, a three-quarter-sized person. Alex's normal-sized father must be a giant. "She just left to get something to drink from the vending machine. She'll be back in a second." Hillary Johnston glanced at Candy's stomach as she spoke.

"I just wanted to talk to her for a minute. I'll come back later."

"You girls have no idea, do you?"

"Huh?"

"Of the pain you cause."

"Sure we do." Candy heard herself. She sounded like a smart-ass.

That wouldn't help anything. She lowered her gaze and shoulders, feigning deference or depression. Something that might please Alex's mom.

"Alex likes you. You shouldn't have lied to her. She told me what you did. She could use a friend here. You could help each other. She's sixteen. Who would raise that baby? You girls just have no idea." Then her voice lost its tightness and her jaw loosened, too. "I haven't been much help to her." She looked as if she knew she'd lose no matter what she did. When Alex walked up behind Candy, her mom said she was tired and they should go sit by the pool if they wanted to talk.

Sitting on the side of the scummy pool, their feet dangling in greenish-yellow lukewarm water near a brackish vein of cracked concrete, Alex took a sip of her Coke and held it out to Candy.

"No thanks. Your mom seems pretty pissed."

"She's okay usually."

"She said you're mad at me."

"Duh. You pretty much told me the biggest lie in the world."

"No, I didn't. I'm *not* pregnant."

"But back there"—Alex pointed toward the weight room—"you said you were. You bought that e.p.t."

"I didn't *say* anything, and I didn't *buy* anything either. I stole that test for you. My aunts are wrong. Roger is wrong. It's the power of suggestion. That can be really strong, you know. I saw a PBS show that talked about women who had imaginary pregnancies. They actually got huge and puked and had labor pains and everything. But that's not me. I'm not pregnant. I'm not imagining I'm pregnant. I've never even had sex. I don't want to be pregnant."

"Me either on that last one."

"So you're going to get rid of it like your mom wants?"

"I didn't say *that*." Alex looked down at her legs dangling in the water. Magnified and refracted, they looked as if they should be attached to somebody else. She kept her head down when she spoke. "I'm not okay about anything. And my mom is all messed up about it, too. I don't know how I let this happen. I don't even like having sex that much. I just did it because my boyfriend, Keith, wanted to. He didn't force me or anything. It wasn't like that. I met him in a chastity class at school. Everybody in the class had to sign cards saying we'd stay virgins until we got married. How stupid is that? It's like they're telling a bunch of sixteen-year-olds to get married."

"I go to Catholic school. A nun teaches sex ed. She says your virginity is like a locked safe and you take something out of it if you have sex before you get married. But if you wait, your husband opens it on your honeymoon and it's full. So it's like he gets paid. I, myself, don't understand how that doesn't make him a prostitute, by the way, but Sister Miriam kept telling us to 'keep the safe locked, girls—don't give out the combination—save your riches for your husband.' "

"For me and my boyfriend, sex was sneaky. We only had it five times. I counted. We always did it fast and in places that weren't comfortable, like a car or one of his friend's bedrooms that smelled like dirty clothes—you know, when the friend's parents were out of town. I didn't even mind when the first time wasn't romantic or anything. But after that, I wished we'd figured something out. My parents never go away, plus I have four brothers and sisters. Keith's brother got his girlfriend pregnant last year, so his mom wouldn't leave us alone at his house. Keith is going to be an engineer. He'll probably get a scholarship to Marquette—he's really smart." Alex pounded her fist on her thigh.

Candy thought Alex might be hyperventilating. She talked too fast and she made grunting sounds as if she might explode. She sounded gross. Alex looked directly at her then and told the rest of her story.

"I'm pretty sure I got pregnant from the time we did it in a closet at a party. A closet, like we weren't good enough for light or even air to breathe. And I was drunk and I puked an hour later. What kind of way is that to start a baby?" Alex pounded both legs now.

Candy stared at her own feet in the pool. The nail polish on her toes was chipped and when she wiggled them they glinted like bits of tropical fish swimming by. "My mom was probably drunk when she got pregnant with me and I never even knew my dad. But the mom is mostly what matters and my mom ended up great. And look, I'm fine, too. You can be a good mom no matter where your baby started."

"You think?" Alex whispered.

"I know. Those things aren't related. They aren't important. What's important is that it's not right for you to go to some abortion clinic unless you're sure you want to."

Alex lifted her head. "But that's the problem. I'm not sure about anything. And what about my mom?"

"She shouldn't force you to do this just because she had too many kids."

"I just found out I was pregnant two weeks ago. It's all too fast. I'm only eight weeks. I can feel it though. I can already feel it. It's like a wave inside me."

"I've got a plan that could buy you some time."

"Why do you care?"

Candy shrugged. "I like a challenge."

"What's your plan?"

"You're pregnant. I'm not. That's the truth, I swear." Candy reassured her as Alex tilted her head and squinted. "Everybody just thinks I am. But we can use that. What we'll do is we'll make up some story about how we're not really sure after all that we're pregnant and we want to take a pregnancy test together—like for moral support—in front of your mom and Elizabeth. And then I'll switch the tests around. My negative test will become yours and your positive one will be mine. I'm good at sneaking. I have excellent hand-eye coordination. I can pull this off."

"I already took one of those tests at the health clinic last week. That's why I'm here today. My mom won't believe it."

"They're only ninety-nine percent accurate. It says so right on the box. That's why I stole it for you. Your mom believed it when it said you were pregnant. She'll believe it this time, too. It's what she'd rather believe. People always find evidence for what they want to believe."

"Let's say you can switch the tests. Then what?"

"Then, you leave Lovely, fast, while your mom is thanking God that it was all a big mistake. You get to go home and think about it without your mom pressuring you. That was your first mistake, telling her before you knew what you wanted."

"It sounds too simple. What if they take us both somewhere and do a blood test instead?" Alex looked suspicious again, like her mother.

"Sure, it sounds simple. But all kinds of things that work are simple. A three-on-one fastbreak. A free throw. You want complicated? Trust me, there're plenty of ways to fuck up simple and make it that way, fast. And that might happen, but this is worth a try. If we have to do some blood test, I'll try to switch the test tubes instead. Or I'll figure out something else."

"Well, instead of all that, why don't I just tell my mom, 'No, I don't want an abortion.'"

"Well, yeah, Alex. I mean, why don't you?"

Alex's cheeks turned rapidly pink as if she'd been dipped in dye and her voice came out cracked. "I don't even blame my mom for wanting me to do it. I mean I really understand."

"Forget about your mom. You need to make your own decision. That's what this is about. This buys you time without her breathing down your back and trying to make up your mind for you."

"I like my mom. I never lie to her."

"Sometimes a person doesn't have it in her to do the right thing up front, and when that's true, it's okay to do the right thing anyway she can." Alex looked unconvinced, so Candy pressed. "You *never* lie to your mom? Are you telling me your mom knew you were drinking beer and having sex in that closet?" Alex looked as if she'd cry, and Candy pressed harder. "If you can't lie to your mother to save your baby, than maybe you don't want the baby after all. But if you do want that baby, you should go through at least this much trouble to keep it. I don't care either way. But you should care. Either way, Alex, this is too important not to be sure."

"It will never work."

"Well, all you've got to lose is that baby. I'm just trying to help you figure out if that's too big a price to pay."

"Did you really not have sex with that big guy, your coach? Or are you lying about that, too?"

"Please Alex, that picture is way more than I can handle. Trust me. Until recently, I wasn't much of a liar either."

Elizabeth stood at the window of room 107 and watched the girls at the pool. Glo had moved the one chair in the room to the illuminated corridor between the two beds and she knelt, leaning her forearms on the seat of the chair, her prayerbook open before her. She wore a nightgown and bathrobe, and every once in a while, she lifted her arm and looked at her bicep, clenching it and smiling. When she saw Elizabeth looking at her, she protested, "What?"

"You're a regular Iron Lady."

"I'm not ashamed to be strong."

"I can see that."

"You're judging me, Elizabeth. Stop doing that."

"For what do you think I'm judging you?"

"For something I haven't done yet."

"Yet?"

"You know what I mean, young lady." Glo put down her prayerbook. "Don't be smart with me, Elizabeth. You, of all people, have no right to judge. And you judge all the time. Everybody. You judge everybody."

"That's not true."

"That priest in Flint, Roger, Anita Prokoff—"

Elizabeth stopped her. "But they're all awful. You thought that priest was phony. I don't like any of them." Hearing how her defense proved Glo's point, Elizabeth added, "I'm hard on myself."

"That doesn't make it right."

"This is really choice. You and your one way. Your one church. Back there at the Prokoffs' house you actually say to Candy, you don't just *think* it, you *say* it, that she's responsible for her mother's death, and now you're lecturing me about judging?"

"That came out wrong. I should have explained."

Glo looked pained. Elizabeth saw that, but she kept at it, defending herself by indicting her aunt. "Forget explanations. You should have apologized and instead you're attacking me, and it's because you feel guilty."

"Elizabeth, I'm sorry. The truth is I don't want you to spend your life making lists about what's wrong with others. That's all I'm trying to say." Glo moved away from the chair and toward her niece. Her palms were open, her shoulders back and down. With her posture, she asked for something.

But Elizabeth didn't know what. "You're ready for bed. I'm going out for a walk."

Once outside, Elizabeth walked to the weight room. She'd seen a pay phone there earlier. She dialed Leo's number. Her old number. He picked up after one ring. She hesitated, waiting for background noise, Molly whining, the dog barking, something that would signal this a bad time and give her an excuse to hang up. But, except for Leo's repeated "Hello?" there was nothing. Finally, she spoke, "Leo, do you think I'm judgmental?"

"Elizabeth? What's going on?"

"This trip. It's hard. Just answer me."

"Is your niece okay?"

"I don't think so. Don't dodge, Leo. Am I judgmental?"

"What's the deal? You don't talk to me for nine months and now a visit, a phone call, a therapy session on demand?"

"I want an answer. An honest answer. I trust you for that, Leo."

"Yes. You're judgmental. You're very judgmental."

"Jesus, Leo, how about a little hesitation, a little thought. You know, contrary to public opinion and your Mr. Mom act, you're no saint either." Elizabeth thought about her inclination to indict almost everybody and then grudgingly allow them to prove her wrong. Glo and Leo were right.

"Elizabeth, are you still there?"

"Leo, why did you marry me? What possessed you? I'd been divorced twice. That was not a good bet."

"When you put it that way, statistically speaking, the odds were that it would work out."

"And look, instead, I lose. I make you lose."

"You didn't make me lose anything. You judge yourself harder than you judge anybody else—"

"See, that's just what I was telling Glo." Elizabeth rushed toward vindication.

That wasn't his point. "But that only makes it self-destructive. You have instincts, Elizabeth. Granted, some are pretty bad, but if you need to fix something with yourself or with your relationship with somebody else, quit examining it and just do it."

"Just do it? That's what you come up with? A Nike slogan? You and Glo think you're so smart. But you're just like everybody else, Leo—you think you're better than me because you have a kid, but what does that make you? I'll tell you what, judgmental. I feel sorry for that little girl of yours. She has a judgmental father."

"You called me. You insisted I answer. And now you're purposely misunderstanding me, Elizabeth." She heard the static *zzzst* of the connection broken. He'd hung up on her. That was not like him.

The girls turned as they heard steps approaching from behind. Elizabeth limped to the pool. Candy watched her. She wondered if maybe there were something wrong with Elizabeth. Something she hadn't told anybody. Elizabeth's eyes were bloodshot, the rims of them red and irritated. It must hurt to even look out of them. Her lips were swollen, pulpy with blood right underneath, as if they'd been soaked in salt, and yet the rest of her skin seemed smaller and tighter than it had the day before—tomorrow it might not even fit her face. Her right shoulder drooped a little, though she slumped so much that was hardly the first thing you noticed. Her bit of burnished hair, usually a glimmer, looked as if it had been coated in wax, dull with a matte finish. And she should have put on a pair of jeans instead of shorts because her bruise, softball-sized now, was a ring of hot pink speckled with deep red blots that circled around a shocking white center. In the Mar-Jo parking lot, with dim light leaking from the pool and grimy light fixtures over every flimsy door, it looked as if all Elizabeth's blood were being drawn to the four-inch-diameter bruise on her leg. The colors on her skin—red, white, and pink—announced all the trouble she was in. Candy started to stand, to bring Elizabeth a chair, and then caught herself and shook off the wisp of understanding before it took shape as kindness. She had no reason to help her aunt instead of herself or Alex.

Elizabeth dragged a tattered lawn chair toward the lip of the pool and grimaced as she lowered herself into it. "I can't believe you're putting your feet in that botulistic-looking water. What are you talking about?"

"Our babies. What are you doing out here?" Candy looked up at her and smiled beatifically. Her aunt looked as if she might, any minute, leak blood from her eyes or lips or leg.

"Glo is about to go to sleep. She snores and my leg is killing me and you're too young to be talking about babies."

"Well, we're not too young to have them." Candy kicked her feet in the water, creating froth.

Elizabeth ignored her. "So Alex, how are you doing? How's your mom?"

"She has a lot on her mind."

"I'm sure she does." Elizabeth put two fingers to her temple and rubbed it. "Candy, you're going to have to ignore the sermons that

Glo and her new friend Roger will give you. You've got a big decision to make, and you have to make it soon. I'll help you with whatever you decide. Have you seen a doctor and confirmed this? How far along are you?"

"I have to get rid of it. I don't want a baby." As Candy said this Elizabeth sat straighter, obviously suspicious of her matter-of-fact tone, so Candy added, "Amy Prokoff and I have talked about it a lot. She's a really good listener. I think it will be the right thing for me. I'm not even as far along as Alex. Hardly far along at all. I didn't even take a test yet, but I can feel it, you know? Well, I guess you really don't know the feeling, but I'm sure I'm pregnant. I missed my period a few weeks ago. But I need to take a test. That's why I bought one today. Or maybe I'm wrong and I'm not really pregnant after all." Candy ran on, making no sense. How could a girl make sense when she was pregnant?

"Maybe I'm not either. I think I messed up my test. My hands shook." Alex joined in.

Elizabeth thought that in all her years as a high school counselor, she could count on one finger the number of girls who didn't sound as stupid and naïve as these two when faced with pregnancy. "You're both engaged in wishful thinking. But Candy, what do you mean you haven't taken a pregnancy test yet? You need to do that right away, so you know what you're dealing with. And, Alex, you haven't seen a doctor?"

"We're going home on Thursday. I have an appointment on Friday."

"I'll talk to your mom. Tests can show false positives. Candy, you need to take one right away. You might be wrong. We'll get a couple tomorrow. And Candy, remember what I said about Glo and Roger.

You don't have to volunteer information to them or to anybody as you decide what to do, and you don't have to sit still if they attack you with their values. Just walk away if you need to."

"I kind of tune out when Glo talks." Candy kicked her legs slowly in the water, feet together, finlike, creating a slow-motion wave. She hadn't looked at Elizabeth during the whole conversation. Like she'd told Alex, people were happy to believe your lies if you told them what they wanted to hear.

"Well, I guess that's settled then." Elizabeth looked up from Candy's disembodied legs in the filmy water. "So, I'll leave you two alone. I really am tired. Don't stay out here too much longer. Glo is waking us at seven. She wants to take us out to breakfast. Come with us, Alex, and invite your mom. Candy, do me a favor, and when you come in tonight, if Glo is still snoring, give her a kick and tell her to roll over."

Candy jerked her head up and looked directly at Elizabeth. "I will not. She's old. She deserves to snore in peace. You're so mean to her."

"All right already. I'm tired of hearing from everybody about how mean I am." Elizabeth hoisted herself out of the chair and hobbled back to room 107.

Watching her aunt's retreat, Candy kicked her legs slowly again, feeling the resistance, the tug down as she lifted up, the pull back to water created by the weight of her own flesh and bones. She kicked harder, creating a white froth that licked her calves. When she kicked harder still, Alex joined her, and soon the pale green Mar-Jo pool water rose and christened them both.

CHAPTER 14

EARLY AUGUST MORNINGS in northern Michigan came swaddled in all kinds of weather. One dawn might break with heat so dry it scorched the throat, another might drive in hard on rain gritty with sand the wind had shaved off the dunes, and there were even some where scythe-edged cold, defying gravity and the *Farmer's Almanac,* rose up from ground riven with frost. One old-timer in Lovely talked about the three feet of snow that came on August 1 back in 1930 when he was a boy, and even discounting that as faulty folklore (meteorological records showed no evidence of snow that deep that early), everybody old enough to zip her own down jacket or lace up his warmest boots had to admit that once in a while an early August morning in Lovely called for long johns and a hat.

But not that one. On that morning when Glo, Elizabeth, and Candy waited in the smoky Mar-Jo lobby, the air was so stout with humidity that Elizabeth felt she might devolve, her skin and lungs becoming more, or would it be less, sophisticated until, amphibious, she straddled two worlds. It was only 7:25 and she'd done nothing more physical than walk across the parking lot from room 107 to the lobby, but already her shirt clung to the cleft of her chest, and her glasses had a fringe of steamy vapor around the lower parts of the lenses. That August morning in Lovely was laden with rain just aching to fall.

They'd met as scheduled. Glo's breakfast invitation was a command, not an option. Glo wore her Sunday best, though it was Monday. Her hair was smooth, as if she'd given it standing orders to defy the humidity, and her handbag hung on her arm like an ornament. Elizabeth's clothes, T-shirt and linen shorts, were creased in odd places because they had not been folded neatly when packed. She looked crumpled and used—tired before the day had begun. Only the bruise on her calf pulsed with purpose—it had deepened to purple, and plum-colored filigreed streaks invaded its background like the alternate routes on a road map. The saturated air made it glisten and shine.

Elizabeth had risen at 6:45 when Glo shook her shoulder. She showered and drank a cup of the Mar-Jo's lobby coffee, which even freshly brewed was more than half bad, by 7:15. Crumpled clothes, foggy glasses, aching body, and bad coffee aside, this early in the morning, Elizabeth felt modestly hopeful. For what, she couldn't exactly say. But she knew that as the day crept on, the possibility would leak out, leaving behind the sediment of reality—a talc of little things gone wrong or often something more abrasive.

Candy had shaken off Glo's first four admonitions to wake. After the fifth, she'd opened her eyes, sat up, stepped into the same clothes from yesterday, which were the same clothes from the day before, now mealy with wear, and within thirty seconds announced herself ready to go. With no time to tend it, her hair, if it hadn't been in dreadlocks, would have looked as if it were. She smelled as if she'd traveled to Lovely in a Greyhound from California, instead of a Cadillac from Detroit. As they left room 107, Candy grabbed the basketball from the closet, and Glo and Elizabeth looked at each other, thinking maybe they were getting to her after all. Or maybe not—Candy didn't dribble or spin or bobble the ball, she girdled it to her belly.

In the lobby, Elizabeth listened as Roger gave instructions to Janine, his replacement for the morning. Roger talked fast, telling her which rooms were still for rent, which needed cleaning, and which guests were checking out when. Janine wore glasses on a silver chain and she took them off and put them on continually, as if she were changing her mind about how clearly she wanted to see what he pointed out to her. "Now Janine, after I have breakfast at Granny's with the ladies, I have to go to Copperwood, and then I have the Guadalupe shrine meeting later this afternoon." Roger took a deep draught of air—he wore a Breathe Right strip across the bridge of his nose; at first glance Elizabeth thought he'd been in a fight—and then he herded Glo, Elizabeth, and Candy out of the lobby.

"Roger, wait." Janine ran out to the parking lot, her glasses clattering against her chest. She held up a blue smock—a large yellow HELLO, MY NAME IS ROGER button pinned to its neckline—"put this in your car so Julie doesn't have to write you up again on your next shift." She perched her glasses on the tip of her nose and explained to Glo, "My granddaughter, Julie, is his boss at Goods. She said Roger has improved his attitude since she talked to him about it last month. Makes me laugh sometimes—she's just nineteen. She's his boss there. He's my boss here. The younger ones bossing around the older ones. Nothing is like it used to be."

Roger grabbed the smock and dismissed Janine, walking fast across the parking lot.

"So Roger, Goods? What's that?" Elizabeth hurried to his side, sensing the smock was something he'd like to hide.

"It is nothing. It is none of your business either."

"I'm sure your nineteen-year-old boss doesn't think it's nothing." Claudia had said Roger wasn't so bad. How had she put it? *He's ours,* she'd said, *he has his troubles like everybody else.* Leo said she had instincts good and bad, but even Leo wouldn't expect her to be nice to a man like Roger. She couldn't help herself, she snatched the blue smock out of Roger's hand and read the slogan embroidered on the left breast pocket: GOODS-4-LESS—WHERE SMART SHOPPERS SAVE MORE. "So you're a clerk at a motel and at a discount store? Your mother must be proud."

Roger grabbed the jacket back. "I *manage* the Mar-Jo. I work part-time at this store for financial reasons that are beyond my control." He turned his back to her. "Gloria, thank you for inviting me to break bread with you and your beautiful nieces this morning." Elizabeth and Candy, standing alpinelike on either side of him, rolled their eyes as if they'd been cued to do so. Roger set his briefcase on the hood of the Cadillac, opened it, and took out a crumpled pack of cigarettes. "Now, Gloria, normally I would rather not drive a car painted like a hot dog. I have an image after all, but for you, I will make an exception. It will be my pleasure to drive you lovely *señoritas.*" He held out his hand for the keys, and Glo opened her purse as if hypnotized.

As Glo extended her arm to give him the car keys, Elizabeth reached in and plucked them from her hand. "Don't be silly. I'll drive. This car is mine, Roger."

"Well, not yet. Not officially," Glo said.

"Close enough. And I wouldn't want people who usually see him driving that," Elizabeth pointed to his car, a brown Ford Taurus with a hubcap missing on the left rear tire, "to see him slumming behind the wheel of a Coupe de Ville."

As they got into the car, Alex ran up, almost breathless. "Hey, can we come, too? Me and my mom? She'll be ready in two seconds."

Elizabeth waited for Glo to protest, and when she didn't, she answered the girl. "Sure. Tell her to hurry."

Roger helped Glo into the backseat and then sat in the front with Elizabeth, placing his battered brown briefcase on the seat between them. As she turned the key in the ignition, eager to turn on the air-conditioning, he lit a cigarette. His exhale of smoke curdled around the flesh-colored band on his nose. "Oh no"—Elizabeth looked for the button that would open all the windows—"no smoking in the car."

"Is it *legally* your car to make the rules, Elizabeth? Did your good aunt transfer the title yet?" He blew smoke in her face as he spoke.

"Glo"—Elizabeth looked at her aunt in the rearview mirror— "tell him to put that out."

"You used to smoke as I remember. You and that second man you married."

"Ben, Glo. His name was Ben."

"At the wedding, you both had cigarettes lit almost the whole time. It was very unattractive. He burned my arm during the Hokey Pokey." Glo leaned forward to display the faint remains of Ben's carelessness.

Roger stuck his head out the window that Elizabeth had opened and talked back over his shoulder. "You are very hostile, Elizabeth."

"You give me plenty to be hostile about." Elizabeth coughed dramatically as she searched the radio for something other than static.

"I have placed my *cabeza* out the window. What more do you want from me?"

"Forget your *cabeza* and get your ass out of the car. Glo, tell him to stop. Isn't the smoke bothering you?" Elizabeth coughed again.

"Language, please. He's got his head outside. It's fine."

"It's not fine for Candy. Candy, are you okay?" Candy sat molded to the corner, her eyes closed, her arms cradling the basketball to her stomach. With a wave of her hand, she told them to be quiet. Or maybe she told them she was fine. Elizabeth couldn't be sure. Candy hadn't spoken to her yet that morning.

Roger, cigarette smoked to its fiber filter, flicked the butt across the parking lot and turned to Candy. "How are you and your unborn baby feeling this morning?"

Candy put a finger in her mouth and gagged. Glo slapped her hand. "That's enough of that. He's being nice to you. There's no need for disrespect."

"Me and my unborn baby feel like puking. He asked and we answered. Don't blame me. I'm going to go get a Coke or something while we wait for Alex and her—"

Glo stopped her. "There's no time for that. And before the shrine rehearsal this afternoon, you need to clean up and put on some decent clothes. You're going to be the Virgin Mary for goodness sake."

"Gloria, this is a very nice car on the inside." Roger passed his hand over the leather seat and the state-of-the-art dashboard. "If it were mine, I'd trade it for something smaller. I know somebody in Copperwood who would give me ten or fifteen thousand for it plus a Neon or a Geo. I could drive there this minute and trade it in for another car and the cash. Even with the unfortunate painting on the side. Used-car dealers always like a Cadillac."

Thinking that through aloud, Roger had surprised himself with the possibility. Elizabeth saw it in the sudden tilt of his head and the narrowing of his eyes as he pressed the buttons on the stereo system. He was laying a claim. "Hold on, cowboy. It's my car. Not your ticket to fifteen thousand dollars."

Roger tapped ash out the window. "I am out of cigarettes. I hope you do not mind if we stop for more along the way."

When Glo said of course, Candy muttered, "Me and my unborn baby should have asked for a smoke."

In the rearview mirror Elizabeth saw Alex and her mother approaching. The woman walked slowly and carried a large umbrella, planting its tip in the ground, a drag against Alex, who pulled her arm. From a distance, she looked like a teenager herself. Candy had mentioned that Alex had four sisters and brothers. Elizabeth wondered how a woman so tiny had carried a baby and then done it four more times. Her feet were so small—hooflike, as if they'd been bound at birth—how had she not toppled over at nine months? Elizabeth looked down at her own size tens straddling the accelerator and brake. Her feet would have been capable of carrying a litter. Alex and her mom stopped near the pool and argued for a minute, their voices raised. The woman's sharp-featured face, fully made-up, stiffened when she pointed toward the Cadillac, but then she walked quickly toward the car, distancing herself from Alex.

Elizabeth twisted—a bad move, it hurt—to face Alex's mom after the woman slid into the backseat. She grimaced as she introduced herself.

"Hillary Johnston." The woman grimaced back and brushed Elizabeth's extended hand with her own. "And I don't know why you invited him along when we've got the girls here, when we've got this situation." Her voice smacked back at Elizabeth.

"Let's all forget our disagreements this morning, shall we Mrs.

Johnston?" Glo, her voice calm, turned her face to the window and looked at the scenery, and for the next two minutes as they drove down the road to Granny's for breakfast, the only sound in the car was the hypnotic tryst of tire and road.

"Uh-oh." Claudia's freckles scrunched together on her forehead when their group of six walked into Granny's. She took Roger aside, but spoke loudly enough for them all to hear. "Mary is here. Joe is working breakfast shift. She's drunk and hanging on him and you have to promise not to make things worse because she's already making them bad enough."

When an unnaturally tan woman who wore unnaturally short shorts came out of the kitchen and stood toe-to-toe with Roger, Claudia gave up all pretense of discretion and explained to Elizabeth and the rest of them, "That's Mary, his ex. He refers to her as 'she' or 'that woman.' He says her Christian name is an insult to the Virgin Mother. She drinks. Messy divorce. Money problems. Other things. Her boyfriend, Joe, is our cook. She makes Roger crazy. She causes him a lot of trouble."

"You were married?" Glo sounded as if she'd inhaled helium.

"What's it to you?" Mary whipped her head around at Glo's question. Her voice was low and raspy. Her movements were careful, premeditated, writ larger by alcohol.

"I want to appeal to Rome for an annulment. I just cannot afford to right now. I pay alimony. She lives with another man," Roger explained to Glo and then turned his attention back to Mary. "Would you please just leave me alone? What can I give you so that you set me free? ¿Por cuanto? Name your price."

As Roger defended himself and questioned his ex, Mary stared at Glo, who, suddenly warm, struggled out of her sweater. A button caught the gold cross around her neck. When Roger reached out to help her free it, Mary tried to slap his hand and skimmed his nose instead. His Breathe Right strip went askew with her touch. Glo stepped back from them both and worked on the tangle herself. "It is not something I am proud of, Gloria." Roger looked from Glo to Mary, from pride to sloth. He tried to straighten the strip on his nose and failing, ripped it off and shook his hand violently to be rid of the stubborn sticky thing.

"Is this your new girlfriend, Roger?" Mary reached wildly again and this time miraculously snagged the cross around Glo's neck. "So you finally found a roller holy enough for you. I'll tell you what, Roger, fifteen thousand—that's what Joe and I need. Lump sum, no monthly payment that you can skip out on. Cash up front. You give me that and I'll give up that pitiful alimony you send me every month postage due, and I'll swear to the pope that you're a virgin and I'm a whore." Mary, talking money, sounded almost sober.

"Fifteen thousand?" Roger sounded surprised. "That's all it would take?"

Elizabeth imagined how he felt—it wasn't that much money, and from the looks of her it would be well worth it to sever all legal ties to Mary. Roger was obviously no great bargain as a husband, but he may have received the short end of the deal with Mary.

Melissa had been a pinch-faced drunk, all stripped down muscle and sinew in a brine of booze, but Mary was the opposite. Her eyelids were puffy and her skin distended. Even without her impaired motor skills, her raspy-edged words, and the boozy vapor that rose off her like steam from a simmering stew, it was her face where the skin just didn't fit that gave her away as a drunk. Elizabeth thought if she pricked Mary's bloated cheek with a pin, the woman's head would take off in wild swoops and swaths until it dropped to the floor—*pffttt*—deflated, empty of its alcoholic fumes.

How had Mary and Roger come to marry? Elizabeth thought she should understand this need in people, but like the internal combustion engine or the telephone or photosynthesis—commonplace and fundamental things—the institution of marriage confounded her. Sex. Companionship. Friendship. Passion. Children. Financial partnership. A person could have any of those without marriage. And love, fidelity, patience, constancy, selflessness, commitment. Weren't those essentials in any relationship? Husband and wife. Parent and child. Even aunt and niece. But who could offer all those things all of the time? Or even most of the time? Everybody was setting themselves up to fail. Look at Melissa. Did five good years with Candy compensate for twelve bad ones? Look at Glo. Had she and Stan been happy?

Her strength was that she'd learned her limits. She wasn't one to dive in deep and drown. The better choice was to wade in and stop. She did what she could do around the perimeter. She played her role. If it were a basketball game, as things stood now, with her shoulder and leg injuries, it would be pointless, even harmful, if she drove the lane. She couldn't be effective that way. The defense would collapse on her. It would swarm. She'd lose the ball. If three failed marriages had taught her anything, they had finally taught her this: don't do what you can't do. But then bits of her phone call with Leo played in her head: *you have instincts . . . quit examining it . . . fix something.*

She saw Mary tugging at Glo's chain, and she stepped between them. "We don't care about your marital status, Roger. And you"— Elizabeth pried Mary's hand from the cross around Glo's neck—"better keep your hands off my aunt." Freeing Glo, Elizabeth spoke over her shoulder to Claudia, "How about you take us to our table?"

"Whoa. Are you digging ditches today, sweetie?" Fifteen minutes later, Claudia scribbled to keep up with Candy's order of three eggs over easy, sausage, a tall stack, bacon, a grilled pecan roll, and a large orange juice. Two days into the trip, Candy could have ordered the whole left side of the menu and Glo and Elizabeth wouldn't have blinked, but apparently Claudia wasn't desensitized to such an appetite. The others, battling either morning sickness, general anxiety and depression, high blood pressure and cholesterol, or, in Roger's case, succumbing to vanity, ordered a paltry spread of such things as dry toast and juice and poached *huevos*. The five of them combined barely had one meal as large as Candy's.

"This might take awhile," Claudia warned. "We're short-staffed and Joe's having trouble cooking with Mary in the kitchen. And Roger, not that you asked my opinion, but I don't believe for a minute that she'll give up alimony or help you with an annulment for fifteen thousand or fifteen million. And you shouldn't either."

"You don't know her, Claudia. Money is what she cares about. We had a lot in common that way. Right now, I'd beg, borrow, or steal fifteen thousand if I saw the possibility somewhere. And once I was free of that *puta*, I'd leave this town like that." Roger snapped his fingers. "I'd start all over somewhere else. *Adios, amigos.*"

"You'd leave the shrine unfinished?"

"Somebody worthy would take over. God provides." He noticed Elizabeth. "What the hell are you staring at?"

"You said *don't* and *I'd* and *puta* and *hell*. Who took the stick out of your ass?"

"Language, please, Elizabeth." Glo, confused by new feelings upon learning of Roger's marriage, scurried to the familiarity of reprimanding her niece.

"Well, Elizabeth, if you'd ever had to deal with an ex-husband, you might understand why I resort to profanity when that woman is around."

"You'd be surprised at how much I understand about exes, and it actually wasn't an insult, Roger. Try listening more carefully."

"It actually wasn't a compliment either, Elizabeth."

"Fine. You're Mr. Quid Pro Quo of prayer. If you need money, why don't you make a novena? Pray for the heavens to open and drop it in your lap."

"You should all say a prayer that this order gets filled in less than an hour." Claudia finished up with their table. "Mary is mean today, Roger. Stay out of her way. Don't antagonize her." Her warning red meat to his alpha instincts, Roger followed Claudia to the kitchen.

"So Hillary, in the matter of these girls being pregnant." Elizabeth took advantage of Roger's departure.

"Do we have to talk about this before we've even had coffee?" Glo didn't see why she had to be part of a conversation about two teenage pregnancies. Candy, not Alex, was her business. She reached into her purse for her pill box, snapped open the compartment labeled MONDAY, and lined up her Inderal and Zocor, her calcium and diuretic and aspirin. She looked around for Claudia or somebody who could bring her water.

"Yes, Glo. Actually, we do."

Hillary sat up straighter in her chair. "I don't even know you people. I'm not discussing my family problems with you." She glared at Dexter, who still wore his Tigers cap backward. He cleared the table next to them, picking up the dirty silverware and cups and plates one at a time, as if examining them for antique markings, eavesdropping on their conversation.

"Dexter, get out of here." The boy blushed as Elizabeth reprimanded him, and he picked up his pace and walked away with his tub full of dirty dishes. "Listen, Hillary, I understand how you feel, but it's not only *your family* problem, it's Alex's future. It might make you

feel more comfortable knowing that I'm a high school guidance counselor. I've faced—"

"And I'm a very devout Catholic," Glo interrupted.

". . . this situation before," Elizabeth raised her voice over Glo's,
"and what we have going on here is that these girls have obviously
bonded." Candy and Alex nodded. "They're friends. And what's the
old saying, 'Friends double our joy and halve our grief.' " Hillary
snorted. Elizabeth, thinking better of her for it, explained. "Sorry.
Some parents like bromides."

Alex spun her knife on the tabletop, and it twirled out of control
and landed in Hillary's lap. "Oops. Sorry. Mom, I'm thinking maybe
I'm not pregnant after all."

"Honey, you can't wish away this baby." Hillary reached across
the table and pushed aside a strand of Alex's hair that had crept behind her yellow-lensed glasses. "I wish you wouldn't wear those. They
make you look liverish."

"No, Mom, what I mean is that Candy hasn't even taken a pregnancy test yet, and I was telling her about how you do it, and as I told
her I realized I might have messed up my pregnancy test."

"What do you mean, 'messed up'? You told me you went to the
county health clinic."

"I did, but the nurse there was really busy. There was a lot going
on. I think there was a line in both the little windows of my test stick,
but maybe there wasn't in the circle one. And I don't think the nurse
checked it out very carefully. This other guy was bleeding all over so
she mostly paid attention to him. My stick was sort of shadowy. And
I did it the way where you're supposed to stick the stick in a cup for
three minutes, but I think she might have lifted the stick before then."

"Alex, the tests are easy. Foolproof. I'm sure there's no mistake.
And we're going to the doctor back home on Friday. You'll get an-

other test there. Honey"—Hillary placed the knife back in her daughter's hand—"I know you'd rather not be pregnant. And rather not have to do anything about it. I understand that."

"But, Mom, if I take a test with Candy here now, we might not have to go to the doctor on Friday. We could know sooner instead of later."

"Maybe she's not pregnant, Hillary. That would be good, wouldn't it?" Candy wedged her basketball between the table edge and her stomach and joined Alex's plea. "Plus, I could use a friend. I don't really want to take the test. I'm scared."

"You pee on a stick, Candy—there's nothing frightening about it." Hillary spun her own knife and it pirouetted across the table toward Glo as if they played a truth or dare version of spin the bottle—speak next at knifepoint.

When Glo smacked her hand on the table and stopped the knife, her careful row of medications jumped and fell off the edge. She'd heard enough. "Urine? Pregnancy? Is this acceptable table talk? Where is Claudia? I need water. Where is our coffee?" She leaned down to search for her pills.

"Hillary, why not let Alex take the test again? Really, it wouldn't hurt her and it would help Candy." Elizabeth thought the girls' plan was a good one. Alex and Candy together on this could make each girl feel less desperate, more willing to listen to reason.

"Fine. Let's *all* take pregnancy tests! Elizabeth, how about you? How about your aunt? Maybe she's pregnant, too."

Glo came up from under the table at that. "How dare you? I'm a widow." She looked at her ringless fingers. How could Roger have married that woman? She put her hand to her throat, remembering Mary's clumsy motion toward it. Stan used to touch her there. "You watch your tongue, Mrs. Johnston. Just because you have a promiscuous daughter, you should not insult me."

"My daughter is not promiscuous."

"Your daughter is sixteen and pregnant. I rest my case." Glo turned to Alex. "I'm sorry to speak this way, and just so you know, I'm not implying that my own grandniece has not behaved just as self-indulgently and irresponsibly as you have." Glo remembered Suzy at the Frosty Cream in Mayville, propping her magazine against her bulging belly. All these girls and babies.

During her forty years working in high schools, Glo had held dozens of newborns. Every young teacher on maternity leave thought it her duty to stop by and show off the blanketed bundle that fit in the crook of her arm. Glo didn't know if it was hormonal instinct or social convention that drove the new mothers to seek approving "coos," but either way, the St. Mary's staff and students were dovelike in their welcome. Everybody liked a baby after all. The visiting mothers often turned to Glo first—"Would you like to hold her?"—bypassing nuns and students, as if they saw only Glo as other, as lonely for a baby, for something more. And she tried to do her part, tried to feel some kinship or comfort or need for the baby, whether it was still or squalling, but standing in a dim, tiled hallway, surrounded by a covey of girls and women breathing out soft "ahhs" of appreciation, Glo felt she might as well cuddle a sack of groceries. To make up for this, she bounced the babies up and down enthusiastically and chucked their tiny chins with too much gusto, causing their mothers to reclaim them quickly.

Suzy at the Frosty Cream and now Candy and Alex were too young to see any further than the very moment they faced, too cocky to admit how naïve they were, too impatient to see that someday soon enough they'd become themselves instead of what some boy thought they should be: willing to have sex with him. But then, Glo wondered, what about touch? What about the skin on skin that led them to this point? Glo thought of Stan, of the rush of feeling that had blotted out the embarrassment of the first time she'd had sex with him. The first time she'd had sex at all. She remembered the feeling of Roger's hand on her back in the weight room last night, and heat rose to her cheeks. He'd been married—that was a blow. A different heat, this one scorching, advanced to her forehead.

That woman, Mary, had seen her for what she was: a sixty-three-year-old woman who'd mixed up desire and devotion. Glo knew her better self was the one who prayed. But what to make of the other self that had laid with Stan, and that wanted to do so still? Had she used the rigor of her faith as compensation for that need unfulfilled?

That morning at Granny's, Glo felt the heat of her own temptation, and with the rise in temperature something loosened in her understanding. Temptation. That's what happened to these girls. To Candy and Alex. They were tempted, too. Could she really upbraid them for not waiting until they were forty-nine? Would she have wanted them to experience such a lonely stretch of time, during which their desire for sex was overtaken by their fear and embarrassment at not yet having it? She felt ashamed of the hard line she'd spoken a moment ago, and she offered something else this time. "All these girls? They'll have their babies"—Glo looked at Hillary, Elizabeth, Alex, and finally Candy, one by one—"and we must help them."

It was quiet around the table when Glo finished. Candy played with packets of sugar, Alex picked at a split end, Hillary pushed her thumbs into the sides of her head as if there were tacks there and her temples were corkboard.

Elizabeth considered how truly distraught her aunt must be. Dur-

ing the past twenty years, along with the prayer booklets, church cal-
endars, and plastic rosaries that Glo had sent Melissa and Elizabeth,
she'd also included anti-abortion literature in various degrees of grue-
someness. One packet had arrived when Melissa was pregnant with
Candy, though her sister hadn't even known it yet. It was as if Glo had
been an early pregnancy test herself—hundreds of miles away in
Chicago, sending a large brown envelope full of warning to Melissa in
Detroit.

"It's another manifesto from Glo. I should throw these directly in
the trash," Melissa had said as she tossed the unopened envelope on a
table. She and Elizabeth were on their way out to a bar where Melissa
knew the bartender would load them up with free kamikazes if some
guy in the crowd didn't get to it first. They drank and played darts all
night, and then they fought over who was less drunk as they stumbled
out to the parking lot, both of them loaded and determined to drive.

Almost twenty years later, Elizabeth didn't remember who'd won
that argument. Even the morning after, she hadn't remembered who'd
won the argument. What she did remember was shuffling slowly, each
tiny slide of her feet upsetting her stomach, making her head feel as if
somebody had pulled an iron band around it a notch tighter. Everything had been tentative and wobbly and painful and hazy—she didn't
know where her glasses were. She couldn't see much without them.

As she walked into the sunny living room of Melissa's apartment,
she made out the shape of her sister kneeling on her haunches and
drinking orange juice (probably enhanced with vodka, though Elizabeth wouldn't have guessed that at the time). Glo's envelope, addressed in block letters with black Magic Marker, was at Melissa's
side, the contents strewn around her like paving stones. Bloody, grisly,
gruesome paving stones from various right-to-life organizations' most
horrendous tracts.

Elizabeth remembered how, barely stable on two feet, and with her vision impaired severely by her hangover, by her lost glasses, by her extreme myopia, she had smelled the freshly showered redolence of her sister, but she couldn't see well enough to know that Melissa was all right. Instead, she saw a sea of red that swirled and lapped at the edges of her sister's blue terry-cloth bathrobe, the scent of her cream rinse mingling with the less fragrant waves of Elizabeth's alcohol-sodden breath and the smoky clothes she'd slept in. And in that blur of hazy vision and hangover, Elizabeth couldn't tell if Melissa was bleeding to death or surveying the bludgeoned bits of a crime she'd committed in a drunken rage. But she did know, in her muscles, bones, and stomach, that something was wrong. She lurched and then collapsed to her knees as if somebody had taken a tire iron to the bend of them. She'd put her head down, breathed in deeply and focused on not throwing up, willing herself to change the direction of her muscles that were headed toward hurl.

Melissa had walked over to her, put a cool hand on her neck, and spoke in a low soft voice until Elizabeth raised her head weakly and asked, "How much did I drink last night?"

"Enough so that you made out at the bar with a forty-year-old guy and then with an even older one while you danced to Patsy Cline. Come on, get up and sit on the couch and I'll get you a Coke and some aspirin and toast. When you're up to it, we'll go to the Steak 'n Egger. You need grease to soak up the alcohol."

"Forty? Older than forty? Why didn't you stop me? Weren't there any young guys around? How come you're not sick? Didn't you drink as much as I did?"

Melissa took a long pull on her orange juice. "Even more. I guess I have higher tolerance."

"Where are my glasses? What's going on in your living room? It looks like a massacre."

"Your glasses are in the kitchen. That's Glo's latest anti-abortion package. She sent a thick one this month—posters, flyers, brochures—she must have made a big donation somewhere. I think she's compensating because she's never had sex. She could save herself a lot of money if she'd just get laid. She's probably more worried about it all now that she considers us both old enough to have sex."

"Oh my God. Did I have sex last night? Why did I get so drunk?" Elizabeth had smashed her fist to her forehead and shook her head. "Am I pregnant with some old guy's baby right now? Does Glo know something I don't? Do I need an abortion?"

"You didn't. You had fun. You're not. She doesn't. You don't." Melissa answered her frantic questions, keeping it all straight.

Elizabeth took deep breaths at her sister's urging, and then she asked her, "Would you ever have one?"

"One what?"

"An abortion?"

"Maybe. I don't know. I guess so."

It was two weeks later that Melissa realized she was pregnant with Candy. Two weeks later that she stopped drinking for more than a year. Cold turkey. Just like that. She'd stayed sober until Candy was six months old, while she breast-fed her, and then she'd quit that cold turkey and drank a beer.

Elizabeth remembered how Melissa had gone back to drinking in stages. Quantity and alcohol content increasing every year. Just beer, though plenty of it, as Candy crawled and teetered. By the time Elizabeth graduated from Wayne—she'd never made it to UCLA—Melissa was on to stiffer drinks, mostly vodka, but only at night, after she'd come home from work and fed and bathed and read to Candy, who had toddled into kindergarten. By the time Candy was in second grade, Melissa was a full-blown, highly functioning alcoholic, who sometimes went on three- and five-day drinking sprees, leaving her daughter in Elizabeth's care, or a neighbor's, or, once, when Elizabeth and the neighbor were both out of town and Candy was in sixth grade, all alone. And then the five years of sobriety during Candy's junior high and high school years. The first two years when she went to AA every day, Melissa called Elizabeth often—called to tell Elizabeth stories that she didn't want to hear, offer apologies that she wasn't ready to accept, report progress that made her jealous of how deep-rooted it seemed.

Because by that time, Elizabeth had two busted-up marriages and troubles of her own. And even a year later, when she was with Leo and knew she finally had a marriage that was worth the trouble of keeping whole, when it came to Melissa, she'd remained suspicious. What if Melissa began to drink again? What if Melissa went for Leo, the way she'd gone for Ben? She'd allowed all the "what if"s to distract her from what *was*. Candy, for instance. She'd sold out her niece for the price of indulging her fears. And between her distrust of her sister and the three hundred some miles between Detroit and Chicago, it had been surprisingly easy to do.

Hillary's voice, over the din of Granny's patrons, brought Elizabeth back to the table. "What Alex and I decide to do is none of your concern." Hillary pointed her tiny finger at Glo.

Elizabeth played peacemaker. "She's only trying to help, Hillary. Let's take it a step at a time. After breakfast, Candy and I have to meet Coach D, but why don't you and Alex go to the store and buy a couple of pregnancy tests, and we'll just deal with what we find out from those later today. Okay? Everybody?" She pushed her hair off her forehead so that, Einstein-like, it appeared to flee from her scalp. Her golden streak flopped over her restraining hand as she waited for their acquiescence or for more protest. She looked out the window and a fat splat of rain bounced off it. A half dozen people walked toward Granny's. Elizabeth watched as they stopped, fifty feet from the restaurant door, and held out their hands, palms cupped. They looked puzzled, as if they couldn't place the substance that fell from the sky. As if summer rain—a common Midwestern occurrence—had never actually fallen before.

She turned back to the table, to see them all nodding in answer to her question. Candy and Alex eagerly. Hillary grudgingly. Glo unsteadily. Elizabeth sat back, satisfied at the truce and plan of action she'd brokered. She looked out the window again and in the bounce of artificial light reflected there, she noticed Coach D, alone at a table. He read a newspaper, and as he turned the pages slowly, the movement of his hand and the wafting newsprint seemed a benediction. He saw her staring into the window and she continued to watch his reflection as he got up and came to their table. She turned and faced him when she heard his voice.

"Good morning, ladies. Golden, remember, you're meeting me at the Rec Center in an hour. We'll shoot around." Coach D looked at his watch.

"I'm coming, too," Elizabeth said.

"I don't have a problem with that." Coach D pointed at the rain out the window. "You know rain in the air causes unusual human behavior. People would be wise to expect trouble when it's about to rain. Instead of being surprised by it, I mean. People do strange things in the rain. Birds, too." They all looked at him as if they'd just realized the village had an idiot.

Coach D rocked back and forth as he spoke. With his belt tightened below his inflated gut, he looked like the pregnant one. Candy, who knew him well enough not to be surprised by the crazy things he said or did, laughed at his bird comment. He was only thirty, younger than Elizabeth, but you wouldn't guess that by looking. Candy and Kim McVitty had called him the old man during their sophomore year on the team. That's the part he played: he drove a station wagon; he didn't have a girlfriend; he lectured them about opening their own sodas at a party so nobody would slip in drugs while they weren't looking. Sodas? At a party? Kim and Candy had rolled their eyes at that one, though truth is they had not yet become girls who drank anything *but* soda at parties. (Candy had seen her mother too drunk too often to be tempted, and Kim was scared she'd get caught.) Between his looks and lectures, Coach D may as well have been fifty. It was insane that anybody, even a nun who didn't know shit about it, would think she'd have sex with him. Candy laughed again unnaturally, mortified.

"Birds, Coach? Candy, what's so funny?" Elizabeth asked.

"Nothing funny about birds. I take them seriously." Coach D tipped an imaginary hat at them all. "Enjoy your breakfast, ladies."

After that, Elizabeth set out the agenda for the day. "Alex and Hillary, we'll meet back at the Mar-Jo before the shrine meeting this afternoon. Glo, will you be okay alone for a few hours? You can join us at the Rec Center if you want. We're going back to the motel first, anyway."

Claudia returned to their table then, plates stacked step-style up her left arm, coffeepot in her right hand, and Candy yelped with pleasure at the feast about to begin and Claudia's being so wrong about how long it all would take. But Claudia swept past them with the bounty, correcting herself. "Where's my head this morning?" She moved on to another table of six—a man and a woman and four young children, all girls, the oldest, perhaps eight, already looking maternal for all the gathering and shushing she did. Elizabeth watched as the woman tied a bib printed with Christmas trees around the neck of the youngest child, who banged an orange plastic hammer on the tin tray of her high chair and then leaned down and tied another little girl's yellow tennis shoe. The oldest girl reached over and gathered a little sister's flyaway hair into a ponytail, pushing and pulling it through a thick purple, polka-dotted, elastic band in three quick swipes before the toddler could let loose a whine she had clearly been contemplating when she saw her loose ends trailing through a puddle of syrup that another sister had spilled. After attending to all that, the mother and the oldest girl stared out the window, not noticing that the baby spilled her juice.

"Did you notice that Claudia has freckled *lips*? I wish she'd bring *our* food," Candy said.

"It's not her fault that our Spanish-speaking muscle man's ex-wife showed up to mess things up in the kitchen." Elizabeth defended Claudia, and then she jumped as Hillary, startled by a stupendous smash and shatter that came from the kitchen, knocked over her glass of ice water. Those events were punctuated by a smaller, closer confusion as Claudia veered sharply right to avoid the orange plastic hammer hurled by the bib-wearing baby. Candy grabbed the hammer before it hit Glo's forehead. Claudia, wobbling under the bounty on her left arm, held the coffeepot high with her right. Lateral movement sure, Candy was at Claudia's side within seconds. She grabbed two plates that wobbled on Claudia's forearm, and used her elbow to push a heavy bowl that held a steaming glob of oatmeal away from the hammer-throwing baby's head. Claudia lost control of two other plates on her arm, and a stack of pancakes fell butter side down on the carpet, while a hamburger and fries flew into the air like confetti. But, thanks to Candy's intervention, the coffeepot stayed aloft and right side up.

The room was deeply quiet for an instant, as a room is in the split second following an unexpected occurrence, before the neurological impression of the event morphs into material questions: What just happened? Is anybody hurt? How bad is this?

Glo broke the silence with a cluck. "A hamburger for breakfast? It's no wonder a child in such a family throws things."

It seemed clear to Elizabeth, once confusion became informed a little, that Claudia and the family of six she waited on were fine—sticky and spattered, yes, but no third-degree coffee or oatmeal burns or blood spurting from arteries severed by broken glass. And it was even clearer that Candy had reflexes so sharp that even with her Teva flapping loose she had helped save them. But clearest of all, from more crashing and now some yelling in the kitchen, was that they were not going to get breakfast at Granny's anytime before lunch. As if to prove the point, Roger came back to the table and said, "It's a mess back there—I think we should leave."

"Roger, for once, we agree." Elizabeth rose. "Glo, are you sure you'll be okay alone for a few hours while Candy and I go to the Rec Center?"

"She won't be alone. She'll be with me," Roger said.

"Why would she want to be with you?"

"Your aunt is a grown woman, Elizabeth. If she wants to be with me, she can be with me, and if she doesn't want to, she'll say so. Gloria"—he offered his arm—"would you be kind enough to drive me into Copperwood so I can pick up my paycheck?"

"You have a car, Roger. Why does she have to drive you? Why don't you get your ex to drive you?" Elizabeth wouldn't drop it.

"Hush, Elizabeth." Glo turned to Roger. How could she blame him for leaving such a wife? "Of course I'll take you on your errand."

"*Gracias,* Gloria. It's my great fortune that you care." When he reached up and straightened the cross on her neck, which had become entangled on the button of her sweater again, she leaned toward him, accepting his help.

They split up outside Granny's. Roger and Glo dropped off Candy and Elizabeth at the Mar-Jo and then left for Copperwood. Hillary and Alex walked to the IGA. But first everybody took a biscuit from the stash that Candy held before them, opening up a dish towel that she'd stuffed full after detouring through the kitchen on the way out. They were all hungry. Nobody gave her any grief for taking them. Glo said they'd even up with Granny's some time later, and then added, as she brushed crumbs off her chest, that this was certainly not the breakfast she'd expected.

CHAPTER 15

BACK AT THE motel, Candy showered and changed clothes. Furloughed from two days of traveling grime that sluiced down the mildewed Mar-Jo shower stall drain, she put on her favorite T-shirt—a tie-dye that Jerry Garcia and the Grateful Dead had designed to help raise money for the Lithuanian basketball team in the 1992 Barcelona Olympics. Her mom had given it to her—a large even though she was just a little kid back then. It had grazed her knees. Candy wore it now with the sleeves cut off and the bottom chopped to her waist.

She inhaled with gratitude as she pulled the clean shirt over her head. Candy would give Anita Prokoff props for her laundry skills. She looked at herself in the steamy mirror and seeing only a swirl of red, yellow, blue, and green tie-dye, she cleared a path through the mist with her forearm. There it was on her chest—the bony-assed black-eye-socketed skeleton dunking the ball, which hurtled through a flaming net. The bleachers in the background were full of cheering skeleton heads. Had her mom even liked the Dead?

She lifted up the T-shirt and poked her stomach. Its flat and sinewy track of muscle and skin was going soft. She wasn't surprised they all thought she was pregnant. How much longer would it take to turn into a total fat-ass? How long to lose her shot? Her legs? It had been almost a month since she'd played with any intensity.

The basketball court had always been where she'd been able to peel away everything else. But now, on court or off, she couldn't forget something as insignificant as sex she hadn't had, a baby that didn't exist, and aunts she knew better than to count on. She'd played through years of her mom drunk, through the past nine months of her mom dead. But now? How could this—gossip, lies, a coach who ran away, her aunts just doing what they'd done forever anyway, namely *nothing for her*—mess her up? Why wasn't the court big enough for all that?

She was nervous about meeting Coach D over at the Rec Center. Before she'd quit—actually, it was before Coach D had quit, she reminded herself—she'd shot more than 40 percent from three-point range during games. During practice she could sink twenty threes in a row once she'd stepped into her groove. How much had she slipped since she'd worked out seriously with Coach D in June? Gone to Red Star in July? She took another deep breath. The skeleton on her chest bent its bones as she inhaled. God, it smelled good. Anita Prokoff was a genius.

Candy came out of the bathroom to find Elizabeth on the bed with her leg propped up on pillows. Reading a magazine. No, holding a magazine. Her hands moved up to her hair, down to pat the mattress, over to smooth the bedspread. She wasn't even looking at the page. Her calf, bruised and swollen hard as if packed with wet sand, was wrapped in a towel full of ice. It was the only thing about her that was still. Candy had sprained her ankle badly in the last minute of the second quarter in a game against Lahser her sophomore year, taped it tightly, gone back in halfway through the third quarter, and scored fifteen more points. Elizabeth's bruise was the least of her problems.

"Candy, I don't think you should go meet Coach D after all. I want to talk to him alone again, first."

"I don't think you should even bother to offer an opinion, Elizabeth." Candy reached for the bag of pretzels and Coke that she'd left open on the dresser.

"You're eating too much sodium. This article right here"—Elizabeth flapped *Newsweek* in Candy's face—"says that salt leeches calcium. It actually dissolves bone. For every extra teaspoon of salt you eat per day, you dissolve one percent of your skeletal bone a year. That's ten percent over a decade. You'll be shorter than Roger by the time you're thirty. I'm careful with my salt intake."

"So you're the advertisement for strong bones?" Candy went to the closet and got her basketball. "I'm going to the Rec Center."

Elizabeth hoisted herself off the bed and trailed behind.

The morning cloud cover hung low still, and as Candy and Elizabeth walked to the Rec Center, the soggy air was a weight on the napes of their necks, promising and threatening a weather-altering storm.

Arriving, they saw Coach D in the distance, walking in the cemetery, a golf club on his shoulder, just like the day before. He stopped and leaned down and looked more closely at some bushes. Then he brought the binoculars around his neck up to his eyes and aimed them at the branches of the old and leafy trees. He didn't notice their approach.

"Has he been into birds for a long time?" Elizabeth reached out for Candy's arm, holding her back.

"I guess. I really don't know much about him off court." Candy sucked in her stomach when she saw Elizabeth looking at it. "Contrary to gossip."

They moved closer but Coach D, preoccupied with his quest, didn't see them. They were also partially obscured by a border of shrubs and a large oak tree. He tilted his head to one side, ear up, expectant, listening to a thin piping sound—*phoe-be, phoe-be*—over and over again. A sparrow-sized bird flew off the end of a dead branch in a tall maple the coach stood near, dive-bombed at an insect flying by, and returned to the branch, hiccuping *phoe-be* again. They watched as Coach D pulled an index card from his shirt pocket and made a note with a stubby pencil. A bird with deep red–tipped wings that looked as if they'd been dipped in candle wax and tail feathers that were capped in yellow scrabbled its way out of a bush and perched not five feet from him. About to call out a greeting, Candy felt Elizabeth tug her arm. Her aunt put her finger to her lips.

They stayed hidden as Coach D dropped to his hands and knees and rooted in the damp ground. They saw him hold up a worm, swing it like a pendulum at a robin that had flown to the ledge of a tombstone nearby, and then slurp it up in pantomime. He tossed it aside as the bird took flight.

Candy ignored Elizabeth's silent plea for silence after that. She didn't want to see him do something even weirder. "Hey Coach."

He jumped when he heard her voice, and then he looked sheepish. "Hi Golden. You been here long?"

"She's here, too."

Elizabeth came out from behind the oak and limped toward the coach.

"You've got to RICE that bruise, Elizabeth. It's like I told you—rest, ice, compression, elevation. You shouldn't be walking around on it. Let me take a look."

When Coach D leaned down to stare at Elizabeth's calf, she stepped back. "Let's just worry about Candy. Do you have a catchy acronym for her problem?"

"My guess for why you're hurt right now is that you're paying too much conscious attention to yourself. That throws your balance off."

"I'm hurt right now because you shanked your shot. You're lucky I have some consciousness left. If you'd hit it higher, I'd be in a vegetative state."

Candy interrupted. "So Coach, you had something you wanted to talk about?"

Coach D rested his fingertips against his temples, moving them slightly as if he were tuning in a radio station, and then he looked up as two of the red-winged yellow-tailed birds flew directly at each other—suicide bombers playing chicken. They passed safely, mere inches between them. "Folklore says that's a good sign. Those birds flying at each other. Especially if it's raining."

"It's not raining, Coach." Candy stuffed her hands into her pockets and extracted them as her waistband cut deeper into her middle.

"It will be soon enough. Listen, Golden, I wanted to explain. Why I left the team. And why you can't."

"You had your reasons. I have mine. Not that I'm saying I quit like you did. I'm just not playing for a moron like Morrisey—I have principles."

"Golden, if I'd stayed, it would have been worse for you. Really bad. Believe me, I wouldn't be your coach. I'd be the guy who people thought, well, you know," he waved vaguely at her torso, but his voice was direct. "I'm telling you, whatever they said about me and did to me, they would have done ten times worse to you. I'm not trying to be a martyr here, but they would have picked you apart if I'd stayed at All Saints."

"News flash, Coach—the vultures are circling anyway."

"Don't insult vultures." He reached for her arm, and then he stepped back, miming support instead. "I keep a basketball in the bushes there"—he pointed to a prickly thatch of shrubs next to a crumbling gravestone—"if you ever forget yours. If you ever need one. Golden, once you're back on court and shooting fifty percent and grabbing ten rebounds a game and winning a State title and getting a scholarship to the best places—I'm talking U Conn or Tennessee or Stanford—they'll forget about everything. Or they'll move on to some-body else. Of course, a lot depends on, you know, your condition." His voice wavered as he pointed again at her stomach, and this time he blushed.

"Oh God, forget the stupid baby. Quitting the team has nothing to do with the baby." As far as Candy was concerned, Alex couldn't get out of town soon enough so that she could come clean about this fake baby.

"Candy, will you listen to him? He doesn't want you to give up everything for him. He doesn't want you to give up *anything* for him. He's good with your playing next year for that other guy." Elizabeth turned to Coach D. "Tell her. Tell her again that you really want her to play for that other guy, for the moron."

"Golden, if you decide not to play, I mean after you decide what to do about your situation, it would have to be for a better reason than thinking Morrisey is a jerk, which he is." He looked at Eliza-beth—"She's one hundred percent right about that"—and then back at Candy. "But you can't use loyalty to me as your excuse. I reject that. I don't give you permission to use me as your reason. If you don't play it has to be about not playing for yourself. So, really, *why* aren't you playing next year? Is it just your condition? Or is it something else? Think about it, Golden. Can you tell me why?" A rumble of thunder punctuated his words and when a crack of lightning followed, he threw his golf club aside as if it were a live wire.

Just her condition? It was a baby. Never mind that it wasn't really. They thought it was. And listen to them—talking about basketball. Coach D had helped her when her mom died, but that was then. Right now, he did not have his priorities straight. She had quit because she was pissed—a decision or, she'd admit it, a reaction that was lit by anger. But now there was more to it than that. She was tired of being labeled. Like her mom had been for years: drunk and not taking care of her kid. Like Elizabeth was now: depressed, divorced, and wouldn't have a baby. Like Glo: devout and wearing clothes that matched. This is what people saw her as now: basketball star and teenage nympho with weird hair and cool T-shirts. And she wanted to be seen as more. She *was* more. It was just as well that none of them wanted to live with her. At least she didn't have to get up every day and face their misconceptions.

It began to rain with intent—the soaker that had been promised all morning. Coach D herded her and Elizabeth forward without actually touching them. "Come on. I have a place we can go to stay dry. There's something there I want to show you anyway." He wrangled them toward a large mausoleum. The one that Candy had stared at last night in the moonlight. Candy read the name MOONEY etched in chipped white marble above a corroded iron door. When a feather floated into her mouth and caused her to sputter and step back, Elizabeth's hand on her back steadied her.

Coach D smiled, but the line of his lips looked a little trembly. What had he been doing in Lovely since he'd run away from Detroit in June? Why was he hanging out at a cemetery every day? There had to be better places to practice golf. And why was he shoving his shoulder against the rusting mausoleum door until it scraped open against the crumbling cement threshold? Everybody else thought he was weird. Candy had always figured the weirdness was on the surface and didn't have much to do with the important things, the things that couldn't be seen. Now she wondered if everybody else was right. She laughed nervously and followed him tentatively, glad for Elizabeth's breath on her neck. Coach D pushed the door shut behind them with a clang and darkness dropped like a cloth. Candy felt him walk past her to the back corner, and then she heard a click and he pointed a flashlight at the ground.

She heard a sound in the corner. Something familiar. It was the motorized hum she'd heard faintly last night when she was sitting at center court staring at the cemetery. It was louder, but she recognized the buzz and whir. Coach D walked toward the sound, pointing his flashlight at it, and Candy saw a small generator. The air smelled bad but it felt good, as if it were broken in, softened with use. Something floated around her head and then she spat out another feather. What was going on? She slapped the basketball nervously palm to palm. The surface beneath her feet was spongy, and when she looked down at the gauze of light created by the flashlight, she saw that the stone floor was covered with a square of Astroturf propped up on one end on wood blocks so that the hole cut into it fit over a small cup. He'd made himself a putting green on the floor of a crypt. Is this what he wanted to show them? It wasn't all that strange, considering five minutes ago he pretended to eat a worm. She saw more golf clubs in the corner.

Coach D walked toward them, and she heard another click and then fluorescence squirted from a shop light strung on a hook in the ceiling of the stone room. She saw an urn on an altarlike slab against the back wall of the room. That must be a dead Mooney. A crack of lightning fissured through the stone walls and Candy jumped, then shivered. The recessed upper walls on either side of the mausoleum formed chest-high stone shelves. She saw a vase, a rusty crucifix, and a large mirror on the shelf to her right. That was odd. What she saw in the mirror's reflection was even odder: Two bronze-colored hens, sitting quietly, their throats rippling in swallowed clucks. One perched like a knob atop a bluish-green Flintstone-sized egg, too small to cover it adequately. The other rested on something also, but she covered it completely. Candy looked at Elizabeth, who stared the other way, at the hens not the reflection, but her mouth gaped, too.

"They're Cochin bantam hens, ladies. Very broody. They'll sit on anything. The mirror makes them think they're in a full hatch—that's good for their frames of mind. This one"—Coach D pointed to the hen that covered the contents of her nest—"is trying to hatch a Titleist golf ball. I kid you not. I set it up there while I was doing something else, and the next thing I knew, she was clamped on it. I can't get her off. She went for my eyes when I tried. But this one"—Coach D gently touched the brown feathers of the placid hen—"she's doing hero's work. Aren't you?" he questioned the hen, who stared at her reflection in the mirror across the way.

"What the hell are you talking about?" Elizabeth spoke before Candy could ask the same question. The beady-eyed birds stared at Candy's basketball.

"This egg. I'm talking about this egg." He pointed to the four-and-a-half-inch oval. When Candy reached out to touch it, the hen squawked and Coach D intercepted her hand. "Hands off, Golden. Do you know how important this egg is? I'm making birding history here. I'm hatching a baby condor. This is a condor egg. A California condor. They're almost extinct, you know." Coach D stood straighter as he said this, as if he were about to salute.

"Good God," Elizabeth muttered.

"I found it in a hollow log behind a grave site. They've got a captive breeding program out west, and they've lost track of most of the birds. It's not impossible that a few got completely lost and made it to Michigan. They're the largest birds in North America. The largest vultures. They're related to storks. They have ten-foot wingspans." He speeded up his park ranger recitation, heading off their unspoken disbelief. "They can fly fifty-five miles an hour. They're powerful. They could make it to Michigan. They've found condor fossils as far east and north as New York. It's possible. This egg's mother probably died right after she laid it—I bet she was exhausted from the cross-country trip or maybe it was too cold for her once she got here. I'm hatching it for her. A few of these birds full-grown can work together and drag a bloody grizzly bear a half mile." He spoke doggedly, reciting, as if he'd memorized the speech in preparation for this audience of doubters, as if he wished he could open his robe and invite them to touch his side.

"Grizzly bears? California condors? In Michigan? Earth to Coach D." Candy waved her hands in front of his face, and then continuing the balletic movement pointed at the urn. "And this place you're hanging out in? Those are dead people. Coach, you shouldn't even be in here." She thought he must not be serious.

Coach D shook his head. "I've studied this egg. I'm convinced. I had to do it here to have any chance at all—I couldn't move it far. In case the mother came back, though at this point it's clear she won't. And so what if I'm wrong? What difference would that make? But I've thought it through. This *is* a condor egg. It's been incubating since I got here in June. Almost sixty days. It will break out any time now. We'll see what you say when I've got a baby vulture in here screaming for meat. But listen, they don't kill anything—they only eat what's freshly dead. They group together. They don't compete. Different kinds eat different things. So, the condor, because it's so large, goes for internal organs. Then, medium-sized ones go for skin and tendons, and the smallest go for scraps and bones. It's all very efficient." He reached out toward the bantam and stroked the broody hen tenderly, tip to tail, his hand soothing unruffled feathers, murmuring encouragement, taking a break from his birds-of-prey tutorial. Candy looked at her aunt, ready to run out of the small space with her, but Elizabeth looked hypnotized.

Watching Coach D from behind, Elizabeth thought that she'd be able to pick him out in a crowd simply from his posture. His feet turned slightly inward, his shoulders drooped in a permanent slump, and his hands were usually in his pockets. He didn't gesture when he spoke. He used his hands to shoot a basketball or whack a golf ball or coddle an egg or pet a hen. He wasn't one to bother with inessential motion. She'd met him twenty-four hours ago, and she knew a lot about his habits already.

Habit could be contagious. When she moved out of their house, she noticed she'd brought along certain practices that she recognized as Leo's. The way he peeled a grapefruit as if it were an orange. The way he tied socks in a knot as he folded the laundry. The way he washed spinach, moving it back and forth three times in the sink, and drying it on a towel spread on the kitchen table, a portable fan blowing gently on it. When she'd first seen him do these things, she'd thought them silly, odd, and now she did them herself. What had she passed on to him? Did he think of her as he twisted a grocery bag into a plastic rope and then tied it into a loose knot so that it could be stored efficiently? Did he tear credit card solicitations into small bits so that nobody would steal his junk mail from the trash and entangle him in debt? Did he think of her as he cut the grass and shoveled the snow on a diagonal line?

"Darwin watched the condors from the *Beagle.*" The generator hummed as Coach D spoke.

"What?" Elizabeth wondered if he talked about birds during practice. How had his teams done so well? It couldn't be *only* because of Candy.

"Darwin—he studied the condor in South America. They're very heavy sleepers—hundreds of years ago they were captured alive while they slept. Hunters slipped nooses around their necks. Darwin watched them for half an hour straight and they never flapped their wings. They sail on air currents." Coach D took his hands from his pockets and spread his arms wide.

"That sounds nice. The sailing part, not the nooses." Elizabeth rubbed the back of her neck, imagining deep sleep.

The generator-lit dimness of the crypt felt as if it had burrowed through Candy's skin, leaving no boundary between the fetid air, the dead Mooney family that she didn't even know, the talk of nooses, and the hens sitting dumbly on any vaguely circular object placed under their butts. She pressed the basketball harder against her stomach. And then she bolted. The hefty, rusty, creaky iron door was no match for her determination to be anywhere else.

Once outside, she expelled a deep breath she hadn't known she'd been holding and sprinted to the Rec Center court. The rain had stopped for now. But the sky wasn't done with all the weather it held. The court had a large puddle on one end. She didn't care. She'd rather dribble through dog shit than be in that tomb. She set herself up outside the three-point line on the puddleless end and lofted shot after shot after shot, paying no attention to form or success, just heaving the ball up.

When she turned to grab a rebound that angled sharply right, she saw Elizabeth and Coach D walking toward the court. She sank five threes in a row while they murmured to each other on the sideline. In the quiet before each shot, she overheard fragments of their conversation. "At least you're here with her now." Coach D patted Elizabeth's arm awkwardly as he said that. "I mostly came because Glo promised to give me a car." Candy heard Elizabeth correct him. At least Elizabeth hadn't tried too hard to pass herself off as something other than what she was.

After a few more minutes, Coach D came out on the court and rebounded for her, feeding her from the baseline. Candy let him because he didn't say anything and she was tired. The humidity was thick—she felt as if she were playing in a dim sum basket. When she lifted her T-shirt and wiped her face, Coach D looked away.

After draining threes for ten more minutes, Candy faced off with Coach D, who'd moved to the top of the key, stuck a hand in her face, and challenged her to some one-on-one. She dribbled at him, crossed over, stepped back, and sank a three. Elizabeth sat on the damp grass on the sidelines. She hollered instructions every now and then and clapped at the good shots. Candy drove hard, working mostly her left hand, spinning and reversing, using her off arm and shoulder to create space, curious if she'd lost anything on this, her less dominant side. A few times she heard a low whistle from Elizabeth, once after a reverse layup that left the Coach swatting air and another time when she faded back, and went glass (or, more accurately at the rundown Lovely Rec Center, went splintered, weathered, wood backboard), banking a shot so cleanly from such an acute angle that Euclid would have scratched his head.

Elizabeth was on her feet by then. Coach D was stronger than Candy, and he moved nimbly for a big guy. Candy fell for his head fakes more than she should have—maybe it was defense, not offense, that she'd lost.

"Don't jump, Golden. You're leaving your feet too soon. Don't commit so quickly. Play with your chest on my left shoulder. The double would come from the right." Coach D head-faked again three plays later, but Candy didn't fall for it and stuffed the ball back at him. Elizabeth hooted from the sidelines and came on court to slap Candy on the back.

"How about doing something slower so I can play."

"Not a good idea. You shouldn't be putting weight on that." Coach D pointed at her leg.

"I shouldn't do a lot of things."

"And you should do a lot of others." Candy passed the ball hard at Elizabeth as her aunt talked to her coach. It bounced off Elizabeth's shoulder and ricocheted off the court. Coach D left to chase it down.

She should have thrown it at him instead. Drilled it at him. Right at his face. She couldn't believe Coach D was wasting his time on a stupid fucking bird. A stupid fucking *imaginary* bird. She didn't know what was in that egg, but it sure wasn't a vulture from California. He was like those stupid hens—attaching himself to the wrong thing. She'd been an idiot to defend him. A condor? He should have been in Detroit coaching the Ravens. And was Elizabeth actually buying that bird shit? Why had she stayed in there with him? The two of them together made Glo and even Anita Prokoff look good. At least Glo was predictable—she'd say her prayers, she'd complain about the way people dressed, but she wouldn't go pledge allegiance to some egg or take seriously a guy who did. She could count on Glo to be always like Glo. Glo wouldn't go off and do something strange with a bird.

She looked at her T-shirt, imagining her mom as one of the skeleton heads in the stands watching her play. She should know if her mom had liked the Dead. What other simple stuff didn't she know about her mom? If her mom were alive, she would support Candy's decision to quit the Ravens. Then again, if her mom were alive, she wouldn't be here in Lovely being asked to defend it. She wouldn't have spent so much time with Coach D in the gym in the first place. Anita Prokoff wouldn't have sniffed around. There wouldn't be any decision to defend.

Her mom's dying had started this whole thing. And almost nine months later, Candy thought that this—*quitting*—was the best way to keep the game as something she could count on for her future. She couldn't risk the game's letting her down the way they all had. If it did, she'd have nothing. Better to give it a break, a breather. If she left now, she could *choose* to come back when it would be strong enough to sustain her again.

Why aren't you playing? Coach D had asked. That was why. But she wouldn't tell him or any of the others. Nobody else need know what she held close. Look at him with those eggs. He'd told the truth, what he believed to be the truth, about them and what did he get? She and Elizabeth thought he was crazy. They didn't believe it. Important things should be carried alone. Don't tell anybody what really matters. Keep it to yourself. She shook her dreads, but slowly, more tired than pissed off.

And then Elizabeth was in her face again. "Candy, remember how we used to play Horse."

"That was a long time ago."

"I taught you how to play. Don't you remember?" Elizabeth wouldn't let it go.

Neither would Candy. "I remember everything. You're the one who forgot."

CHAPTER 16

*T*HE CADILLAC'S SEAT-POSITIONING system was NASA-like in its complexity. Roger pushed a button, lifting himself higher. He pushed it another way and moved himself closer to the steering wheel. Another button, and his pelvis was tilted up and back. Finally, one last control, temperature—his rear end made cooler or warmer—his pleasure at his command.

Glo watched the millimeter-by-millimeter adjustments that raised him high enough to see out the windshield. He massaged the steering wheel, stroked the dashboard, and rubbed the empty space between himself and Glo. She examined his hands as he did so. His fingers were thick, his nails cut square, corners sharp. His veins were plump, as if they'd been pumped full of air.

"Gloria, this is an amazing automobile."

"It was my husband's."

"I hope Elizabeth appreciates such a generous gift."

"She doesn't think much of the hot dog."

"She and I agree again." Roger touched the dashboard and with a digital click, the radio surround-sounded them and suddenly they were riding down the road taking it easy with the Eagles. He stretched in his seat, enjoying the smooth rub of leather on his shoulders, the instant response of the steering wheel to his fingertips. "Elizabeth is very strong for a girl—I wouldn't admit this to her, but she almost beat me last night in the weight room. She's too angry, though. In fairness, I have that effect on certain ladies."

"Her life is lonely. I wish she'd go to church."

"Was your husband devout?"

The sun temporarily broke through the clouds, which were sure to rain on them soon. Glo looked out the window as they passed a barn that was weathered to gray. A dog slept in front of it, absorbing the unexpected and eroding shadow of noon's approach. "He was not."

"Neither was my ex-wife. You can imagine. You saw her back there."

Glo clarified, feeling disloyal. "I never said Stan was anything like that." But then she felt she owed Roger, too. "Was Mary always that way?"

"Nobody is ever *always* that way. But I met her when I drank, so my judgment was not keen." Roger looked straight ahead, though the road that Monday midmorning was empty.

"You drank?"

"I stopped ten years ago. And then I converted."

Glo thought she would like to take his hand to show her support, to congratulate him on his sobriety and his conversion, but he gripped the padded steering wheel at ten and two. "Was it difficult?"

"What? The stopping? Or the converting?" Roger accelerated and passed a panel truck that struggled on the slight upgrade. "The drinking part *still is* difficult—the temptation. I'm a compulsive person. I know this about myself. But the conversion, truly that's not even the right word. It wasn't a conversion because I was nothing, religion-wise, and then I was Catholic. So I gained. It's not difficult to gain something good. I wish more people realized that. But for a long time with sobriety it felt as if I were only losing. There were benefits to it, but I compared them to the benefits of drink. And the comparing? It doesn't help anything. It's still not easy. That's why I work out and volunteer to take care of things like the Guadalupe shrine and have two jobs. I need to be occupied and active. I need to be involved."

"Candy's mother drank. I prayed for years that she'd stop."

"Did she?"

"Yes, but I don't think my prayers had much to do with it. We sent her to Hazelden for a month. And then she continued with AA. The program worked very well for her."

That had been five years ago. Glo had arranged the intervention that propelled Melissa into rehab. She and Stan had driven to Detroit from Chicago to be part of it. She'd talked to Candy about it before-hand and got the names of her mother's sober friends—there were three—who also came. At the last minute, Glo had called Melissa's boss and he had come, too. Her niece was going to lose her job either way, and Glo thought there was a better chance if more people were present.

They'd confronted Melissa in her own living room after she got off work. Candy, twelve, had been there. The Hazelden advisor said that could work or backfire, that somebody who knew both the mother and daughter well should decide what would be best for

Candy and what would most likely guarantee success in the intervention. Success? Defined as getting Melissa to agree willingly to walk out the door with Glo and fly to Minnesota.

Arranging it all from Chicago, Glo had called Elizabeth, who had moved to the city from Detroit just a month earlier. "Elizabeth? Melissa was arrested again yesterday. They've taken away her license. She needs to be in a rehabilitation hospital. We need to go to Detroit and confront your sister."

"Half sister."

"Stan and I are driving in tomorrow morning. I'm making all the arrangements for an intervention. If we're successful, I'll fly with her to Hazelden. We're doing it when Melissa gets home from work tomorrow evening. I'm not sure if Candy should be there. I don't want to harm her any more than she's been harmed. You know the girl best. I need your advice."

"Mel is defensive about how much she's messed up with Candy, and that could make her mad, instead of agreeable. But as far as harming Candy, it's not as if she hasn't seen and heard it all from Melissa."

"That sounds like a 'yes' on the Candy question. So I've got Melissa's three friends who don't drink, and her boss said he'd come, and Candy, and Stan, and me, and you. Will you drive in with Stan and me? Or would you rather go alone?"

"Me? I'm not going."

"Of course you are. After Candy, you'll be the most important person there. We need to face Melissa directly and tell her what she's done to us and how she has let us down and how we love her and want her to get sober. I'm reading from some literature the hospital sent me, by the way."

"I left her and Detroit one month ago. One month, Glo. She

knows how she's let me down. Even drunk, she can remember that far back. I'll go to the next intervention we do for her. I promise."

"What do you mean, 'the next intervention'? There will be no next anything."

"Of course there will be. I've watched Melissa do this for eighteen years now. You don't actually think she's going to stop drinking because a few people gather around and tell her she's hurt their feelings?"

But she had. Glo had flown to Minnesota with Melissa and handed her off to Hazelden staff and then flown back to Detroit the next morning. Stan, retired, had stayed with Candy that month while Glo went back to Chicago and work, and Melissa made her first guided steps toward sobriety. Glo took the train in on weekends and helped with cooking and cleaning, and Stan drove Candy to school and basketball practice during the week. After Melissa had been at Hazelden for a while, they'd allowed her to talk to Candy. Glo had listened, discreetly, to Candy's end of the conversation. She couldn't see her grandniece's face during that call, but she heard a half note of hope climbing the wall of wariness in Candy's voice. After the call, the girl tucked herself into her bed, limbs folding awkwardly like a heron returning from flight.

Glo had wanted to go to Candy after that first phone call. She'd gathered her rosary and prayerbook, but Stan had held her back. "Leave her be for now, Glo. Pray for her quietly on your own. She knows we're here." And he'd been right. Candy emerged from her bed an hour later and did her homework at the kitchen table while Stan read the paper and Glo made dinner, and the next time Melissa called, Candy had been less wary. And the next time even less than that, until the wariness became the note that interrupted the hope, and the hope became the wall she eagerly scaled.

Glo hadn't thought about all that in a long time and talking to Roger about it, she was reminded of a mission accomplished, of a mother and daughter saved. "I think her daughter was the biggest part of the reason she finally sobered up." She turned to Roger as they drove past a cemetery.

"And now the daughter is pregnant. Frankly, Gloria, these young girls having babies? Where are their morals? Even drunk, I had morals."

Glo was glad to be speaking honestly and less formally with Roger. "I can't think about the baby right now. It's too much. What will she do with it? She'll have to give it up for adoption. She's too young. How will she play ball if she's pregnant? She'll have to sit out this year and play next year. Elizabeth knows about that sort of thing. She'll have to work it out. Someday when Candy is married she can have another baby and raise it." Glo asked and answered her own questions, and then posed two she needed help with. "Do you have children, Roger? Will you marry again?"

"I see myself as a leader, not a father. As to marriage, that's not up to me, I'm afraid. Rome doesn't hand out annulments like penance. I need an ex-wife who will agree that the marriage didn't exist. Mary says she won't insult our years together by swearing they never were."

"But this morning, at Granny's? I mean she obviously doesn't care for you."

"We had a good year or two in the beginning. We loved each other back then—at least while we were in a bar at midnight drinking bourbon we did. What about your husband? Did you have a good marriage?"

Glo stared out her window again. She didn't want to talk about

Stan with him. She saw a sign on the shoulder of the road: CROSS IN THE WOODS—NEXT EXIT. "Roger, let's go there."

"Where?"

"The Cross in the Woods. Take the next exit."

"What about your nieces? Aren't you going with them? Isn't that the whole point of your trip?"

The point of the trip? Twenty-four hours ago the point had been to keep Candy at the Prokoffs' house and on the basketball court and to make amends for the wrong she'd done Stan. The trip she'd packed and planned for so carefully had become something much different. The point had changed. Glo put her hand on Roger's arm. "They'll forgive me."

"I haven't been to the Cross in more than a year. I could do a little research for the Guadalupe shrine." He considered it, but then looked at his watch, and pointed at the dashboard clock, its razor-thin green segments glowing with the news that it was too late. "I'm sorry, Gloria, but my paycheck. I need the money today. The Guadalupe meeting is at two. We don't have time to do it all."

"I have plenty of money. We won't stay long."

The Cross in the Woods was immense, huge, massive, large-scale. Some might even say monstrous. It had side shrines of minor saints and religious figures—Our Lady of the Highway, St. Peregrine (the cancer saint), Blessed Kateri Tekakwitha, and St. Francis of Assisi. And it had the way of the cross—fourteen stations of prayer, depicting Jesus' suffering—scattered through the grounds like bread crumbs for those who'd lost the way. The Cross in the Woods also had a gift shop, which was home to a "unique doll museum" that displayed what was believed to be the largest collection of dolls, more than 525, dressed in the "garb of religious orders of women who worked for the Lord in our country." The shrine had a chapel, a family center, an outdoor church, and an indoor church, as well as its own staff. The Cross in the Woods also had dozens of iron-slotted collection boxes waiting for the clank of a visitor's alms, and of course ample parking.

Glo knew all these things about the Cross in the Woods because she'd studied the brochure she'd been handed by a beatific young girl in an iridescent orange plastic vest who waved her onto the grounds from the entrance on M-68, after commenting on their "nifty" car. She knew the rest of it from looking. Even on a humid, dreary, murky morning, the Cross in the Woods radiated organized, well-endowed, smoothly running splendor.

When Roger and Glo pulled into the lot, it was filling with tour buses and minivans and SUVs and run-of-the-mill Chevys and Fords and Chryslers. People who came to the Cross in the Woods bought American. It had started to rain, but groups of boisterous agile teens from summer youth camps still hopped off some of the buses. Clusters of senior citizens stepped gingerly off others, grasping air as they searched for a helping hand below and then, on solid ground, dodging raindrops as if their synthetic sweatsuits were made of the finest cashmere.

Roger took notes about it all, using his briefcase as a lap desk. He'd have to be a saint not to be jealous. "I'm sure your shrine will be good, too, Roger."

He curled the left side of his upper lip. "I forgot there was such excess here."

Glo checked the brochure and then her watch. "There's an eleven o'clock Mass. Shall we?"

Roger snapped his briefcase shut and reached for the umbrella in the backseat. "We shall, Gloria. Come. We will raise our voices to the

Lord." He held the umbrella high, but its ribs still brushed the crown of Glo's head. He tucked his briefcase under his armpit. He took her hand. Glo bowed her head and bent her knees as, together, they entered the church.

The priest's voice was stentorian as he intoned the postcommunion prayer. Glo thought such a voice was wasted on the tourists surrounding her. These were laissez-faire Catholics, or perhaps not even Catholic at all. She could sense it from their fidgeting, could see it in their dress—T-shirts and sandals, bright Hawaiian shirts matched with odd-colored shorts—they did not comport themselves as if they were someplace sacred. She would have preferred to be in a skirt and pumps herself, but she excused herself since she was traveling, ignoring the obvious—the others were, too.

The church was modern. Its interior walls were brick and the pews and huge beams that held up the vaulted roof were made of gleaming cherrywood. The brick pillars that rose to the peaked heights of the unadorned church framed panoramic windows and were garnished with gilded letters that stated the obvious: ALLELUIA and HE IS RISEN. The great panes of glass, Windexed to high shine even with the rain, looked out on the eponymous crucifix—a seven-ton bronze-figured Jesus nailed to a fifty-five-foot Oregon-redwood cross—and the benches making up the amphitheater-like bowl that faced it outside. On more temperate days, Mass was celebrated outdoors. On that drizzly Monday morning, the monumental panes were impotent, unable to gather light so diffuse.

At St. Viator in Chicago, the small windows cut into the stone walls up high were stained with dark-colored glass, so that whether gloomy or sunny outside, inside little more than dim murk from the windows and forty watts (which was at least twenty watts too few) from the gilt-edged filigreed chandeliers fell on stone statues of saints. Form met function and rested on the heavy bowed heads of the parishioners. But these new churches? Shadows did not become them.

Kneeling, nose between her steepled fingers, Glo looked up from her silent prayer. The little boy in the pew in front of her was old enough to sit quietly and fold his hands in supplication, but instead he pushed a yellow plastic truck along the pew, making *vroom vroom vroom* noises while his mother smiled down at him and his father raised a camera and took a photo of the giant cross outside, looming gloomy in the rain.

Roger was suitably reverent. He knelt next to her, his thumb and forefinger pinching the bridge of his nose, head bowed, eyes closed. He smelled of tobacco and smoke. She breathed in deeply, surreptitiously, separating the sharp-cut edge of tobacco, which she liked, from the secondhand smell of smoke. As she watched, he leaned back in the pew and removed his notebook from his briefcase, adding to the list of things he needed at the Guadalupe shrine. Glo read a few: pretty girls as ushers, multicolored devotional candles, communion wine. Roger's covetous notes and smoky exhalations were reminders of his shortcomings, but look at what he'd done—sobered up, converted, sought an annulment. On balance, Glo judged him to be a very good man.

"The Mass is ended, let us go in peace to love and serve the Lord." The priest opened his arms to the visiting congregation, adding that he welcomed them to the shrine, and that he and other shrine staff would be very glad to answer any questions they might have as they toured the grounds. Glo looked out at the rain through the window behind him. Only a few people milled about the giant crucifix or sat on the outdoor pews in front of it.

Roger insisted on holding the umbrella again as they left the church, and again Glo stooped to accommodate his chivalry. She thought back to the beginning of this trip. She never would have expected to be alone with a man like this (or a man like anything) when she left Chicago two days ago. Roger spoke, and she bowed her head to listen; his breath in her ear was welcome, warm—his voice a whisper. "We'll pay our respects at the Cross, and then I'll drive you back to Lovely by the scenic route." She felt his heart beat. Or maybe it was her own. They were that close. He twirled the umbrella when he was finished speaking and raindrops exploded like sparks from the tips of its ribs.

The rain that morning went from mizzle to drizzle to downpour and back again, and Glo and Roger shared the umbrella the whole time. After visiting Tekakwitha and Peregrine and a half dozen stations of the cross, they sat in the first row of the outdoor church, at the base of the giant crucifix. By now the rain had stopped, and Roger made a note about a display of votive candles that flickered, protected by a green awning emblazoned with a yellow banner proclaiming, SUGGESTED DONATION, $2. Glo, seeing him so occupied, and thinking movement might be the answer to the sciatic string of pain that, lubricated by the damp day, traveled in a tangle from her lower back to her right knee, walked behind the Cross.

The backside was not as carefully tended as the front was. It had bare dirt patches and crabgrass and a decrepit cyclone fence that leaned in and out at various points, marking a wavering boundary to the shrine's land. It also had dozens of handmade devotions, most of them in the shape of a cross, fashioned from odd bits and pieces that people must have dug out of their backpacks or handbags.

Among the many tributes, Glo saw red licorice sticks bisecting each other and tamped into the dirt; hot pink bubble gum stretched on the post of the cyclone fence, another cross shape, holy in form if not content; white stones gathered and placed in the shape of a heart with more cross-shaped licorice waxy red in its middle; perpendicular palm fronds laced through the aluminum thread of the fence; two drinking straws held together with a butterfly hair clip; and a series of small twigs Band-Aided together and propped against a shrub.

Objectively speaking, these were leftover, secondhand devotions. But that wasn't the feeling they engendered. At this backside of the shrine, out of pristine public view, people had also left elaborate home-spun memorials to their beloved dead. Glo counted a dozen such tributes in the form of bouquets of carnations dyed too brightly and placed next to holy cards weighted against weather with a stone, the brief explanation for the memorial printed on them: *Dear son, killed in an auto accident; Devoted mother, please rest in peace; Darling Annie, you were too perfect for this world.* That last note was placed next to a picture of a smiling toddler, who, Glo imagined, may well have been.

Glo thought about how she'd judged these shrine visitors as she'd sat in church a half hour earlier, and now she felt ashamed of it and humbled by these sugary confections and cheap flowers. This was heartfelt homage, no matter what these people wore or whether their children played with trucks during Mass. In that moment, Glo had a glimpse of the potent mix of religious-tinged nostalgia, loneliness, and loyalty that caused people to worship in ways so different from her own. She thought of Stan and his scrapbooks of Chicago memorabilia. He would have understood these homemade devotions. She should have brought him here.

These past few days, surrounded by all these people—Elizabeth, Candy, Roger, Hillary, Alex, that coach—who had made mistakes right and left, she saw herself more clearly. She'd been too quick to condemn others and commend herself. She was no great bargain. She'd made a mess of her marriage—a secret mess, a private one, but a mess nonetheless. She thought of Roger and his wife and their public disputes. Roger, rising above it, or trying to, in his own fashion, with his sobriety and his two jobs and his homemade shrine and his struggles for an annulment. She admired that.

A crow cawed and landed a few feet from her, pecking at and picking apart an aluminum-foil gum wrapper that bound two twigs in the shape of a cross. Another crow sailed overhead, mimicking the shrill beep of an alarm clock as it flew. Roger came around back and joined her just then, stamping his foot and running toward the pecking bird, shooing it away from the crucifix twigs. It flapped up in a flutter, and followed the electronic call of its friend.

So Roger must feel it also. Must feel the need to help protect this holy homespun place. Or maybe it was something else he felt. Because there in the mist, after staring at a mini-shrine to a sixteen-year-old girl killed by a drunk driver, Roger put down his briefcase and looked up at Glo. When he rose on his tiptoes, placed his hands on her shoulders, and pulled her toward him, she didn't pull away. When he kissed her, she allowed that, too. Glo was tentative, conscious of the public place they occupied, though they were alone in it, and the irony of remembering Stan one moment and kissing another man the next. She'd come to the Cross in the Woods to ask forgiveness for all the ways she'd failed her husband. But this was something Stan would understand.

This? At least she'd never disappointed Stan in this. She missed this. She moved closer to Roger. He moved closer to her. His hands came off her shoulders, moved down her back, and pressed her to him. Her hands, eager for all of him, pressed back. He called her *"mi señorita linda."* She felt as if they could, as if they should, inhabit each other. Her skin and bone felt permeable as feeling flowed unimpeded.

Her breath was short. Her pleasure long. It began to rain again, but they didn't pull apart.

Then the crow. Again. It swooped near, almost skimming Glo's head. She and Roger drew apart and looked up at the pitch-black bird. Beak, feathers, feet—all black. Perhaps it was the one that Roger had shooed away moments before. Another just like it flew toward it in the light rain. Their wedge-shaped tails cut a wake in the saturated sky. One carried something shiny, and Glo looked behind Roger, worried that the birds had desecrated some naïve devotion and that they'd collide head on. But they hadn't and they didn't. The birds' staccato glottal caws merged into a solitary chord and then they disappeared from view.

As long as there are girls, boys, men, women, as long as lips and hands and legs meet lips and hands and legs, as long as there are physiology and pheromones, as long as there are need and desire, as long as there is simple touch, there will be sex or love, biology or destiny. As long as there are cars, large or small, parked on roads less traveled, sex or love will sometimes happen there.

Thirty minutes after leaving the Cross in the Woods, Roger drove the Cadillac slowly down an old logging road that led nowhere anymore. He and Glo sat close together in the front seat, their hips colliding as he steered clear of the worst ruts. Her left hand was on his thigh. His right hand massaged the small of her back. When he stopped and turned off the ignition, they faced each other.

The Cadillac, out of traffic, offered sanctuary. He asked if he could kiss her again, and she answered by kissing him. The sweep of desire Glo felt for Roger eclipsed all else. It blocked all the reasons not to take what she felt skin deep to even further depths. He pressed her closer.

"Gloria? Are you certain about this?"

She kissed him again.

"Gloria," he said again, his hands roaming across her back, her shoulders, her face, his touch insistent, "a woman such as yourself—you must be certain."

She wondered if his nicotine could seep through her skin. She felt potent. She traced her finger along a prominent vein that rivered its way along Roger's right arm. Cold blue, it looked as if it would burst with the pressure of her touch, but it was warm and pliant. *Certain?* He was divorced. They were not married. They were in a car in the middle of the day. She remembered the brush of Darcy's tail on her leg two weeks ago. She needed more than that. Of *that* she was certain. She kissed him again and felt intoxicated, her head swimming with all she'd missed since Stan died. They moved to the backseat. Glo felt a welcome wobbliness. She was ready for time number 417.

No. That was wrong. She pulled away from Roger momentarily, thinking of Stan. But Roger reached for her and his lips pressed against hers and she felt such liquid pleasure that she wanted to kiss him for hours. Losing track of time, she wondered if she already had. He removed his shirt and helped her out of her blouse and sweater, undoing her buttons easily. She shrugged her clothes off her shoulders. She tried to catch her breath, which raced ahead of her, and breathe in rhythm with him. He said *"Tengo hambre por tu"* and then he kissed her and laughed at his own mangled Spanish. Glo laughed, too.

Though they'd been ungainly under the umbrella, they dovetailed in the backseat of the car. They undressed, eagerly, giddily. She rubbed his chest and then he put his head to her breasts. The close quarters left no room for embarrassment and self-consciousness. Glo was struck by the surprise of their bodies unclothed. He had a farmer's tan—white and brown bisected biceps. His torso was compact. His legs too short. Varicose veins bulged on the hollowed under-side of her left knee. Her skin was everywhere slack. He was divorced. They were not married.

None of that mattered. Body alive, vision obscured, jolts of sheer feeling enlivening her limbs, Glo thought to herself that this was fine. This wouldn't count.

CHAPTER 17

"So your coach? That egg he's hatching? He really is odd, isn't he?" Elizabeth tightened the towel full of ice, which she'd wrapped around her calf again, and crammed a pillow under her leg.

"I don't have a coach. Don't need one. And you looked like you were into it back there in that henhouse-slash-tomb."

Elizabeth and Candy were back at the Mar-Jo, on one of the beds together. Candy pounded her thigh with her fist to the beat of some percussive music she'd found on the clock radio on the nightstand next to her. She jabbed the air on the downbeat. Later that afternoon, when Glo returned from her errand with Roger, they'd go to the shrine meeting so Candy could practice her role as Virgin Mother-to-be. Meanwhile, they waited for Alex and Hillary to bring over a pregnancy test so that Candy could verify that she was perfect for the part.

Elizabeth leaned over Candy and lowered the volume, bobbing

and weaving so that she wouldn't turn into her niece's punching bag. "Coach D is right about your defense. Your center of gravity needs to be lower. Keep your feet moving. Quit looking around so much. More feet, less arms. You got burned more than you should have. You can't fall for those head fakes during a game."

Candy cranked the volume and announced over it, "Hello? Are you listening? No coach. No games."

"So are you hungry? How do you feel? Queasy still?" Elizabeth adjusted the volume to a compromise level and continued their habit of off-kilter conversations.

"I'm starving, but otherwise I feel decent. Considering, I mean. It helps to have Alex around. We'll both be fine. I just have to figure out what to do. We're young, you know—Alex and I. And it's not easy to be a mom when you're young." Candy continued to jab the air and punch her thigh to the beat while she said what she figured were the right things, but she might as well have been talking about a haircut or makeup, she was so nonchalant. She stopped punching and added, "You know, my mom never even considered having an abortion. That was something I thought about when I was twelve and my mom was drinking and you left Detroit and there was nobody around for me most days. I thought it meant that however shitty my life was, I was really supposed to be born. Because when you think of it, my mom wasn't married, she was pretty young, and she only had you around for help. It really would have been logical for her to not have me. Just like it is for me or Alex. Isn't it sort of ironic, Elizabeth? Here you are again. Isn't it ironic that I have you around, *for this.*"

Elizabeth ignored her niece's sarcasm. "So you and your mom talked about that stuff? She told you she never thought about having an abortion?"

"She wanted me from the instant she knew she was pregnant."

Candy was sure. "But she wouldn't hold it against me if I made a different choice. My mom wasn't like that."

"You're right. She wasn't like that at all." Elizabeth remembered Melissa's change of heart at the Michigan State Fair. She was surprised her sister hadn't told Candy the whole truth. Maybe she should have. If Candy knew her mom had had second thoughts about her pregnancy, she might feel more comfortable having second thoughts of her own. Not that Elizabeth wanted the girl to have the baby. She didn't. But even more than that, she didn't want Candy to feel forced not to have it. If she told Candy about that day at the Michigan State Fair, her niece would know something else, too. She'd know that Elizabeth was the one who had urged Melissa to think twice and then some. That she had been a big part of Candy's life right from the start. "Actually, when your mom was pregnant . . ."

Candy spoke at the same time, "Coach D has gone to a lot of trouble for that stupid egg."

Elizabeth thought of Coach D in the dim stone mausoleum, coddling his egg, protecting something he imagined to be an endangered species, while she was about to pull another thread from her niece's skimpy security blanket just to make herself look good. Not even good, just less bad. Melissa had sobered up and cared for Candy. Her sister hadn't needed to feel regret for all the wrong she'd done. Melissa had asked for forgiveness. It was Elizabeth who hadn't given it. It was Elizabeth who should feel regret. Sitting in the Mar-Jo with Candy, she did.

"I screwed up with your mom. I wish I could change that."

"Too late. You can't." Candy pumped up the volume and music crashed through the room, obliterating anything else they might have said.

"Couldn't you go sit there?" Elizabeth pointed at a wobbly

straight-backed chair. "Or there?" She pointed at the other bed, which was neatly made and covered with Glo's things laid out in orderly fashion (the Mar-Jo was short on dresser drawers). There were Glo's prayer materials, a nightgown folded in a perfect square, a pair of beige pants, a bra and a pair of white underwear folded neatly and tucked under them, almost out of view, and a light blue blouse. As Elizabeth shifted her weight, chasing comfort, the hollow headboard knocked against the wall, and Candy sagged toward her. "Come on, Candy. Turn the radio off. My head hurts. And go sit over there on Glo's bed. My leg hurts, too. It's bad enough we have to sleep together. Give me some space when we're awake. Just push Glo's stuff aside."

Candy had changed out of her sweaty Dead T-shirt. Her new T-shirt was bright red, tight, cut off at her midriff, and read HELLRAISER in black block letters. She scratched her stomach as she looked at Glo's clothes. "I will not. She's careful with her stuff. You should show her more respect."

"How much respect does she show us? Putting us up in this pit."

The only defense against the offensive Mar-Jo Motel room was sleep or absence. The room was large enough so that it didn't feel crowded by the two saggy-mattressed double beds it held, but the space only emphasized how empty it was of anything pleasant. The beds faced a cinder-block wall, the porous gray cement painted white. The carpet was flat-napped, tarnished, and gold-flecked with an unintentional tinge of cigarette ash, muddy shoes, and spilled drinks. The only window in the room was small and faced the parking lot. It was covered with a thin, red-white-and-blue-striped cotton curtain. One wobbly lamp teetered on the nightstand between the two beds. The lampshade had a cigarette burn and when Elizabeth twisted it so the burned spot faced the wall, it spun wildly—the bolt on top was missing—and the burned spot faced her again.

The red-and-blue polyester bedspreads were faded, the quilted tracks of fluff between the stripes had gone flat many Mar-Jo customers ago. The bed frames squiggled and squeaked every time they sat on them or when one of them rolled over at night. It was surprisingly quiet with both of them on the bed that afternoon. Elizabeth looked down at Candy. No wonder it was still—the girl had fallen asleep, her face free of the scorn or disinterest she displayed like a merit badge during most waking hours.

Candy had been young, maybe seven, the last time Elizabeth watched her sleep. Elizabeth helped Melissa move that day. Her sister had been evicted, again, her landlord fed up with her excuses about the rent. It was her fifth such move in as many years. Each time, Melissa said it was for the best, that she and Candy needed a change of scenery, a better school district, an easier commute, but Elizabeth knew better. By that time Candy must have, too.

Those were the years when Elizabeth had come to understand that nothing she did or said would make her sister sober up. That particular moving day, Melissa hadn't had a drink in two weeks, and she'd sworn to Elizabeth that this time she'd quit for good. That she really meant it. That she didn't need AA or anybody else's help like all the other drunks did. That she was made of stiffer stuff. Elizabeth didn't believe it for a minute, but at that time she hadn't yet discounted the *possibility* that Melissa might stay sober. So she just said, *good luck* and *I hope so* and *are you sure you don't want to go to a meeting?* and promised to help on moving day.

Melissa worked hard preparing for that move. She found an apartment that was nicer than her previous place. It was in the same school district so that Candy didn't have to transfer again. During the hours when she typically would have been at a bar or drinking alone at home in preparation to go out and drink yet more with others, Melissa wrapped vases in sweaters and placed them between pillows that she stuffed in boxes—creating a nest for her few fragile possessions, trying to buffer them through the upheaval. She'd placed some of her shabbier furniture in the alley for the regular trash pickup, including the battered, flattened futon that Candy had slept on for years.

In the futon's place, Melissa had bought Candy a bed. A bed in a box for $89.99 and all you needed to put it together was a hammer and a screwdriver. A loft-bed. An escape on high. Something every seven-year-old dreamed of. Elizabeth remembered how excited her sister had been about the surprise for Candy.

"Will you stay and help me out a while longer, Elizabeth?" Melissa asked near the end of the moving day when she and Elizabeth and the two teenaged dropouts she hired for fifty dollars each had finally finished bringing everything into the new apartment. "I thought we'd be done sooner, and I want to go to Kmart and pick up new sheets for the loft. After that, I'll swing by school and bring Candy home. If you could put the bed together while I'm gone, it would be the perfect surprise for her. The guy at the store said it's a half-hour job. Candy hated that old futon. I want everything to be different at this new place." Melissa checked her watch. "It's one-thirty. I'll be back with her by three." Elizabeth, tired from the move they'd begun at seven that morning and not handy at all, said yes, of course she'd put the bed together. It was a sweet thing for Melissa to have done for her girl. When her sister left, Elizabeth opened the box.

Three hours later, crying in frustration at not being able to get it together after all, Elizabeth kicked the box the bed had come in. EASY-TO-PUT-TOGETHER LOFT BED it proclaimed. Liars. The directions were in German or Danish or some other guttural language that looked cruel in print. Smudgy diagrams that had arrows and numbers, which monolinguists like her were expected to follow, accompanied the foreign instructions. She stared again at the line drawing of a corner she was trying to square. She couldn't do it. She sat cross-legged. Her head felt heavy as a bowling ball.

She looked at her watch. Melissa and Candy should have been home more than an hour ago. She heard a door open, and then silence followed by a timid, "Hello . . ."

"In here," Elizabeth called, afraid to disrupt the fragile mess she'd created on the outside chance she'd done something right.

Candy appeared at the doorway, her face a storm, her hair tangled, and her shoes untied.

"Where's your mom?"

Candy shrugged.

"But she went to pick you up."

"I couldn't remember for sure where this new apartment was. I've been walking home looking for it. I knocked on four other people's doors. I'm only seven." Candy shook her head, too young for this truth. She noticed the box, the tools, the lumber. "What's that?"

"It's a new bed. It's for you. Your mom wanted it to be a surprise. She's buying you new sheets—that's where she is now. She must have run into traffic. I'm putting this together. Look at the picture. It's going to be great."

Candy stared blankly at the unconnected pieces strewn about the floor, and then closely at the picture on the box. "So I'll have to climb a ladder to go to sleep?"

Elizabeth abandoned her false cheer—her niece deserved better. "Let's forget the stupid bed. I've got a basketball in my car. We'll go shoot somewhere." Elizabeth struggled to her feet, pushing aside the tools and bolts and pieces of stubborn wood. When she reached out to put her arm around Candy's shoulders, her niece crouched to tie her shoe.

When Melissa came home that night—at two in the morning—Elizabeth and Candy were asleep on opposite ends of the couch. Melissa shook Elizabeth awake and pointed at the loft leg that propped open the door to Candy's new bedroom. Her rebuke was a whispered hiss, "I ask you to do one thing for my kid."

Elizabeth, knowing better than to try to defend herself against her sister's drunken rant, in whatever volume it was delivered, rolled over and faced the back of the couch, first draping a leg over Candy on the other end, sensing that her niece was also awake, and wanting to remind her she wouldn't leave. Melissa stumbled to the kitchen where she knocked over something and then broke something else. Candy coiled herself tighter with the thud and shatter. Elizabeth stayed awake for another hour, until she heard the steady wheeze of Candy's sleep and the silence in the kitchen that told her Melissa had passed out drunk again.

Elizabeth left the next morning after she gave Candy breakfast and pointed her out the door to school. She didn't bother to wake Melissa to tell her that she couldn't keep doing it. Drinking, that is. Deserting her kid, that is. Because the truth was, Melissa could. And Melissa would. And for a long time, Melissa did.

Ten years later, Candy, asleep next to Elizabeth on the saggy Mar-Jo mattress, her fraying twists of hair marking the dingy pillowcase like ruts in an unpaved road, looked like what she'd been back then—a tender-headed young girl—instead of a problem uncoiling wildly only to twist into trouble again. Elizabeth got off the bed carefully so as not to wake her. She paced. She looked out the window. She looked at her watch. Noon. Where was Glo? And how much longer could she sit still in this dingy room and do nothing? Not one more minute. Elizabeth shook Candy's shoulder. "Wake up."

"What?"

"Let's go see if Alex and Hillary are back yet. You and Alex have to take those pregnancy tests."

"You go. I'm tired." Candy pulled the pillow over her head.

"Come on, please? I don't like talking to anybody I don't really know well unless I absolutely have to." Elizabeth lifted the pillow and pulled Candy's hair.

"Ouch. Quit it. Hey, Elizabeth, do you have *any* friends in L.A.?"

"Not yet."

"Here's a clue. The not-talking thing? That could be the problem." But Candy got out of bed and grabbed her basketball, waking up as she thought of the sleight-of-hand challenge ahead. This was it. Her chance to help Alex. She walked out the door, Elizabeth at her heels.

Candy dribbled backward, watching Elizabeth as they walked to Alex's room at the other end of the Mar-Jo. If she were going to pull this off, she had to study her opponent. She had to know her weaknesses, her strengths. Elizabeth had a messed-up shoulder, a disgusting bruise, and she was old. Physically, she was no match. But this wasn't only about strength, this was also about mental acuity, and her aunt was not a total dumb-ass. Candy crouched, dribbling short and hard, facing Elizabeth, going backward, keeping a beat. Her broken Teva strap flapped, but Candy was surefooted, even on cracked cement. Backward, forward, sideways, blindfolded, fingers tied together, she would not falter or miss a beat. The knock of the ball lengthened to a chime as Candy stood from her crouch and dribbled from her full height. Now and then, Elizabeth reached in to swat the ball away, but Candy protected it easily. They didn't notice Alex and Hillary sitting by the pool until Alex yelled hello.

"That's a nice picture," Elizabeth said.

Candy took a look. "Depends what you see."

"I see a mother and a daughter coming together during a hard time."

"And I see a mom forcing her daughter to make the biggest mistake of her life."

"Come on, Candy. Does Alex *really* want a baby? Hillary has a good point. The girl is sixteen for God's sake. Maybe Alex should listen to her mother."

"Of course you'd think so. Look at you. You're a freak. Married three times, no kids. You're like an unnatural woman or something."

"Aren't you tired of treating me like shit? Aren't you ever going to forgive me?" Elizabeth reached in and snagged the ball.

"You've never even asked me to." Candy looked at her with a combination of pity and disgust.

Elizabeth considered stepping up to the challenge Candy had hung in the Lovely air: *Will you forgive me?* Was that it? Was that all she had to ask her niece? But in the moment of thinking of asking, Elizabeth understood that there must come a time when she wouldn't consider asking, but would, instead, simply say the words. That's what she owed Candy—not feeling that was fretted over and wrung through the rollers of duty or regret, but feeling that was soaking wet, dripping true. She had hoarded forgiveness when it came to Melissa because she had been sure it wouldn't be the last time she'd be asked to give it. She hadn't understood what was clear to her now—forgiveness, whether given or received, replenished itself.

She held out the basketball, a silent offering. Candy took it and ran away fast, dribbling as she disappeared around the corner of the Mar-Jo.

Elizabeth ignored Alex and Hillary, who still waved from poolside, and walked around to the back of the Mar-Jo. The weight "room" was empty. She felt as dumb and heavy as the plates of weight and the barbells Roger had neatly racked. She sat on the bench where just the night before she had doomed them all to stay in Lovely.

That look Candy had just given her was one Elizabeth had seen before. One she'd given before, too. The dissolution of a marriage doesn't occur without signals of intent. The dissolution of *three* marriages offers that much fuller a range of expression. The relative ease of her first two breakups had heightened the distress of the third. She had not known that sadness could penetrate her. Could seep into her skin and turn every breath into a lament. No, worse. Not *every* breath. She could have girded herself against that expectation. Instead, some days it was every other. Other days, one in ten. Still others, only when she was confined in small spaces—the shower, the car.

Their whole last year together, when she and Leo could have accepted the inevitable and essential split to come by acknowledging all the good they'd had together, hadn't worked that way at all. Every time they'd had sex, she'd imagined that Leo had wanted to cry at the waste of it and that had made her angry at him. The act, steeped in the one thing wrong between them that couldn't be fixed, became painful, and then it became something even worse—a duty, a chore, a habit. So they'd had sex less and less often until finally, with the tacit, then spoken, acknowledgment that they were divorcing for a no-fault reason, they went back to playing their roles in the less important arguments of their married life, the ones that had, for a while, taken a backseat to the pressing issue of wanting versus not wanting a child. The mundane arguments about how she was a pessimist and he didn't follow through, he dried the dishes immediately and she stacked them precariously, she was disorganized and he liked to plan. Specks of discord with which they could have lived happily ever after.

Elizabeth left the weight room and walked in a field of stubbly grass and weeds. There was no sign of illicit life in the field—no beer cans, cigarette butts, or condoms. The Lovely kids and lowlifes must hang out elsewhere. She saw something white up ahead. It was the e.p.t. Candy had punted over their heads last night. Elizabeth stooped gingerly, testing her calf to see if it could hold her weight. She looked at the soggy e.p.t. box. The test inside was sealed tightly—unaffected by the morning rain. She looked at the price tag. Too bad she hadn't taken this walk earlier, she could have saved Hillary $12.99.

Thirty minutes later, Hillary and Elizabeth sat in room 107 of the Mar-Jo. Hillary waved away Elizabeth's apology about how messy it was—"The mess improves it." When Alex and Candy had gone into the bathroom, each holding a test kit, saying they wanted to do this together for moral support, Hillary had said sure, go ahead. The girls were casual in a studied way that Elizabeth thought suspicious, but then it wasn't the first time she'd seen high school girls keep each other company in the bathroom, so she didn't protest either.

Without the girls in the room, Elizabeth felt awkward. Was Hillary a guest? Was this a social situation? She supposed she should say something. "So, Candy said you have five kids."

"I do."

"How old are you?"

"Thirty-six."

"That's a lot of kids for somebody so young."

"How old are you?"

"The same. Thirty-six."

"But no kids?"

"I'm like Bartleby the Scrivener. 'I would prefer not to.'" Hillary look puzzled, so Elizabeth added, "It's a short story by Melville. He wrote *Moby-Dick*. That's a famous novel . . ."

"I know what *Moby-Dick* is. Just because I live in the UP and have five kids doesn't mean I'm stupid."

"I'm sure it doesn't."

"Alex told me you've been divorced four times and that you refused to have children and that's why all these husbands left you."

"Girls that age. They can be so cruel. And they rarely get the facts straight."

"So you weren't divorced four times?"

"Three."

"She also said that you and Mrs. Dreslinski deserted Candy and left her all alone in Detroit when her mother died."

"Wrong again. She wanted to stay there and play basketball. She lived with her best friend's family. Glo lives in Chicago, and I live in L.A."

"With no kids? No husbands? Right? Actually, if either of you'd had kids you probably would have been more likely to do the right thing by Candy—you would have stayed with her or brought her to you. An understanding of basic family values is one of the benefits of motherhood."

"From what I hear, you're pushing for a mother-daughter trip to the abortion clinic. Those are real family values in action."

Hillary flinched. "If you did have kids, I'd feel sorry for them. Women like you are just selfish."

Most women didn't say such things to Elizabeth out loud, but she sensed they were convinced that she had no idea of the deep fulfillment of motherhood—deep fulfillment she was missing. And Elizabeth couldn't argue. She *didn't* know that fulfillment. But then she didn't know the fulfillment of being a missionary or a public defender or a hospice nurse or a liberal senator. She didn't have a dog. But people didn't automatically think any less of her for any of that. Or did they?

She'd known all along that her ovaries were appendix-like in their irrelevance, and when she was younger, she resented what she interpreted as a matronizing attitude. Resented all these women who looked at her with a mixture of curiosity and pity or who protested too vigorously that they respected her childless choice, all while flashing photos of their chubby babies and sharing information about Gymboree and chicken pox. But as she became older, Elizabeth realized that they weren't judging her, it was just that they so deeply loved their children and identified as being mothers to them, that they simply could not conceive that life without them could be any good at all. Once they'd become *Mom,* the thought of not being that to their specific, individual, needy, loving children was beyond their ken. The emotional and biological roles were welded to create an impenetrable armor against that possibility.

It was only once in a while that a mother, some stranger, dared to show Elizabeth a truth equally powerful. At such times, the woman, weighted with children, would turn to her in the cereal aisle of the grocery store or at the crosswalk or whatever inconsequential place she happened to be. The child on display might be a two-year-old in full limb-locked tantrum, fighting some danger only he could sense, or a newborn shrieking raucously, undeveloped neurons misfiring, unable to ask for the specific comfort she desperately needed. At these moments, flailing in the uncontrollable surf of her life with her children, the mother would turn to Elizabeth, beseeching. And when these women looked at her so nakedly, Elizabeth wished she could whisper some word that would act as a narcotic for the rigid little boy, making his limbs pliant, or that she could take the fuzzy rind of the squalling infant's head in her hands and soothe both mother and child. A blessing bestowed by a stranger passing by. A miraculous bolt of good from out of the blue. But instead, at those times, Elizabeth averted her eyes and walked away quickly.

Hillary was right. She should have stayed.

She attempted amends. "Hillary, I'm sorry for what I said about the clinic trip. I don't know what I'm doing. I don't know what's best for Candy."

"Forget about it. I'm just hoping that my good intentions count for something"—Hillary picked up Glo's prayerbook from the nightstand and rubbed the worn satin ribbon marker that was sewn into the binding—"or that bad ones are forgiven." She pulled the ribbon taut and opened the book to an onionskin page of the prayerbook. "I'm also willing to accept a miracle."

The girls came out of the bathroom then. Each held a test stick and looked scared. They placed them on the nightstand; Candy put hers next to the bed she and Elizabeth slept in. Alex put hers on the side closer to Glo's bed. Three minutes later, the results were clear.

Hillary spoke first. "I didn't expect . . . Alex, get me the instructions so we're sure." Her voice came out a giddy treble, which she tried to suppress. "Honey, I'm sorry, I mean, I'm not sorry . . . What I mean is that you're so young. You have years for this. And I know you didn't want to have to choose . . ." She stopped talking and held Alex's hand, staring at the wand on the nightstand, its square window bisected with a vivid pink line, its circular window empty, nothing uncertain about it. Alex blinked repeatedly behind her yellow-tinted lenses.

"So there, see. I was right. I'm going to have a baby. And look, Alex isn't." Candy's voice sounded almost as giddy as Hillary's. Elizabeth didn't think of her niece as the type who would be stupidly happy about an unplanned pregnancy. Candy looked up and pointed her chin toward Alex, in discreet acknowledgment of something.

"Wait a minute." Elizabeth reached into her back pocket and brought out the e.p.t. she'd picked up in the field. "Candy, here's the one you punted last night. I found it out back. Let's make sure you're not that asterisked one percent you're so worried about." She held the box out toward Candy, then toward Alex, and then Candy again. She stopped and thought for a minute, a conductor with a baton, suspending her orchestra. "Candy," Elizabeth said, "retake the test. Use a plastic cup and place the test stick in it this time. Then bring it out here."

"I can't go again so soon."

Elizabeth pointed around the room at four Coke bottles in various stages of emptiness. "Try."

"Then Alex should come in with me and take it again, too." Alex hopped up and went to Candy's side.

"There's only one test in the package." Elizabeth gave Candy the test kit and a half-full Coke, and then she inspected the bathroom, making sure the toilet was flushed. "Alex stays out here with me and Hillary."

Grumbling, Candy closed the bathroom door and then leaned against the shower stall. She could plead a shy bladder, but Elizabeth would only make her take the test later when they were alone. She had a better chance of creating confusion if she did it now. She'd have to distract them and use some sleight of hand after all. The first round of tests were on the nightstand. All she had to do was to swap her soon-to-be negative stick with the positive one and then knock one of the two negatives behind the nightstand and get it later. Fine. She would. She could. This was not a problem.

Neither was peeing again. With cup in hand half full, and the e.p.t. wand swizzle-sticked in it, Candy mentally diagrammed the placement of the beds and the nightstand she had to get to. She remembered where Elizabeth and Hillary and Alex had been sitting or standing when she'd left the room. Who was she kidding? They weren't going to take their eyes off her and her pregnancy-hormone-free offering. She had nothing.

She looked at her watch. A minute left. Elizabeth hollered for her to hurry up and then Candy heard a thud and then her aunt swore. Elizabeth must have tripped and bumped into something again. She was awfully clumsy for somebody who was decent at sports. Maybe that was the answer. What if instead of easing her way to the nightstand, she tripped and bumped her way there? She looked at her Teva—the perfect excuse. She was so used to its coming undone that she could wear it on court and maneuver with ease, but they didn't know that. The half cup of urine she held was as good as a grenade. If she tripped and it went flying, they'd all turn and duck for cover. Then she'd make the switch—pick up Alex's pregnant stick, and knock one of her own not-pregnant ones behind the nightstand. She'd sweep them all up later when nobody watched. She checked her watch again. Twenty more seconds. She took a deep breath and looked at herself in the mirror. She straightened her dreads. She put her game face on.

Cup in hand, she opened the door and walked out of the bathroom.

"Well?" Elizabeth waited outside the door.

"Ten more seconds and you'll have your additional proof that you're going to be an aunty. A grand-aunty." Candy lifted the cup. "To hormones." She telegraphed her confidence to Alex, but her friend wasn't receiving. Alex looked as if she'd just stood in a puddle and stuck a knife in a toaster—her eyes were glazed, her body rigid. It was just as well that Alex was clueless. It would make her reaction believable.

Hillary sat at the foot of Glo's bed, Alex stood next to her, and Elizabeth paced in front of them both. Candy announced, "It's time," and then she took the wand out of the cup, and walked toward the nightstand to place the evidence under the light. When she stumbled on the strap of her sandal, she turned her body toward Glo's bed and her audience. Everybody instinctively gasped—bodily fluids spewing or splashing in public having that general effect—and then they backed away from the contents of the cup, moving toward the door. Candy was sorry to sacrifice Glo's neatly folded clean clothes, but if Glo thought it would help save a baby, she'd probably invite a dog to use her pant leg as a hydrant.

While Hillary, Alex, and Elizabeth ducked and watched the cup's contents splash into the air, Candy recovered from her stumble and reached out for Alex's true stick, pink lines bright and affirmative in both the square and circle window, and put down her new stick, a twin to the other on the nightstand, square bisected, but circle clear of any baby-welcoming pink. Then she knocked the old negative test off the stand. When Alex and Hillary and Elizabeth crept out of the corners of the room, Candy stood in front of the nightstand waving her test stick like a magic wand and pointed to her broken sandal strap with it.

Elizabeth knew something was wrong. Candy could go one-on-one in the WNBA with her sandal strap flapping and keep control of the ball. Something else was going on. She tried to look around Candy at the test stick on the nightstand, and the one that had fallen to the floor, but her niece blocked her view.

Meanwhile, Alex pushed her mom toward the door, opened it, and said good-bye in a falsely hearty voice. Elizabeth ignored her at first, but Alex's second big gasp of the day drew Elizabeth, Candy, and Hillary to the door where they all looked out at Roger leaning into Glo, and Glo leaning against the Cadillac. The squirt of relish on the Skipper's red hot dog complemented Glo's mint green sweater and pants. Her arms were wound around Roger. His hands touched her face. They kissed and came even closer together. When they disengaged, they talked for a while, and then Roger drove off in the Cadillac. Glo turned and looked at her audience at that point and—perhaps this was the most miraculous of all—simply smiled.

Elizabeth felt as if she'd fallen down the rabbit hole. Or maybe everybody else had. Glo was involved in a public display of affection with a divorced man younger than herself whom she'd met twenty-four hours ago. Candy was going out of her way to prove she was pregnant. Coach D was convinced he was hatching a nearly extinct, carnivorous bird. Down was up and up was down in Lovely. She'd go to the shrine-planning meeting that afternoon, but after that, promise or not, Elizabeth, the de facto voice of reason, would pack her aunt and niece in the Cadillac and get them out of Lovely. Fast.

CHAPTER 18

GLO WAS LATE for the shrine meeting. Roger was even later, which gave her time to compose herself further. She worried that she'd feel awkward around him, but when a mix of heat and desire shot through her, she realized that awkward or not, she'd drive away with him right then if he pulled up and beckoned. She put her hand to her mouth and smiled behind it as she remembered the feeling she'd had with Roger in the backseat of her car—the liquid state of her body within the solid state of her skin. She put a hand to her chest and felt her heart beating there, faster than usual, she thought. She must remember to take her medication later. She'd never found it under the table at Granny's that morning.

She searched for Roger again, just to be sure, in the crowd of twenty or so volunteers who'd gathered at the makeshift shrine. The large red-and-white tent's guylines were pulled taut. The canvas sides were raised and rolled as tightly as grade-school maps. Metal folding chairs leaned against an oblong packing crate, which held the statue that Roger's cousin had sculpted. A few unadorned folding tables were placed haphazardly around the tent. The lighting consisted of bare bulbs on tall metal stands in each corner of the canvas-covered slab. The metal, the cement, the canvas and ropes—the Guadalupe shrine had all the ambiance of a prison camp.

Glo walked out the open north side of the tent, facing Main Street, Route 51, the only way in or out of Lovely. She put her hand to her brow, and looked in a half circle west to east, like a pioneer woman waiting for something good to come clear in the distance. Roger might drive down the road in the Cadillac any minute, or perhaps he'd walk over from the Mar-Jo as she and the girls had. Or would he come from home? In what direction was his home? She shook her head, impatient with herself at all she had to learn about him. She felt the slosh of giddy warmth again. She knew important things about him already.

She noticed movement down the block, and she put her hand to her hair, smoothed her shirt, and turned that way, but it was a couple approaching, not Roger. As they came closer she saw it was Mary, the ex, who, like Glo, knew the pleasure of Roger. She walked next to a solidly portly man, shorter than she was, so that his arm reached up to hang around her shoulders. Glo blushed. Tall women—was that Roger's type? Short men—was she in some way like this other woman?

Claudia, a silver whistle on a cherry-red lanyard hanging around her neck, came up to her. "Mrs. Dreslinski, have you seen Roger?"

"And why would I have seen him?"

"I thought at the Mar-Jo, maybe? It's not like him to be late. He asked me to bring him a whistle for this meeting." Claudia yanked on the lanyard as she spoke. "He really wants to rally the troops."

Glo relaxed. Claudia wasn't insinuating anything after all. The teenage busboy from the restaurant this morning and the weight room last night—Dexter, that was his name—walked past her and smirked. She stiffened again. They *were* insinuating. All of them. They'd seen her kissing Roger in the parking lot. Or what if somebody had walked past the Cadillac parked on the old mill road? Glo flushed hot from cheeks to shins, but her extremities were ice cold. She was probably already the subject of gossip, the butt of a joke, as far away as Copperwood. That's how these small towns worked. The people in them weren't nice at all, they just pretended to be. The sun, stabbing from the west, spotlighted a constellation of acne in the form of a chalice on Dexter's cheek and neck. She grabbed his forearm. "Young man, what's so funny?" He wrenched his arm away and backed off as if she'd demanded his money.

After five more minutes of waiting for Roger, Claudia took matters into her own hands and blew the whistle, pointing to this, then that and directing people to move it here, then there. The statue of Our Lady of Guadalupe, direct from Roger's Milwaukee cousin, was in its packing crate in the middle of the floor, in the aisle created by folding chairs that the shrine volunteers arranged in preparation for the inaugural Mass. People stepped over or around the coffin-shaped crate as if it were a natural obstacle, a rock or a tree stump.

Candy and Alex unloaded folding chairs from a cart on the far side of the tent. Or mostly, Alex did, while Candy played with her basketball, twirling it on a finger, shuffling it from palm to palm. Dexter hovered nearby, his baseball cap on backward, annoying them as they worked, snatching the ball from Candy, and pretending to throw it in Alex's face. Watching him, Glo shuddered. A boy that age was the father of the child Candy carried. As soon as Glo returned Candy to Detroit, she'd make calls to Catholic Social Services about adoption. It's what Candy must do. If it came to it, Elizabeth would move back to Detroit and live with Candy until the baby came. Or Candy would move to Los Angeles with Elizabeth. That might be best, come to think of it. In the old days, girls in her situation were sent away—no need to reinvent a perfectly acceptable method of saving face. They shouldn't expect Anita Prokoff to operate as a home for an unwed mother.

Glo didn't know if any of this was what Candy had in mind, but the girl was seventeen. She wasn't mature enough to raise a child that was the result of her pleasure. She'd committed a sin. A few days ago Glo would have felt mostly anger and impatience about that. But now? She'd just committed the same sin with Roger—her nonfunctioning ovaries didn't make it something other—and she wanted to stay swamped in the feeling of it, of Roger, of desire indulged. And there were mitigating factors. What she'd done with Roger was holy in essence. It was only the timing that was off. She would ask for absolution later. Meanwhile, Glo considered the possibility that Candy had her good reasons, too.

The air was saturated with good intentions as the shrine volunteers worked to turn the plain tent into a place of worship. A dozen or so volunteers wore name tags that read SUNNYVIEW SENIOR CENTER. Glo watched two of them work together to lift and open a folding chair, while Henry, the large man who had lifted the giant-sized dumbbells in Roger's class the night before, arranged Queen Anne's lace and black-eyed Susans in a vase and then placed it next to a pair of silver candlesticks on the makeshift folding-table altar. This was the altar over which the visiting priest would preside during the ceremony to officially christen the Guadalupe shrine. After spending the morning at the well-endowed and organized splendor of the Cross in the Woods, Glo felt sorry for Roger and these volunteers whose penny-ante display would do nothing to obliterate the looming shadow of a fifty-five-foot-tall redwood crucifix.

When Claudia blew her whistle again, Glo, startled, almost stumbled over a chair. Elizabeth, coming up behind her, steadied her aunt.

"So where's your boyfriend, Glo?"

"Don't say such a silly thing. I'm not in junior high." Glo smoothed the front of her T-shirt, which was really Elizabeth's T-shirt, the lucky State Class A basketball championship T-shirt that had kept Elizabeth aloft so far.

Elizabeth and Candy had been surprised at how unconcerned Glo was when they explained about the pregnancy test and the accident and why Glo had better not wear any of the damp clothes folded so carefully on her bed. "I want to shower," Glo had said. "Elizabeth, lend me something to wear. Candy, gather up my clothes. We'll find a Laundromat later."

Once Glo had closed the bathroom door, Elizabeth and Candy discussed her behavior. "She took a shower last night. Old people don't usually shower that much." Candy picked up Glo's damp blue blouse, which had soaked up most of her staged e.p.t. accident, by the tip of its collar and tossed it on the floor.

Elizabeth thought it odd, too. "Maybe she smells his smoke on her skin. They were going at it pretty good in the parking lot."

"How smoky could she be? She kissed him. She didn't have sex with him in the backseat of the car." They laughed at the thought.

But it didn't add up. So, at the Guadalupe shrine, with Roger missing in action, Elizabeth teased Glo, trying to get the truth. "So, Glo, if it's not your 'boyfriend' you kissed in the parking lot an hour ago, who was it? He's not your lover, is he? You don't strike me as the type to have a 'lover.' Besides the whole mortal sinfulness problem, it's a gilded word, not you at all."

Glo didn't think language was up to describing the feelings she had for Roger—feelings so strong they were almost tactile. You might as well try to hammer a nail with a toe shoe as talk about what she and Roger had done. Elizabeth was right—she certainly did not have a "lover." "Not now, Elizabeth—later—let's talk later." She walked away and joined the Sunnyview Seniors, watching Mary and Joe out of the corner of her eye, keeping her distance from that other woman who'd had sex with Roger.

After they'd worked for an hour, Claudia whistled again and told them to help themselves to the sandwiches and snacks that she and Hillary had set up on the side. Elizabeth waited until Candy and Alex and Dexter had filled their plates. She'd had enough of the girls for one day, and the teenaged boy, stupid and rude, was a reminder of Candy's condition. A condition Elizabeth still found suspicious. Candy was in an awfully good mood for being pregnant and Alex didn't seem relieved enough by her lucky break. Hillary, on the other hand, was giddy with the news that she wouldn't be a grandmother after all. Elizabeth watched her open folding chairs and dust tables and cut sandwiches. Hillary literally whistled while she worked. She also smiled at the Sunnyviews and waved across the tent at Alex every few minutes.

The lunch spread was unimpressive. A heaping platter of sandwiches—soft white bread with American cheese and bologna—an industrial-sized bowl of potato salad; a half dozen liter bottles of Sprite; a gallon-sized jar of pale green, sandwich-sliced, dill pickles; and a bowl of mustard, the yellow cut of color shocking next to the other placid tones. Elizabeth grabbed a sandwich, not bothering with a plate, and walked toward an empty solitary chair near the folding-table altar, where there were no pregnant teenagers conniving or giggling or making smart-ass comments.

Glo stopped her when she was halfway there, maneuvering her into an empty seat. "Here's my niece, now." The older people Glo sat with turned expectantly, and Glo patted Elizabeth's head, then smoothed her niece's golden streak. "She came all the way from Los Angeles to be with me and help out with the driving on this trip. She's a high school guidance counselor at a very good Catholic school." The seniors murmured congratulations. Elizabeth, puzzled by Glo's show of pride, smiled feebly.

The Sunnyview Seniors bragged about their grandchildren in between forks full of potato salad. Then they set forks down and dug in their wallets for school photos of children who either hadn't yet grown into, or had already grown out of, their features—each of the kids had ears, noses, or chins that were too large or too small. The proud grandparents proffering the photos also had insufficient or exaggerated features, noses that monopolized their faces, flesh that hung loose on scrawny necks. Maybe it was this mismatch that so often made kindred spirits of kids and their grandparents—a hey-you-look-funny-too recognition. The Sunnyview Seniors' knees and elbows were bare in the heat, and the skin there hung wrinkled and loose in puff-pastry-like folds as their bones and cartilage slowly eroded, leaving less joint for the undiminished flesh to cling to. Elizabeth wondered if that's what Glo would look like in ten years. In twenty? She looked at her own smooth, tan knees. How many years before she looked like that, too?

When Claudia blew her whistle and announced that they should all get back to work, the Sunnyviews immediately put down their plastic cutlery, as if their eating were choreographed, and moved to Claudia en masse. Elizabeth and Glo were alone again.

"You patted my head, Glo."

"I'm sorry."

"Oh, it's okay."

"I wanted them to see that I had someone, too. It's those school pictures. All those grandchildren—this one plays the trombone, that one is a Brownie. Any seven-year-old can be a Brownie, and in my experience, a twelve-year-old who plays the trombone is a social outcast. Trust me, when you're my age, you'll have had it up to here"—Glo chopped her throat with the flat of her hand and then reached up and smoothed her hair—"with other people's grandchildren. How's your leg, Elizabeth?"

Elizabeth looked down and examined the progress of her bruise. Hot to the touch, it looked as if an oil slick had congealed on her calf. It was dark and glistening with faint splotches of sickly yellow and murderous red that shimmered through when the light shined directly on it. "It could be worse."

"Oh, I agree. It could almost always be worse." Glo put a hand on Elizabeth's head again, though there was no one there to see her do so. "I'll pray for you. More than I already do." Then she joined the other volunteers who had gathered around Claudia.

Elizabeth felt the stamp of Glo's hand on her head. Was her aunt capable of considering a person as something other than a sinner, a saint, or a soul to be saved? Did Glo have feelings for Roger? Elizabeth had seen evidence for answers on both sides of both those questions. She wondered which picture of Glo was true. After only two days with her aunt, she no longer assumed she knew.

She heard the screeching pull of hard matter yanked from something even harder and looked up to see Henry, with Claudia directing, leaning on a crowbar, his biceps inflating like balloons as he tried to pry the lid off the crate in the aisle. After the first few nails gave way, the shanks of those remaining dug in harder, resisting his muscle. Henry pushed and grunted, leaning harder on the crowbar, until finally he motioned for help. At that, Candy pushed aside Dexter, who was moving forward, shoved her basketball into Glo's hands, and rushed to Henry's side.

With Henry and Candy leaning on the crowbar, one by one the four-inch nails gave up their hold and the lid popped off the crate. Glo stood at one end of it, propping the basketball against her protruding hip as if she were a player, while the dozen or so other shrine volunteers lined up on the sides of the crate and stared down as if they were looking into a grave. Elizabeth inched closer, still outside the perimeter, but curious.

Claudia and Candy and Henry scooped out armfuls of packing straw, revealing a white-sheet-swaddled oblong shape that shimmered through layers of tightly packed bubble wrap. When Candy reached in and began to rip off the plastic cushion, Glo grabbed her wrist with her free hand and yelled, "Halt," as if she were a German prison guard. "Roger should be here. Let's wait a while longer. All this"— Glo let go of Candy's wrist and gestured around the tent—"is his work. He deserves to be here for the unveiling. It means a lot to him."

As she finished, they all heard Mary laughing. "Now that is a waste of a Cadillac. And it looks like that bastard is leaving town in it."

Alex and Hillary, standing near Mary, turned from the statue to the street, and Alex said, "It looks like he's moving all his stuff," and then Hillary called Elizabeth over and pretty soon everybody turned from the shrouded supine statue and lined the side of Main Street and watched as Roger Sallee drove by in Glo's car. The Cadillac was

weighed down with boxes and suitcases—visible in the backseat—
and as if to remove all doubt about what he was doing, the bare bulb
of a floor lamp stuck out the passenger window of the front seat. As
Roger passed the shrine going west on Route 51, he tapped ash from
his cigarette. He kept his eyes on the road, ignoring the openmouthed
people who lined the street and gawked as if he were the circus come
to town.

The crowd was quiet after Mary's initial outburst, so the smack
of the basketball on the Guadalupe shrine slab as it slipped from
Glo's hip was magnified, and as it bounced from lower and lower
heights, it echoed and the shrine sounded like the holy place Roger in-
tended it to be.

Claudia was the first to ask a question on everybody's mind:
"Where's he going?"

Dexter asked another: "Is he stealing your car?"

And then everybody turned to Glo as if she, a Lovely visitor for all
of twenty-four hours, was Bonnie to his Clyde, or, more likely she
thought, feeling her cheeks go scarlet, Hester Prynne to his Reverend
Dimmesdale. Her chest burned, and she moved her hand there protec-
tively. She felt her heart's thumps, percussive, in her throat and
eardrums. They all knew. Three hours earlier she'd had sex with
Roger Sallee in the backseat of the car he was stealing from her now,
and she knew that they knew. His ex-wife. The smart-aleck boy.
Candy. Elizabeth.

The languid satisfaction, the edgy anticipation of seeing him
again, the well-being, the whole mix of conflicting emotions that she'd
felt earlier, turned to straightforward shame at having her intimate
moments displayed on Main Street. She remembered how Roger had
registered her wealth when she'd first met him, his eyes blinking as

rapidly as a cartoon character with dollar signs for pupils as he'd picked up her checkbook. He'd told them just that morning that he could get cash for the car. He'd looked so surprised when that ex-wife, that Mary, had said she'd give him what he wanted for fifteen thousand dollars. He'd listened to her carefully, he'd taken that seriously— in the confusion of feeling at Granny's that morning, that much had been clear. Elizabeth hadn't trusted him. Glo remembered his hands on the upholstery of the Cadillac. She'd thought he was stroking it as if it were a reminder of her. She'd gotten it backward—her arms and legs had substituted for the leather he coveted. She looked frantically for her purse and saw it hanging on the back of a chair. She wondered if her checkbook and wallet were still in it, were still here, with her, in Lovely. Roger Sallee had sex with her because he wanted her money. She understood that now. Everybody in the tent must, too.

Claudia confirmed her fear. "What a shit, and after you were so nice to him, Mrs. Dreslinski. I thought you two were really getting along."

"Stupid, too. I mean, dude, there's a hot dog on the side of the car you're ripping off." Dexter scratched his neck as he spoke, altering the sacred design.

Alex and Hillary looked at Glo with cow-eyed pity. Pity! A pregnant teenager found her pitiful. Glo's hands flew up to her chest again and she pressed hard to calm herself. She was actually glad when Mary spoke—it had become too quiet again. "If he sells it and sends me the money, I'll keep my word and marry you, Joe. It's the honorable thing to do."

Elizabeth waited for Glo to explain or to take some action. Had Glo lent him the car? Did she want Elizabeth to call the police? But Glo was quiet, eerily still, except for her throat, which twitched as if she'd swallowed something that tried to claw its way out. Her aunt had kissed this man in public—he'd taken her for some kind of ride. Glo needed her help. Elizabeth stepped up. "He's not stealing it. It's my car. Not my aunt's. I lent it to him—he told me he needed to move a few things. If you all have an issue with Roger not being here for your meeting, that's your business, but don't worry about the car. That's no big deal." With Elizabeth's explanation, Alex and Hillary looked even more sympathetically at Glo, as if she'd just been given a round of chemotherapy while her relatives insisted the tumor was benign.

That was just like Elizabeth, Candy thought. Lame-ass. Everybody knew that Glo had been dumped on Main Street after she'd probably had sex with a guy on the first date. Hardly even a date, they'd gone for a drive. That shouldn't happen to anybody, sixteen or sixty. Candy didn't need the details to know that one way or another Roger had screwed Glo, and she couldn't let that be the thing that everybody in Lovely remembered.

Candy yanked the whistle around Claudia's neck, pulling it until Claudia's head was almost on her chest. She blew it sharp and hard while Claudia covered her ears. When she had everybody's attention, Candy announced, "Forget that loser. Forget the shrine for now. We're taking a break. We're going to the Rec Center to play some ball. I"—she jabbed herself in the chest with Claudia's whistle and Claudia's head bumped her chin—"will teach you how."

The Sunnyview Seniors laughed and said no way, but they followed Dexter and Hillary, who went gladly, and Joe and Henry, who lined up on either side of Mary, and told her to come along so they could shoot around. Candy cajoled and urged and herded them all until they were gathered to cross Route 51, which was busy with traffic for a change—Aramark food service trucks taking goods to the Cross in the Woods, tourists heading for the nice hotels closer to it. Candy, in charge, wasn't about to wait until it cleared. Instead, she held her arms out at each side and stopped cars from both directions, as if she were Charlton Heston and the traffic were red Jell-O. She marched forward, not looking back until they'd all crossed Route 51, and walked up the wide graveled Rec Center driveway and onto center court.

Once there, she remembered that Glo had dropped the basketball back at the shrine. She told Claudia to keep everybody on court, and she ran to the cemetery, leaping the drainage ditch that separated the rundown and neglected Rec Center from the dead. She looked for the gravestone near the patch of bushes where Coach D had told her he always left a ball. There it was. She dropped to her knees and pushed aside the brambled branches. She swore as she scratched her hands. Why did he have to hide the ball in the first place? It's not as if anybody in the cemetery were alive to steal it. She inched her hands in deeper and finally reached the scuffed ball, pulling it out in a swoop that scratched it and her. She stood up, woozy with the sudden change from crouch, and then she yelped as she bumped into something that yelped back.

She whipped around, elbows out, protecting the ball. "Damn. Don't sneak up on me, Elizabeth." Candy dropped the ball to her hip and rubbed the back of her head, which she'd knocked against her aunt.

"I didn't sneak up. You didn't hear me. What's going on with you? With Alex? Tell me the truth."

"It's not only my truth to tell. Don't worry about me. We need to think about Glo." Candy looked over at the basketball court, searching for Alex, for Glo.

"We'll get to that. But right now she won't even let me call the cops and report the car stolen. She's not thinking straight. And neither are you. Did you really quit your team because you're having a baby? Or because of Coach D? It doesn't seem that's what this is all about."

"It's none of your fucking business. *That's* what this is all about."

"Having this baby is not your only option."

"So, you're going to force me to choose some other option?"

"I didn't say that."

"You'd probably think I have to have an abortion just to prove I'm pro-choice."

"A girl your age with a baby to raise or a pregnancy to go through? You need to think about it. You'll need help. So I'll help you—whatever you decide." Elizabeth's leg ached, and she looked down at it, not at Candy. Candy made a sound, disgusted. Elizabeth heard herself. No wonder her niece didn't believe her. Her offer sounded as if it were being winched out of her—her voice a taut line on which the burden tugged.

When Elizabeth had left Candy in Detroit, she'd packed her car as tightly as Roger had packed Glo's. She'd been eager to be on the road to Chicago before noon, but she had slowed down as she got closer and closer to putting the final box in the trunk. Once finished, she'd have to face Candy and say good-bye. Melissa, too, she supposed. She couldn't put it off any longer if she wanted to get into Chicago and unpack her belongings before midnight.

She'd gone to Melissa first. She dreaded that less. She was easy to find. It was two in the afternoon on a Saturday. Elizabeth went to Taffy's, the neighborhood tavern where Melissa's friend Judy tended bar. The sun came through the windows at Taffy's, insistent, and the patrons squinted into their drinks. Melissa sat at the end of the long wooden bar. She and Judy leaned in toward each other, talking fiercely, their figures creating a steeple.

"Mel?" Elizabeth tapped her sister on the shoulder. "I'm leaving now and I wanted to say good-bye." Judy walked away as Elizabeth spoke—she thought Elizabeth was a prig.

"So, you have a place to live in Chicago? Or are you staying with Glo?"

"I have a place. I told you that already. I gave you the address and phone number. Did you forget? Did you lose it? Already? It was last week."

"I have a lot on my mind, Elizabeth."

"Yeah, a lot. On your mind." Elizabeth pointed to her sister's glass.

"Oh Christ, Elizabeth. Quit being the alcohol police. This is my first drink. I'm relaxing and talking to my friend. I'm fine."

"Your daughter isn't."

"My daughter is on the honor roll, is the MVP of her basketball and baseball teams, saves all the money she earns baby-sitting, does the dishes every night, and keeps her room clean. I think my daughter is doing just fine, too."

"Where is she now?"

"Heilmann—she's playing pickup ball with some boys."

"I'll go there and say good-bye."

"Do what you have to do."

"You too, Mel. Remember what you have to do. Don't make Candy raise herself."

Melissa had raised her glass. "Why not? Unlike us, she's doing a damn good job."

Elizabeth had gone to Heilmann next. She would have even without Melissa's pointing her there. It was Candy's favorite place to be. Elizabeth stood on the sidelines for a while watching a group of boys who, even working as a team to trip up Candy, could only slow, not stop, her. The high school student who was paid to half-referee half-chaperone these younger kids' weekend afternoon pickup games ignored what was happening on the floor, and the boys became more and more physical with Candy. They'd stop, but only if she cracked. And Candy, at twelve, refused to crack. She also refused to acknowledge Elizabeth's presence, although Elizabeth called to her and tried to wave her over.

After a few minutes, Elizabeth went to the young guy who was supposed to be watching the action on the floor. "Do you think you could put the magazine down and actually do your job? They're beating up that girl out there."

"She's okay. If she wants to play with boys, she can't be a baby about it."

"I'm not asking you to baby her. I'm asking you to make sure she doesn't fracture her skull."

"You're not her mom." It was more statement than question, Melissa's reputation reached far.

"Aunt."

"Relax, Auntie. She has to learn to handle it on her own."

Elizabeth, with her bags packed in the car in the parking lot outside, knew he was right. And instead of interfering or assisting, she walked away. She actually walked away from Candy without saying a thing. One hour later, one day later, one month later, five years later, she admitted this. It was yet another thing that added to her thicket of shame. But Candy hadn't allowed her to go quietly. She'd come running out to the parking lot.

"You're leaving?" Candy shivered and folded her arms into the old Bill Laimbeer jersey that hung almost to her knees. Her bangs were soaking wet, her bare legs goose-bumped.

"I've got a long drive. I tried to get your attention on court, but I guess you didn't see me."

"I saw you."

"Oh, well, I just stopped and said good-bye to your mom. She's hanging out with Judy at Taffy's. She said she'd pick you up at four."

"I'll be walking home before that."

"Candy, I know that none of this is easy for you. But you have to understand that it won't always be this way. It won't always be like this."

"I do understand that." She pointed at Elizabeth's car, packed to the roof with boxes and suitcases, a floor lamp inching out the window. "Now it will get even worse."

And it had. But only for one more month. After that, Glo had effectively kidnapped Melissa and taken her to Hazelden, and Melissa had gotten sober.

Thinking back to that day in the Heilmann parking lot when her skinny niece shivered with cold and trepidation, Elizabeth felt that of every mistake she'd made in marriage, everything in her life that she'd ever done that was wrong, and every other thing that she'd done right—helping Melissa during her pregnancy, helping her raise Candy, protecting Candy during some of Melissa's worst binges, making a good marriage with Leo, and then breaking it off for good reason—all of those things, when added up, were obliterated by her choice to leave Candy alone on a cold day in Detroit, with her mother at a bar and a bunch of boys on court determined to hurt her.

That day at the ditch in Lovely, Candy reminded her again. "I don't need your help. I wouldn't even want my baby to know somebody like you and your fifty-two ex-husbands. You left my mom. You're useless. You're no help to Glo, either."

"I tried. You heard me covering for her about the car and Roger."

"And you fucked up. I had to do it. And now I have to get back there and take care of things again." Candy turned away. She was not like Elizabeth. Alex, Glo, those people from the old folks' home—she would do something for them. They could count on her. Her mom would be proud, yes, she was sure. So far, her mom would be very proud.

She ran back fast, leaping over the ditch. She heard Elizabeth following. Her aunt's breathing was heavy and she said *goddamnit* as she jumped the ditch. Candy looked over her shoulder and saw Elizabeth falling, her hands thrown up in surrender, her feet scrabbling for hold. Candy kept running.

CHAPTER 19

CANDY SENT THE Sunnyview Seniors to the sidelines to cheer. No offense to them, but she didn't want a bunch of old hearts failing on her court. She needed somebody to ref, though. Somebody old might be able to do that. Somebody who was good at keeping track of things. She saw Janine, the old lady from the Mar-Jo front desk, mingling with the other old folks, talking to them while she cleaned her glasses with the hem of her shirt. Candy called her over. "Do you know anything about basketball?"

"My granddaughter plays for the fifth-grade team at St. Thomas Aquinas. I went to every game last year. She plays the flute, too. My grandson is in the chess club, and he . . ."

Candy snapped her fingers at Claudia and pointed to the whistle around her neck. "Give me that." She turned back to Janine, who was now blabbing about another granddaughter's finger painting, and swung the whistle in front of her. "Put those glasses on. You're the ref." Janine held her hand up to her brow, protecting herself from the intermittent silver glint that shot off the whistle in the fickle Lovely sunshine. "Don't worry about ticky-tack fouls. Only call big stuff. Like if somebody trips or pushes somebody or runs a mile with the ball. Otherwise, let us play."

Still talking, Candy tossed the ball to the big, tall guy who'd needed help opening the crate. He caught it easily with his left hand and dribbled a few times. Good, he could handle it. She'd put him on the opposing team—he might be mild competition for her. She pointed to Alex, and then to the guy who had an arm around Roger's fucked-up ex-wife, and then to Claudia. "You three are with me. You," she turned to the big, tall guy again and he interrupted her.

"My name is Henry."

"Okay, Henry, and you"—she pointed to Dexter, who would be crazy speedy on court and cause trouble—"and you"—she tapped Mary, who smelled like her mom after a night at the bar, on the shoulder—"and Hillary"—better to keep her away from Alex—"are all on the other team. Listen to Henry, he knows what he's doing."

"Where do you want me?" Elizabeth, having climbed out of the ditch like an amphibian evolving, limped onto the court and pulled her hair into a ponytail, wincing at the creak of pain in her shoulder as her arms went above her ears.

Candy looked at her aunt. Good question. What if Elizabeth hadn't stashed her at the Prokoffs' house nine months ago? What if she'd never left five years ago? What if she'd forgiven her mom? Standing on court with all these people she hardly knew surrounding her, Candy felt unconnected to Elizabeth. And then in a fritz of feeling that originated in her chest and announced a circuit broken, she became disconnected from herself. Since her mom died, she'd had these moments when she felt as if she were separate from her own breath and bones. One part of her just watched the things the other part did. She worried lately that the two parts would become so distant that she'd never be just one person again. On court last season, she'd been able to run hard and catch up to herself, but this year she wouldn't have basketball. She blamed Elizabeth for that, too. Both parts of her were pissed at her aunt. Where did she want Elizabeth? As far away as possible.

Her aunt spoke again: "I'll be on your team, okay?"

Candy looked at Elizabeth coldly. "No. Their team." She pointed toward Henry, Hillary, Dexter, and Mary. She'd take care of Elizabeth on court.

Glo came off the sidelines and tapped Candy on the shoulder. "Where should I go?" Glo clutched her purse to her chest and her lips hardly moved as she spoke.

"Over on the sidelines with them." Candy waved at the Sunnyviews.

"But I don't have any grandchildren who play trombone."

"Huh?"

"I'm too young for the sideline. I don't live in a senior center."

"You don't play basketball, either. And you have a sore back. And you take ninety-five pills a day for your heart. And you're wearing the wrong kind of shoes."

"Are you saying her shoes are better than mine?" Glo nodded at Hillary, who kicked the ball, which had rolled her way, with her orange espadrille. "And look at him." Glo pointed at Dexter, who picked up the ball, beat at it with his fists, and then ran after it as he too kicked it away. "Surely he'll be no help to anybody."

"You're right. But a person your age can't run around in the heat."

"I'm sixty-three, Candy. A person my age can do all sorts of things."

Candy put her hand on Glo's arm. "Glo, instead of playing, why don't you go back to the Mar-Jo, call the cops, and tell them Roger stole your car?"

Glo's cheeks flushed. Roger had left town. Left her. After having sex with her. "No police. He might come back. You have no idea of what I can do in the heat."

"Glo, the game will be fast and hard."

"I'll be fast, too. I'll be hard." Glo lowered her voice, "Please, Candy, don't send me over there." Glo pointed at the knot of Sunnyviews who wore visors and sunglasses and rubbed sunscreen into their skin, papery thin or leathery, wrinkled no matter its thickness. "If you let Elizabeth play, you've got one less on your team. You need me."

Candy saw the opposite was true. Glo needed her. Glo's cheeks were red, then white, her voice wobbly. Candy recognized that meeting of shame and anger and pride that made a person need to *do* something. She'd felt it after Jimmy knocked her down and whispered in her ear in the Prokoffs' backyard the other day. The physical lash back at him had given her relief from the creeping understanding of what everybody thought about her. Glo, who was more like a nun than anybody Candy knew, had done something with Roger and he'd repaid her by stealing her car. Glo needed to do something now. Candy understood that.

"Okay, Glo. But be careful. Try to stay out of the way."

Candy calculated. Alex and Hillary would both suck, and being on opposing teams, cancel out each other's mistakes. Henry would be good for Elizabeth's team. Dexter, also on Elizabeth's side, would be stupid and reckless, but he'd accidentally do some things right. Mary would be aggressive, but teetering on the line between drunk and hungover, she'd mess things up for Elizabeth. On Candy's side, Claudia might not have good form, but Candy had seen her handle a half dozen orders of pancakes, and she'd do just fine with one basketball. And the guy with Mary—Joe, he'd said his name was—thick in the middle with his stubby legs, would be a bulldog. Guys like him thought they could take care of anything, that's why they hooked up with drunken women. That left her and Elizabeth, and as good as her aunt was, as fundamentally sound as her game might be, she was no match for Candy, an All-American, almost twenty years younger, and injury free. Candy's team could absorb Glo.

Candy raised her voice, "Okay everybody. Listen up. We're playing full court. One point a basket to eleven. You have to win by two. She"—Candy reached out for Janine's whistle—"is blowing this when anybody does anything really wrong and stupid, but otherwise we're just going to play. If you don't know how to play, don't worry, Elizabeth will explain stuff to you guys and I'll help my team. Here"—Candy took the ball from Dexter and tossed it to Elizabeth—"no jump balls. No shots on fouls. Just possession. You guys take it out first."

Janine gave two wavery toots as Elizabeth gathered her team and handed out defensive assignments. They'd play man-to-man. She didn't have time to explain a zone. She'd guard Candy. She put Henry on Claudia, Dexter on Joe, Hillary on Glo, and Mary on Alex. She put the ball in Henry's hands so he could pass in to her from the baseline, and told them all she'd bring it upcourt and that they should move to the pass instead of standing around waiting for the ball to come to them.

Henry threw in and raced ahead. Once Elizabeth crossed center line, she passed back to him six feet ahead of her on the wing. She cut across the key, in the big hole carved by Alex, who stood stock still, useless, unless you counted it useful to look as if you were about to cry. Henry's pass back, a good idea, give and go, sailed high over her outstretched hands, and directly into Candy's hands, which were held even higher, so no alley-oop there. Candy took off, running upcourt. Only Elizabeth trailed her flight to the hoop. The others, however ignorant they were of the game, must have realized they were seeing something special, that Candy embodied something rare—grace, speed, agility, strength, ballet, game—call it what you will. They watched as she drove to the basket and leapt high. There were no defenders to outwit, but Candy showboated with a sweet reverse, left hand leading, and her team scored first.

Henry took out the ball again, passed to Elizabeth again, and they moved upcourt side by side. Janine trotted along, whistle in lips, clapping her hands to urge on no one in particular, and everyone in general. Once she'd crossed center line, Elizabeth called to Hillary and bounced a pass to her. The ball hit her in the chest, her hands fending it off instead of catching it. Elizabeth shouted encouragement: "That's okay, Hillary. Next time keep your eye on it." Hillary saluted and laughed. Alex trudged upcourt next to Mary. They both looked drained—their presence of little value to anybody.

Claudia took the ball out at the sidelines and passed in to Joe, who was better than Candy expected. He handled the ball easily, as if it were attached to his palm by a string, and then he shimmied around big tall Henry, who was out of position at the top of the key. Seeing Glo open underneath the basket, dumb luck, he lobbed the ball there. Elizabeth rushed over to defend, but stopped well short of her aunt, unwilling to initiate contact. There was no need for it anyway. Glo heaved the ball up, missing the rim and even the backboard by three feet, effectively passing to Mary, who looked irritated to be holding a basketball instead of a cocktail in her hands.

Dexter scooted over and plucked the ball from her. Then he zig-zagged upcourt, blind and deaf to his teammates, especially to Hillary, who stood alone under the basket calling for the ball. Dexter crouched low and looked fierce as he dribbled, as if he faced Visigoths or guard dogs, though no one was on him. Elizabeth and Candy, close to each other at half-court, laughed as he neared the basket and flung himself upward in a spasm of limbs and ball that went in the general direction of the basket, then hit the backboard with a wallop.

Candy rearranged to serious before Elizabeth did and sped toward the rebound, corralling the ball so that Dexter, lunging, couldn't stick his Gumby limbs around it. She walked upcourt, dribbling to a steady beat that calmed everybody, and slowed the tempo of the game, which after five minutes stood at 1–0, with three spectacular airballs. Candy reviewed the court as she moved, checking if there were any surprises, such as Alex actually moving or somebody cutting to an open passing lane. Elizabeth sidled up to her, but played off. She had deflected one of Candy's passes already, and she made it tough for Candy to get a good look at the basket. She'd give Elizabeth this much: her defense was solid.

Elizabeth, keeping a healthy distance from Candy so her niece wouldn't get a step on her so far from the basket, coached her team as she backpedaled, defending. "See what I'm doing? Everybody? You want to stay between your player and the basket."

Nearing the three-point line, Candy drove left, but Elizabeth stuck with her—she wouldn't be shed that easily. Candy stepped back and dribbled crisscross once, then twice, between her legs, looking for an outlet pass, but her teammates, even Joe, who obviously knew bet-ter, stood still.

Elizabeth crouched low, her bruise throbbing from the stops and starts of the game. Her ankle was wanky from her slip into the ditch as she'd chased Candy moments ago. Her shoulder already hurt again—that skinny girl who'd knocked her down so long ago in June had done a lot of damage. June, only two months ago—when Candy was *not* pregnant, *not* quitting basketball, *not* sleeping next to Elizabeth in a grimy motel room, and *not* trying to fake her out on court and everywhere else. She wanted Candy to be settled in her choices—baby, basketball—either one, neither, both, she didn't care anymore. It had nothing to do with sparing herself the day-to-day duty of it or of lessening her guilt at duty shirked. She simply wanted the girl to be all right.

Glo called to Candy for the ball, and when Candy hesitated for a split second, Elizabeth reached a hand in, but not cleanly. She hacked Candy on the forearm, hard, and Candy said, "Fuck you," loud enough for the Sunnyviews on the sideline to *tsk tsk* and look at Glo sympathetically.

Janine, gaining confidence on the whistle, blasted the game to a stop and wagged her finger in Candy's face. "You're an awfully pretty girl to have such a filthy mouth."

Still, it was Elizabeth's foul. But no free throws. Candy told Claudia to take it out on the sideline. Glo scooted over toward the ball and caught Claudia's inbound pass. The Sunnyviews came alive on the sideline—one of their own generation was part of the play.

Glo hadn't played a game of any sort since she and Stan had miniature-golfed in Florida three years ago. She had natural grace, but she had not, in all her sixty-three years, until that moment played basketball. She heard the Sunnyviews clapping in unison on the sidelines, their makeshift cheer—"Go Glo. Glo Go"—leaving them tongue-tied and laughing. The ball felt large in Glo's hands, and she noticed that it was pocked with grit, dirty, and unwieldy. Claudia stood nearby waving her right hand in the air, as if she were begging the teacher to call on her, but Glo wanted to move the ball forward on her own. She tried to dribble, paddling the ball, and it careened up higher than she expected, to her shoulders, so she slapped it softer the next time and it only came up to her shin. Finally, like Goldilocks, she got it just right. She ran forward, bouncing the ball to her waist, crossing the center line, and then she stood at the top of the fading semicircle painted on the cement, breathing hard in the thick humidity. Having no idea what else to do, she heaved the ball up over Hillary's arm in the general direction of the basket, where Candy, Joe, and Alex gathered. Candy leapt and plucked it at the top of its arc, just an inch higher than Elizabeth, who leapt, too, and then she redirected the ball through the hoop, and ran back toward Glo, high-fiving her for the alley-oop. The Sunnyviews cheered on the sidelines, the men punching the air, the women kicking like showgirls. All of them yelling approval for Candy and Glo.

And then the tenor of the game changed: Candy and Joe, with common sense from Claudia, relentless commitment to at least do no harm from Glo, and disinterest from Alex, took over on one side, while Elizabeth and Henry, with Dexter offering bursts of reckless speed, Mary proving herself sober enough to stay out of the way, and Hillary's glee about not becoming a grandmother at age thirty-six resulting in an enthusiastic and perfectly timed swat or two, got down to business on the other.

First Candy and Joe and then Elizabeth and Henry displayed solid foot- and handwork that resulted in crisp passes to the open shot— easy jump shots, wide-open looks from downtown, and sure-handed layups. It was surprising that a game could come out of the mess of inexperience and ineptitude that cluttered the rundown court. But it did.

Elizabeth stuck to Candy and made her work as hard as she ever had. No shot went uncontested. No look was clean. Elizabeth played as if it mattered. She ran faster, jumped higher, tried harder than she had in months. She muscled into the game in a way that made her forget the complications that existed elsewhere, in Detroit or L.A., in head or heart. She gave all with an integrity she couldn't muster off court. Her moves were made in sunshine, her blocks were clean, her appreciation of Candy's prowess unweighted with other concerns.

Candy got around her anyway. She was responsible for most of her team's points and boards, but there were no gifts. She slashed and cut and slapped at her aunt. She bumped and butted Elizabeth. She told her with hip, hack, and head fake that she couldn't make amends that easily. That she had a price to pay.

Glo was as preoccupied as her nieces were present. She moved up and down the court with the flow, but her mind was on Roger, on Stan. Both gone. What had she been thinking with each? She could have trusted Stan with her doubts, with everything. Stan hadn't been taunting her with his kindness or his lack of faith. She could have talked with him about how difficult it was to reconcile the warmth of him lying next to her in bed with the disappointment she felt on Sundays when she went to Mass alone. He had cared for her deeply, and she saw now how much that mattered to her, no matter what Stan did or did not do on Sunday. She needn't have let Stan's choice chafe her so. She needn't have felt at war with him or with herself for wanting him. At half-court in Lovely, she forgave herself for that. As to the way she'd misjudged Roger, she smiled ruefully. She shouldn't have trusted him with anything. She'd always felt so sure and certain she was right—about everything—but she saw now that she was a cornucopia of imperfection. She forgave herself for that, too.

Glo came back to the game when Candy, bringing the ball up-court on an 8–6 possession, straight-armed Elizabeth so violently at the top of the key that Elizabeth spun and reeled five feet before landing on her rear at the free-throw line. Janine whistled and play stopped. "You"—she pointed at Candy—"are not going to get away with that a second time. Clean it up young lady, or I'm ejecting you." Candy gave her the finger when she turned away, and Glo reached over and smacked it down, though more gently than she might have earlier. Janine, hearing the slap, turned and glared, but Candy leaned down to tighten the strap on her sandal, and Glo looked the other way.

After thirty minutes, Candy's team, up 10–9, had the ball. One point to go and they'd win. But Henry reached behind Joe and cleanly volleyballed a pass directly into Elizabeth's hands. She was off, with Candy trailing her, though not by much. Elizabeth cranked it up and got an extra step on Candy as she crossed the center line. But Candy only bided her time. She increased her speed, lengthened her stride easily, and, like that, she was at Elizabeth's side—her seventeen crisp years effortlessly catching up to Elizabeth's broken-in thirty-six. A second later, she was a step ahead, in front of Elizabeth as her aunt uncoiled and sprang to the basket. Elizabeth stretched in the air, reversed at the last second, a twist and switch to her left hand to avoid her defending niece, whose mission was to go for the ball and deny her the chance to score. As it should be. Ascending, Elizabeth was proud of Candy's tenacity. She'd taught her well.

The others stayed back, catching their breath, knowing they couldn't overtake the two driving players. Glo, moving in from the center line, was closest to her nieces. With Glo looking on, and Elizabeth hanging in the air, taut, vulnerable, and looking to tie, Candy leapt to protect her lead—her arms held high like scepters, her quads muscling her up, her hamstrings stretched taut as a tripwire. Candy, seventeen. Candy, her body unscathed. Candy, who was not pregnant, was also not going for the ball. She went for Elizabeth. She would not let her aunt even the score.

There is no more vulnerable moment for a player than the one when she moves midair, fully extended, to stuff, finesse, or settle her shot. She is irrevocably committed. Her muscles and ligaments are consumed with vertical leap. Her vision contracts to encompass the rim she stretches toward. Her fingertips feel the ball, but not the rush of air she brings about with her motion, or the heat her exertion creates. She doesn't taste her salty sweat or sense the closeness on the court, which she, in that instant, commands. She hears, if she hears at all, the sounds of the crowd only as murmuring background. The sharp suck of her own in- and exhalation is what she rises toward, as if only by going airborne can she catch up to her breath.

The defender must not take out such an opponent in midair. Even the dirtiest players rarely do it. The defender who would do such a thing may go airborne, too, but she's prepared to leap and land. She'll recover and spot herself after contact. It's the offensive player who won't know what hit her. She is bound to land badly. In a twisted heap. Her head first? Her elbow? Her shoulder, knee, or ankle? It's anybody's guess. But it won't be pretty. It will hurt.

At the first thud of body on body, of Candy driving into Elizabeth, the Sunnyviews sucked in their collective breath, an "ohhhhh" that highlighted the moment. As she saw the midair collision, Glo sped up and reached the top of the key. She had to get to these girls. No, these nieces—her family—who had limbs long like hers and were affected by her neglect, her criticism, her prayer. The lineage was clear. They were hers. She need not judge them by their religious state. She needed to care for them whatever state they were in. She hadn't done that so far, but she'd do so now. As her nieces descended, arms and legs extended, becoming sunlit silhouettes, logos against the Lovely sky, Glo moved fast, heel toe, heel toe, heel toe, then faster, Miss Clavell–like, rushing to disaster.

As Glo picked up her pace to a skip, Candy came down beyond the baseline, safe, in a three-point stance, loose and graceful, absorbing the shock of concrete by springing up again a bit, no harm to her from the flagrant foul she'd just committed.

Elizabeth, exposed in flight, incredulous, offered a meek "oh" of her own as Candy assaulted her midair. Her breath became a question. Her body, which would best have gone limp in preparation for the fall, stiffened. Elizabeth would land brittle, not pliant, and that would make it worse. She hurtled down, lost in space, her sense of where she was confused with where she'd been. She tried to protect her head, and the sharp protuberances of knee and elbow and hip, needing more time to sort it out as the concrete came into view. At the very last second, she sensed another presence falling forward, toward her. Elizabeth twisted, trying to get out of the other body's way, but disoriented, she fell into it.

They both landed hard. Elizabeth's left side bore the brunt of the blow, as she came down with legs and arms splayed, then immediately contracted, in pain. But they moved—all her limbs moved. She smiled weakly, certain she was fine, and looked over to see who she'd brought down with her.

Glo, because of Elizabeth's last-second maneuver, absorbed a hard blow that knocked her back as she'd been falling forward. She hit her head once, with force, and then she lay still on the cracked-up concrete, eyes open to the Lovely sky.

Candy, seeing Glo flattened from her hand, her hip, her fault, looked around frantically. Glo down? That was not what she'd meant to do. That was wrong. The ball. She'd swatted it when she'd attacked Elizabeth. She'd go get the ball. They needed the ball. She ran after it as it rolled down the slight incline toward the cemetery. She counted back as she ran away—Anita Prokoff, Sister Anne, Ms. Hogan,

Hillary Johnston, and Elizabeth—she'd pushed aside every mother-aged woman (plus that asshole Morrisey) who had the nerve to think she got a vote on Candy's future. That was all fine. She felt entitled to do all that. She remembered the sickening thunk of Glo's head on the cement. To that she had not been entitled. There was no way to feel fine about that.

The ball had rolled into the muddy ditch that Elizabeth had slipped into before the game. Candy jumped into the ditch and landed softly. Glo was laid out on cement. Glo was too old to be a mother. Too old to be knocked down. She replayed the picture of Glo falling forward—she was sure of it. Glo had been falling forward before Elizabeth knocked her back. What had happened there? What had she done to her old aunt?

She scrambled out of the soggy ditch, frantic for firm ground. She heard her name: "Golden, come here. You've got to see this." Coach D stood at the mausoleum door, calling her. She could not go back and face the damage she'd done on court. She went to Coach D.

CHAPTER 20

*T*HE RUSTY SCREECH of the heavy hinges reverberated as Candy stood on the threshold of the Mooney mausoleum. She held her breath as a shroud of fowl air billowed her way, and she felt the weight of her choice to enter the dark stone room. She stepped back, but Coach D, behind her, pushed forward. She inched in, taking half steps that matched the *cluck cluck cluck* of the brooding hens and the rustle of shifting straw.

"Come on, Golden. What's your problem? Quit mincing. This is going to be good." Coach D brushed past her and clicked a switch on the utility light that hung from a hook in the ceiling. He dialed up the temperature on the space heater and the coils, eager to perform, glowed immediately red. The generator buzzed in the corner.

"Hurry up. It's happening. My baby condor is about to be born."

"Coach, this place is going to catch on fire with that heater and all this stuff in here."

"What stuff? There's no 'stuff.' The room is made of stone. I've got a handful of clean straw here." He picked up a wisp from the floor and held it to his nose. "Your aunt should be here, too. Where is she? This would lift her spirits." He took a deep breath. "It smells good, doesn't it?"

It smelled like chicken shit. Candy dug a toe into the AstroTurf putting green that ran the length of the room. More than Elizabeth's spirits needed lifting right now. She lay flat on court again—probably with something broken, not just bruised. The golf ball–hatching hen, six inches from her ear, screeched, and Candy jumped. What had she done to Glo?

Coach D beckoned her, insistent, like a cop at a busy intersection. "Get over here."

Candy heard a peep from the stone shelf where the hens sat. The bantam stood to the side and watched the pale bluish-green oval she'd tended for the past two months. Her head was cocked and her beak jerked up then down, as if she were angry at this thing she'd sat on for weeks. As if it were being disloyal. The egg vibrated visibly. Candy heard a telegraphic click from inside the shell.

"It's using its egg tooth to peck a hole. Then it will work its way out. It's pure instinct. Pretty soon it will use its hatching muscles and bump against the shell with its head. This is history, Golden. And you're here for it. You're a lucky girl." Coach D stared at the egg as he spoke. When the hole in the shell was the size of a dime, the chick used its head to push against the top. How hard had Glo fallen? Candy didn't feel lucky. The chick kicked a leg to the side every now and then.

When the baby bird squirmed out of the fragmented shell, it was covered with soft light-colored down. It opened and closed its beak. Coach D grinned and rubbed his hands together. He went to a six pack–sized cooler in the corner and took out a package of Ball Park franks. Candy watched as he cooed and fed bits of hot dog to the newborn.

"Hey, Golden," he said without turning from the baby bird, "turn up the heater. Then come over here and feed her. Hmmm hmmm." He hushed the little bird with a throaty hum as it let loose a series of thin high chirps. He fed it again, tearing the hot dog into tiny morsels that he dropped delicately down the bird's chutelike beak.

Candy watched him instead of the bird that couldn't be a condor. His forehead was creased, his attention focused. He'd concentrated like that on her during practices, or in the huddle during a game. Elizabeth had looked at her like that, too, intently, wanting to know her secrets. Coach D dropped another bit of Ball Park in the baby bird's beak. He murmured to and fed a bird that he thought would grow up to eat dead meat. Lucky bird. Stupid coach. The bantam brooder sat on the side, her job complete, clucking every now and then. The coils on the space heater insisted, still glowing orange-red, and the generator hummed. The second bantam, stubbornly attached to her golf ball, paid no attention to the baby bird just born, biologically programmed to miss it all.

Candy stepped back. "So, Coach, what will you do now?"

He motioned her closer and handed her a hot dog. "Break it into tiny pieces. Drop them in her beak, carefully." Candy, nervous, hungry, took a bite before she did as told. The bird's eyes bulged as it swallowed, larvalike, as if there weren't enough room in its body for the tiny morsel.

"I wonder if it's warm enough in here for her. Did you turn up that heater? I have to e-mail the Audubon Society again. Maybe they won't ignore me this time."

"Do you really think it's a condor, Coach?"

"I do."

"What if you're wrong?"

He shrugged.

"But what will you do? You left the Ravens. You quit your job over something that didn't happen. And now, this vulture condor thing? It makes you seem like a crazy guy. It makes you seem pathetic." Candy wanted to figure it out.

"People leave important things all the time, Golden. But they come back, too. At least some of them do. I'll coach again, and you'll play again." She shook her head no, emphatic, but he held up his hand. "You won't always feel this way. And this little one"—he stroked the air around the chick—"will be whatever it is. There's nothing it or I can do to change that. So what if I'm wrong? I'm just trying to help the bird along its way. What's pathetic about that?" He turned away from his bird and looked at Candy's knees. "So how about you? Are you okay? What will *you* do, Golden?"

"I'm fine." Then understanding his lowered gaze, she answered what he really asked. "I'm not going to have a baby."

His gaze moved up to her elbow. "You sure? That's a tough choice to make. Elizabeth will want to help you with that. With arrangements and counseling and all that."

The baby bird squawked again. Candy didn't correct his mistake. Let him assume Elizabeth would actually help her. She thought how stupid it was to think everything would ever be the way you wanted it to be, even if you could figure out what that way was. Then, as she watched Coach D feed the goopy little bird again, she thought it was probably just as stupid to think nothing ever could be.

He had been wrong to leave her and the team the way he did. But all those nights in the gym after her mom died? When the season was over? When she had nothing? Leaving in August did not cancel out what he'd done for her in February, March, April, and May. Maybe he was right. Maybe people could return. If she had written off her mom those first twelve years of her life, she wouldn't have had her the last five. Her mom had worked hard to get it finally right. Candy picked up her basketball, propped it on her hip, and went back to what she'd left on court.

The instant before she had reached Elizabeth, on her way to save her niece, and well before Elizabeth's hip and shoulder had butted her own, Glo felt it. Her neck and jaw locked—her hand snapped to her chest where something weighty seized her. Her legs gave way. Not just her legs. Her shoulders and arms, her torso, her hips, her knees, her fingers and toes. It was as if the linchpin that held the shaft of her spine to the axle of her hip had just been pulled.

She knew it was some ventricular insurrection that was responsible for this sudden deflation of muscles. This collapse of bone. This elephantine press on her chest. Her doctor had prescribed against the possibility of such an attack for the past three years with Zocor and Inderal LA, and hydrochlorothiazide. How odd, Glo thought, *I'm having a heart attack and I'm thinking about the names of the drugs that didn't stop it*. The doctor had assured Glo there was no reason to live as if she were about to die. "Just take your meds and live your life. You'll be fine." The young woman had looked up from Glo's chart in the middle of her scripted pep talk, and, as if seeing Glo for the first time, repeated, "You look good. I mean it. You'll be fine. Take an aspirin every day, too."

Glo's forward momentum placed her squarely in Elizabeth's path of descent, but it was not her niece's body that knocked Glo down and out. The blow from Elizabeth merely pushed her back so that she landed faceup, instead of down. Her efforts to make her body do her bidding, to do anything other than fall back in collapse, were useless. She might as well have tried to practice Wicca.

She heard shards of conversation, tops and bottoms, but lost the middles in the echo of the cauldronlike space where her head used to be. That place felt light, empty, floaty. Was that a word? She didn't know. She didn't pray. She thought once more of Stan. All those years that she'd wondered if she'd been mistaken in marrying him, sent him out to smoke in the garage, dreamed of his dying? And he'd loved her anyway. Ah well, it turns out she'd loved him, too. She'd stayed with him. It was more than she'd done for the girls. For Melissa and Elizabeth. For Candy. She'd had a fantasy that she could make or break commitments, those connections to Stan and the girls, but the truth was she was bound to them, completely committed with every breath she took, with no exit and no choice. She couldn't squirm out of it no matter how she tried. Candy, Stan, Elizabeth, Melissa—Glo had broken some commitments, hadn't lived up to others, had been blind to still more. But that didn't negate their existence. Commitments simply are—you might as well pick up the ones placed before you. They aren't going away. She hoped Elizabeth understood that sooner than she had.

She heard Elizabeth say "911" and then "fucking," though the sound was distorted and it could have been somebody else. Elizabeth swore entirely too much. Candy did, too. Glo shrugged. Or would have if she had any influence on her own body. Let them. Let all these girls swear up a storm. Let them have babies, abortions, five marriages, six affairs. Roger had condemned her nieces, she had, too, but she finished what she'd started at the Cross in the Woods that morning and forgave herself for that. Elizabeth and Candy were here with her right now. Weren't they? She hoped so. That's what she wanted.

Laid out flat on court, Glo's peripheral vision receded gradually, from the edges to the center, her eyesight narrowing from panoramic to tight spot, and then even that dimmed. Glo felt herself being extinguished. Fading to black. She was the star of some slow motion enactment of what? Was she dying? Glo was.

Elizabeth knelt beside Glo. The sounds around her were amplified in the narrow tunnel of her concern. She murmured a quiet mantra, *breathemove, breathemove,* one word running into another, more wish than prayer.

"Call 911," she shouted at no one in particular in the crowd around her. She heard murmuring, but no call to the police. She looked up. "Nobody has a cell phone?" She hated cell phones. She looked back down at Glo. "Why don't I have a fucking cell phone?" She hated herself.

"I'll call. I'll get help." Hillary shouted over her shoulder as she ran off court, back toward the Mar-Jo, her feet, even in espadrilles, up to the task. Alex ran ahead of her, faster.

Elizabeth pressed her hands together and closed her eyes and pursed her lips against Glo's fate. Her own left elbow was raw and bloody, the skin hanging from it in shredded strips, matching her right, and her hip felt as if somebody had taken a tire iron to it for how hard she'd landed on cement, but she ignored that pain. Glo was quiet. Glo was motionless. Glo's pupils were large and fixed. Elizabeth thought she'd gladly barter a limb for the relief of seeing her aunt stir, of hearing her aunt moan.

A dog howled. In the crowd that circled Glo and Elizabeth, a wave of concern swelled and then broke into individual voices. Claudia warned against moving Glo, and then she knelt next to Elizabeth on the cement. Joe told everybody to back up and give her room to breathe. Mary reminded him that she fell and hit her head all the time and look, she was fine.

Dexter did a play-by-play on the collision, ". . . and then the old one landed on her wrist like all bent over and her head clunked down. Bad day for her. Guy steals her car. I think she broke her neck or something."

Another voice, quivering, added to the recap. "I watched closely. She was falling forward well before that younger one fell into her."

Dexter talked over her. "That one with the bruise who did the bench press, she seems like she'll be okay. Man, if Candy did that flagrant shit in a real game, her ass would be suspended and fined big. And that lady is like her grandma or something, so how cold is that?"

Elizabeth didn't hear Candy's voice in the undercurrent of concern. Maybe she wasn't there. Elizabeth couldn't look up from Glo to find out. Two derelict aunts down for the price of one vicious foul. Candy was probably celebrating somewhere. The quivering voice spoke again, and Elizabeth placed it. It was Janine, the clerk, the referee. "She had a heart condition, you know. I do, too. We both took Zocor. We talked about it. I don't think she hurt her head. This is all heart business."

Of course. Janine was right. It was Glo's heart, and she wouldn't last until an ambulance arrived. She needed CPR, something Elizabeth knew. With back, hip, leg, shoulder, and head all hurting from the blows she'd received, Elizabeth put her ear to Glo's face, straining to hear breath, and then she knelt upright again. She shook Glo's shoulder. "Glo, can you hear me? Glo, do something." Glo made a grunting, gasping sound that ended in a snore. Elizabeth had used her Red Cross CPR training once before, three years ago, when a bellicose dad had dropped in the bleachers midcurse, angry that his daughter had been ejected for swearing at the ref. These sounds from Glo were not breathing. They were distress.

Elizabeth tilted back Glo's head and listened again, but only agonal breathing, a rattling strain, met her ear. She pinched Glo's nose and covered her aunt's lipsticked mouth with her own. She breathed in twice, long deep breaths, two seconds each, that propelled air into Glo's lungs. Then she began chest compressions, forcing her aunt's blood to do its job and carry oxygen to her brain. Claudia joined her at Glo's side and took over the compressions, pushing down firmly with the heels of her hands. Capable and counting. Two breaths. Fifteen chest compressions. They tag-teamed for two rounds—Elizabeth breathing, Claudia pressing—performing the most essential manual labor, pumping blood and pushing breath into Glo's body.

Elizabeth looked up during the third round, as Claudia compressed Glo's chest, waiting for the lament of an ambulance siren. A crow swooped over the court with a harsh raucous cry and landed with a flutter and folding of wings on the iron rim under which Glo lay. Elizabeth looked at it, wishing she could interpret it as something other than a deadly sign. The bird was pitch-black against a swab of cloud in the sky that had cleared since the morning rain. Another crow landed, facing it, and they became quiet. They flew away five seconds later, their feet hanging limply, like laundry on a line, their cacophonous duet becoming faint. Another sound, the ring of ball on cement, came close, then closer still. Once more, Elizabeth looked up, this time to see Candy returning, driving the ball down an aisle the parting crowd created. Elizabeth flinched at the momentum coming her way.

She needn't have. Candy stopped her dribble a foot from Glo's head and crouched down on the other side of her motionless grandaunt, across from Elizabeth. "She's okay, right?"

"She had a heart attack."

"I didn't do it."

"It's her heart, Candy."

Candy sat on her basketball and put her hands on Glo's chest, next to Claudia's, which were doing compressions. "I can do that."

Claudia spoke between counting. "Forget it, Candy. Three. You don't get to dribble back here. Four. And be the hero. Five. Elizabeth and I. Six. Can handle this. Seven." Eight counts later, she pushed Candy's hands away again.

"I didn't mean to hurt her," Candy explained, though she needn't have. Everybody knew whom she'd meant to hurt.

"You should have thought about collateral damage. Jesus, Candy, what kind of shitty thing was that to do?" Claudia, kneeling upright and steady as stone, yelled at her while Elizabeth breathed for Glo.

"But she's okay, right, Elizabeth?" Candy wobbled on the ball.

"And then what? You ran away?" Claudia was not done assigning blame. "No, Candy, look at her. She's not okay at all."

Candy fell off the ball and landed on her ass. Her thick ropes of hair escaped the bit of twine that she'd used to hold them off her neck. The heat was palpable. She wiped sweat from under her eyes. This was bad. She'd paralyzed Glo. No. Killed her. No. Elizabeth had. Candy got up and knelt across from Elizabeth. She wanted to reach over Glo and punch her aunt—hit her so hard that her brain would rearrange and she'd see how she'd caused this. It was Elizabeth's fault that everything got so fucked up. She traced back to Elizabeth's deserting her five years ago, to her mom's dying nine months ago, to Glo's falling flat on the basketball court. She could put it on a graph. She could prove it. The reason for all the trouble knelt across from her. A swell of self-righteous anger swamped her, but she grimaced at facts that also swept by. She'd quit her team, which is what had made them come running toward her in the first place. She'd looked at the map and pointed her finger at Lovely, hoping to find Coach D. She'd let them think she was pregnant and then schemed to prove the lie true. She'd thrown the flagrant. Claudia was right. Glo out cold on court was on her.

Elizabeth, who had finished another round of breathing for Glo, saw Candy's expression turned from bravado to anger to remorse. She reached over Glo and took Candy's hands. "It's okay."

Candy shook her off. "I knocked her down."

"No, I did." Elizabeth corrected her.

"I took you out on purpose."

"She has a heart condition. Hillary is getting help. She shouldn't have been running around in the heat. You tried to stop her. You didn't want her to play. She insisted. She never did a thing she didn't want to do."

"I broke her neck."

"No. It's her heart."

Elizabeth breathed into Glo's mouth twice, and then knelt up and pushed Claudia's hands off Glo's chest. "I'll do that now, Claudia." She pumped twice. "Look at me, Candy. Help is on the way, Candy. You have to breathe for her after I do these compressions, Candy. You didn't do this to her, Candy. She had a heart condition, Candy. This isn't your fault, Candy." Elizabeth pressed down on Glo's chest with the heel of her hand, counting two, three, four.

Candy heard her name. She watched Elizabeth pushing on Glo's chest, her hands covering the letters that announced the basketball championship that Elizabeth's team had won twenty years ago. She saw Glo's chest sink two inches under Elizabeth's hands. When she heard a creak and crack in Glo's chest, Candy let loose a thin whine, a sound that came unbidden, a disturbance in the air.

"That's cartilage. A rib maybe. It's okay." Elizabeth continued counting.

Candy imagined Glo's blood underneath, pooling and stubborn. This whole trip, this whole nine months, this whole five years, Elizabeth hadn't pretended to be there for her. She hadn't offered much of anything, not praise, or promises, or a place to live. She hadn't bullshitted Candy before. She said this wasn't Candy's fault. Candy wanted to believe her. But look at Glo. Look at Glo not moving.

"I'm almost done, Candy. Get ready. Twelve. Thirteen. You'll breathe for her after fifteen. Pinch her nose. Cover her mouth with your own. Two long breaths. Push the air in. Two seconds each."

At Elizabeth's signal, Candy pinched Glo's nose, leaned down, and blew hard into her mouth. She closed her eyes. She didn't want to see the obvious—Glo's glassy stare and her complexion tinted blue beneath her makeup. Her exhalation was a prayer that Glo would sit up and swat her hair away. She heard Elizabeth murmuring *not your fault, breathe, not your fault, breathe,* pardon and plea.

Candy couldn't forgive herself that easily. Nobody should forgive herself that easily. As she finished breathing for Glo, Hillary and Alex ran back, shouting that an ambulance was on the way. Candy looked at her friend. She'd done the right thing for Alex. Her mom would have been proud of her for that. Her mom? She whiplashed back to angry at Elizabeth. "Once in your stupid life, for five minutes, you actually stayed. Glo's dead and you're beating on her chest, and you think that makes up for everything?" Candy felt as if she were going crazy, as if every thought she had was both false and true.

Elizabeth bowed her head. She'd been gone too long. It didn't matter that she happened to be there now, or that she'd been there in the beginning. She had held Melissa's hand then, rubbed her back, and fed her ice chips through thirty-six hours of labor. By hour thirty her sister was a mere impression of a woman, little more than a pool of pain, hardly human anymore. One day turned into another but the pain held still.

She and Melissa had gone into labor and delivery determined and upbeat. During the first twelve hours, Elizabeth referred to her notes from the Lamaze class they'd taken. Amid the bulleted points about early labor and cleansing breaths and back labor and relaxation techniques, she found the asides that tied her firmly to her sister. The ones about the things they'd both found absurd. The ones that might relax Melissa more than "modified valsalva breathing" and "deep cleansing breaths." Things such as the advice from the earnest teacher standing at the blackboard, chalk dust on her beige flax vest, telling them that "the cure is birth, ladies," to a question about how long the pain might last. She and Melissa had driven home that night discussing the grungy visual aids the woman used—a ratty ski cap as cervix with a scuffed up softball as baby head pushing up against it. A smudged plastic-headed baby doll with a soiled floppy cloth body passing through a foam-stuffed pelvis mended in two spots with duct tape. It was an expensive class. Why did the teacher's props look like she'd found them in a Dumpster?

But she couldn't make Melissa laugh during that day that turned to night and day again. And she couldn't make her focus either—her sister's right eye rolled slightly up, as if she were about to have a convulsion. And finally with a second dose of epidural wearing off on the one side where it had taken, and Melissa crashing and losing every physical sensation except exhaustion and pain, the doctor announced that the baby's head couldn't make it past the pelvic bone.

The room became a hive of consultation. The two doctors, the resident and her boss, the attending, huddled about what to do. "Forceps," said the junior colleague. "Not until the head is down plus two," said the one officially in charge. Their back and forth was well-modulated, but Elizabeth, finely tuned to discord even then, understood that the disagreement was deep. There were no C-section rooms available. The anesthesiologists were all busy relieving other women of their pain. *No* rooms? *All* the anesthesiologists? They couldn't agree on how to get the baby out. Her niece or nephew was at a literal impasse.

Elizabeth, nineteen, disbelieving, spurred by fear, made demands beyond her years. She took charge. She raised hell while Melissa whimpered. The last two hours of pushing had wreaked hellish pressure on the finer ports of her sister's vascular system. Melissa's cheeks, spotted red with broken blood vessels, could have been a pointillist's canvas. The fine skin under her eyes was damaged, too. She looked as if she had gone ten rounds with Ali. Elizabeth thought her sister was dying trying, giving all of the nothing she had left. She jabbed her fingers into the attending physician's name, Bocelli, which was monogrammed on her white coat pocket. "Help her. You find a room or an anesthesiologist or whatever you need and you help her *now*. Or you listen to her"—Elizabeth pointed at the resident—"and quit being a chickenshit and use the fucking forceps."

Elizabeth and the junior doctor got their way. The resident would do a forceps delivery, the attending would watch. Somebody pulled an anesthesiologist off another case and into Melissa's room for five minutes, and Melissa received one last blast of epidural relief. They would bring forth the baby.

The doctor and nurse scrubbed. Others, doctors and nurses in specialty teams, came into the room, glomming on to the difficult delivery that was so much more interesting than an uneventful arrival. Melissa rested and cried while they prepared themselves and her. Her face was red and white and black and blue and sad. Her legs wobbled feebly, and when her muscles were too depleted to follow the doctor's simple command to hold them open, Elizabeth grasped her sister's knee.

She was aghast at the sight of the forceps, though she tried to hide it. Metallic, blunt, and prehistoric-sized, they were out of place amid the flexible curve of plastic tubing and sterile beeps of fetal monitors. She listened carefully to the resident who demanded Melissa's attention as she inserted the forceps. "You need to concentrate on me. Don't breathe. Don't push. Until I tell you to."

It was clear to Elizabeth that this place Melissa resided was not somewhere a woman went with anybody else—not with sister or mother or friend or even father of the baby to be born. This labor was Melissa's only. She held her sister's knee and hand harder, but she understood that was only for herself. She could not help her sister.

Elizabeth's intake of breath was a blade as the baby's bloody head, eyes welded shut, protruded so stiff and solid it looked like a totem. The resident's hands, forceps discarded, grasped it firmly, guiding. Forty seconds later, Elizabeth exhaled when, with one more push from Melissa, the baby's shoulders came free and the baby, still bloody, still *still*, came free, too. Somebody said, *It's a girl.* And then terrified that nine months and thirty-six hours had brought only this stillborn creature, Elizabeth held her breath again and said a silent prayer, *breathemove,* begging for motion, for sound, and there it was, finally, the baby's limbs jerked in a spasm, and the baby announced her presence with three cries, layered, thick, and low.

Her young mother, her younger aunt, her nurse, and the forceps-wielding doctor all let loose breaths held (and fear held tighter) and laughed or cried or smiled or sighed. Everybody welcoming the baby born. At last.

Melissa, after her daughter was Apgar-scored and swabbed and swaddled and returned to her, held her fast to her chest, lowering her head to brush her contused cheeks against her baby's sleep. And her expression, her gaze on her daughter, was not what Elizabeth expected. It was not satisfied or proud or happy or relieved. It was as sad a look as Elizabeth had ever seen, as if her sister understood from the very beginning all the ways they'd disappoint this girl.

Melissa looked up at Elizabeth then, her blackened eyes and outstretched arms asking an unspoken question. And Elizabeth accepted the tiny burden, the expansive gift from her sister that came with no strings attached, no questions asked. What other choice could she make?

Elizabeth, making another round of compressions on Glo's chest, looked down at Glo and then across at Candy and a swell of confidence broke over her. Glo had been right after all—she only needed to pick up what was placed before her. She need not worry about whether it was a burden or a gift, about whether she was capable or not. "Candy," she said, "I can help you with the baby. I won't leave you alone with it."

Candy shook her dreaded head. Back there with Coach D, as she'd watched him tend his baby bird, she'd had some momentary understanding of why you could stick with them even when people let you down. But here on court, she couldn't conjure that feeling. Everything she cared about was gone, and now Elizabeth offered to help. She didn't understand why Elizabeth had left her, and she had no faith that she'd come back now. Candy felt exhausted by the things she'd carried all alone. She relinquished a little bit of truth, and picked up a bigger bit of responsibility. "There isn't any baby. I'm not pregnant, and we wouldn't be in this town if I hadn't lied. She wouldn't be here like this"—Candy leaned forward and bowed her head over Glo—"if I hadn't lied."

Elizabeth leaned in toward Candy until they formed an apex over

Glo. She grasped the muscled knots of the girl's shoulders and she wouldn't let go, though Candy tried to shake her off. Elizabeth told her again. She insisted. "This is all on me, Candy. I'm the one who did this, Candy. Glo never did a thing she didn't want to do, Candy. It wasn't you, Candy." Again, she repeated her niece's name over and over again, assuring her that she knew who she was. Knew who she was talking to. Heard her. So there would be no doubt.

The sun, angling more acutely west, shined on Glo's face, so that her pupils, large and fixed, aggielike, shined, too. Elizabeth checked her watch. They'd been at it for more than ten minutes with no response. She heard an ambulance siren. It was too late. Glo was dead. There could be no doubt about that either.

*T*HE EMOTION THAT is left to those behind? It can transform to something other at a question overheard: *Where will the girl live now?* Or at a touch uninvited on shoulder slumped, head bowed, or cheek turned. One moment, a mourner is anchored in her spot, dense with sorrow. The next moment, she feels a stiletto of uncertainty at that question or that touch, and she sets her shoulders and breathes in sharply, defensively. Still, penitence eventually will escape its chamber and be replaced by compunction. Remorse may follow, though such self-reproach and mental anguish does little good. Contrition. Forgiveness. These wait their turn. They'll claim their place.

Returning to Chicago from Lovely for Glo's funeral, Elizabeth and Candy accepted condolences from Glo's former colleagues and current parish and neighborhood friends. Anita Prokoff sent a floral tribute, a fanlike display of white mums and aggressively red and pointy flowers, which Elizabeth asked the funeral home director to place in a dim corner. The card attached blessed Elizabeth and Candy for their loss and offered prayers for the repose of Glo's soul. Candy, hiding in the corner to escape the whispers and looks full of pity or disapproval, plucked the card from the arrangement and tore it into little pieces that she dropped on the floor and ground into the carpet. When she turned to face the crowd of Glo's old friends again, she whacked her elbow into Elizabeth's chest.

"Ow." Elizabeth rubbed her clavicle.

"You're doing it again. Quit sneaking up me." Candy rubbed her elbow.

"We need to talk."

"I don't want to talk."

"It's about where you're going to live."

"I'll go back to Amy's house."

"You can't do that."

"Why not?"

Elizabeth pointed at the bits of shredded card on the carpet. "Because you really don't want to."

"Does that matter?"

"I want you to live with me." Elizabeth, self-conscious, placed her hands on Candy's shoulders, but when she felt her niece's muscles tighten spasmodically, she quickly shoved her hands in her pockets. "I mean, would you, please?"

Candy tugged at her dress, which was deep red and short and tight around her stomach and hips. Then she gathered her dreads in her hand and held them up off her neck, so that her dress hiked up again. She looked over Elizabeth's shoulder to the front of the room, where mourners murmured and knelt before the urn that held the proof that Glo once had corporeal form. She shivered involuntarily, remembering the breath she'd forced into Glo. "No. Forget it. That's not a good idea."

Elizabeth followed Candy's gaze. "I didn't expect that she'd want to be cremated. She was full of surprises. She had secrets. But some things she didn't hide. When Glo and I drove to Detroit to pick you up last week, she told me she was ready to go at any time. She said she wanted us with her when she died. She got what she wanted."

"Lucky her." Candy draped herself in attitude to deflect her confusion about Elizabeth's invitation and concern.

"I'm moving back here, Candy. To Chicago. I'll fly back to L.A. and give notice at my job and take care of a few things, but then I'll be back. Glo left me her house."

"Lucky you."

"She left everything to us. Equally. She told me she was going to do that, too. Her lawyer called this morning. He needs to meet us. Apparently, she and Stan were in much better financial shape than I'd ever imagined possible. You'll have money. It's in a trust. You'll get it when you turn twenty-one."

"Lucky me."

"You can't live alone right now. If you won't live with me, we'll have to figure out something else. Something that you think is okay. Something that you want." Elizabeth reached out to brush the hair off Candy's shoulders, but, thinking better of it, pushed her own hair off her forehead instead and changed the subject. "Leo is here. He and Glo were friends. I want you to meet him. He's brought his daughter with him. I told you about her, right? Her name is Molly. She's the one with problems."

Candy looked over Elizabeth's shoulder and saw a little girl whose tangled hair was held off her face with one blue and one green barrette.

She held a man's hand with both of hers and pulled him toward the urn full of Glo as she whined *no* at a high pitch, the word only stating the obvious as every straining muscle in her stubborn little body clearly telegraphed refusal. "Hmmm. That girl, Molly? Not so lucky."

A half dozen pumpkins, carved in anticipation of Halloween, a week away, littered the bright blue steps of Leo's front porch alongside an upended red bike, wheel spinning, and a child-sized yellow canvas director's chair, also upended. It looked like a tiny tot battlefield. Elizabeth parked the Cadillac in front of it, hot dogs parallel to the kindercare of colors on her old front porch. It was warm for October, seventy degrees, but she tied her jacket around her waist. She wished she hadn't worn shorts. This wasn't L.A. It was six o'clock already. The sun would set soon—she'd be cold in twenty minutes. She heard noise from the back, so she walked that way, bypassing the obstacle course on the front steps and the cold-tiled entryway to which she'd given up her keys in August.

Leo knelt on the side of the house, a spade in one hand, a bulb in the other. He stood as he saw her and came toward her, brushing his dirty hands on his jeans. "Hey! Elizabeth. When did you get back in town? Why didn't you call? How did you get here? I would have picked you up."

"I flew in last night on the red-eye. I've been unpacking. Airing out the house. Glo left it spotless, but you know how dust blooms. I drove the Cadillac over. Glo gave it to me before she died."

Leo walked past her toward the front of the house and then turned around and laughed. "So that's the hot dog Cadillac. What did you end up doing with that guy who stole it?"

"I had second thoughts. So I told the cops that there'd been a misunderstanding—that I realized Glo had lent him the car, which, it turns out, is what he had told the cops, so the stories meshed. I saw her kissing him. I figured she wouldn't really want him in jail."

Elizabeth had called the police and reported the theft of the car after Coach D had driven them to the hospital from the Rec Center basketball court. He'd run over from the mausoleum to tell Elizabeth the news about the baby bird, just as the EMT team arrived in an ambulance. Elizabeth and Candy sat in the backseat of his old Ford Escort wagon, and he followed the ambulance that carried Glo to Copperwood General Hospital. The ambulance had traveled at the posted speed limit—there was no need for sirens. Coach D had been quiet during the thirty-minute drive. The atmosphere in the car hummed with low-voltage grief.

Elizabeth had watched Candy intently as they followed the ambulance. She wasn't careful in her concern. Coach D had been with Candy the day Melissa died, too. How long did it take before such a memory didn't cause constriction of blood vessels, expansion of tear ducts, loss of hope? Longer than nine months. Elizabeth felt sure of that. In the backseat of Coach D's car that afternoon, even Candy's lips were pale.

After taking them to the hospital in Copperwood, Coach D went back to the Mar-Jo and waited while Alex and Hillary packed Elizabeth's and Candy's and even Glo's things, which he then brought to the Copperwood Best Western, where they'd stay while arrangements were made for Glo's body to be transported back to Chicago for the cremation and funeral. Coach D drove back and forth that day, quiet and calm and unhurried. When he finally left for good that night, Candy had gone out to the balcony of their third-floor room, which overlooked the parking lot.

"Hey Coach," she called down to him. Elizabeth, on the phone with the police at the time, had closed the sliding-glass door behind Candy.

Coach D looked up and shielded his eyes from the sun setting behind her. "What is it, Golden?"

"I hope your baby condor makes it through the night."

"Thanks, Golden. Me, too."

The next day, Elizabeth and Candy walked to the police station, a half mile away. Hillary and Coach and Claudia had all called and offered to come over and drive them, but Elizabeth, despite her aching leg, wanted to walk. It would give her time alone with Candy. The cops had called that morning also. They'd caught Roger easily. Actually, they'd caught him before she'd reported the car stolen the night before. He'd tried to trade the car in, just as he'd said he would, but his crooked dealer friend was neither crooked enough nor friend enough to help him. The guy had not only refused the Cadillac but had called the police as soon as Roger left the lot.

When Candy and Elizabeth arrived at the police station the next morning, there was the Cadillac, in the parking lot, still packed with Roger's belongings, including the floor lamp that stuck out the window. Elizabeth thought about how her niece had hated her that afternoon as she drove away from Heilmann, her car packed for her move. Hated her almost as much as she hated her mom at the bar down the street. Candy's loathing for them both had been palpable. Her hopelessness had been, too. Yet with all the neglect Melissa had heaped on her daughter, Candy had forgiven her. Elizabeth thought of all the things she'd done to her niece. All those things could never be undone. But what about the thing she hadn't done? She hadn't stayed.

At the Copperwood police station that morning, Elizabeth dropped the charges against Roger. He wasn't the only one who'd taken flight when he shouldn't have.

"You should have called me, Elizabeth." Leo returned from his inspection of the Cadillac. "I could have gone over to the house yesterday and aired things out. Or I could have brought the girls there to-day. We would have helped you unpack."

Elizabeth ignored his concern and went directly to her own. "So, how's Candy? You're working on her to go back to school, right? To play ball again? She's not just a free baby-sitter for your Tasmanian Devil, is she?"

A few days after Glo's funeral, Candy had agreed to live tem-porarily with Leo and Molly and to help him out of his child-care jam, but she'd been noncommittal about finishing high school. And she refused to play ball. When Elizabeth and Leo first suggested the arrangement to her, she'd looked at them as if they were speaking Farsi, and then she'd turned suddenly and glared at Molly, who stood behind her, tugging on her dreadlocks. As the little girl, un-fazed, pulled Candy's hair again, Candy had put her head in her hands and lowered it carefully to the table. After a while, Candy had looked up and nodded yes.

"Molly calls her 'mean cousin Candy.' They argue about almost everything. It can be amusing sometimes, even touching. Of course, it would be better if they weren't both so pissed off for real most of the time."

"What's Molly's story?"

"Mom overdosed. Dad unknown. In and out of foster care since she was abandoned two years ago." He was interrupted by a scream from the back of the house. Elizabeth jumped, but Leo didn't blink. "That's my girl. Candy hasn't talked much yet. I don't push it. She seems comfortable here. I still think it's a good plan, and not only be-cause it's helping me out these few months. I'm on half-days at Lane, by the way, so Candy has her alone only in the morning. I've got Molly on three different waiting lists for child care. Places with good teacher-to-kid ratios, so she'll get enough attention. Something will open up soon. Meanwhile, between me and Candy, she's got one-on-one attention almost all the time. It will make a difference. I know it will. It already has." He waved his spade. "Go back there and say hello to them while I finish this." Leo knelt and placed a bulb in a hole he'd dug.

Elizabeth's jacket, tied loosely, fell from her hips as she walked past Leo, and when she crouched to pick it up, she and Leo were face to face and he spoke again, an afterthought. "She gets a lot of phone calls from a girl named Alex."

"That's somebody we met up north. She's pregnant."

"I know. I guess the boyfriend-father pulled a disappearing act once she decided to have the baby. I shouldn't know all that, but Candy talks so loud. One other thing, her old coach from Detroit called. He'll be in town for an Audubon Society meeting next week. He's coming by to talk to her on Tuesday."

"Coach D? Why didn't I know that? How come nobody tells me things?"

"Maybe because you never answer your phone. Anyway, I'm telling you now. And that's okay, right? He's been cleared of everything, right?"

"He's eccentric but harmless. Think Phil Jackson meets Mike Krzyzewski meets Andy Kaufman. And he looks like a younger Bobby Knight."

"He told me to tell you and Candy that the Cochin bantam killed the condor."

"No kidding?" Elizabeth clucked.

"Is that some kind of code?" Leo noticed her calf then and visibly started. "What happened to you?"

Still crouching next to him, Elizabeth touched the muddy puddle of purplish-brown that stained her leg. She shook her head, rueful at how fascinated she'd been with the progress of her bruise. She'd gone to the doctor when she got back to L.A. It was a hematoma—a blood tumor. She'd have a permanent discoloration, a ridge of scar tissue, and a slight declivity in the muscle of her calf. "It's nothing. Just a bruise."

She stood, and he did, too, and she looked him in the eye, wanting to be sure he heard her and understood what she was about to say. "I want her to move into Glo's with me, Leo. You promised you'd help persuade her to do that. This is just a way station. My sister wanted her with me. I was in the damn room when she was born. Don't forget that."

Leo tamped a mound of dirt around the bulb, firmly, with his foot, and then he brushed his hands on his pants again. "I put up a basket on the garage off the alley. Candy is back there now teaching Molly and two other kids how to play. They're four, and she treats them as if they're in boot camp. Go watch. You'll enjoy it. Shoot around with them. That's how you and Candy got to know each other in the first place. Don't forget that either."

"Molly, quit being a baby and get your butt over here with the other kids," Candy yelled at the scowling little girl, who crouched and dug up clumps of the neighbor's tiny back-alley patch of sod.

Molly looked up at Candy, startled, as if she had assumed she were invisible, and then she laughed, throaty and deep, in a register beyond her years. "You said *butt.*" Molly, still laughing, tightened her ponytail, pushed her bangs out of her eyes, and wiped her nose with the back of her hand, leaving traces of dirt on her forehead and cheeks, painted for the game. Another little girl reached up and petted Candy's twisted hanks of hair as if they were puppies.

When Candy felt the girl's hand on her back, she whipped around and swatted it away. "Don't do that, Danielle." She blew the whistle around her neck and shouted, though the girls, even AWOL Molly, were within a whisper's distance. "You girls suck. You need to work at this if you're going to be good. You need to get serious. You need to practice. You need to be tough. Let's run through it again." Molly had joined the other girls, and Candy placed her in front of the basket, facing away from it, ten feet out. "I'm going to dribble toward you, Molly. You're going to defend against me. Moving backward. One arm out. One up. I'll shoot over you, and you'll turn to the basket, block me out, and grab the rebound."

As Elizabeth slipped through the gate, Candy dribbled slowly toward Molly. The little girl rushed at her, swinging her arms wildly, swatting any bit of Candy she could get her hands on. She pulled on Candy's T-shirt, which was bright orange and read LUCKY GIRL #48, and then she lowered her shoulder and tried to headbutt Candy out of the way. The other girls laughed.

Candy stopped dribbling and put one hand on the charging girl's forehead and held the ball aloft with the other. "You see this, you other kids? I want you to pay attention. Molly is ruthless. Molly cares. Once Molly learns the rules, Molly is going to be great on defense." Without looking up, Candy lofted a one-handed shot. The ball cut an elegant curve in the sky, but, spinning a scintilla too much, it rattled into the rim and popped up and out as if it had been shot back.

Elizabeth, seeing the ball heading over the fence and into the neighbor's yard, darted across the alley to save it. She leapt and got a hand on the ball. She bobbled it between her long fingers, and, fighting, gained control before she came back down, hit cement, and found her balance.

Then, with all these girls watching, Elizabeth planted, took her look, and from thirty feet out launched her shot, wrist bent, arm a scepter—her follow-through sound. The ball arced toward the net, its rotation steady, and hung lunarlike for an instant against the dusk-accepting sky.